PRAISE FOR LIZ TALLEY

"Talley packs her latest southern romantic drama with a satisfying plot and appealing characters . . . The prose is powerful in its understatedness, adding to the appeal of this alluring story."

—*Publishers Weekly*

"Relevant and moving . . . Talley does an excellent job of making her flawed characters vastly more gray than black and white . . . which creates a story of unrequited loves, redeemed."

—*Library Journal*

"Talley masters making the reader feel hopeful in this second-chance romance . . . You have to read this slow-burning, heart-twisting story yourself."

—*USA Today*

"This author blends the past and present effortlessly, while incorporating heartbreaking emotions guaranteed to make you ugly cry. Highly recommended."

—*Harlequin Junkie*

ROOM
TO
BREATHE

OTHER TITLES BY LIZ TALLEY

Come Home to Me

A Down Home Christmas

Morning Glory

Charmingly Yours

Perfectly Charming

Prince Not Quite Charming (novella)

All That Charm

Third Time's the Charm

Home in Magnolia Bend

The Sweetest September

Sweet Talking Man

Sweet Southern Nights

New Orleans' Ladies

The Spirit of Christmas

His Uptown Girl

His Brown-Eyed Girl

His Forever Girl

Bayou Bridge

Waters Run Deep

Under the Autumn Sky

The Road to Bayou Bridge

Oak Stand

Vegas Two-Step

The Way to Texas

A Little Texas

A Taste of Texas

A Touch of Scarlet

Novellas and Anthologies

The Nerd Who Loved Me

"Hotter in Atlanta" (a short story)

Cowboys for Christmas with Kim Law and Terri Osburn

A Wrong Bed Christmas with Kimberly Van Meter

Once Upon a Wedding with Jamie Beck, Tracy Brogan, et al.

ROOM
TO
BREATHE

Liz Talley

Text copyright © 2019 by Amy R. Talley

Published by Montlake Romance, Seattle

www.apub.com

Amazon, the Amazon logo, and Montlake Romance are trademarks of Amazon.com, Inc., or its affiliates.

ISBN-13: 9781542008631
ISBN-10: 1542008638

Cover design by David Drummond

Printed in the United States of America

To my mother, Jane Elizabeth, who prepared the child and not the path. Thank you for letting me read instead of nap, and thank you for letting me be creative, run a little wild, and learn independence. I'm thankful for your love and teachings every single day (especially when I hear myself say your words).

CHAPTER ONE

Daphne Witt had always done everything by the book. She took dry-clean-only clothing to the dry cleaner. She always washed the dishes before she went to bed. Her limit on wine was two glasses. No more. She even rinsed out her peanut butter jar for recycling . . . and that was a huge pain in the rump.

So the very idea that she was standing in her recently gutted bathroom lusting after the twenty-five-year-old man measuring the space for the soaker tub she'd bought on clearance was mind-boggling.

But she couldn't seem to stop imagining how his defined abs would feel beneath her fingertips or the way the sweat sheening his neck might taste on her tongue.

It was raunchy, disturbing, and honestly, a bit of a relief.

Because when her then-husband, Rex, had pulled out of their driveway two years ago, loaded down with his worldly possessions, that part of herself—the one that got all gooey when Rex wrapped his arms around her and kissed her nape while she scrubbed the lasagna pan—had withered up dry as bird droppings on hot pavement. And her desire, libido, or whatever drove a woman to wear a lace thong that disappeared into kingdom come hadn't shown back up until, well, *now*.

And danged if it hadn't shown up like a Cat 5 hurricane.

"I think the tub you bought will fit fine," Clay said, the metal tape measure snapping into place, sounding louder than normal in the hollowed new addition that was open to the October heat. He turned toward her with a congratulatory smile. "Nice find on that tub, by the way."

Clay Caldwell was almost young enough to be her son. In fact, he'd taken her daughter, Ellery, out a few times in high school. So Daphne shouldn't be admiring the way he filled out his Dickies work pants. Checking out a guy who was about fifteen years her junior was wrong.

Way wrong.

Still, it wasn't like she was doing anything more than admiring a handsome, very fit man. No harm in that, right? After all, Clay seemed to be asking for it, parading around without a shirt, rubbing his hand over those washboard abs, and cracking smiles like a frat boy popping beers.

Wait? Was this sexism?

He was asking for it.

"Mrs. Witt?" Clay poked her arm.

Riiiiight.

Mrs. Witt. Old lady Witt. Washed-up Mrs. Witt. Bringer of the juice boxes and name tags at Bible school Mrs. Witt.

"Sorry. Why don't you call me Daphne?" she said, pulling her attention from her ridiculous thoughts back to the very real present. Clay was her contractor. Period.

He shrugged his sun-kissed shoulders. Shoulders that invited touching. *Damn it. Focus.* "Sure, but it feels weird calling you Daphne."

"I'm not collecting social security . . . yet," Daphne joked, trying not to be offended. Of course he didn't want to call her Daphne. He'd always known her as Mrs. Witt, and as a good ol' southern boy, he'd call her Mrs. Witt until she turned up her toes, no doubt.

"You're funny, *Daphne*. Of course you don't look like you're even close to social security checks. You look my age. In fact, you should know you were all the guys' favorite MILF when we were in high school." His dark-blue eyes twinkled and then widened. "Oh crap. Ignore that. So inappropriate."

She knew what a MILF was, of course, but she'd never thought she'd ever been one. Okay, so she had always been the youngest in the mom crowd, but she'd never worn tight clothes or put out any "boom chicka wow wow" vibes when she volunteered in the PTA.

What did a woman say to being told she was someone that younger guys wanted to . . . uh, do? "I don't even know what to say to that, Clay. Uh, thank you?"

Clay laughed. "Sorry. I mean, it's true. You were always the prettiest mom, but, yeah, inappropriate to mention. I'm trying hard as hell to be professional here. My brother's always riding my ass about that. But, hey, I don't want you thinking you're out to pasture or anything. You're still pretty . . . um, pretty."

Was Clay flirting with her? No. He was just being sweet. Tossing her a bone. Besides, even if he were flirting, Daphne wouldn't know. She'd gotten married at the end of her junior year of high school and never learned "single gal at the bar" skills. She wouldn't recognize an innuendo if it slapped her in the face. Daphne had married the boy who sat next to her in kindergarten and ate paste. From day one Rex had been as obvious as mud on white pants.

Nearly four years ago, Rex had started seeing a therapist for anxiety, an affliction that had cropped up shortly after Daphne landed an unexpected book deal with a children's publishing house. After a few years of therapy, Rex declared Daphne emotionally and physically unavailable. Supposedly her emotional abandonment left him no choice but to load his gargantuan pickup truck and drive away from twenty years of marriage.

Daphne would have been more upset if she hadn't been so exhausted from a deadline, making Ellery's costume for sorority rush, and the other multitude of tasks sitting heavy on her shoulders. To be honest, her first thought was at least now she didn't have to iron his shirt for work the next day . . . and she could watch what she wanted on TV that night without argument.

Daphne had always loved Rex, or thought she'd loved him. But perhaps she'd merely settled because that was all she'd been offered. When she'd gotten pregnant at Winter Formal (thanks to a five-year-old dry condom Rex had been toting around for the special occasion), both Rex's father and hers insisted they marry in order to keep the baby.

So they had.

There had been good times and not-so-good times. That was marriage. Daphne had been content raising Ellery, baking cookies for fundraisers, and being the perfect wife she'd pictured in her mind for so many years—self-sacrificing, ever smiling, always comforting. She'd worked at a preschool to make ends meet, balanced the books at Rex's AC-repair company, and tried to make the little things count. She'd gone all in on the American dream.

Until the day she made copies of a silly book she'd created for her pre-K classes and one of the moms sent it to her cousin, who happened to be an editorial director at Little Red Barn Books. Daphne's world had busted wide open into a dream she'd only ever nurtured in the darkest recesses of her heart.

Ever-obvious Rex could say whatever he wanted about emotional abandonment, but the truth was he didn't know how to handle Daphne becoming a successful author. At first he'd patted her on the head, assuming she had a new hobby like the time she decided to try scrapbooking. Then she got an agent (she had an agent!), another book deal (six figures!), went on a book tour (hello, San Francisco!), and Rex didn't have his dinner on the table every night at six o'clock.

And one evening Rex delivered a well-rehearsed diatribe on what *she'd* done wrong and why that had led to him leaving her. Oddly enough, Daphne hadn't collapsed on the ground, heartbroken.

Nope. She'd merely shrugged and said she understood how he felt. And she had. Because until he'd uttered those words—*I'm not happy, Daph*—she'd thought she *was* happy. But she wasn't. Her career had brought her a satisfaction she'd never thought she needed. She'd changed, and she hadn't wanted to go back to the person she was.

So maybe she *had* emotionally abandoned Rex when she'd claimed herself.

"You're not mad, are you?" Clay asked, interrupting her thoughts.

"At what?"

"Me saying that stuff. I mean, it was a compliment, you know." He looked worried.

"I know it was. It's fine," she said, trying to brush the whole thing off with a wave of her hand. "Makes this ol' gal feel good to think at one point she had it going on."

"Hey, now, Ellery's mom has got it going on." He sang it. Then he winked at her.

Heat flashed through her. That had been a popular song back when Ellery was a child. Daphne used to sing it into Ellery's hairbrush when she got her dressed for school. To feel such pleasure at Clay's words was pathetic—so very pathetic and embarrassing—but she couldn't help herself. It was nice to feel like she wasn't a dusty old bag waiting for the chariot of death. This was way different from being declared the hottest little number since Marlene Dietrich by her dad's cronies at the assisted-living complex. Some of those guys didn't see too well.

This was a young, half-naked, hot man in a tool belt. A guy not even Daphne's accomplished, gorgeous daughter had been able to catch. Not that Ellery would ever admit it.

Clay clipped the tape measure onto his low-hanging jeans and looked out the opening of the new addition where a few other men hammered on things. A saw in the background whined, and dust kicked up. Little pieces of sawdust clung to Clay's bare shoulders. She wanted to brush them away, but that would be way too personal. Or mom-like.

"You're not having issues with dust in the house, are you? Or too much heat leaking in? I think I got a good seal," Clay said, looking at the heavy plastic he'd used to blockade the work area from the main living quarters. Sweat ran in rivulets down his chest. She tried not to look. He noted her trying not to look. Pulling the cooling towel from around his neck, he swiped at his torso.

"It's too hot to be doing this. Maybe we should have waited until next month," Daphne said, averting her eyes.

"Nah, it's always hot in Louisiana. If we stopped working every time we started sweating, we'd only work two months out of the year," Clay said, walking toward the opening and then pulling on the chambray shirt he'd draped on a sawhorse. "Let me show you our progress. We've been lucky. This dry weather has us on schedule."

Daphne followed him outside, where several other workers did construction things. What, she had no clue. Clay worked with his older brother, Lawrence, in a newly formed construction company, Caldwell Contracting Services. They specialized in remodels and additions, and though they were young, Daphne knew they were more than competent. Lawrence had graduated with a degree in construction engineering technology while Clay had skipped the traditional four-year college and taken drafting and electrician courses. Both boys had worked their way through school working for a large-scale construction company before forming their own last year. Daphne was happy to support guys she'd watched grow up.

Which made her feel extra perverted for practically salivating all over Clay.

It was that stupid book's fault. Tippy Lou had given her a book regarding female arousal and orgasms and then bugged her for months about reading it. Finally, Daphne had pulled it from beneath her stack of decorating magazines and started.

This was what she got for doing what Tippy Lou suggested—horny.

"All this looks great. I can't believe you were able to match the siding," she said, marveling at how seamlessly the new addition blended with the old farmhouse. She and Rex had been gifted the house by her grandparents the day after they'd married. Strange to think her grandparents had just given their old house to two teenage kids, but her grandparents had been even younger when they'd married fifty-one years before.

The small farmhouse had three bedrooms, a small living area, and an even smaller kitchen. Having only one bathroom had turned into a nightmare when Ellery got older, so Rex had turned a storage closet into a half bath for Ellery when she was in middle school. But the blueprint had remained the same until two months ago, when she'd hired Caldwell Contracting Services.

When Daphne had called to list the house, bouncy Shelly the Realtor had suggested a remodel. Shelly hadn't actually turned up her cute nose at the hand-painted apples on the kitchen backsplash, but she'd certainly made a face. She'd prescribed a weeklong viewing of HGTV for Daphne, who'd never realized how important open living spaces, en suite bathrooms, and big walk-in closets were to potential buyers. Oh, and heaven forbid someone have carpet. Berber and white appliances were the kiss of death.

"We're going to leave this open until we get the tub and vanity inside, then we'll close her up and work from the inside. But, yeah, it's looking good."

"When will you be totally done?" Daphne asked, thinking about Ellery's upcoming birthday at the end of October. Her daughter would be turning twenty-three. How was that even possible? When Daphne closed her eyes and thought about her daughter, she saw a little girl in pigtails, stamping her foot over not getting the fluffy puppy behind the pet store glass. Her daughter had grown into a beautiful, complicated, creative young woman . . . who still wanted her mother to bake her a chocolate cake and throw her a fun party. But with more weeks of construction left, Daphne would have to figure out something else for Ellery's birthday.

"About a month. Probably the second week of November if everything arrives on time. It's going to be dusty and messy until then, but in the end, you'll have a gorgeous place."

"Perfect. I need buyers, and Shelly promises it has a better chance at selling with these changes. I hope I can recoup the money invested." When Daphne had decided to move into town, she'd offered the house to Ellery and her fiancé, Josh, but her daughter hadn't wanted to live in the country. With her career in fashion up in the air after a missed internship, and Josh potentially going elsewhere for residency, it didn't make sense to hold on to the family property. Time for someone else to make a home in the farmhouse.

"You'll recoup and then some, but I can't believe you're selling this place," Clay said, looking around at the bucolic pasture with the old barn that she still needed to clean out. "We had some good times out here."

"Yeah, well, Ellery's not too happy about me moving, but she doesn't want the house, so . . ." Daphne wiped a hand across her brow. They needed a cold front soon. October in north Louisiana often felt like coming out at the wrong end of Saint Peter's gate.

Clay chuckled. "You mean Ellery's not getting her way?"

Daphne snorted. "Shocking, right? I don't want to live out here by myself any longer. Time for a new start for me and Jonas."

Hearing his name, the old hound rose from the shade of the oak tree and ambled over. He pressed himself against Daphne's leg, sat down, and issued a big sigh.

Both she and Clay smiled at the older dog. Jonas, named for Ellery's favorite boy group when she was younger, would soon be settling his old bones at the new small patio home being built in Bordeaux Village. Daphne was excited about this next step in her life. With clean lines and a gorgeous cobbled courtyard, her new place would be the blank slate she needed to launch a new Daphne. No longer was she merely Ellery's mom or Rex's wife. She was a successful artist and author. Every time she remembered that, she wanted to pinch herself. It was almost like a do-over for her life.

"A new start's always good. Still, this place is just what I want when I get ready to settle down," Clay said, longing lacing his words.

"You're too young to settle down," Daphne said, glancing at him. His shirt still hung open, and the sunglasses he'd pulled on when they'd walked away from the house kept her from seeing his emotions. He looked exactly like what he was—a guy with the world in his hand.

"Not that young. I'm twenty-five, and I've played pretty hard for the past few years. Kind of tired of that life." He shrugged a shoulder. "Even Ellery's getting married."

"But not yet," Daphne said, thankful her daughter hadn't insisted on a wedding within the year. With Ellery's fiancé in med school and her own career on hold, the last thing her daughter needed was the hassle of planning a wedding. Once Ellery got a satisfactory job and Josh got through at least his second year of medical school, they could look at planning a wedding.

"Yeah, but I'm tired of the life I'm leading. It gets old, and I'm ready to find someone who wants to stay home and not party," Clay said, hooking a thumb in his waistband, which, of course, drew her attention to the lighter skin revealed at his waist.

She pulled her gaze away and vowed to complete the dating profile she'd started on MadeForMe.com but never finished. No more looking at Clay Caldwell like he was . . . a man. He used to swipe beer from her fridge and play badminton in the side yard, for heaven's sake. He was a kid. Okay, not technically. But a kid.

"Well, I need to run some errands. I can put Jonas in the laundry room if you want," she said, smoothing her damp hands against her shorts. She had planned on tackling a new proposal for the holiday series but had gotten distracted by boxing up the kitchen. Updated tile and kitchen counters would go in once Clay finished with the bathroom and closet. So much to do to get ready to turn the house over . . . but she needed to drop off her father's new medication, then pop in to her ex-husband's heating and AC–repair company to leave him a few tax files he'd orphaned in the hall closet and called about.

"Nah, leave him outside. That's what you want, right, boy?" Clay gave Jonas a scratch behind his ears. The dog immediately flopped over and offered his belly to be scratched. Clay squatted and obliged.

"Now you've done it. He'll have you giving him belly rubs every day," Daphne said, brushing a hand through hair that had frizzed with the heat of the day.

Clay looked up at her, his mouth curling into a lazy grin. "I'm good at scratching an itch."

She didn't think he was talking about Jonas.

Holy hell.

"Uh, I better get going," she said, pressing her hands against her shorts again. She knew she looked rattled. Hell, she *was* rattled. Not because Clay Caldwell had pretty much started flirting with her, but because she had a sudden inclination to roll over.

And that was unacceptable. And stupid. And dangerous.

All things Daphne Witt had never been.

CHAPTER TWO

Dear Miss O'Hara,

I love the way you described the sun setting on Caddo Lake. Guess that's what authors do, huh? I've always thought it was like God finger painted an ending to the day. Soothes me. You say you have a place on the lake? Must be nice to get away for a few days when you want. I'm sure it's easier to write your stories when you feel at peace. We have a small lake on the vineyard property that I sometimes visit to fish or just connect with myself. You know we have a house that people can rent. Of course, I prefer the bed and breakfast since french roast coffee is steps away, but we rent that house out fairly often. If you ever want to plan a writer's retreat, it's a good option. We host lots of writers. They like the quiet and the wine. Ha. I'm not giving up on getting you to come speak. As the only male chairperson for PTSA, I've promised to deliver

big on Book Week. You're my ace in the hole . . . if
you'd just say yes to me.

Don't make me tell the world Dixie Doodle is really
a hound named Jonas.

Best,
Evan

Ellery Witt stared at the blinking cursor and wondered if she should
confess her crime.

Which technically wasn't a crime. Just a deception.

After all, pretending to be her mother was expected of her as
Daphne's assistant. She pretended to be her mother on social media, on
blog posts, even on one phone interview when her mother had a killer
migraine and couldn't reschedule. Being Dee Dee O'Hara, the creator
(and owner) of Dixie Doodle a Southern Belle Poodle was ironically
something Ellery was good at.

That's what a degree in fashion design got a girl—pretending to be
someone else. And working on the floor of Selber's department store
for minimum wage.

And that's what rubbed her ego until it was a tender blister. She'd
done everything she was supposed to do in college. Yeah, she did the
sorority thing, even becoming Rush Chair, but she'd skipped going
to keggers in order to get her design projects perfect down to the last
itty-bitty detail. She'd participated in every showcase, gone the extra
mile, sat on committees she didn't want to all so she could get a leg up.
And . . . nothing.

She could admit that putting all her eggs in one basket had been a
mistake. She hadn't pursued internships with any other companies like
she should have because she had been so certain J.J. Krause would hire
her. When she'd Skyped in for her interview with the design company,

she'd been shocked to find that Jaclyn Joy Krause herself was conducting the interview. Ellery'd had a sizzling, connective energy with the up-and-coming darling of the fashion world—they'd even finished each other's sentences. J.J. had all but told her she'd be flying Ellery to Milan for the next show as her intern. But then J.J. had gone with a total poser famous for his epic cocktail parties and snarky blog posts. The guy had visited Italy a few times, and suddenly he had his thumb on the pulse of European fashion? Please. The dude was from Minnesota. Ellery had been crushed when J.J.'s assistant had called to get her address so they could send her a conciliatory last-season clutch.

All her hard work hadn't amounted to beans. She should have gone to the parties and written dumb Snapchat stories about ugly shoes. Maybe then she'd be working for a designer instead of selling ladies daywear on the floor of the local department store and being her mother's minion.

And she wouldn't be so scared that everything she wanted would never be hers. Because that was what she felt—frightened that she couldn't do what she'd always said she would do. Everyone expected her to succeed, to be the best, to wear the right clothes, marry the right man, and have the fabulous career.

Or maybe that's what she expected from herself.

"Hey, have you seen my clinic jacket?" Josh said, riffling through the laundry basket sitting on the love seat. "I need it tomorrow."

"Haven't seen it," Ellery said, covertly watching him but pretending she was engrossed in her mother's email. Her fiancé had come home late, and the dinner she'd fixed to celebrate their eighteen-month anniversary had congealed into something inedible.

"Damn, effing Forester wants us to wear them tomorrow. He does this crap, making us jump through his hoops, so he can humiliate someone. Forecast for tomorrow: a wet one for the schmuck who forgets the jacket," Josh said, not bothering to look her way as he next went for the small coat closet.

Ellery had tried to punish him with her silence, but he hadn't even noticed. She and Josh had gotten engaged at the end of the summer when they'd gone with her father and his girlfriend, Cindy, to Seaside, Florida. The marriage proposal had been expected and perfect—a sunset, a table set with champagne, and waves crashing in the distance. The engagement ring was almost ridiculously too big, and Josh had dropped to a knee even though she knew he hated getting his pants sandy. They'd moved into the adorable town house in August, and Ellery had carefully constructed a tasteful, fun vibe for the place. Clean lines, whimsy, and comfortable furniture they could use once they bought a house. Everything should be gravy.

Except it wasn't.

Because Josh had spent every waking moment of the last month and a half either studying with his study group or studying by himself. He ate breakfast while tapping on his computer and came to bed long after she'd turned off her bedside table lamp. They'd had sex once since medical school had started. And it hadn't been great. More like an afterthought.

"Maybe you left it in your car?" she asked, tapping the icon that would close the email from Evan McCallum.

"Nah, I already checked there," he said, going into the kitchen and opening the fridge to take out the bottle of wine she'd been saving to celebrate their eighteen-month anniversary. It didn't escape her that he was uncorking a bottle from Evan's winery they'd purchased at the farmers' market.

Evan McCallum had emailed her mother months ago, asking if she would be the guest author for his daughter's school's Book Week in the spring. He'd written a clever email to Dixie Doodle, inviting the flighty poodle to attend and bring her owner if she must. Ironically, Evan's email had landed in her mother's overflowing in-box the day Ellery had learned J.J. Krause had given her position to Frankie Rizzo. And really, who even made up a name that bad? And wore fedoras and wing tips with rolled-up jeans. Can you say *Trying too damned hard*?

So the email had felt prophetic.

She'd written Evan back as her mother, apologizing for being months late in answering and then explaining she couldn't commit to the spring date until she heard from her publisher and the network. Ellery had been clever herself, writing as the poodle, which had amused Evan. Right after she emailed him, she'd looked him up on Facebook. She wasn't even sure why. Maybe because he lived fairly close. Or maybe because she'd been searching for something to distract her. Evan didn't have a personal page, but his vineyard had one. There were pictures of a handsome man with a too-engaging smile wearing a cowboy hat and directing workers harvesting the vines. In one picture an adorable red-headed little girl clung to his leg. She looked at that picture four times that night. He seemed so . . . intriguing.

Then she'd seen his wine at the farmers' market, and it felt like the universe was telling her something. What that was, she had no clue. But since then, they'd been exchanging emails almost daily, and she'd found herself telling Evan things she'd never told anyone else. Like about her nightmares, her fear of failure, and how frustrating rejection had been. She'd even mentioned the problems her "daughter" was having with her career and engagement. She wasn't sure why she did this. He was a stranger, but somehow it felt safe, as if he weren't real. Like the harmless fan mail she'd sent weekly to the Jonas Brothers when she was twelve. The boy group had been nebulous, too far away to be relevant in her life.

Of course, the problem was Evan lived only a few hours away . . . and thought Ellery was her mother. Not to mention she'd been bordering on flirtation in her emails. Oh, and, yeah, she was engaged to another man.

Ellery looked up at her fiancé, who was pouring the delicious red wine they'd bought on a rare morning when Josh had agreed to skip study group for the farmers' market. Josh was wholly gorgeous—blond, blue eyed, with a cute swoop of hair that looked preppy and edgy at the same time. When she'd seen him across the room at the frat house, she'd known she'd found the perfect complement to her own style. She'd made her way toward him, skirting a guy gatoring on the fraternity house floor, which had been covered with sticky spilled drinks and God only knew what else. When Josh had turned toward her and rolled eyes that were the exact same shade as hers, she'd known they were meant to be.

Things had been so good—football tailgates, fraternity formals, ski trips—and then Josh had been accepted to med school in her hometown. The fates had stamped their futures together. Ellery finished up school, applied for the internship, and waited for glory to find her. She'd work in the city—New York City—while Josh completed medical school. Then they would reunite and begin their life together. Josh would be a plastic surgeon, and Ellery would own her own company or work for Neiman Marcus; either way she'd blossom into greatness. Easy peasy lemon squeezy.

Oh, she'd gotten the lemons all right.

"This is good wine. Where'd you find it?" Josh said, holding the goblet to the light. They'd taken a wine-tasting class this past summer—Josh's concession to help Ellery feel better about not getting the Krause internship—and he loved to show off what he had learned.

"Look at the label," she snapped, feeling annoyed he hadn't remembered he'd picked out that particular wine.

"One Tree Estates? Is this what we bought a few weeks ago?"

"Yeah, back when we actually did things together," she said, closing her computer and setting it on the glass-and-cypress coffee table Josh had bought without her. She'd wanted to protest him picking out a coffee table without her approval, but she couldn't because the thing was gorgeous and exactly what she'd pick anyway. "I'm going to bed. You coming?"

He sank onto a barstool. "Don't be mad, baby."

"I'm not mad," she lied. She'd known med school would be tough on both of them. Just not this tough. She hated feeling the way she did.

"You sure? Because I don't want you to be mad at me."

She nodded. "I'm not."

"Good. I'm going to run over to Drew's. I borrowed his notes for a class. Besides, I think I left my coat in his trunk."

"It's almost eleven o'clock," she said, standing and smoothing the men's undershirt tank over her baggy gym shorts. Her bun was falling out, and she wore the glasses that made her look smart. Josh loved when she worked the sexy nerd vibe. Or he used to. Back before they got engaged and he became so consumed with being at the top of his class.

On one hand, she was enormously pleased at how driven Josh was; on the other, she wished she mattered as much as his career goals. He rarely made time to be with her anymore, unless he counted sitting on the couch typing on his laptop as quality time with her. She couldn't remember the last time they'd actually looked each other in the eye and had a conversation about something other than what had happened at school that day. Ellery wanted Josh to *see* her.

Maybe she was being selfish. Josh was such a good guy, and he loved her. She knew this, but she'd never been so lonely in her entire life, which was strange because she had moved back to Shreveport, a place where her family lived, where she knew people who were happy to meet up for happy hour.

So what was wrong with her?

Perhaps if she'd gotten the internship, she wouldn't have time to be so introspective or discontent. She would have been too busy to miss her man. She'd be Ubering to fashion week locations and meeting designers at intimate parties. New York City and J.J. Krause had betrayed her.

If wishes were horses, beggars would ride.

Her mother had told her that all her life, but Ellery hadn't had to hear it all that often. She'd gotten what she wanted—the cute car, head cheerleader, the "right" sorority, good grades, and the perfect fiancé. Until recently.

Oh, cry me a river, sister, with your #firstworldproblems. You didn't get something you wanted. Welcome to life.

Josh set the goblet on the counter and rose, jogging her from her self-pity.

"I know it's late, babe, but this has to be done. You go on to bed. I'll be back soon. Save me some kisses." Josh smoothed his hair in the foyer mirror as he picked up his car keys. The man had been studying or whatever he did for hours and still not one hair out of place. At that moment Ellery didn't feel like a rumpled sex kitten; she just felt rumpled. Maybe she even needed a shower. She quelled the urge to sniff in the direction of her armpit.

Josh jogged over, gave her a quick peck and a light slap on her butt. "Later, fancy pants."

Ellery summoned a smile. "Don't work too hard. I worry about you, you know."

"Don't worry," he said, opening the door and stepping out into the fall humidity. "I'm doing this for us. It's going to pay off, you'll see."

When the door closed, she stared at the dead bolt for a full ten seconds, wondering if his words would prove true. They'd planned a future, laying it out like a house plan. Here's where we'll do this. Over there we'll do that. Foundation, walls, heated floors so their toes would be toasty in the winter. Yet she wondered if they'd started building on shifting sands. What if she and Josh weren't right for each other? What if they were making a mistake?

No. They were perfect together. Everyone said so.

Turning, she picked up her laptop and climbed the stairs.

She should come clean with the winemaker tonight. Just tell him she'd been lonely and hadn't meant to mislead him by pretending to be her mother. But the thought of no longer exchanging emails with him made her feel even lonelier.

Emailing another man as her mother wasn't *too* wrong. Wasn't like she was cheating. She just maintained a dishonest friendship with a gorgeous man who probably didn't deserve to be duped.

As she climbed the steps, she traced the apple on the cover of her laptop. She'd tell Evan the truth.

Eventually.

CHAPTER THREE

"Hey, honey," Daphne said, lifting Ellery's ponytail from her neck and giving it a tug. She loved her daughter's hair—a gorgeous shade of blonde Ellery highlighted. Her baby girl was too pretty for her own good. "You want lunch from Cush's today?"

Ellery brushed her hand away and tapped on the computer. "No, thanks. I need to start cutting back if I'm going to look good for my wedding. I plan to be a size zero come next spring."

"Elle, a size zero is ridiculous. People will want to *see* you in your dress, not wonder if it's Day of the Dead or something." Daphne tried to keep her voice light, the way she always did when she tried to suggest something to her daughter. Ellery always bristled at any hint of criticism, but lately it had been worse.

"Real funny, Mom." Ellery clicked on the graphic and dragged it to a tiny folder, where it disappeared. "I'm going to look healthy. I'm working out at the Barre four times a week. I'll have the body of a goddess. You want to come with me? They have a beginner class."

"What are you trying to say?" Daphne asked. Ellery always tried to get her to go to exercise classes, but Daphne preferred running most days. Organized classes had never appealed to her. Exercise was her escape, a time she could jab in her earbuds and listen to podcasts or a book that didn't feature poodles and tea parties.

"That you isolate yourself out here. Hanging out with Pop Pop and Tippy Lou isn't exactly being social. You can make friends in these classes, plus use muscles you never knew you had." Ellery rose and smoothed the T-shirt swing top she wore over a pair of ripped boyfriend jeans. Several strands of delicate gold chain were layered around her neck. Her daughter somehow managed to look stylish and trendy in sloppy clothes. Daphne always looked . . . well, sloppy in sloppy clothes.

"Maybe," she conceded, only because her daughter was unfortunately correct. She enjoyed visiting her father and playing dominoes with his friends, even if they were out of her age range. And her neighbor Tippy Lou Carmichael, while delightfully droll and enigmatic to the point of oddness, wasn't going to go shopping with her or out to drinks. Tippy Lou preferred herbal tea on her front porch while she watched the feral cats she fed every morning chase lizards and laze about in her garden.

Daphne had always been the type of person to have only a few close friends. Though she'd cultivated friendships with many of the other teachers at Saint Peter's Day School, where she'd worked as a teacher's aide for fifteen years before staying home to write, she'd never been good at being social. She had church friends, a book club, and knew a few local writers who wrote professionally, but her best friend, Karyn Little, had moved to Idaho with her new husband over a year ago.

In a few short years, she'd lost her husband to self-centeredness and her BFF to the land of potatoes.

"Not maybe. Definitely," Ellery said, looking over at her.

"Maybe I'll try it." Going to the class with Ellery might help their relationship, something that Daphne couldn't seem to get back on track. She didn't know what was wrong, how she should act, whether she should have given Ellery a job or not. Daphne had only wanted to make things better for Ellery. That's what every mother did, right?

But Ellery had grown more and more distant over the past few months. Daphne suspected that it had something to do with something Rex had said, but Ellery wouldn't open up. Any time Daphne asked her what was bothering her or if she wanted to talk, her daughter would tell her everything was "fine." She'd begun to hate that word.

"I'm pretty much done for the day. I have to mail these packages. These are a few of the winners from your online party." Ellery picked up a bag full of colorful pink envelopes.

"I had an online party? When did you do that?" Daphne asked.

Ellery rolled her eyes. "Mom, I know you're happy to dump a lot of this stuff on me, but you have to keep tabs on your fans so you know what they want. That's something many retailers get wrong—they lose touch of who their consumer is. Your goal is to sell books and broaden your reach. It's important you don't get too far away from your readers. Go on your interactive website. Check out the games the kids are playing. We just started a 'Design Dixie Doodle's New Collar' contest. Some of the entries are seriously cute."

"Dixie's getting a new collar?" Daphne asked, miffed her daughter had designed a contest without her approval. Dixie Doodle was her damned poodle. She decided when the fictional purebred got a new collar.

"Her winter collar. Maybe you can even include the collar that wins in one of your upcoming books," Ellery said, walking out the door and right into Clay.

"Whoa, hey, Elle," he said, grabbing her elbow and steadying her. "I haven't seen you in forever."

"I saw you last week at Elmo's," Ellery said, shrugging off Clay's hand. "But I guess you were too trashed to remember?"

"Hey, I was celebrating a new contract, but, yeah, I guess I had a few too many."

"Honestly, Clay, it's time you grew up," Ellery said, pushing past him before spinning back. The Tom Ford scent she wore tickled Daphne's nose.

"Guys never grow up, do we?" Clay joked.

"Some don't." Ellery gave him a flat look.

Her daughter had dated several guys in high school but had been tight-lipped when it came to information on what had happened between her and Clay. Daphne vaguely remembered a dustup with the head cheerleader for a rival school. Ellery had been only a sophomore, and Daphne remembered Clay being her daughter's first heartbreak. Ellery had rebounded quickly with the quarterback for the Riverton Falcons. She had an uncanny ability to hook a new, even cuter guy after each successive breakup through high school and college.

Point in case—Josh was so pretty angels sang when he walked by.

Daphne still didn't know her soon-to-be son-in-law very well because he was always studying, but he seemed to truly care about her daughter. And that was what mattered most.

"I'm out, y'all." Ellery disappeared.

Clay turned his pretty blue eyes on Daphne. "Sorry to interrupt. I wanted to get your opinion on the marble. They sent two different samples in your color range. One has a lot of movement, the other is pretty simple."

"Sure, I'll take a look," Daphne said, following him outside her office and into the heat of late morning.

Ellery tossed the bag of packages into the narrow back seat of her sleek new Lexus and gave them an absentminded wave.

"She's a firecracker," Clay said with a smile before jogging down the front porch steps. Today he wore a T-shirt. Thank God. The jeans fit him like a second skin, though. So now she had to contend with the butt thing.

Not only had she practically drooled over a shirtless Clay yesterday, but she'd actually rated the bag boy's backside that morning at the grocery store. Thankfully Steve the bag boy was older than Clay, but she was now convinced her libido had written a memo titled "Take Care of Your Sexuality before You Mount the Bag Boy." She wondered if something was wrong with her hormones. Or maybe she was ovulating. Something other than going middle-aged crazy.

Wait, was turning forty years old hitting middle age?

Nah. And technically she was still thirty-nine for the next two months.

She just needed a man her own age, a nice companion to take her to dinner, to watch TV with her, and to give her regular sex so she didn't do anything crazy. Too damn bad there wasn't a plethora of decent fortysomething-year-old men waiting for a fortysomething-year-old woman needing a booty call.

Clay walked her out to a sheet of plyboard sitting on two sawhorses, forming a makeshift desk. He had a clipboard, a few tools, and two white-and-gray Carrara marble samples. Picking up one, he traced the veins. "See? Lots of movement here. I think it will look good since you went with the gray cabinets. Now this one has less movement, but it will look good, too."

"Which one would you choose?" she asked, noting how masculine his hands were. She fanned herself, wishing the blasted heat would go away. *It's October, Mother Nature. Get a damned clue.*

"Well, I like a lot of movement in stone. Hides flaws and, I don't know, seems to have more life. It invites you to touch it." Clay stroked the white marble with the smoky swirls again. She wasn't sure if it was the poetic words or the actual caressing of marble that beckoned her libido forth again.

She swayed toward him.

"Hey, you okay?" Clay said, looking at her with concern.

"Oh yeah. It's just hot out here." She lifted her brown, curly hair from her sweaty neck and told herself that was the truth. It had nothing to do with the way Clay—who was practically a child—was stroking the damned marble. Something had to be wrong with her. Maybe she needed to make an appointment with Dr. George.

"A cool front's coming in tomorrow. Now tell me which one so you can get out of this heat." He tapped the clipboard. "Gotta get this order in to stay on schedule."

"The one you liked is fine," she said.

"You sure? You aren't being picky over this. Most women make me show 'em tons of samples."

Daphne shrugged. "I'm picking this for the new owners. You like this one. I'm going with it. Easy enough."

"You sure aren't like your daughter. She gets her panties up her crack if a guy breathes wrong." His words should have been an insult, but they held affection. Clay didn't seem to understand that he'd hurt Ellery long ago. Some guys were just oblivious.

Ellery was strong, opinionated, and somewhat manipulative, but she was also warm, generous, and clever. From the beginning, holding Ellery was like holding a baby doll with blonde curls, big blue eyes, and a Cupid's bow mouth. Ellery learned early on how to work things to her advantage. She wielded her dimples like a samurai, and she mastered the perfect combination of head tilt and pout that rendered most adults helpless. It didn't hurt that her daughter was classically gorgeous—a combination that drew people close and allowed her to walk a smooth road to any destination. But having everyone wanting to bask in her glow had drawbacks—Ellery expected people to fall into line with her ideas and stubbornly refused to accept anything less than *her* vision. Clay Caldwell hadn't bought into her vision, and Ellery still nursed the slight.

"I've learned to pick my battles," Daphne said, reaching over and tapping the sample he held. "And this isn't one of them."

"You smell good," Clay said, actually inhaling near her hair.

Daphne snapped back.

Ignore the hum of whatever is awakening.

"I showered," she said with lightness in her voice.

Clay stacked the marble samples, his cheeks a bit redder than before. Like he knew he'd crossed a line. "Right. Shouldn't take too long to get this in. The supplier usually has both of these at the ready."

"Perfect," Daphne said, stepping toward the farmhouse. Her newest book—*Dixie Doodle a Southern Belle Poodle and the Disappearing Lights*—called her name, but the noisy construction and whatever this thing was that she had going on with herself, this whole Mrs. Robinson fantasy, were too distracting. "I'm going to run down to Tippy Lou's and pick up the okra for dinner tonight."

"You frying it?" Clay asked, arching his eyebrows in an endearing way.

"I'm thinking about it. Josh and Ellery usually come out. Tippy Lou, too. You're welcome to stay and eat if you want. Your brother, too. Probably the last time I'll cook before you start on the kitchen renovation." As soon as she issued the invitation, she wondered if she shouldn't have. Dinners were for family, but then again, her family had been good at no-showing. Josh studied, her father played canasta tournaments, and Ellery sometimes picked up extra shifts. Last week her daughter had missed dinner to go to book club with Rex's girlfriend, something she'd always blown off doing with her own mother. That had hurt a bit.

Calling Cindy Rutherford Rex's girlfriend felt so weird. Cindy and her then-husband, Paul, had been the youngest couple in their Sunday school class. When Cindy split with Paul, Daphne had been there to lend a sympathetic shoulder. Daphne had also served on the Pioneer Center Centennial Celebration committee with the blonde, not to mention they'd lunched together, partnered for a tennis tournament, and even done a girls' trip to Cabo together. So the thought of Cindy living with Rex, eating his half-charred burgers, and folding his boxers was . . . well, awkward.

It bugged the hell out of her that Ellery preferred to spend time with Cindy over her own mother. When Ellery had moved back, the silver lining to her daughter's disappointment had been the opportunity to reconnect. But something sat stalwart and fat between them. Daphne wasn't sure what it was—blame, anger, or just Ellery pulling away into being an independent adult. But it was there all the same in the way Ellery sometimes looked at her, the shortness of their conversations, and her daughter's general lack of enthusiasm for going shopping or making brownies. Daphne was all aboard her new life plan, but the one thing she didn't want to let go of was the closeness she'd once had with Ellery. Her career and Ellery going to college had been a roadblock, but Daphne had been determined to reestablish their close relationship.

She just wished Ellery had gotten that memo.

"Cool. I'll ask Law, too. If I come, I'll bring dessert," Clay said.

"Now that I don't need," Daphne said, reminding herself that Clay was her contractor and a kid. He wasn't looking at this as anything other than dinner, the same way he would have six or seven years ago when she had tons of teenagers staying over for dinner. Her crazy preoccupation with noticing Clay as a man was *her* problem, and she needed to get it under control.

With that in mind, Daphne climbed into her eight-year-old Acura and drove down the road to Tippy Lou's ranch-style house. When she climbed out, a cat shot out from the porch to curl around her ankles.

"Hey, Butterbean," Daphne said, reaching down to give the fat old tom a scratch behind his ragged ears. Butterbean was one of the tame cats. The ferals skulked about, eyeing her with suspicion. Many had been trapped, fixed, and rereleased. All were well fed and slept in the old barn.

"Howdy, Daphne," Tippy Lou called from the swing on the deck she'd built beneath the shade of several pecan trees. She fanned the smoke and pinched the glowing end of the joint. "I'll put 'er out."

Daphne climbed the steps. "Thank you."

"It's medical," Tippy Lou said, as she always did.

They smiled at each other and said in harmony, "No, it's not."

"But it helps," Tippy Lou said, smoothing the seat beside her. Tippy Lou had been Daphne's mother's best friend, and the woman had stepped in as a mother figure when Daphne lost her mom. Daphne visited a few times a week for tea, advice, and much-needed laughter.

"Helps what?" Daphne said, wrinkling her nose at the potency of the pot. Tippy was also an old hippie who hadn't bothered to surrender the Bohemian lifestyle she'd discovered in the late sixties. Her one concession was she didn't drive her "groovy" van any longer and she'd settled down in her great-aunt Maude's house. She still dressed in wild prints, wore her hair in a long braid, and listened to weird music.

"Everything," Tippy Lou said with a laugh. "You should try some. Loosen up a bit."

"I'm loose."

Tippy Lou's reply sounded half strangle and half cackle.

"I am," Daphne said, knowing she wasn't exactly "loose," even if she tried to master not giving a damn.

"You're as loose as these jeans," Tippy Lou said, lifting her polyester tunic to reveal a flap of skin hanging over her waistband. The jeans looked decidedly uncomfortable.

"How are you even breathing?" Daphne joked, kicking the swing into motion.

"I was breathing very well until you got here, tight-ass," Tippy Lou said, casting a glance at the extinguished joint.

"I'm not a tight-ass. In fact, I invited a twentysomething-year-old man to eat with me tonight." Damn it. Why had she said that? Tippy Lou was astute, always looking for hidden meanings and reading people's emotions. Daphne didn't want to let Tippy Lou sense a crack in her sanity when it came to Clay. The woman had been pushing her to get in touch with her inner goddess for months. Thus the book on arousing her inner female sexuality. Lord.

"Did you say you invited a twentysomething man to eat you?" Tippy Lou said, turning laughing brown eyes on her.

"Yeah, I'm going to strap myself down naked on the dining room table." Daphne snorted.

"I've done that before. Make sure you don't use furniture polish. I had a rash on my ass for a week."

"Lord, Tippy, that's TMI."

Tippy Lou laughed, stopped the swing, and stood. "It's too hot out here. Let's go inside and have some tea."

"Or wine," Daphne said, holding up the portable wine chiller containing the vintage Ellery had bought at the farmers' market and left for her to try.

"Not for me. I've decided to give up drinking anything except whiskey and then only when I have a chest cold. And that's because my grandmother swore by it. Of course, I suspect she was a closet alcoholic." Tippy Lou held open the old screen door.

"Why would you give up drinking? That's what makes life tolerable," Daphne joked, stepping into the house and back in time. Tippy had kept the velour couches, hand-hooked rug, and Home Interiors decorations her aunt Maude had used circa 1982. Even so, the house comforted, like going back and being in one's childhood . . . as long as childhood contained incense and a full-size statue of an earth goddess.

Tippy Lou went into the kitchen, which featured Formica counters filled with a collection of cheerful teapots and stacks of bills. "I got a whole mess of okra out of the garden this morning. They're tender, too." Tippy passed her a wrinkled brown paper bag.

"Thanks, Tippy. You coming for dinner? It'll be the last dinner before they rip my kitchen apart."

"Is it all veggies this time?"

"No. Meat loaf."

"I'll take a rain check. You know I'm opposed to eating things killed with a sledgehammer."

"Thanks for that image," Daphne muttered, accepting the chipped teacup filled with the wine Tippy had opened. Tippy set about making herself a cup of tea while Daphne sipped the surprisingly good wine and enjoyed the absence of whining saws and hammers beating a rhythm on the side of the house.

Tippy plonked down beside her. "So tell me about this guy."

"There's no guy. I was joking. My contractor Clay wrangled an invitation to dinner. His brother, Lawrence, too. You know the Caldwell boys."

"Knew their daddy. He was a hell raiser and filled out a pair of biker pants nicely." Tippy sipped her tea, her blonde eyebrows arching. "I can read you, you know. You sure you don't have something cooking with that boy?"

Boy. Exactly.

"No, he's a kid. Well, man. But you know. He just mentioned liking home cooking, so I told him to stay for dinner if he wanted. No big deal. I was joking earlier since you implied I was a tight-ass. I'm going to complete my online dating profile, and I'm on chapter twelve of the book you gave me."

Tippy studied her for a moment. "You'll find a lot to like about the perineal sponge—it's erectile tissue, you know."

"Please, Tip," Daphne said, gulping her wine.

Tippy Lou gave her a cat smile. "So you'd rather talk about the sexual benefits of a younger guy?"

"What? No." Daphne nearly choked.

"You like him."

"He's way too young for me."

"I'm reading your aura. It projects horniness and confusement."

"*Confusement* is not a word, and I'm not horny," she lied. Because she *was* something. Which again was both disturbing and a relief. "I'll admit I need to start dating—"

"Or fucking," Tippy interrupted.

Daphne made a face. "Language, Tippy."

Tippy Lou snorted. "Sorry, Emily Post."

Daphne rolled her eyes. "You're right. I need something more in my life, but not with *Clay*. Ellery dated him in high school, for heaven's sake."

"Not for long, and is she dating him now?"

"You know she isn't. She's engaged to Josh."

"Who has his own aura issues, but he's not our focus at present," Tippy Lou said, removing the tea bag and taking a sip. "It's not like you'll go to jail for doing the Caldwell boy. He's legal. If you got an itch, and he's willing to do a little tickling, let him, for goddess's sake."

"I will not," Daphne said, setting the cup down harder than intended. Sudden tears welled in her eyes. To even entertain what Tippy Lou was suggesting made her feel dirty. Very, very dirty.

And tempted.

The last two years had been hard on her ego. Rex had found someone else pretty quickly. And yeah, it had been difficult seeing him happy with another woman, but Daphne had elected to ignore dating and sexuality and . . . just emotional complication. She'd spent her time traveling to book signings, attending large conventions, and flying into big cities for meetings at large boardroom tables where they set a bottle of water at one's elbow and then proceeded to talk about obscene amounts of money, production schedules, and foreign rights. She'd gone from wiping up apple juice to nodding her head as if she knew what all those executives were talking about.

Problem was, she'd been Ellery's mom, Rex's wife, and John's daughter for so long that she didn't know how to be just Daphne. Not to mention she'd never had sex with anyone other than Rex. Being intimate with someone else made her feel as if she might break out in hives. What if she wasn't good at it? How would she know if she sucked at lovemaking? Were the backs of her knees wrinkly? Her butt saggy? Her vagina stretched out?

She should probably start doing Kegels.

Tippy Lou gave her a soft smile. "You're so hard on yourself, Daph. You worry about things that don't matter. I'm not telling you to do something that makes you uncomfortable, I'm just saying life is short, honey. I know people say that all the time, but it's true. And in that short life, you deserve some happiness, some comfort . . . some good sex."

"Of course I do, but with the right person," Daphne said, polishing off her wine. She eyed the bottle and thought about having another glass but decided instead to take it with her. Surely a nice rosé would be good with dinner. "I should get going. I need to get started on dinner. You sure you don't want to come down and have a bite?"

"I'm good. Enjoy nature's bounty," she said, eyeing the crinkled bag of okra. "Including whatever the universe brings you in goodness."

Daphne rose and set her cup in the old farmhouse sink, tucking the okra beneath her arm. "The universe has brought me plenty of goodness over the last few months. Dixie Doodle is getting her own show, my daughter is engaged and living in Shreveport, and I have a contract on a new house. I'm enjoying nature's goodness."

"But you're not getting off," Tippy Lou reminded her with a smirk.

"Since you're so obsessed with having an orgasm, maybe you should screw Clay yourself."

"That poor child couldn't handle what I got," Tippy Lou said, pouring herself another cup of tea.

Daphne laughed. "You've smoked too much dope, old woman."

CHAPTER FOUR

Ellery shouldn't have come to One Tree Estates.

Driving west had seemed like a good idea a few hours ago when Josh canceled their lunch date. Again. But now she felt like a thirteen-year-old staking out the hot quarterback's locker.

The gift shop at One Tree Estates had only a few patrons, which made Ellery feel even more exposed. She browsed a rack of snarky wine-centered greeting cards while eyeing the tasting room beyond the sliding barn door.

Maybe Evan was in there pouring wine. Or working in the adjacent distillery, where they made vodka from grapes. Or maybe he was picking up his daughter from school, tousling her ginger curls and laughing about the silly antics of Farting Fredric Mooney, the scourge of the second grade at Hickory Hill Elementary School.

Or maybe Ellery had lost her damned mind for driving an hour and a half away just so she could . . . what? Spy on Evan?

Why was she so intrigued by him? She'd just sent him an email that morning after she'd woken with the revelation that she was trying too hard to make her life perfect when that didn't exist. Of course, knowing this and doing it were two different things. But for some reason she had to tell him her thoughts . . . because he would understand exactly what she meant.

Dear Evan,

Have you ever tried to wear a shoe that doesn't fit? I do that all the time. Or maybe the vision in my head doesn't always match the reality. Take every holiday. I imagine hot cider by a roaring fire, people gathered around singing carols, and everyone laughing at the joy of it all. A crown roast sits on the table, and there are piles of presents under the tree. Like the perfect commercial. But then you wake up Christmas morning, and the coffee machine is busted, you have a sore throat, and someone bought you socks. Reality versus fantasy. Sometimes it's more fun to live in a fantasy world. Maybe that's why I write children's books. It's so much nicer in my pretend world.

Best,
Dee Dee O'Hara

"Miss, can I help you?" a woman with frizzy red hair and a gorgeous silk blouse asked, interrupting Ellery's thoughts.

"Oh, I'm fine. Just browsing."

"Is this your first time visiting the winery?" she asked.

"Yes," Ellery said, placing the card with the monkey drinking from a goblet back in its slot. "I bought some wine at the Provenance Farmers Market in Shreveport a few weeks back. We drank it all. Since I was close, I thought I would come by and pick up some more." And try to catch a glimpse of the owner, like some kind of nutcase who wasn't engaged to the perfect—albeit distracted—guy.

"That's awesome. We had good success at the farmers' market there. We're working hard on expanding our distribution and letting people know there's a stellar winery here in East Texas. I'm glad we made such a good impression," she said, sticking out her hand. "I'm Marin Dorsett. My brother and I own the vineyard."

Ellery put her hand in Marin's. The woman's grasp was cool and firm. "Nice to meet you. I'm Ellery."

She intentionally left off her last name. Better to be on the downlow. Just in case.

"Have you visited our tasting room? We have several varietals here that we don't normally distribute. Our anniversary white blend just rolled out last month. It's really complex but refreshing. You can only buy it here."

"I'll do that. So tell me about owning a vineyard. Working with family is always hard, right?" Ellery asked, hoping her question sounded nonchalant and not like a fishing expedition for info on Marin's brother.

Evan's sister had rounded cheeks, a sprinkling of freckles, and bright-blue eyes, which made her both adorable and chic at the same time. "You could say that, though I cannot lie, my brother, Evan, is pretty spectacular. My father actually started the vineyard when we were children. Our mother left for greener pastures, and my dad, Bear McCallum, bought this acreage. It had been crosscut, and only one scraggly tree stood in the middle."

"Thus One Tree Estates?" Ellery asked.

"Exactly." Marin chuckled. "The name was a no-brainer; the actual building of a vineyard, inn, and restaurant, a little more difficult. My father knew how to grow oranges—he was originally from Florida—but not grapes. Big learning curve, but as you can see, it worked out. My brother went to college, majored in business, and then spent a few years working in California and Oregon vineyards, learning everything there is to know about growing grapes. Once he came back with all that knowledge, we expanded, adding more grapes and buying more land. We're really proud of what we're doing here."

"You should be. The wines are good," Ellery said.

"That's good to hear, especially from someone so young."

"I'm not that young," Ellery said, hating that she did indeed look so young. "It's the ponytail. I'm turning twenty-three in ten days."

"Oh Lord, sugar, that's young. I'm thirty-three and feel like I'm fifty years old. Three kids will do that to you. Well, it was nice meeting you. Buy some wine. Tell your friends. Bring them back with you. We love new patrons."

"I will," Ellery said, smiling as Marin disappeared through the tasting-room doors. Quickly, Ellery grabbed two goblets embossed with the One Tree Estates logo and walked to the register.

The woman working the gift shop wrapped up her purchases and handed her the bag with a smile. "No wine?"

"I'm going to the tasting room before I buy."

"Why don't I hold these for you then? That way they don't accidentally get knocked over and broken. Not that anyone in our tasting room ever gets a little sideways." She rolled her eyes and chuckled. "What's your name, honey?"

"Ellery. Just Ellery is fine," she said, then walked toward the tasting room, preparing herself to see the handsome man who sent her daily emails. But Evan wasn't behind the bar. A young guy with a faux-hawk wearing a Soundgarden T-shirt stood polishing glasses and conversing with two older men in business attire. He looked a little older than her, but definitely under the age of thirty.

He nodded at her when she entered. "Welcome to the tasting room."

"Well, hey now, things are looking a lot prettier around here," one of the businessmen said, giving her a crocodile smile.

Being friendly was a Texas pastime, but she was not in the mood to be hit on by guys skipping out on work for a late liquid lunch. "Thank you, sir, and thank you," she said to Faux-Hawk.

"You sure you're old enough to drink?" Faux-Hawk asked, eyeballing her.

"You sure you're old enough to serve?" she countered, showing her dimples.

The older guys hooted. Faux-Hawk's mouth flatlined. Who wore a faux-hawk anymore, anyway? That was so last decade, and even then it had been stupid. But it suited this guy in some way. Maybe because he didn't seem to be the kind to give a rip what anyone thought about him.

"Saucy, ain't she?" the other business guy commented.

"Don't worry, I'm old enough," she said, scouring the list of pours, deciding the two old guys reminded her of the cranky guys on *The Muppet Show*. "I'll try the anniversary blend Marin recommended."

Faux-Hawk looked as if he might ask for her license, but then shrugged and pulled a bottle out of the iced bin lining the back wall. He handed her a glass with a very small pour. Maybe she shouldn't have been such a smart-ass.

The wine was good—light, crisp, with a taste of pears or something. She tried to remember her tasting class. *Chalk*, *lime*, and *smoke* were words she remembered being batted around. She hadn't paid a great deal of attention because her palate obviously wasn't sophisticated enough to discern differences.

"Mm," she said, draining the glass. "That's good."

"You're supposed to taste it, not shoot it." Faux-Hawk gave her another sample.

"I know how to do tastings. I prefer to skip the swishing and spitting." But she took the second sample and spent more time rolling the vintage on her tongue. It was acidic but not terribly so. And maybe she tasted Texas sunshine in the second pour.

"What do you think?" the plumper of the two businessmen asked.

"It's good. Nice and bright," she said, happy she'd remembered that particular term from the class. It was one Josh liked to use when they went out to dinner. *It's too bright. I prefer a more subtle wine.*

"Try this one," Faux-Hawk said, taking the glass she'd set down and pouring a sample from another bottle. "This is our rosé. Little dry but has a nice finish. Perfect for hot fall afternoons."

"You sound like you memorized that," Ellery said, sticking her nose in the glass so she looked like she knew what she was doing. "Nice bouquet."

Faux-Hawk quirked a dark eyebrow as if he knew she had no clue about wine.

Ellery sipped the rosé, trying to not toss it back and get out. This guy made her uncomfortable with his discerning gaze and smoldering Adam Levine vibe. "I like it."

"Want to try something else? The Syrah? We have a red anniversary blend."

"Yeah, that's good," one of the business guys commented.

All three watched her. "I think I'll just take three bottles of the first one. The white anniversary blend."

Faux-Hawk nodded and wrote the order down, collected the wine, and placed it in a cardboard carrier. He had nice forearms and a tattoo on his biceps—a swirl of ink dipped below the edge of his T-shirt sleeve. She wondered what the tat was. She almost asked him when he took her credit card, his fingertips brushing hers, his mouth quirking at the Minnie Mouse on the card.

"Disney fan?" he asked.

"Yeah. I get points. What? You don't like Disney World?"

Faux-Hawk shrugged a shoulder. "Never been, but it seems . . . I don't know . . . kinda basic?"

"Yeah, basically fun," she drawled, trying not to prickle at his comment. He looked like the kind of guy who thought climbing mountains or biking through a desert was a vacation. She preferred mouse ears and Dole pineapple whips. Nothing wrong with a little Fantasyland.

Ellery signed the pad he flipped over with her finger. The wine was more expensive than she expected, but pride kept her from asking him to take a bottle off. Faux-Hawk flipped the pad back and handed her the receipt. "Thank you for your patronage, Ellery."

"You're welcome."

The two older guys looked at each other. Then one of them looked at Faux-Hawk. "You should get her number, Gage."

Ellery's eyes widened, and she stepped back.

Gage shook his head. "Ignore them. They've had samples of everything, which means"—he turned to the two guys—*"they're buying at least a case."*

"No worries," Ellery said, lifting the carrier. "I don't live here, anyway. And I'm engaged, so there's that. Not that your whole gruff, bossy wine-pourer thing isn't attractive."

"I'm not bossy," he said, his dark eyes drilling into her.

"It's okay. I'm not, either," she said.

The smile that curved Gage's lips changed his entire face. He had green eyes, a scruffy jawline, and the whitest teeth she'd ever seen. He could do toothpaste commercials with that smile. "Yeah, you don't seem bossy at all, and don't worry, I wouldn't have asked anyway. It's obvious you're not my type."

Ouch.

The two businessmen looked like Bambi in headlights. One lifted his eyebrows and looked away. The other picked up his cell phone and pretended to check messages.

Ellery felt the heat rise in her cheeks. This arrogant ass had just shoved her into a slot. "I'm assuming your type is someone similar to yourself? And since I'm not an asshole . . ." She shrugged one shoulder and turned away.

She crackled with outrage.

How dare he assume she was a type? He knew who she was by five minutes of her tasting wine? Ha. She didn't think so.

What an insufferable, pompous jackass. She knew who she was. Yeah, she liked nice things, as evidenced by the Lanvin bag she'd scored at a bargain basement sale in New Orleans. And maybe she spent too much on her hair products and the lash extensions. Hey, she had stubby lashes. So she wore expensive perfume and got pedicures? That made her discerning, not a type. And who didn't like Minnie Mouse?

A terrorist, that's who.

But whatever.

She pushed out into the Texas heat and stomped down a winding set of steps toward the gravel parking lot where she'd left the cute white Lexus RC 350 her daddy had bought her for college graduation. And though she loved the clean, sporty lines and the shiny chrome, the sight of her car made her stutter-step and her thoughts flash back to the lean smart-ass who'd just stereotyped her. She drove a luxury car her daddy had bought to make her feel better about failing at getting the internship. She worked a job her mother had given her so she could pay her half of the rent on the town house. She'd spent forty dollars on a blowout with money she needed to pay off the loan she'd taken for the furniture she'd bought for the guest room. She was a walking stereotype of a spoiled southern debutante with no responsibilities.

And, yeah, she'd even *been* a stupid debutante.

At that moment she despised herself, because maybe Faux-Hawk had seen exactly who she was. And maybe she didn't like who she was but didn't know how to change. Because that would mean admitting that all she'd so carefully planned could be totally . . . wrong. She felt shaky and afraid to let go of the life she'd always clung to.

Ellery sucked in a huge gulp of humidity and unlocked her doors, shoving the box with the wine into the narrow back seat. Then she climbed in, cranked up the AC, and rolled back the sunroof. Better Than Ezra, a vintage Baton Rouge rock band, poured through the speakers. She shifted gears, wishing she'd never driven west toward the high sun in order to escape her life. Wishing she'd not been so . . . curious about Evan. She hadn't even seen him, which was probably a good thing because her fascination with him was wrong. All she'd gained in the process was being insulted by a glorified salesclerk, three bottles of a good white blend she could barely afford, and guilt over not being able to run her own damned life.

As she rounded a large curve, she came upon a redheaded girl riding a bike. She wore a pink bike helmet and a wrinkled school uniform. Jogging behind her in a running tank was Evan McCallum. Even red-faced and sweaty, the man made something odd rise up within her. He raised a friendly hand as she passed them, a small twitch of his lips fading as quickly as it appeared.

Ellery glanced into her rearview mirror as he jogged around the corner, following behind his daughter. The view was pretty dang good, which made Ellery even angrier at herself. He was an older man with a kid. And she had a fiancé.

"Stop being a stalker," she muttered, wondering if she had indeed done something totally stalkerish. Did driving all the way to Deacon Point, Texas, in order to catch a glimpse of Evan qualify as stalking?

No. That was ridiculous. She had needed to get away from her world and think, and One Tree Estates was right off the interstate. Buying good wine for her birthday was on her list anyway. Surely her mother would do something fun for her birthday—she always did. Ellery's mouth watered when she thought of the Texas chocolate sheet cake with bright sprinkles Daphne always made. This time Ellery would bring the wine, so her trip had nothing to do with her inordinate interest in a man who was too old for her. Had nothing to do with the fact she felt ignored by the man she was supposed to love.

Supposed to?

No, *did*.

She loved Josh. They were going to have the perfect life together just as soon as he got through this first year of school. The first year was always the hardest, so all she had to do was hold it all together for one year. By the time May rolled around, she would have the perfect new job, and Josh would move to his second year. They'd both be closer to their ultimate goal—a successful power couple living in a gorgeous house, doing meaningful things, and being their most fabulous selves.

Looking at the clock, she mentally calculated the time it would take her to get back to Shreveport, take a shower, and make it in to work. She had to work until 8:00 that night in the miniscule couture section of Selber's. Today they would have gotten in new shipments. She'd snagged a pair of funky velvet slippers to display with the leather designer jeans they were getting in. She wanted something edgy in the display for the boutique clothing, paired with something more conservative. Something Saint John–ish. Maybe she'd add several strands of gold from the Roberto Coin jewelry collection.

Just the thought of designing a look for the winter displays soothed her. This was where she felt in control. Creating tasteful designs and hand-selling Stella McCartney and Rag & Bone were easy for her. She could see what worked for what customer, sell the dress a woman would wear time and again, pair the best accessories, and find the perfect statement pieces. Ellery Witt had been made to create and sell clothes. J.J. Krause had missed the boat.

And as Ellery angled her college graduation present onto the interstate, she remembered the wineglasses she'd left behind the desk of the gift shop.

But she wasn't going back.

Her phone rang. Her mother.

Ellery sighed and pressed the Bluetooth button on the steering wheel. "Hey, Mom, what do you need?"

"Hey, baby. I just put the peas on. You and Josh are coming to eat tonight, aren't you?"

"Oh shit. I forgot to tell you. I switched shifts with Margaret. I'm working tonight," Ellery said, changing lanes. Her mother had decreed Thursday night a sort of family night. Ellery resented that her mother had tried to revive something they'd done when they had actually been a family. They weren't a family anymore, so why bother to pretend something that wasn't there? Besides, she saw her mother nearly every day now that she worked as her assistant. Wasn't like they needed any more time together.

Part of her not wanting to be with her mom all the time was because Daphne was suffocating. When Ellery was in that house, she still felt like a little girl, like her mother was still mopping up after her. Ellery hated herself for letting Daphne assume control, she hated herself for taking the job her mother had offered. She wanted to be independent, but being her mother's assistant had been easy money and something she could use on her résumé. And it wasn't hard to do.

The other part of her aggravation with her mother stemmed from what her father had told her last summer when they'd gone to Seaside. Something she didn't know how to deal with, how to bring up to her mother, a woman who felt more like a stranger to her now.

Daphne sighed. "You sure y'all can't come? I think Clay and Law may stay for dinner. Josh can meet some of the guys you grew up with."

"I'm sorry. I'll try to leave next Thursday free."

"This will probably be the last dinner for a while. I just enjoy seeing you."

"You see me almost every day."

"But that's different." Her mother sounded sad. Ellery felt guilt crawl around inside her. Her mother always made her feel guilty. Like she didn't do enough to be a good daughter. But Ellery hadn't been the one who'd decided to change. Her mother had done that when she decided to pursue a career. That decision had toppled everything in their lives, breaking apart all Ellery had known. And now her mom was selling their house and hadn't even asked Ellery if she minded. Well, she'd asked if she and Josh might want to buy it, but that was it. Two weeks later she had a Realtor out, and a FOR SALE sign was hanging out front.

Everything felt . . . too much too fast.

"I bought some good wine today. I'll bring it by before I head into work," Ellery said, hoping her gift of wine would absolve some of the guilt for taking a shift on "family" night. Of course, her mother would probably insist on reimbursing her for the wine, which would make her feel like she couldn't pay her way. Then again, Ellery could use the extra money. Damn it, adulting was hard.

"That would be nice. I'm happy to pay you for it."

"Sure. Bye, Mom," Ellery said, switching off the phone, wishing she could keep driving past Shreveport, past Louisiana, going anywhere other than where she was now.

CHAPTER FIVE

The corn bread hadn't cooked enough in the middle. Still, it would have to do. Daphne didn't have time to make another pan—something that bothered her. She didn't cook as often as she once had, but she liked her final product to be perfect. Of course, the corn bread would taste fine with the purple-hull peas she'd bought at the farmers' market. Last bushel they'd had for the season. Daphne had gotten lucky, since peas had been scarce all summer.

Daphne pushed open the screen door. Her decorator had gasped when she'd seen it. Soon the anachronism would be replaced by french doors. Even so, Daphne liked the old-fashioned screen door with its creak and ensuing thump when closed. Took her back to her grandmother's house when there was always cold sweet tea and the sound of her granddaddy playing his guitar to an audience of field crickets.

The end of the day had brought her a cool breeze. Insolent fall was finally stepping in line. Headlights swung up the drive and Daphne checked her watch. Late, but not ridiculously so.

Bumping up her drive was the contractor's truck. *Please, Lord, let him have brought his brother.* She squinted, praying to see the shape of Clay's brother, Lawrence. Nope. Only one door opening.

Damn it.

"Hey, sorry I'm late," Clay called, climbing out of the pickup. Hooked in two of his fingers was a brown wine bag. He slammed the door. "Where's everybody?"

"Ellery's working tonight. Which means Josh won't be here, either. Is Lawrence coming?" *Please say he's on his way.*

"Nah. He said to thank you for the invite, though."

Clay stomped up the back steps. He'd recently showered, because the curls that brushed his ears were damp. He wore a gray T-shirt and a pair of jeans that were worn soft on the thighs. Cowboy boots completed his look, and the scruffy beard didn't look unkempt but instead reminded her of lazy days in rumpled sheets. That beard would provide delicious friction against—

"I brought some wine," he said, interrupting her really, really wrong thoughts. *God, Daphne, chill out and stop going there, pervert.*

Her mind zoomed to that stupid book—*The Mystery of Female Arousal.* Tippy Lou had cleaned out her shelves, and among the books on healing minerals and transcendentalism, she'd found that gem. She'd handed it to Daphne, who had just admitted she hadn't missed having sex for the past two years all that much. Tippy Lou had been aghast and insisted Daphne read it and give her reports on each chapter. She'd also mentioned masturbation and recommended a site for sex toys. Not wanting to listen to anything more about the importance of self-pleasure, Daphne had tucked the book into her bag and promised to read it.

Then tried to forget about it.

When Daphne had finally picked the book up off her nightstand weeks later because she'd read everything in her TBR stack, she'd learned about her own desires, what turned her on, some clitoral-wishbone thing, and all kinds of scientific mumbo jumbo on how to get turned on and climax for days. Okay, not really, but it had felt like that. As a result, the idea of fulfilling sex thrummed right in the middle of her cerebral cortex, which in turn told the hypothalamus to secrete testosterone and something . . . something about the amygdala. Whatever. All she knew was that reading that book had made her hyperaware that no one had touched her body for a long time. A very long time.

"How thoughtful of you," she said, taking the bag and opening the screen door. "Come on in. Everything is ready."

"Smells delicious." Clay walked past her, taking up more space than she'd estimated. His shoulder brushed against her, and she warned herself to stop thinking about sex, that book, the way he smelled, and the fact that she could probably have her panties around her ankles in 1.4 seconds.

"I hope it's good. I've been so busy, I haven't cooked much lately. Plus, it's been so hot." She pulled the wine from the bag. It was a pink zinfandel and had a lizard on it. Daphne had seen that bottle at every store that sold wine . . . even the local gas station. But no matter, the man had brought wine, which was most gracious.

"I didn't know what to get. I don't drink the stuff usually. I'm a beer guy, but the girl behind the counter said she liked this." Clay shrugged his shoulders and gave her a sheepish grin.

"It's fine. Ellery dropped some wine by earlier, and it's already chilled. So I'll just tuck this away for later." She shoved the bottle in the fridge, thinking Tippy Lou might like it. But wait, her friend had given up drinking. For now.

"Can I help you with anything?" Clay asked, setting his hands on his hips. The action made him look even more masculine. The loaded question didn't help, either. She could think of a lot of things he could help her with.

"Nope, I've got it. I usually serve family style, but since it's just me and you, I'll fix the plates and bring them into the dining room." She turned and picked up two of the stemmed glasses from the six she'd set out. "You know, on second thought, you can open the wine and pour us both a glass."

He looked at the bottle chilling in the marble wine cooler, grabbed the opener, and stared at the bottle as if perplexed. Daphne fought the inclination to take it from him and show him how to do it because it would make her look motherly. Or bossy. Or practical. So she turned and took the plates from the cabinet. The kitchen surrounding her was familiar; the man struggling to cut the foil from the top of the bottle was not.

She scooped peas and dished out mashed potatoes, okra, and meat loaf before adding a sliver of not-so-soggy-in-the-middle-anymore corn bread onto plates. Finally, Clay handed her a glass of the crisp blend from the Texas winery Ellery had been raving about for months.

Daphne took a big slug and sighed. Good stuff.

Clay sniffed at his. "They say you're supposed to smell it before you drink it. Saw that on TV one time. I don't know why. I mean, unless it smells like cow patty, you're probably going to drink it, right?"

Daphne smiled. "Oh, you know fancy people. They like the bouquet."

"Guess you ain't fancy people," he teased, nodding at the fact she'd already had two big sips.

"You would be correct," she said, handing him her glass and picking up the plates. "Follow me. I'm starving."

Clay did as bid, trailing after her as she pushed through the swinging door (another thing that would change because, duh, open concept demanded everything be visible—even the dirty dishes) and set Clay's plate across from her usual spot. She'd intentionally handed him her glass of wine so she could choose his place for him. Didn't want him right next to her where she could smell him or accidentally brush his arm.

Whether anything could actually happen between her and Clay was up for debate. The man's earlier words had felt flirty, but Daphne wasn't sure if he was being nice or was truly attracted to her. She'd heard rumors about him from Ellery. He liked to sleep around with various women, so maybe he wasn't so choosy. Or maybe she just wanted him to want her. Pathetic as it was.

"Wow, you set the table and everything," Clay said, handing her the glass that was now in need of replenishing. Maybe she'd gulped it a bit too fast.

Daphne glanced at the slightly faded zinnias she'd gathered from the cutting garden beside the barn and the pressed linen tablecloth she'd tossed on the table earlier. Gleaming flatware sat upon trifolded russet napkins. "I always try to make it an occasion. Probably silly, but it's my way of holding on to a family tradition."

"I think it's nice," he said, leaning around the table and pulling out her chair.

"Oh," she said, taken aback at the gentlemanly and somewhat date-like nicety. "Thank you, Clay."

"You're welcome. Hey, I know how to treat a lady," he said, giving her a grin that made her libido wriggle in delight.

Stop it.

"Um, prayer?" she inquired after picking up her fork.

He arched an eyebrow and shot her another grin. "Are we going to need it for some reason?"

More loaded words. She could be in deep trouble. Or totally imagining the innuendo. Cheerful teasing seemed to be Clay's nature. He did this with everyone—the grocery clerk, the lady at the lumberyard, all his female clients. "Nope. Dig in, I guess."

Clay did as suggested. "Oh man, this is even better than my nana's meat loaf. Don't tell her, though."

"Now I can blackmail you. I will so tell your nana if I don't get everything I want," Daphne said, stabbing her empty fork toward him. See? She could tease. Then she realized what her words sounded like. "I mean on the house. What I want on the house."

"Oh, so you set this up so you could get dirt on me? You're a devious woman. Exactly the kind I like." His eyes danced, and his dimples made an appearance.

Holy Hell. Dimples.

Daphne decided flirting was too dangerous, so she took another sip of wine and shuffled the peas around on her plate. "So tell me about the work you're doing downtown. I think I heard y'all were doing loft apartments?"

He took a sip of his wine. "All we've done so far is gut the old Blanco Biscuit company building. We got the bid just over a month ago, but it's a big project, so we needed some extra help. We're hiring right now. It will be fairly modern but have some rustic elements, too. Think we'll have five full-floor loft apartments and ten floors with duplex style. The guy who bought it is going to even hire a doorman."

"A doorman? In Shreveport?"

"Well, more like a security guard but, yeah, total uptown." He shoveled in a few more mouthfuls of peas and chewed thoughtfully. "It would be great for a woman like you—career-focused and single. They'll be upscale and safe, so you might want to check into it."

He thought of her as a single career gal? Something about that idea struck a chord in her. Moving off the farm and into a more manageable patio home had felt like conceding to her age and lack of a man in her life, as if she were admitting that the house she'd lived in for twenty-three years was too much for her to take care of alone. Daphne had consoled herself with the fact she was being practical and giving herself that blank slate for a new life. Clay made her sound . . . smart, successful, and not so on the shelf. Like the heroine of her own life, rather than a stuffy children's author who hadn't gotten laid in over two years. "I've already put money down on a place, but I think that sounds like a great project. Always good to bring new life to downtown."

"Yeah." He swiped the last bite of corn bread into the remaining juice left by the peas and popped it into his mouth. "That was incredible. You're a terrific cook."

Daphne looked at her own plate. She'd barely touched anything despite professing she'd been starving. Her stomach felt too jittery. She pulled a piece of corn bread free and popped it into her mouth. The buttery goodness wasn't what she wanted.

Clay pushed back his chair and went into the kitchen. "More wine?"

She looked at the one sip left in her glass.

Remember: two-glass limit, sugar britches.

"Sure," she said, eating a few more bites so he didn't notice she'd barely eaten. "I made a chocolate pie, too."

"Lord, woman, you're spoiling me. I usually eat Subway or pick up a salad from Whole Foods most days," Clay said, returning with the bottle and filling her glass nearly to the top. He sat down and poured the same amount into his. For a few minutes, they both sipped the crisp wine and allowed words to remain unspoken. Daphne tried not to down the wine too fast, but her nerves were back. Or maybe they hadn't left. She knew exactly what she'd allowed to happen by inviting Clay to dinner. Maybe she was setting this up on a subconscious level—her inner "goddess" putting all the pieces where she wanted them. So she could have exactly what she desired.

Or maybe she was thinking too damn much. The wine warmed her, curled around her like an old friend, making her feel mellow and a little sleepy. She took the last sip and set the empty glass down like a statement.

Clay set his own empty glass on the table, his eyes on her. "You know, I just don't get something."

"What?"

"Why are you out here all alone? A woman like you is the total package—smart, beautiful, successful, and"—he tapped his plate with the tines of his fork—"a good cook. I don't know how Rex let you get away and why someone else hasn't already snapped you up."

Daphne blinked several times, trying to think how to answer that loaded question. Total package? Felt more like she was a banged-up box in the return cart behind the counter. A last-season return that would be immediately tossed into the clearance section . . . or maybe she'd clung to that notion because it was safe to feel that way. After all, she'd had men show interest, but that was only after they found out who she was.

Oh, she was no celebrity in this area. People in North Louisiana were more apt to know the name of amateur dirt-bike racers than they would a local author. Still, she'd gotten a lot of press with the Disney deal, and that brought some fellas out who would normally not look her way. Opportunists weren't what she was looking for, so she'd ignored any overtures and focused on her career while giving her heart time to "get right" before diving into something.

But Clay wasn't like those guys. If anything, he was quite the opposite, with his unassuming manner, boundless enthusiasm, and generous compliments. Still, he was not the right guy to jump back into the dating pool with. Or whatever pool they were skirting around, occasionally dipping a toe into.

She folded her napkin next to her plate. "You're sweet, Clay, but in December I'll turn forty years old, and in case you're not up to speed, that's not what most single guys my age look for in a woman. Men my age want pretty, young things."

Clay tilted his head, reminding her of Jonas, who was in the laundry room and would have to be fed shortly or he'd start barking incessantly. "Are you crazy? Of course men want women like you. You don't play games or use guys to get free drinks or tickets to Dierks Bentley. You don't take constant selfies in a bikini or kiss every guy at the lake because you drank too many vodka tonics. No, you're independent, smart, beautiful. If guys your age don't want women like you, there are other guys who do. Guys who are fed up with dating immature, shallow women. Guys like me."

Daphne had wondered why Clay had been flirting with her. Now she understood. He was tired of swimming in his own dating pool. Still, his words were too much for her to handle. Oh, they were good words . . . words she'd secretly wanted to hear, but still dangerous. "I think you're painting me as something I'm not."

Pushing back her chair, she grabbed her plate and started for the kitchen. As she rounded the table, he reached over and laid a hand on her arm. "Hey, I'm not blowing smoke up your ass, Daphne."

She raised her gaze to his. He looked sincere, God help him. "Sugar, I know you're trying to make me feel good about my husband leaving me and then finding someone younger and . . . uh, bouncier . . . lickety-split. Like I said, it's sweet, but—"

Clay's laugh interrupted her. "Are you kidding? I'm not being sweet. I'm trying to get in your pants, Daphne. Maybe *you* aren't up to speed on how this works, but let me fill you in. A guy forgets to tell his brother about dinner, and then he prays Ellery and her fancy fiancé are too busy to show. Then he uses as many ways as he can to let the woman he's been thinking about for weeks know he wants her. He brings her wine, compliments her cooking, and maybe pours a little too much extra in her glass, hoping that it loosens her up a little. He tries to make her understand that he *wants* her . . . and he prays she lets him"—he took the plate from her hand and set it on the table—"kiss her."

He tugged her toward him.

"Clay, I don't think—"

"That's the problem, Daph. You're thinking." He stood, quick as a cat or some other really fast animal. A puma. A striking snake. Something dangerous and sexy slamming into her with intention. Clay cupped the back of her neck, and she looked up at him. His blue eyes were half-lidded, and they were studying her lips. He lowered his head, and when he was a mere inch or two from her lips, he whispered, "How about we don't think?"

Then he kissed her.

Clay Caldwell kissed her, and damned if her knees didn't buckle at the rush of hunger unleashed inside her body. The torso beneath his T-shirt was rock hard. This was no Rex, soft and slightly pudgy. No, this was a fantasy . . . a young, hot, hard man who knew how to kiss a woman.

The hand he'd rested on her lower back moved down, hauling her body closer to his. The fingers at her nape exerted slight pressure, tilting her head so he could deepen the kiss. His tongue invaded, causing something hot and slithery to invade her belly. No, not her belly. Lower. Deliciously lower.

He used his mouth to punish and then tease, gently sucking at her bottom lip before deepening the kiss.

Daphne, held hostage by the desire rampaging like Godzilla ripping through a city, could do nothing more than knot her hand in his shirt and hold on.

The alarm on her phone dinged. **Feed Jonas.**

Daphne tore her mouth from the delicious assault. "Clay, wait. Stop."

He did. "What's wrong?"

"We can't. We have to stop." Daphne released his shirt and pressed the wrinkles out. Her ragged breaths matched his, and she was certain her body was calling her a total idiot for halting what had been the best thing it had felt since . . . forever.

Clay sank down into his chair. "Okay."

Okay?

"It's just that this is crazy. I'm too old for you. You used to date Ellery."

He made a face. "Yeah, in high school. And we went out, like, three times."

Daphne rubbed a hand over her chest. Her heart was pounding, her nipples were hard, and the throb in her pelvis hadn't faded. She was primed like a Formula 500 engine waiting to tear around the track. "Still. This is a bad idea. You're my contractor."

"We're both adults, and it's just sex."

Just sex.

Daphne ran an unsteady hand through her hair. "Uh . . . um, how about some chocolate pie?"

Jesus, she was so lame. How about some pie? What kind of dorky, lame-ass woman who needed to have multiple orgasms yesterday turned down hot, no-strings-attached sex with a guy like Clay? The man had abs of steel, sexy blue eyes, and wanted to *do* her. And instead of shucking her drawers and climbing aboard, she'd offered him dessert.

Clay's mouth twitched. "Sure. I like pie."

Daphne all but bolted for the kitchen, thankful for the swinging door and what it could hide. She leaned over, clasped her knees, and pulled in three deep breaths.

This was crazy and she couldn't do it. She wanted to. She really, really wanted to be the kind of person who said to hell with it and let things take their course. But she was Daphne Witt, former secretary of the PTA, current children's author, and soprano in the Saint Peter's Episcopal Church choir. She couldn't. It would be so wrong.

So, so, so wrong.

But Clay could probably go all night, not the usual five minutes of thrusting before ejaculating and then rolling over and falling into a chain saw snore. She knew this from his kiss and the way he'd moved his hands slowly. He hadn't ground his pelvis into hers or rushed through the kiss so he could get right down to business. No, he was a pro.

He'd be good at sex. She knew this like she knew her checkbook would balance. Some things were sure bets.

Daphne straightened, opened the refrigerator, and removed the pie she'd baked that afternoon. Before she closed the door, she grabbed the second bottle of the white blend Ellery had brought by. Just one more glass, and then she'd shoo Clay out. Tell him she had to be in bed early because she had to take her father to the doctor tomorrow.

Exactly. She was a responsible, decent, God-fearing woman who wasn't going to let her passions rule her decisions.

Even if she really wanted to.

CHAPTER SIX

Dear Miss O'Hara,

Sometimes I like to create fantasies, too. I know what you mean about reality being tough. I'm thirty-five years old and still can't believe all the things I've been through in my life—a change in career, the death of my wife, the Dallas Cowboys losing to the Redskins. Just kidding about the last one. I'm over it. Mostly. But I get you. Sometimes you just want life to be easy and pretty, the way it is in the movies. But there's something good about those bad times. They shape us and make us into something we never thought we would be. I've learned these lessons as a wine grower. Timing is everything. When to harvest, when to lower tem-peratures, when to leave the grape on the vine. Every decision has a consequence, but you won't know the result until you uncork the bottle. Reality

can be sweet, but sometimes you don't realize it
until you look back.

Best,
Evan

Ellery looked up from her phone and surveyed the display she had
been working on for the last ten minutes. It was lacking . . . something.

"Hey, Rach, the new gloves are on the back shelf. I think it would
be better to move them to this table. Will you grab them? Oh, and then
can you fetch the hand forms from the back? We'll use those crocheted
Loro Piana gloves on one, and the long Sacai striped on the other."
Ellery shoved her phone into her pocket as Rachel went to fetch the
gloves. She and Rachel Maneri swapped out working boutique and
accessories, and because they were a good twenty years younger than
any other salesclerk, they'd bonded quickly.

Ellery scooted the white marble table with the gilded legs away
from the aisle. She'd used a half-torso mannequin and wound a soft
angora shawl around the form, securing one of the flaps high on the
shoulder with a Gas Bijoux crystal insect pin. A fuchsia Inverni cashmere beanie sat atop at a jaunty angle.

Rachel set the box down, and Ellery looked at her new friend.
"What do you think?"

"It doesn't look very fallish," Rachel said, eyeing the display Ellery
had created. "Shouldn't we use fall colors?"

Ellery rolled her eyes and faked a French accent. "Oh, darling,
you're so provincial."

"Well, excuse me. I didn't go to design school. Whoop-dee-doo."

Ellery laughed. "Point taken, but you don't have to go to design
school to see that sometimes a punch of the unexpected draws attention, makes the customer feel whimsical, fashionable, and daring. But

you're not wrong—an element of fall would be good. What about those fluorescent pumpkins? Those could be funky and sexy at the same time."

Rachel looked at her like she'd gotten into the cooking sherry. "Oooh-kay."

Ellery closed her eyes momentarily and took a moment to miss being with her design friends from college. They would have totally understood what she meant.

But she couldn't blame Rachel for thinking her pairings odd. After all, Rachel majored in accounting or something else number oriented. Right from the beginning Rachel had remarked on the silliness of high fashion and said she worked at Selber's only because her grandmother, who worked in bridal registry, had gotten her a job over the summer. Summer had faded into autumn, and Rachel decided she could handle a part-time job and school, even though she thought everything in the store was overpriced and ridiculously frivolous.

For some reason Ellery's mind drifted back to Faux-Hawk and his assessment of her. So she appreciated couture? The Ralph Lauren, Diane von Furstenberg, Carolina Herrera, and Stella McCartney collections often made her stop in her tracks and trace the satin seams or brush the fine wool. Nothing wrong with liking nice things. Or Minnie Mouse.

Rachel trudged to the back for the hand forms. The store had closed to customers fifteen minutes before, and Ellery still hadn't heard from Josh. It was Thursday night, and she'd ordered him to pull away from studying long enough to meet her at Sutton's Steakhouse for a drink before the bar closed. She'd used a sexy Bitmoji and then an actual Snapchat of her giving him a Marilyn Monroe–worthy pout. But he hadn't responded.

Her stomach growled.

"Hungry?" Rachel asked, plonking down the hand forms, grabbing the striped glove, and threading it onto the longer form.

Ellery pressed a hand against her stomach. After she'd left the vineyard, she'd found a protein bar in her glove box and had that for lunch.

She thought about the scents in her mother's kitchen when she dropped off the wine, taking the stupid money for it even though she'd told herself she wouldn't. But when your mom held out three twenty-dollar bills with a smile that said "Whatever you want, baby," it was hard not to snatch the cash and make excuses for why she took it. The wine had been good, but the memory of Gage the barkeep's knowing smirk and the way he'd looked down on her like she was some silly piece of frippery had soured her. Not to mention the whole reason why she'd gone—snooping around a guy she had no business snooping around. "Yeah, I'm starving."

"You want to go over to Jason's Deli when we're done here? I think they're open until nine thirty."

Ellery didn't want a salad and iced tea. She wanted vodka and her fiancé. Her face must have portrayed that.

"If you don't want to, no biggie. It's not like I can't meet up with my friends." Rachel's defensive words were drizzled with hurt. Rachel had been a few years behind Ellery in school, and she vaguely remembered her as slightly emo, a little nerdy, and totally disdainful of the cool set, of which Ellery was one. So any hint of a slight was met with defensiveness. Ellery understood. She remembered high school and what a war zone it had felt like sometimes. No one came out unscathed.

Even her. Hadn't the only boy she'd truly crushed on made her look like a fool? Clay's betrayal had hurt more than she'd ever told anyone. She'd been a sophomore and he a senior, and as the bomb dot com of high school, Clay had been "the" guy to hook and reel in. For months she'd tried to get his attention at weekend parties, but he'd always been wrapped up in older girls. Then she'd worn a half shirt with shorty shorts to the lake, and he'd homed in on her. Lord, he'd been fine as a fox, so Ellery had tumbled hard for him. When he'd cheated on her with that skank cheerleader, her heart had spider-cracked, and her ego had plummeted from the penthouse to a dirty tenement in Loserville.

That was why it was hard to be nice to Clay now. For him, it was water under the bridge. For her, it was still a stinging dam of hurt that held back forgiveness.

"I know you can, Rach. I just miss Josh, is all. I asked him to meet me at Sutton's, and he hasn't texted me back yet." Even as she uttered the words, she knew she sounded vulnerable—something she despised being. She didn't want anyone to see her cracks. But at her admission, Rachel's gaze softened.

"He's still studying all the time, huh? That sucks." Rachel pulled the stack of cashmere wraps from the box at her feet. "Maybe you should surprise him at school. Take him some cookies or cupcakes or something like that."

Ellery tilted her head. "That's not a bad idea. If the mountain won't come to me, I'll go to Muhammad."

Rachel snorted. "You may have gotten that backward, but, yeah, go to him. He'll know how much you miss him."

"Rain check for Jason's? You know I love their chicken salad," Ellery said.

Rachel nodded, seemingly appeased. "Sure. I'll finish this up. You better go if you're going by a bakery."

Ellery rushed through the return rack and settled the receipts with the manager. If she were fast enough, she could stop by Maggie Anne's bakery before it closed and pick up the salted-caramel cupcakes Josh loved along with some coffee. Oh, and she could get extras for his study group. She envisioned herself arriving with the treats and everyone acknowledging how lucky Josh was to have her. He'd beam at her, give her a cute kiss on the nose or maybe a pat on the bottom. Ellery Witt, epitome of the understanding fiancée. Even though she really, really wished he'd push away his notes and pull her into his arms and give her his full attention. His cadaver got more action than she did.

"Thanks, Rach. I'm off," she called out to Rachel, who'd stopped to chat with Fiona at the makeup counter. Fi was showing Rachel the new

Christmas gift sets that came with the purchase of a perfume. Normally, Ellery would be all over the new shades of eggplant and olive eyeshadows, but she had the role of best future wife ever to play.

After she hadn't gotten the internship and resigned herself to coming back to Shreveport, she'd rationalized that being with Josh would be a great testing ground for their upcoming marriage. She wasn't giving up on her dream, but since her fashion goals were on hold, she would work on balance and providing emotional support for her future husband. This would be another step in creating a solid relationship, one like she'd thought her parents had.

When Daphne and Rex had asked to speak to her before she went back to college for her junior year, she'd been shocked to learn they were getting a divorce. Her parents had seemed rock solid. Well, at least until her mother had gotten a new life, one that didn't include her or her father. Ellery couldn't lie and say it hadn't hurt to feel as if she'd been relegated to the back burner and left there while her mother went to book festivals, conferences, and three-day meetings with attorneys and her agent. Overnight her mother had become a different woman. Like literally. Her agent talked Daphne into writing under a different name. Two blinks later, the former preschool teacher had a fan club and multiple offers from networks looking to adapt her children's books for a new television series. Suddenly her mother wasn't just her mother. She was Dee Dee O'Hara.

Ellery hadn't realized her father felt the same way—forgotten. Her father had gone to therapy to deal with being abandoned and set aside for her mom's unexpected career. He'd told her all this when they were at the beach, about how he'd felt diminished and lonely. Ellery had always been under the impression her father had ended the marriage, but Dad had implied that things had gotten so bad that he thought leaving was the only avenue left to him. Sitting there that night on the beach, her father had wiped tears away when he told her he'd driven away hoping that his action would wake her mother up to the problems in their marriage, but Daphne hadn't seemed to care. She'd shrugged and said she didn't love him anymore. Ellery had felt something inside her break at the sadness in her father's voice.

And then he'd told her about his suspicions . . . about how secretive Daphne was. About the man who'd answered the phone one morning in her hotel room.

Until that moment, she hadn't realized how hurt her daddy had been. He hadn't asked for his wife to become the next Society of Children's Book Writers and Illustrators rock star, and when Daphne refused to change her new direction even the slightest or fight for their marriage, her father had no recourse but to step away in order to protect his own mental health.

Well, Ellery wasn't going to stop fighting for her and Josh.

She had all the pieces she needed to put together both a successful marriage and eventual career. What was happening now was a speed bump, and she knew how to roll right over those. Nothing between her and Josh had changed. When they'd graduated from UGA, they'd sat under a big oak tree, holding hands, grad gowns tangled about their legs, and declared that they were in this together. Whatever came their way, they could handle. She even remembered his words.

"We're doing this, right?" He'd looked so intense at that moment.

"Yeah. I think as long as we stick together, everything we've ever wanted will be at our fingertips," she'd said, squeezing his hand, her heart so full at having this man's love. Josh made her so happy.

"I know you think coming with me is right, but I think you should go to New York."

"I can't. I don't have a job, Josh."

Josh looped his arms around her and kissed her forehead. "Babe, it's going to be hard my first couple of years. The classes are intense, and I'll have to study a lot. Go to New York and do your thing. If you go with me, you won't see me much. I know the deal with that Krause woman fell through, but there are tons of other designers. You are charming, beautiful, and determined. You'll get something."

"It's too late. Everything's filled. Besides, how pathetic would I look schlepping in and dropping off résumés like some loser? I'd end up as a temp or in the mail room. I can't afford to live in Manhattan on that kind of pittance." Every time she envisioned herself in NYC, it had been with J.J., being the Andy to her Miranda Priestly. It would be hard but worth it to wear the sample sizes, meet fabulous people, and become absolutely necessary to the fashion icon. She wasn't going to answer phones for some start-up that would probably close in five years, all the while dining on ramen noodles.

"You're being remarkably stubborn." He rolled his pretty eyes.

"I can go to Shreveport with you, save my money, and get some practical experience at Selber's. My dad's girlfriend is best friends with Charlotte Rolfstein, who owns the store. Her mother, Mrs. Catherine, is well respected in the right Manhattan circles, and she can get me some looks from some houses next year. It's called a gap year for a reason. Plus, you'll need me to make you homemade mac and cheese and rub your back when you're super stressed."

Josh had smiled, looking so handsome she'd almost whipped out her phone and snapped a picture. *Look at my boyfriend. Cat's meow. #solucky #eatyourheartout #prettierthanme.*

"Fine. Do whatever you want. You're going to do it anyway," he'd said, drawing her into a hug.

So she'd done just that, and it wasn't so bad.

But it's not good, either. None of your best friends are in town, you hang with your mother, and you make ten dollars an hour. Oh, and your fiancé hasn't had sex with you in forever and a day.

Cupcakes would work. Those salted-caramel ones made everyone feel a bit frisky. Or at the very least, Ellery could pretend there was magic in sugar.

Thirty minutes later she pressed the button on the elevator that would take her up to the gross anatomy lab. The security guard had given her a hard time about not having a student ID with her, but she'd flashed her baby blues, given him a cupcake, and left her car keys at the front desk. Oh, and she'd also been patted down just in case she was a nutcase with a gun. They'd had those before. Psych patients who'd masqueraded as doctors or students. Ellery didn't want to think about the words *necrophilia* and *cannibalism*, but she'd heard rumors about both happening at other medical centers. Reality was sometimes stranger than fiction.

The smell of formaldehyde assaulted her when she stepped onto the floor. She knew that the fluid was necessary to keep the cadavers viable so the students could properly learn anatomy, but it literally permeated the entire floor . . . and all of Josh's clothing. Poor dead people. They were essentially pickles for first years to poke and label. Ellery would never consent to donate her body to science. She'd heard the nicknames the med students had secretly given their cadavers.

No way.

She balanced the coffee—four piping-hot autumn blends with cream and sugar on the side—with the box of cupcakes. Thank goodness she'd sold her wine to her mother, because the dang cupcakes had cost an arm and a leg.

Better not to joke about body parts up here.

She stared at the double doors to the anatomy lab. Did she knock? Someone appeared to her right.

"Hey, you looking for someone?" The person asking her the question was tiny, Asian, and wore smart glasses that made her look adorable. She didn't look like a med student. She looked like a middle grader.

"Uh, yeah. Josh Prince? I'm his fiancée, and I brought him a study snack." Ellery lifted the box and gave her a smile. *Aren't I the best?*

"Oh, yeah, he's not in there. I think he and Drew are down in Dr. Spell's lab studying. They already finished with their study group, like, an hour ago," the woman said, pointing down the hall before pushing into the lab. The closing door shut quickly, causing a puff of air to blow Ellery's hair. The smell was . . . indescribable.

"Ugh," Ellery said, trying to not make a face. After all, dissecting bodies was necessary for future physicians. They had to know what nerves, tissues, and organs looked like. Unless they were going to be psychiatrists. Ellery could see herself as a psychiatrist, legs crossed, the cute glasses the med student had been wearing perched at the end of her nose. *Now tell me, Mr. Mahoney, why did you sneak into the school and eat the left pinkie of cadaver number thirteen?*

Eh, maybe not.

Ellery started down the hall, peering at each placard, looking for Dr. Spell's name. Finally, she found it at the end of the squeaky hallway.

She rubbed her lips together, hoping her lip gloss was still glossy, and tossed her golden mane so it fell into place and didn't look flat. Stomach in, smile donned, she pushed the door open, and immediately thumped into something.

A yelp and crash ensued.

"Oh no!" she exclaimed as Josh yanked the door open, his eyes wide in alarm.

"Ellery," he breathed, his gaze darting to where Drew sat at the table, notes spread out before him. Another notebook sat beside it, obviously Josh's place. "What are you doing here? You scared me to death."

"I'm sorry. I was just bringing you a snack for studying." She held up the box of cupcakes and set the tray of coffee on the small table near the door. When she'd pushed the door open, she'd knocked a rolling desk chair into the table holding some sort of equipment.

"Oh," Josh said, his face flushed and his hair a bit mussed. He always twisted his fingers in his hair when he studied, and it was sort of adorable. "Why didn't you just knock? I was rolling the chair to the other side when you opened the door. You could have caused a serious accident or broken something."

Ellery felt flustered herself. And hurt. She hadn't meant to make a scene. "I'm sorry, honey." Ellery handed Josh the box and grabbed the chair, pulling it from where it had wedged between two lab stools. "I wanted to surprise you."

Josh glanced back at Drew, who looked not at all rattled by the chair slamming into the table. Drew held out his hand. "I'll take a snack."

Her fiancé handed the box over to Drew and then picked up the coffee and set it beside his notebook. Then he grabbed the chair from her hands. She let it go without a fight. "I shouldn't have overreacted. You just startled me, and I'm just tired and cranky and—"

"—mad I came by," she finished for him, a slight catch in her throat. She shouldn't have come and interrupted him. Josh was so serious about his studies. Cupcakes now seemed like a stupid idea.

"No, I'm not mad, babe. Just trying to keep my heart from A-fib. You should have called."

"I did. I texted you, like, three times."

He glanced down at his phone, which sat near his notebook. "We were doing a lot of texting with McCurdy's group. Sorry. The texts probably got buried."

Drew seemed oblivious to the tension and pulled out a cupcake, licking his fingers. Icing had gotten on the sides when she'd jumped back seconds before. "Damn, I love these freaking things."

Josh had met Drew at orientation and had raved about how funny the guy was. Drew was tall and broad shouldered with a cleft chin and dark-brown hair that was cut a tad too short for his wide face. He had sideburns and a bad habit of picking at his teeth, but he was nice looking in a rugged, rough-around-the-edges way. He and Josh were mirror opposites, with Josh polished like a new penny and Drew more like a crumpled dollar bill discovered in the pocket of sweaty gym shorts.

Josh took her by the elbow and moved back toward the door. "Sorry I didn't call earlier. We've been swamped, but it was very thoughtful of you to do this for us, babe. I'll see if some of the other guys want some, too."

He wanted her to go.

She hadn't expected him to take the coffee and cupcakes and escort her out in mere seconds. No, a little time together wasn't too much to ask. Maybe a mini make-out session in the stacks? There was a library somewhere in the building, wasn't there? "You're welcome. I was hoping that maybe we could go somewhere and talk?"

Josh's color had returned to normal, but she still made a mental note in her future-spouse notebook that Josh didn't like surprises.

"Why? Is everything okay?" he asked, glancing back at Drew, who had already polished off one cupcake and was working on another. Ellery tried not to frown at the sight of Josh's friend wolfing down the expensive cupcakes she'd bought for her fella.

"I thought you could take a little break. Hey, maybe you can show me your cadaver." She didn't want to see a dead, cut-up body. Definitely didn't want to see that, but she would if it meant he threw her some attention.

"You aren't allowed in there, babe." Josh directed her back toward the door. "Here. I'll walk you to the elevator."

"Oh, okay. I guess this is goodbye." Ellery turned and waved to Drew. "Enjoy the treat."

Drew saluted and, with his mouth still full, mumbled, "I will."

"Be back in a minute," Josh said, holding open the door for her.

Drew had already gone back to his notes. Josh shut the door behind them. The hallway was thankfully empty.

"Josh, I'm sorry if I distracted you. I thought you might want to see your girl. I haven't talked to you in, like, days." She wasn't truly sorry, though. Distraction had been her goal. That's why she'd unbuttoned the top two buttons on her blouse, a Nanette Lepore silk blouse in a gorgeous raspberry that looked terrific next to her peachy skin tone.

"Oh, come on, Elle. I see you every day . . . and I sleep beside you," he said, walking more quickly toward the bank of elevators than she would have liked.

"Josh," she said, grabbing his elbow. "Stop for a minute."

He did. "What?"

"You say you see me, but you don't. Not really. We spend hardly any time together. Don't you miss me? Don't you miss us?" she asked. Her voice sounded pathetic, but she couldn't seem to help it. He'd ignored her for days, slipping out of bed and taking a shower before her alarm clock even sounded for the first round of "punch the snooze button." She'd finally rise, only to stumble into the kitchen to find an empty coffeepot and crumbs from his English muffin on the counter. This morning he'd left a note on the fridge, and her heart had leaped in expectation of something sweet, but it had merely been a reminder to get more milk. They were like an old married couple who weren't even married yet.

Josh pulled her into his arms. In the weave of his lab coat she could smell formaldehyde, his citrusy cologne, and something she couldn't place, but it didn't matter because she was in his arms. "Of course I miss you. I totally do, sweetheart, but I told you this year would be grueling. It feels as if there are not enough hours in the day for all the work I have to do."

"You're telling me," she drawled and looked away from him. She didn't want to be hurt. They'd talked about what med school would be like, but she hadn't realized that she'd be this damned lonely.

"You know I would rather be home with you, watching Netflix and nibbling on these delicious earlobes." He playfully nipped the shell of her ear and gave an exaggerated growl.

Ellery closed her eyes and snuggled into him. "I know. It's terrible, but it will all be worth it in the end. I know it will."

He gave her a final squeeze and then released her before dropping a kiss on her forehead. "I'll be home soon. Maybe another hour or two more. Take a bath and open some of that good wine. We'll toast to being survivors and do more than sleep in that bed, okay?"

"Really?"

He brushed his lips across hers. "Really. We've got this, right?"

She nodded. "We do."

"Good girl. Now scoot. I'll put my nose to the grindstone and be out of here before ten." He glanced at the TAG Heuer watch his father had given him for graduation. "Maybe ten thirty."

Ellery stepped onto the elevator, gave him a winning smile, and then unbuttoned her shirt, exposing her lacy white bra. She ran a hand between her breasts. "I'll be waiting."

Josh laughed as the doors closed. "Vixen."

Ellery's own laughter echoed in the tinny elevator, small company for a lonely woman with her blouse undone. She made herself presentable just as the doors parted in the lobby. Donning a determined grin, she walked toward the security desk.

"Mission accomplished, Ernie. I fed a few med students and partially seduced my fiancé," she said, holding out her hand.

Ernie shuffled around to the back side of the desk and pulled her keys from the drawer. "Well, he's a lucky guy."

"Only if he stays awake for what I have planned," she said with a conspiratorial wink. Her words were empty, but she tried to sell herself on them. Ernie didn't care. He still had ten more hours on his shift.

"Like I said, lucky guy." Ernie grinned, flashing a bit of silver. He looked like that guy on *Home Alone*. The short one. The one that lost the crown.

"Good night," Ellery said, pushing out into the darkness. Her car sat alone beneath the strained glow of the fluorescent light. A few other cars sat far away, and Ellery figured it was indicative of her life. Alone but not alone.

When she climbed into her car and pressed the lock button, she pulled out her phone. Nothing from Josh. No sweet "thank you for being the bestest fiancée in the world" text. That was the old Josh. The one she'd fallen in love with when he left her flowers he'd picked in a field beside the gas station on her front porch. The one who was obviously long gone.

As she was about to toss the phone into the gaping yawn of her bag, a ding sounded.

E. McCallum has sent a message.

Her finger found the mail icon before she could start the car.

Ellery clicked the browser shut because she wanted to read the email after she'd pulled on her jammies and tucked herself into bed. Then she could type a witty response, something that would make Evan smile and marvel at how humorous and sexy she was.

Leaning forward, Ellery leaned her forehead on the steering wheel.

What was she doing? But she knew. She was filling her loneliness with something . . . not quite naughty but in the ballpark. The intrigue, secrecy, and sheer pleasure she took in playing his confidant sucked her good intentions under every time. Exchanging harmless emails with a man wasn't truly cheating on Josh anyway.

Ellery started her car and her phone dinged.

Josh.

Don't forget to pick up milk.

Exactly.

CHAPTER SEVEN

The morning light slanting in the tiny crack of Daphne's bedroom-window blinds landed right between her eyes, an insult normally borne when she hadn't drunk an entire bottle of wine. But she'd drunk a lot last night. Too much, if her pounding head was any indication.

"Nooo," she grumbled, squeezing her eyes shut and turning over. The whomp, whomp of the ceiling fan seemed more pronounced than normal, and her mouth felt like someone had stuffed it with wool socks. She needed water . . . and aspirin . . . and . . . something else niggled her right as her big toe grazed something solid.

Oh. God.

Daphne cracked an eye and saw an expanse of tanned back at the same time she registered that she was naked as the day she'd been born.

She hadn't . . .

No . . .

But yes. She had. Twice, if she remembered correctly.

"Clay," she whispered, poking him and then immediately closing her eyes because when she moved too quickly, the room spun a little.

The man didn't move.

"Clay," she hissed, cracking an eye and peering at her bedside table alarm clock. It read 7:28.

"Mmm?" he muttered, lifting his head slightly before letting it fall back onto her 450-thread-count sheets she'd splurged on when she'd taken Ellery to Dallas that past spring. His tousled brown hair and incredibly gorgeous smooth skin looked odd against the soft ecru-and-honey peach matelassé coverlet.

"Wake up." She poked him again.

Clay raised his head and waggled his eyebrows even as his eyes remained closed. "I'm up."

"No, you're not. Your eyes are still closed. We have to get up. Eller—"

His hand slid up her thigh and curved around her backside.

Daphne squeaked as he dragged her to him. "No, no. Stop that. We have to—"

Clay opened bleary eyes and then kissed her naked shoulder. "One more round?"

Beneath the covers, his hands were busy, cupping her butt and squeezing. Daphne, even though she felt dizzy and slightly nauseous, felt her body respond. That yummy, gooey warmth began to spread in her pelvis as he dropped kisses on her collarbone, moving toward the curve of her breast. His erection pressed against her stomach as he nudged her with his pelvis and pressed her onto her back.

His lips circled her nipple just as he used a knee to nudge her legs apart.

"No, Clay. We have to get . . . oh. Oh . . . mmm," she said as he sucked her nipple into the heat of his mouth.

"Come on, nothing starts the day better than—" He dipped his hips, and his erection slid against a part of her that obviously wasn't connected to her damned brain.

Daphne pushed hard against his chest. "No."

Clay flopped back, taking the sheet with him, leaving her naked in the morning light. Daphne squeaked and grabbed at the sheet. Clay held it tight with a knowing gleam in his sleepy eyes. "Nu-uh. If I can't touch, the least you can let me do is see what I'm missing."

He rolled over and looked at the body she was trying desperately to cover. "And it's a nice view. I mean, these tits are—"

"Stop it," she said, covering her breasts with an arm as she cupped the other hand between the legs she'd squeezed together. "This is . . . crazy. I can't believe we did what we did."

Clay grinned. "Twice. And as you can tell"—he looked down at the tented sheet barely covering his hips—"I'm more than willing for a third round."

Daphne covered her eyes. "We can't. We just . . . oh."

Clay had rolled over and started kissing her stomach, sliding down, dipping his tongue into her navel. "Oh, but we can. I'm not supposed to be at work for another hour. Oh wait, I'm already at work." He slid a hand up her leg to her thigh, making her nerve endings tingle.

She grabbed his hair and made him lift his head. "Ellery will be here in twenty minutes. You have to leave. If she sees your truck . . . oh . . . my . . . goodness."

His hand squeezed her hip. "So how many times do you want to come this time?"

Orgasms. Yeah, she'd had multiple orgasms both times they'd had sex. Like an engine with a head of steam, once started she couldn't seem to stop. She'd lost track of how many times her body had stretched and then shattered against his mouth, his fingers, his hips. Never in her life had she felt so incredibly alive as she had last night.

But last night was over, and even though she'd finally solved the mystery of female arousal, what they'd done had been a colossal mistake.

"Oh God, I think I may vomit," Daphne said, jackknifing to a sitting position and pushing Clay off before running toward the half-finished bathroom. Then she remembered the water was still shut off, so she reversed directions and steadied herself on the chest of drawers. The room spun a little, and she was certain she should be appalled that she stood naked in front of a twenty-five-year-old guy who could model underwear. She pointed at him. "Close your eyes."

"What?"

"Your eyes. Close them," she said. She swallowed down her nausea and scooped up the robe draped on the chair in the corner.

"Hey, are you okay?" Clay asked.

She looked over at him. His eyes were closed.

"Hold on," she said, taking deep breaths and willing her stomach to settle. She shrugged into the robe and jerked the belt tight, as if that could fix the mess she'd gotten herself into. "Okay."

Clay opened his eyes and slid out of the bed.

"Oh God," Daphne said, averting her eyes from the gorgeous naked perfection. Clay tugged the ecru throw at the foot of the bed and wrapped it around his hips. He looked rumpled and beautiful. Her personal Greek god. The giver of orgasms.

Somewhere in the bowels of the house, a door thumped against a wall. "Morning!"

Daphne gasped. "No! No, no, no, no. She's never early."

Clay blinked. "What? Who?"

"Hide, you fool. Ellery's here," Daphne whisper-yelled, glancing around the bedroom at Clay's jeans crumpled at the foot of the bed. Boots had been dropped by the dresser, and a pair of boxer briefs were wedged in between the footboard and the mattress. Holy hell.

"Yoo-hoo? Mama? Are you still in bed?" Ellery called. Daphne heard the thump of the office door. "I'm going to start on the new promo for the Mardi Gras book. Mark Anderson sent some comps . . . Mama?"

"You have to get out of here," she said to Clay, trying to find some measure of calm and utterly failing. Ellery could not find out what she'd done. Absolutely *could not*. "I'm going out there to keep her from coming in here. You get out."

"How?"

"Uh, the window," she said, pointing at the one that would drop him into the backyard.

"This is stupid. I'm not climbing out the window. You're a grown-ass woman."

Daphne turned toward him as she heard the click of Ellery's shoes coming through the living room. "Please, Clay. I can't deal with this right now. Please."

He shrugged, picked up his jeans, and whispered, "Okay, but this is crazy, Daph."

"Mama?" Ellery called through the thankfully locked door.

"Just a minute, honey," Daphne called.

"Are you sick?" Ellery asked, and Daphne envisioned her backing away from the door. Ellery was a classic germophobe and kept hand sanitizer in every bag. Her worst nightmare was a stomach virus.

"No, no, I just slept in. Had trouble sleeping last night," she said, noting that it wasn't a lie. She hadn't slept much, but when she had, it had been hard sleep, cradled in the arms of a man who'd worn her out.

Clay gave a soft, sexy laugh.

Daphne shot him a quelling look and jabbed her finger at the window.

Okay. She could do this. Get Ellery away from the door. Give her something to do. "Hey, sugar, would you mind putting the kettle on? I desperately need tea. I'll get dressed and be right out."

"Sure," Ellery said outside the door. "If you certain you're okay? You sound weird."

"I'm fine. Promise."

"Well, Clay left his truck here, but I don't see him. You should tell him not to do that. People will get the wrong impression," Ellery said, her footsteps sounding as she moved away from the bedroom door and back toward the kitchen. Thank heavens.

Clay actually had the gall to laugh again.

"Shh!" Daphne's mind raced as Clay tugged on his jeans and looked around for his shirt. Clay's truck *was* here, but what else had he left behind? She'd left the plates in the sink and the glasses on the coffee table. Would Ellery notice? She would. Daphne knew she would.

"Uh, Daph, I think my shirt's in the living room," Clay said, grabbing his boots and then snagging the socks he'd toed off when they'd tumbled into bed.

"Oh shit," Daphne breathed. Last night during their make-out session on the couch, she'd tugged his shirt off him and tossed it somewhere. Where had she tossed it? The back of the couch? She couldn't remember.

"Don't worry. I have an extra in my truck," he said, sitting on the bed and pulling on his boots. His hair was mussed, and he looked even younger in the morning sunlight streaming through her linen drapes. Lord, what had she done? She'd slept with a man-child merely because she'd needed to get sexed up. She was a horrible, horrible person.

Clay sprang from the bed and pulled the cord on the drapes. Quietly as he could, he unlocked the window and eased it up. Daphne walked over and peered out. The house was pier and beam and sat a good four feet off the ground. The window made it six feet at least. What if he broke an ankle? "Be careful."

Clay hooked an arm and pulled her to him. He kissed the indentation in her throat, his tongue coming out for a small taste. She closed her eyes at how good it felt. "Last night was awesome. One of the best I've had. You were incredible."

Daphne could do nothing more than nod because it wasn't a lie. Then she gave him a little nudge. "We'll talk later. Go."

Clay swung his legs out and, with a grunt, landed on the ground beneath. He looked up at her and winked. "See ya in, like, five minutes."

Daphne closed the window, lowered the blinds, and then leaned against the wall. The ramifications of her stupidity slammed into her. She'd slept with her daughter's ex-boyfriend like some horny old slut. What had she been thinking?

Well, she hadn't. That was the problem.

After the kiss at the table after dinner, she'd cleared the table and brought the pie and newly opened bottle of wine to the living room. Her intentions had been clear . . . at least to the rational part of herself. She would have a slice of pie, one more glass of wine, talk about the weather, and then send her hot contractor on his way. No problem. She was a woman in control of her life, decisions, and traitorous body.

But Clay had patted the seat next to him. "Come on. I won't bite you. Unless you want me to." He lifted his eyebrows, the ever-consummate flirt.

"See?" she'd said, choosing the chair farthest away. It had been her grandmother's, and she'd had it reupholstered last year. "You say things like that, and it means I can't sit there."

"Aw, come on, Daph. You're acting like we can't sleep together if we want to."

"Exactly. We can't."

Clay made a face. "Yeah, we can. We're both adults. I want you, and I know you want me, too. And, Daph, I want to do dirty, dirty things to you."

He knew what he was doing, damn him. She watched while he swirled his fork in the meringue and then licked it off the tines. The entire action was Intro to Seduction 101. Daphne's girl parts woke up and started chanting, "Do it, do it, do it."

"You sure are cocky," she said with a roll of her eyes.

He smiled at her then, and it was so devilish that she couldn't help returning the smile. "Okay, so I'm attracted to you. I'd have to be dead not to be, but it would be foolish for us to throw caution to the wind and . . . engage in . . ."

"Fucking our brains out?"

Daphne covered her face with her hands and groaned. "You're too young for me."

She uncovered her face and tried to level a no-nonsense glare at him, but he dipped his fork into the chocolate pie and took another bite. "No, I'm old enough to know exactly what you need and smart enough to understand that it's just about sex."

"Complicated sex."

Clay shook his head. "Sex isn't complicated. It's natural. Lady, you've been turning me on for days. I watch you, and all I can think about is touching you, kissing you, tasting every inch of your body."

At those words, her girl parts stopped chanting and applauded wildly, but it wasn't just those parts of her that needed his words; it was the part of her that had been so hurt when her husband left. Rex had made her feel dowdy, unattractive, and worthless. At first when he left, she thought he would come home the next day and say he was sorry for acting like an idiot. But he didn't come back. A month went by. Then another. A holding pattern that suggested he was waiting for her to do something. The more time went by, the more Daphne knew they were over. Still, her heart hurt, and her ego felt shattered. Especially when Rex took Cindy out for dinner. He'd professed it was because he needed someone to talk to, but Daphne knew.

The next day, she filed for separation.

Rex didn't want her unless she went back to being the doormat she'd been before. Unless she gave up the joy her career had brought her. The signs had been there even before she'd signed the second book deal, but she'd been blind to Rex's neediness, to his snide asides about her career, to his covert jealousy of her success. On the outside, Rex had been a supportive husband. On the inside, he writhed with pettiness over her getting the accolades. At times he was plain mean, talking about her gaining weight or how her author picture made her look older than she was. Other times he moped around, talking about how he should have done something more than AC repair. How he should have gone to college and majored in law like he'd always wanted. Before he screwed up his life having sex with her after formal.

So Daphne wanted to believe the words coming from Clay's mouth because she needed them the way parched earth needed rain.

Clay watched her as he ate another bite of the pie. The way he ate was like he was making love to the damned fork. His perfect lips sucked the chocolate off before his tongue darted out to rescue a tidbit of the flaky crust. Daphne felt herself lean toward him.

Setting the half-eaten pie on the coffee table, Clay leaned back and patted the couch once more. "Come on. I won't touch you."

"Unless I want you to?" She said the words before she could stop herself.

"Exactly."

"Fine. I'm not afraid of you," she said, scooping up her wineglass and plopping down next to him. She had to prove to herself that she wasn't going to do what her body wanted her to do. She was not. No way.

"Thank God, because that would be a travesty," he said, lifting the bottle of wine and filling his own empty glass. He arched an eyebrow and looked at her half-filled glass, and though she'd already had 2.5 glasses of wine, she held out her glass.

"So what should we talk about?" she asked, taking a gulp. Then another. And then another. The room had already started tilting a bit, and her thighs felt oddly numb. Okay, so she was a little drunk.

Clay watched her, his mouth twitching. "I don't know. I proposed that we don't talk, but since you're still clinging to the notion that sex would be wrong, we'll find another topic. How about football? Do you watch football?"

"Nope. Not a fan."

"Okay, politics. You a Democrat or a Republican?"

"Neither. I'm an Independent," she said, taking another drink. Clay wasn't drinking and looked oddly relaxed.

"So do you like to take a bath or shower? Me? I like to shower, but a bath's sexy if I'm with someone else. All that slippery, wet skin and soft parts fitting right up against my hard parts. Some of them harder than others, mind you, but still—"

"Stop," she breathed, swallowing hard. Her mind went to the two of them in that new bathtub. She'd fit right between his legs, and he'd curl his hands around to cup her breasts. Oh, it would feel amazingly good. "Next question."

"Have you ever masturbated in front of a guy . . . or a girl?"

Daphne swallowed wine at the same time she tried to breathe. She plopped her glass down on the coffee table as a fit of coughing ensued. Clay thumped her on the back. "Sorry, I didn't mean for that to happen. I was trying to be funny, not kill you."

Daphne coughed and wiped the tears streaming from her eyes. "That's not funny. I don't masturbate . . . in front of people."

He watched her, something in his eyes that she both loved and dreaded. "We could fix that. You could do it for me. Right here. I wouldn't have to touch you like I promised, but I would enjoy the hell out of it."

And then that thought invaded. She could lean back on the couch and unbutton her dress, then run her hand down to her lace panties and—

Is this what young people did? Masturbate in front of one another? Wait. *Young* people? She wasn't that old. She had to stop thinking that way. Clay was right. She wasn't old. If she wanted to have no-strings-attached sex, she damn well could. "I couldn't do that in front of you. I would rather you . . . I mean, ugh, I don't know what I mean. My brain feels fuzzy, and I'm in uncharted territory."

Clay gave a soft laugh and pulled her into his lap, and even though she tried to half-heartedly protest it, she let herself tumble into his arms. "I thought you said you wouldn't touch me unless I asked?"

"You want me to let go?" he asked, his blue eyes dancing with humor . . . and desire.

Slowly she shook her head.

His impish grin faded as his blue eyes darkened. "You may not want to want me, but you do. So why don't you stop stalling and take what you want?"

"What I want?" she repeated.

He tucked her hair behind her ear and cupped her jaw. A rush of desire so intense punched her in the stomach hard. *What she wanted.* She'd known that from the moment she'd uttered, "You're welcome to stay and eat if you want." It was inevitable. Tippy Lou's words beat a drum in her head. *He's old enough. You're both adults.* And then her own thought. *No one would have to know.*

Daphne brushed her hand against his jaw, then slid her hand around to tangle in his hair. "I want you."

He smiled. "So is this a yes?"

"Yes."

And that was all it took. From that moment on, she surrendered herself to every fantasy she'd ever had about the hot contractor who'd haunted her dreams and filled her days with delicious naked man chest and laughing blue eyes.

And now look where she was, leaning naked beneath her bathrobe against her bedroom wall after having practically shoved the man out the window so she wouldn't get caught diddling her daughter's ex-boyfriend, who also happened to be her contractor.

Daphne was screwed.

Literally and figuratively.

CHAPTER EIGHT

Dear Miss O'Hara,

The sun was so pretty through the changing oaks today that I immediately thought of you. You wrote about how you love sunlight dancing through the orange-y cypress trees on the lake in winter. Wait, is *orange-y* a word? I thought it peculiar that you wouldn't say *burned sienna* or *persimmon*. Righters always seem to have the write words. Oops, pardon my homophones. That's the kid's lesson today in language arts. Maybe your silly dog could tackle homophones in a new book?

I hope you're okay. Usually you respond to my emails, and I have grown to depend on our friendship as a boost to the end of my day. I put Poppy to bed, get a beer, and log on. I always look forward to hearing about your day. Once upon a time, being a man of letters was a true compliment. Not sure that holds true for emails. Still, I hope I will get to meet you soon. Of course, I'm determined you will be our speaker. The PTSA is starting to whisper about me when it's time for my report on Read Across America. Please say you'll come. If not for the kids . . . for me?

Best,
Evan

Ellery clicked off her phone, set the kettle on the stove, and turned on the burner. Next week she'd have to use a hot plate because the kitchen was slated for the tear out. She wasn't sure how they would be able to work with all the noise and stupid Clay stomping around without his shirt. Of course, Ellery didn't have to come in every day to do the job her mother had given her. Most of it could be done on her laptop, but remaining in her empty town house made her feel even lonelier. Plus, it was better to keep office hours. More professional, and when she netted a job next year, she'd already have good habits.

She shouldn't be so ugly to Clay. He was who he was. Like a leopard unable to rearrange his spots. It was generally accepted Clay would never be serious with any girl. He had a rep for chasing after skirts, even back when Ellery had pursued him. Some guys were like that—destined to never be brought to heel. So being irritated at Clay was like being mad at that leopard for maiming a gazelle. And, hey, at least he'd gotten his shit together for the most part—he and his brother had started the construction company and seemed to be doing well. The work they'd done so far on her mother's house had been quality. She should lay off being bitchy to him. Sometimes her emotions ran over her common sense. Okay, often her emotions ran over her common sense.

"You want cinnamon apple or pumpkin spice?" Ellery asked when her mother finally pushed into the kitchen, looking a little under the weather. She hoped her mother wasn't getting sick. She looked tired and flushed at the same time.

"You mean apple cinnamon?"

Ellery suppressed a sigh. Her mother knew what she meant. "Whatever. You left dishes in the sink. You never leave dishes."

"I went to bed early," her mother said, walking to the cabinet and grabbing two teacups, which she slid toward Ellery. "Speaking of early, why are you here at this hour?"

"I don't know. I thought I would go over some stuff with you, get my work done, and take off early. Josh said he'd take me to the movies tonight, so I want to get a blowout and maybe get my nails done."

Her mother leaned against the cabinet, waiting for the teakettle to chirp with steam. "A date sounds nice."

Ellery wished she could tell her mother all her concerns about Josh, but that wedge of something sat between them. She wanted to be mature enough to get past the hard feelings she had toward her mother, but she couldn't seem to let go of the anger, frustration . . . betrayal. Ellery wasn't sure why she still felt so hurt by her parents splitting . . . and by her mother not caring enough to repair her life with Ellery's dad. She told herself that plenty of people divorced and lived with broken families, but deep inside she wished for what had been. Down beneath her "it's cool" facade, she longed to be that little girl whose parents were there to smooth away the hurts, hold her when she was scared, and chase away the shadows from the dark corners of her life . . . as irrational as that sounded.

Or perhaps she was overanalyzing her feelings because she felt so . . . unable to control her own life. Perhaps this was something all mothers and daughters went through when they moved from one stage of life to the next. Daphne had always been a helicopter mom, driving her nuts with volunteering for everything at school, leaving well-meaning inspirational notes on her bathroom mirror, and henpecking her to finish an essay, make her bed, send a thank-you note. When Ellery had been a child, her mother's machinations had been like a straitjacket, but now that she was grown, her mother's little asides and unsolicited advice chafed her.

Ellery decided to change the subject. "So who came to dinner last night? I saw the empty wine bottle and glasses. Tippy?"

Her mother turned to the sink and started running water. "Um, just Clay. His brother couldn't come, and Tippy said she wasn't interested in eating animals. I made meat loaf."

"So just you and Clay? That's kinda weird." Ellery tried to imagine what sort of conversation the two could even have. The image of Clay and her mother eating together made something wriggle in her gut. She didn't like it. Mostly because Clay was Clay.

Her mother shrugged. "Well, no one else I invited bothered to come. At least someone came to eat all the food I fixed."

Of course. Guilt was her mother's favorite weapon. "I told you I had to work, Mom."

"I remember."

The kettle whistled, and Ellery poured the boiling water into the two cups. "I know you asked me to keep that date open every week, but sometimes people do what they have to do. It's a lesson you taught me over the past few years, right? *I don't want to work, but I have to work.*"

"So you're quoting me back to me?" Daphne asked.

Ellery lifted a shoulder. "I'm just saying. Anyway, why's his truck still here?"

Clay had probably drunk too much and had to call one of his bimbos to pick him up. Ellery knew his modus operandi because the couple of times she'd seen him out on the town, he'd slung his drunken arm around whatever woman tickled his fancy that night and sauntered out with her.

"Morning, pretty ladies," Clay called through the screen door.

"Speak of the devil and he shows," Ellery drawled. *Stop. Try to be nice to him.*

"Hope you ladies have some coffee on. I could use a cup or three," Clay said, opening the door and coming inside like he owned the place. Ellery bit her lip to keep from saying something she'd regret.

"We're having tea, but feel free to make some," Daphne said, gesturing toward the empty coffeepot.

"Wait, where did you come from?" Ellery asked as Clay let the screen door fall and started for the coffeepot.

"I took a walk," Clay said.

"You? A walk?" Ellery asked, not believing the man for one minute.

"I like to take walks. Besides, my head was fuzzy. I ate dinner with your mom and she served some good-ass wine that I had too much of. Thankfully, she let me sleep it off in the guest room. Uh, Daphne, I think I left my extra shirt. I'm gonna grab it, then ride down to CW Pantry and get some coffee. No sense in dirtying the pot for me." He did an about-face and headed toward the bowels of the house.

Clay had slept at her house? Okay, not her house any longer, but . . . she leaned over and watched him walk out. When Clay was out of earshot, Ellery hissed, "You let him stay here? In my room?"

Her mother looked guilty and shifted her eyes away. "What did you want me to do? He drank too much."

"Call Uber. Or Bimbo Express. That's his usual way of getting home." Of course, her mother was too polite not to offer her ex-boyfriend Ellery's room. The woman probably did turndown service and left a mint on the pillow. The thought of Clay staying in the bedroom where she'd dreamed about him kissing her made her even more aggravated. Soon the house would be sold, and everything she'd ever known would be gone. Clay didn't get to sleep in what had been hers. Not after he'd cheated on her with Devyn Does Dallas Moss. "Lord, Mom, people will talk."

"About what?" Daphne asked, pulling a new box of tea from the cabinet. Her mother's expression had narrowed. "I'm a grown woman, and I don't care if people talk."

Ellery shouldn't poke her mom with a stick, but she couldn't help it. "It looks bad is all I'm saying."

Daphne turned around. "Don't be ridiculous, Ellery. No one will even know, and if they do, big deal."

"Come on, Mom, you know people in this town love to gossip, and though the thought of you and Clay is ridiculous, people might think . . . I don't know. I just think you want to keep your reputation intact. After all, you're a children's author. People are watching you now."

"So that means I can't date? Or that I can't date someone like Clay?" Her mother's gaze pinned Ellery to the tile behind her.

"Of course you should date, but Clay is, like, my age. Surely you want someone more appropriate. He's my ex."

Truth be told, she couldn't imagine her mother dating anyone. The woman was unwilling to share any piece of herself. She was good at trying to advise others about how to be in a relationship, but she'd tossed her own aside fairly easily and hadn't seemed interested in tossing Ellery or her father a rope.

Instead her mother became single-minded in her determination to build a career. Her books became her babies. Part of Ellery admired her mother for what she'd done. And part resented the hell out of being relegated to second best.

So the idea of her mother dating, being in a relationship with someone was . . . surreal.

"So who exactly *is* appropriate for me to date, Ellery?" Her mother put her hands on her hips.

"Come on, Mom. I shouldn't have said *appropriate*, but you know what I mean. All I'm saying is people will make you out to be something you're not if you let guys like"—she jabbed a finger toward where Clay had disappeared—"spend the night. Even when it's totally innocent."

Her mother didn't say anything. Just stared at her. "And what will they make me out to be?"

Ellery adjusted the teacups so the handles lined up and tried to think how she should say what her mother needed to hear. "You remember Shari Gill? How Mr. Mark left her, and then suddenly she lost thirty pounds, paid for her plastic surgeon's kids to go to college, and started taking selfies in a bikini? She used to wear those ugly Girl Scout shorts and Jack Rogers sandals, for heaven's sake. And then suddenly she's shopping at Forever 21 and dating a stunt double who sells weed to high school kids. It was such a cry for help. I'm just saying that you don't want to become like her."

Clay came back in with his T-shirt balled in his hand. "Found it under the bed. Must have accidentally kicked it underneath. By the way, Ellery, you have some classic copies of *Playgirl* under there that would probably fetch a good amount on eBay."

"I don't have copies of *Play*—"

"Gotcha." Clay laughed, shooting his finger like a gun toward her.

"You're *so* mature, Clay," Ellery said, shooting her mother a look that said *see what I mean*.

Clay grinned like a deranged circus clown. The man took nothing seriously.

"Hey, Daphne, thanks for letting me stay last night. I had a great time," Clay said, tucking his balled-up shirt under his armpit. He walked over to her mother and gave her a half hug-squeeze. "Best, uh, dinner I've had in a while. Be back soon."

Ellery caught sight of her mother's flush before she turned away and shut the water in the sink off. Sudsy bubbles peeked over the rim of the farmhouse sink. The screen door slapped against the frame right before Clay's boots crunched along the drive. Her mother's reaction to Clay's departure was odd.

Daphne turned around. "I'm going to ignore what you said about Shari. Her husband slept with half of Shreveport, and then he called her a heifer at the Fourth of July party in front of everyone. She deserved every implant and every halter top she wore. And, by the way, I don't need you to approve of who I decide to date . . . *when* I decide to date."

"You're right. What I want isn't important, is it? I forgot." Ellery let that hang there. Her mother's eyes flashed with something that might have been contrition. For a few moments, silence as comfortable as a thong bikini hung between them.

The kitchen clock ticked, ticked, ticked.

Eventually, Ellery slid the cup over to her mom. A peace offering. "Look, I don't want to fight. You're right. I don't have to approve."

Her mother nodded, seemingly gratified at the admission, and picked up her tea.

Good. Ellery didn't want today to be acrimonious. She wanted it to be good, set the mood for her date with Josh. Squabbling with her mother wasn't going to accomplish anything. "Hey, I'll help you with a dating app if you want me to. There are specialized dating sites for people your age."

"You know that I'm not even forty years old yet, right?" her mother drawled, eyeing her over the lip of the cup.

Ellery laughed, trying to lighten the mood. "I know. It's just going to take me a little while to adjust to you dating. Okay, so let's talk about something else. Like the upcoming book tour. I talked to Ruth, the new publicist. I think you'll like her. Anyway, she sent me all of the bookstore locations so I can make sure your hotels are close. I've highlighted all the directions, names of contacts, and nearby restaurants so you don't have to worry about—"

"I thought you were coming with me on this one?" Daphne asked, setting the mug on the counter and stirring in one sweetener. She took a sip and sighed. "That's so good. Just what I needed."

"The bookstores will have people at the stops to help you." On one hand, it would be nice to get out of Shreveport. On the other, Ellery couldn't afford the time away. Her supersecret credit card kept knocking on the door of her consciousness, and she refused to let her daddy pay that one, too. Besides, a full week riding through Texas and Oklahoma with her mother felt too . . . something. She didn't feel like wading through excited children to open the books for her mother to sign or hand her coffee the way a good assistant would do. Of course she was proud of her mother, but still . . .

Even as she had the thought, she knew that deep down the attention her mother got bothered her. Childish and petty, true, but still, something inside balked at all the fawning. She wished she could be happy about her mother's new life, but the little girl inside her still cried for what used to be. Life had been so much easier when her mother and father stood in this very kitchen, flipping flapjacks and singing old James Taylor tunes. When she didn't have to think about her mother going on dating websites. When she and her mother still hugged and touched and laughed.

But change happened, and she was dealing with it.

Sorta.

"I don't need you, but it would be nice to spend time together." Daphne leaned against the counter and studied Ellery. "We could shop and watch old eighties movies every night before bed. Remember when we used to do John Hughes marathons? Jake Ryan fan club?"

If only her mom really understood how much Ellery wanted to go back to that simpler time. "Mom, I have a fiancé and another job. I can't leave here to go have fun. I'm trying this adulting thing." *And failing. Your daddy pays your bills, your fiancé is avoiding you, and you're carrying on with another man.*

She flicked the voice of truth away. She *was* adulting.

Sorta.

Her mother's sad smile made her stomach hurt. Daphne tossed her tea bag in the trash and said, "I know. It's just lonely being on the road. I don't know how those traveling salesmen do it."

Now she felt even worse. "Well, my birthday weekend's in a few weeks. We could do something fun then." Her parents had always planned something exciting to celebrate her birthday. For her sixteenth birthday, they'd taken her and her friends to Dallas in a limo. Her eighteenth had featured a bonfire, fireworks, and an ice cream truck. When she'd been in college, she'd come home the weekend before or after her birthday because her mother had always conspired with her friends for something over the top. Once they rented out a spa, and another time they reserved a dining room at a local Mexican restaurant and hired a mariachi band. Ellery would always offer up false protest, but the thoughtfulness her mother put into celebrating her always made her feel so loved.

Once she'd overheard her mother confiding to Tippy Lou that since she and Rex had been unable to have any more children, celebrating the day Ellery had come into their lives had been important to them.

"About that," Daphne said, sipping her tea and rubbing her pointer finger along the grout lines of the tiled counter. "Since I'm in the middle of this remodel and have the book tour, I think we need to go low key this year. I called Josh to see if he has plans, but he never called me back. So what do you want to do? Your fiancé is in school, your besties all live out of town, and you have two jobs, so maybe this year we just have a nice dinner and call it a day? Or do you want to plan something more?"

Even though Ellery didn't want to feel hurt, she did.

A *nice* dinner? And Josh hadn't even bothered to discuss her birthday celebration?

Of course, she *was* turning twenty-three, and she'd just given a diatribe on being an adult, so it wasn't like she could be upset that her mother was treating her like one. But for some reason her mom pretending like Ellery's birthday was just another thing to check off her list felt like salt in a cut—the same way she'd felt every time her mother had canceled on her or had been too busy. Not to mention it was the first birthday she'd celebrate while being engaged. She'd imagined Josh doing something romantic—a picnic and perhaps a nice piece of jewelry—but now she wondered if he'd even given a passing thought to her birthday. Her life felt more and more shitty every day. "Sure, whatever is easy. I better get busy."

A buzz and ding came from the direction of the bench by the back door where she'd left her bag. She grabbed it and her tea and started toward her mother's office, where she had a small table with file folders, a laptop, and tons of padded mailing envelopes for signed books. She looked down at her phone and clicked the text message from Josh.

> Sorry about last night. Make it up 2 U this weekend. Hate 2 do this but can't go to movies 2night. Group's gotta meet. Sorry. I <3 U.

Of course he was bailing. And what was with all those stupid 2s? He was a med student, not a middle schooler.

Ellery fought back the tears threatening to make an appearance. She'd waited up for Josh with the wine he'd asked for, wearing a soft cotton men's undershirt with hot-pink panties and her hair in a messy bun. She'd left scented oils on the nightstand so she could rub his shoulders, but instead of getting the intimacy she'd been craving for weeks, she'd gotten a text that said he and Drew had misjudged the time they needed to study. He'd be later than he'd planned. Oh, and did she remember they needed milk?

Effing milk? The man obviously thought about milk more than he thought about the woman he was supposed to love.

She'd thrown the book she'd been pretending to read across the room, angrily turned off the bedroom light, and lain awake for an entire hour thinking about everything from "accidentally" cutting a hole in his favorite Vineyard Vines waxed canvas jacket to throwing her diamond ring in his face when he finally decided to show up at the town house. Or maybe she would just get the dog she'd threatened to adopt every time she saw a plea on Facebook or Instagram from a local rescue. Then she would let Fido or Lola chew his good wool socks and get dog hair all over his pillow. Finally, with no more envisioned punishments for her beloved, she'd cried herself to sleep.

"Are you okay?" her mother called as Ellery slid past the old baker's rack that held half-dead plants and silly paintings she'd done in grade school perched on easels.

"Sure. I'm fine."

Her mother moved toward her, concern evident on her face. "You don't sound fine."

"I am." But her damned voice trembled.

"Elle, is it the birthday thing?"

"No, I don't care about my stupid birthday." Ellery turned away and blinked up at the fluorescent kitchen lights, trying to hold it together. "It's not that."

"Baby." Her mother's soft voice was her undoing.

One tear fell. Then another. She didn't want to admit things weren't good, but she was so tired of holding everything inside and failing at making things work. "Mom, things are so messed up, and he doesn't even seem to realize it."

"What do you mean? With Josh? Is it . . . cheating?"

"No," Ellery interrupted, wiping a hand across her face. Her emotions were a dam with a crack spidering down the center. Water kept leaking out. "It's just that he studies all the time and never comes home. He cancels all of our plans, even the movie tonight. He promised he wouldn't cancel again. I just feel so . . . so . . ."

"Helpless?" her mother finished.

Ellery nodded, well aware that she looked ridiculous crying over her fiancé doing what he needed to do to make a better future for them.

She was a spoiled princess, a silly woman who couldn't suck it up for a year or two to give her future husband what he needed. *Weak* wasn't even the word for what she was. "It's stupid, but I didn't realize it would be so hard. I mean, I work, and everything's okay when I'm at the store or here. It was hard enough to get past not getting the internship and having to slink home, but I cheered myself up with the thought that I would be here with Josh and that I could plan the wedding, be supportive, get experience working retail, just all the things that sounded so good when I said them, but in reality suck. I've never felt like this before, Mom."

Her mother's arms came around her, and for once she didn't fight against the intrusion. She needed someone to touch her, to give her some comfort. "I know, sugar. Growing up really stinks. Imagine having to do it with a toddler and a husband who was trying to make enough to pay the electric bill. Adulting isn't for the faint of heart, but don't worry. Things will get better. It's just been a hard few months adjusting to a big change."

Even as she took comfort, aggravation reared its head. Of course her mother would compare Ellery's misery to her own . . . and of course her mother's life had been much harder. "I know. I just didn't expect to be so sad all the time."

"So let's plan something that gets us out of town for your birthday. I'm tired of dust everywhere and the hammering going on at all hours. You need a getaway, and so do I. Let me call your friends, and we'll put our heads together for a fun surprise."

"You don't have to do that. And it doesn't have to be a surprise. Dinner is fine."

"You love surprises. Keep the last weekend in October open, okay? Or maybe the first in November. Make sure they don't schedule you to work."

Ellery sniffed and wiped the wetness from her cheeks. "You don't have to do that, Mom. It's silly. I'm too old for—"

"No, I want to." Her mother set her hands on her shoulders and squeezed. "Now go mop up your face and start thinking about a cute outfit to wear for your birthday weekend. Where that will be, I'm not sure. I'll call Madison, and we'll think of something."

She nodded, wishing that she didn't feel so happy at the simple thought of a birthday weekend celebration. God, she should be beyond her mother having to cheer her up. At that moment that guy from the vineyard, uh, Gage, popped into her head. He smirked and shook his head. *Spoiled little girl.*

"Sure. That would be . . . that gives me something to look forward to." Ellery smiled and accepted that though she should be more of an adult, she needed someone to care about how she felt. And her mother may drive her crazy sometimes, but Ellery knew deep down she was loved.

CHAPTER NINE

The morning fog skated around the twisted trunks of the grapevines covering the slopes of the East Texas hillside as the sun welcomed the day with a golden softness that made Daphne's mouth curl up at the edges. Something this serene demanded appreciation.

Daphne had arrived at the bed and breakfast chosen for Ellery's birthday weekend late last night and had slept in, ensconced in the gorgeous mesquite wood sleigh bed, serenaded by the waves from the sound-machine alarm clock. The cup of hot tea in her hand and the promise of quiet on the rustic porch had nudged her into the chill of the autumn morning.

Sommelier House Bed and Breakfast, located on the grounds of One Tree Estates, an East Texas winery, had been the absolute best idea for Ellery's birthday that Madison had ever had. Ellery had been raving about the wines grown a stone's throw from Shreveport for a month or two and had claimed she'd wanted to visit, so it would be a perfect surprise. Ellery's girlfriends were in charge of getting the birthday girl to the vineyard. They would arrive that afternoon after having spent the morning getting pedicures and facials. All Daphne had to do was go over the menu with the catering staff, decorate the living area of the on-site private house she'd rented for Ellery, Josh, and their friends, and maybe squeeze in a tasting in the vineyard's large barn-turned-retail-center. Or she could be talked into a craft cocktail at the adjacent distillery.

Either way, a drink was on her agenda because once the crew arrived, there would be no time for quiet reflection.

The past few weeks had been exhausting. Not only had she been avoiding Clay like the plague, but her entire house was torn apart. Her Mardi Gras book—*Dixie Doodle and the Missing King Cake Strudel*—was coming out in a month and a half, and her new one was due to her publisher in a week, and she had only half of it completed. She'd spent the last week sleeping at Tippy Lou's, which at least aided her in avoiding Clay but hadn't helped her productivity.

Clay Caldwell had been the most pleasurable mistake she'd ever made, but their one night of horizontal mambo had been a mistake nevertheless. A typical one-night stand would have been easier to face the next day. She knew how women did it in the movies—a gal had too much to drink, stumbled up to his hotel room, and then the morning after, hooked her high heels in her fingers and tiptoed to the elevator, never to be seen again. But Daphne had slept with her contractor, a man she saw every day, a man she had to stand beside and pick out kitchen drawer pulls with.

Yeah, she was beyond brilliant.

Her only consolation was that Clay seemed to know the score. After all, his casual remark of "It's just sex" had cemented her tumble into his arms. Sounded crass to suggest she'd been just scratching an itch, but that's pretty much all it had been. And if she needed an itch scratched again, she wouldn't rub up against a guy she could never have an actual relationship with because he was wrong for her in every single way she could think of . . . except maybe in bed. They'd been good there.

Of course, Daphne hadn't made it through the morning after before Clay cornered her on the back patio and flipped her self-assurances about the night before being no big deal upside down.

"Wanna try for some afternoon delight?" Clay had drawled, stomping onto the porch when she emerged not five minutes after Ellery had left.

"What? Uh, I don't think—"

"Come on now, I thought we'd established that thinking was over-rated?" His smile should have made her weaken, but she'd girded herself with guilt, logic, and the image of her daughter's face when she'd talked about "appropriate" guys and her reputation as a sane children's author. Nope, Daphne wasn't falling for his sexy teasing. They were one and done.

"Uh, Clay, I'm not sure that's necessarily true. Thinking definitely has its place in life."

"Aw, come on, babe. I've been thinking about last night all morning and waiting for Ellery to leave," he said, looking around to make certain no one was listening or watching them. None of the workers were because why would they? "I keep thinking about those sweet little sounds you made when you came. And, Lord, Daphne, you *know* how to treat a man."

Daphne moved away from him, trying not to turn the color of the maple leaves that had begun turning a punchy red. *Dear Lord.* She liked making those noises. Really, really liked them. "Uh, Clay, last night was . . . exactly what I needed, if I'm honest. It's been a long time since I felt that good. But you and I, well, it's not a good idea."

He made a face. "Why? Because of Ellery?"

"Yeah, that and the fact that we're not suitable."

He'd laughed, and she'd had to punt away the awareness that he was an awfully sexy man. Her body still hummed when she thought about the night before. But her mind warned that saying yes to Clay would be like trying to put toothpaste back in the tube. It could happen, but it would be a hell of a mess.

Nope. One and done. That was her mantra.

"Come on. Suitable? What's this? A Victorian melodrama?" Clay asked.

"You know what a melodrama is?"

Clay stopped grinning. "You know, most people assume I'm as dumb as a stump. I'm not. I chose to go to vocational school and start my own business because I know my gifts. Doesn't mean I'm stupid, Daphne, and I would expect you of all people to be able to look beneath the cover of the book."

Shame burned in her gut, something she'd grown too accustomed to in the last twenty-four hours. "I'm sorry, Clay. That wasn't kind or fair. I realize that you're more than just a pretty face."

He smiled. "Thank you, but being pretty ain't half-bad, as you should know."

She hadn't felt pretty in so long. Yes, she felt shame for what she'd done, but dwelling right beside it was the pleasure of feeling desirable. She couldn't remember the last time she'd felt that way. If she were guessing, it was a few years back when she'd been walking Jonas and a guy had whistled at her. The homeless man hadn't had many teeth, so she wasn't sure how valid it was. She'd been surprised he could still whistle with such a lack of enamel. "No, it's not, but being attractive is not all you have going for you, Clay. That was unfair."

"Thank you. So why don't you want to see me tonight? We had fun."

Daphne swallowed. "We did, but it's like you said. Just sex. And I, uh, I don't think we should continue to . . . have it."

His gaze narrowed. "So you think it was a mistake?"

Yeah. Big-time. After all, if she hadn't read that book and drunk a bottle of wine, there's no way she would have slept with someone a decade and a half younger than she was. In fact, there was a pretty good chance she wouldn't have even slept with a man her own age. It had been a moment of insanity, born from an unnatural compulsion to have sex, and she wasn't going to give in to something like that again.

"Clay, it's not that it was a mistake, per se, it's that I am not that sort of woman. Nothing about sex is casual to me, and since you and I are more likely to spontaneously combust than enter into a relationship, I can't do what we did again. You understand? It's not that you weren't terrific—you were—it's that I can't be that person."

"So you're saying it was a mistake."

"No, it's just not something I want to repeat, if that makes sense." One and done. One and done. One and—

"So you're looking for a relationship, huh?" Clay scratched his head as if he hadn't been expecting that from her. "I guess that's what all women seem to be looking for. Commitment."

Daphne smiled. Clay said it like most men—like someone had sneezed all over their rib eye steak. "Maybe. I'm not sure. What I do know is that you're young, and what you're looking for is not what I'm looking for."

Clay stared at her for a few seconds and then shrugged. "You got me figured out, I guess. I'll get back to work now."

Daphne watched him walk away and felt uncomfortable with how everything between her and Clay went down. He'd be working on her project for at least a month more, but she'd danced the dance, and now her fiddler was calling for his two bits.

So for the next two weeks, she'd lain low because it felt like the thing to do. When Clay asked something of her, she was friendly and courteous, but she didn't spend any idle time chatting with him . . . or checking out how nice his butt looked in the work pants he wore. She suspected he was a bit miffed or confused by her professional demeanor, but he didn't say much. Sometimes she caught him watching her, but she tried to avoid him as much as she could. As for her libido, Daphne ignored the impulses that arose when she thought back to that night, when she remembered how good it felt to be held and loved. She wanted that again, but she wanted intimacy on the right terms. Sneaking around with a man-child, even one as good in bed as Clay, while fulfilling in the short term, wouldn't sustain her soul.

Daphne longed for a partner who would do just that—a man who would challenge her . . . a man who would sit with her on a cool fall morning, sip tea, and not say a word because none were needed.

Her phone dinged, and she lifted it from the edge of the rail on the screened porch.

Rex.

Coming to vineyard for the kiddo's birthday. Hope that's okay. Madison invited me. Got the last room in the B&B. Hope we can talk.

Daphne closed her eyes. "Nooo."

Since the divorce, she and Rex had managed to be civil because that was what dutiful parents did. Things weren't bad between them, but then again, both of them had given up on each other, and that knowledge sat there like a fat slug between them. Daphne had looked forward to an easy weekend, and nothing was easy about Rex and never had been.

From the beginning, Rex demanded attention. With cherub cheeks and blond locks, Rex had been the boy in class who twisted teachers around his pinkie while manipulating others into doing mischief so he didn't get caught. They'd been in Miss Kilgore's kindergarten class together, and Rex was the kid who always won student of the week, the first-place ribbon in the sack race, and a trip to the principal's office to choose a prize for spelling the most words correctly. Rex laughed loudest, ran fastest, and let the girls catch him when they played kiss chase at recess. His top-feeder status didn't change as they meandered through middle school and arrived in high school.

Daphne had been a quiet, studious girl with ginger pigtails that turned a soft auburn by the time she reached high school. Her freckles faded, her flat chest blossomed into something boys noted as they passed her in the hall, and when she got contacts to replace the thick-lens glasses she'd worn, she'd turned into something of a beauty. Rex noticed. Rex pursued. Rex got the prize.

Even after they'd been married, Rex continued to shine. His parents helped finance the AC-repair business and paid for Rex to get a business degree at LSU Shreveport. Her ex-husband had been a pro at glad-handing local businessmen. He'd joined the Rotary Club, the boards of several nonprofits, and donated to political campaigns to ensure Pinnacle Heating and Air was always in the running for city contracts. When Rex was around, Daphne felt like his shadow . . . or maybe like the person he expected to stand beside him, smile pretty, and hand him a tissue from her purse when being in the spotlight strained him overmuch.

That's why their marriage hadn't worked any longer.

Because Daphne had stepped out of the dark into the light. And Rex hadn't taken it well. Not only had he not taken it well, he'd turned her success back on her. Like everything was her fault. Like she should tell Little Red Barn Books "Thanks, but no thanks" because her husband's fragile ego couldn't handle being second fiddle for one single minute. Didn't matter that her secret dream of writing books had come true. Didn't matter that he'd been the one who'd walked away from her.

Daphne opened her eyes and looked at the message on her screen. She typed back. Okay. Cocktails at 5:00 p.m. Dinner at 7:30. Tomorrow tour of vineyard then barbecue birthday celebration at Round Rock Room at 8:00.

She could deal with Rex. After all, she'd been dealing with him her entire life, and though the divorce papers declared them over, the man would always be in her life.

Because of Ellery.

That's why she'd done most everything she'd ever done. But, of course, her willingness to sacrifice was part of Daphne's problem. This entire weekend proved that much. When faced with a tearful Ellery weeks ago, Daphne should have given her a hug, chucked her on the chin, and told her to stiffen her upper lip. But no. Instead Daphne had done what she'd always done—put aside her needs to make Ellery happy.

Because that's what she and Rex had always done.

Daphne sank into one of the heavy rockers on the private back patio of her room. Sommelier House had an old-Texas feel with rustic wood floors pinned down by antique furniture. The overall feel should have been hodgepodge, but instead it felt authentic and weighty, as if the architect had intended visitors to feel as if they were returning to a family home rather than a bed and breakfast. Daphne liked the vibe.

An hour later Daphne emerged from her room, wearing a sweater tunic, leggings, and some cute flats she'd bought at a trendy boutique, and headed for the dining area that overlooked the rows of vines stretching the property. For once, her waves had settled into something manageable, and the extra sleep had given her a nice glow. So far, so good.

The dining room had large dark-wood beams, three wagon-wheel chandeliers, and walls covered in white shiplap. Very Texas. When she arrived at the small table reserved for her breakfast, she found a vase with daisies and a vellum envelope containing a note scrawled in a masculine hand.

Daphne,

Glad to have you here. Looking forward to meeting you later today.

Evan

Daphne tucked her napkin in her lap and smiled at the waitress. "No coffee, but if you have grapefruit juice, I'll have a glass."

The waitress, whose name was Debi, smiled and scrawled something on her pad. "We actually do."

"Oh, good, and who is Evan?"

Debi blinked. "Evan? You mean Mr. McCallum? The owner?"

"Oh yes. Of course. Evan McCallum." Daphne folded the note and shoved it into her bag. Obviously, Sommelier House was big on hospitality if the owner took the time to welcome each guest. Such a nice touch that added to the charm of the East Texas vineyard.

"Are you ready?"

Sounded like Debi's question was about more than ordering breakfast. *Was* Daphne ready? After all, this weekend would demand the delicate balancing act she seemed to always have to do with Ellery, not to mention her ex-husband was coming to no doubt undermine her every word, and then there was Josh, who'd already delivered a text about how he could stay for only one night and wouldn't be available for social niceties since he had a test in some kind of "ology" the following week. Irritation at the man her daughter was engaged to reared its head. "I suppose I should be."

"No, you should take the time you need. Everything on the menu is delicious."

Daphne smiled. "I'll take the eggs Benedict with the homemade biscuits and local honey. I'll probably need to run a few miles afterward."

Debi laughed. "But it will be worth it."

"I bet," Daphne said. She pulled her napkin into her lap and tapped through her email messages on her phone. She had several from writing friends, which was always a comfort. Writing and illustrating was a solo endeavor, and she appreciated her online groups of other authors who gave her advice, support, and a kick in the pants when she needed it. Her new publicist had sent a few interviews. She forwarded those to Ellery for her to sort on Monday. Her agent had an offer from a foreign publisher for Turkish rights. Daphne smiled at the thought of children all over the world enjoying her high-strung, friendly poodle and her serious sidekick labradoodle cousin Mahalia. Some days she couldn't believe she was an author. No, *every* day she was in awe of the blessings that had come her way.

"Here you go," Debi said, setting down a chilled glass of juice, a plate of fluffy biscuits with a cute jar of honey, and the breakfast Daphne had ordered. "Oh, and Mr. McCallum thought you might appreciate these. I forgot to change them out earlier."

Debi switched the daisies out with a vase of gorgeous ruffled lavender peonies.

"Oh my, how beautiful. Peonies are my favorite." Daphne smiled at the waitress. "I wonder how he knew."

"His daughter is a great fan of your books. I know because she totes them around and reads them to our chef. The child's not supposed to go into the kitchens, but José gives her ice cream, so what are you going to do? We listen to Dixie's adventures and laugh at Sir Ruffles trying to always be so tough. He's a crazy dog."

Daphne's heart warmed at the thought of the owner's daughter loving her books enough to read to the kitchen staff. "Thank you. I love writing about those silly dogs. I'll have to meet his daughter. What's her name?"

"Poppy. She's pretty adorable. I know she'll love meeting you."

"How did you know who I was?" Daphne asked. Most people didn't connect the simple Daphne Witt with the overly adorned, fussy Dee Dee O'Hara.

The waitress shrugged. "I'm not sure, but Mr. McCallum is the kind of person who always knows the details."

Daphne smiled and then looked down at her breakfast. "Attention to details makes a difference."

"Enjoy your breakfast."

Daphne did. The eggs Benedict was well executed, the biscuits light and fluffy, and the grapefruit juice the perfect accompanying tang. She wiped her mouth and pushed back her chair, rising to find Clay Caldwell striding toward her.

What the . . . ?

Her immediate reaction was to hide. Her second one was concern. Had something happened to her house? There was no other explanation for Clay walking toward her, his face apprehensive. Something was wrong. Very wrong.

"What is it?" Daphne said, grabbing her clutch purse from the table, trying not to panic.

Clay stopped and looked confused. "What do you mean?"

"The house . . . is there a problem with the house?"

"Naw, nothing's wrong with the house. The guys finished the demo of the kitchen, and cabinets are going in tomorrow morning." He nodded in what looked to be satisfaction.

"So why are you here?"

"Oh," he said, looking like he was finally clueing in. "Uh, Ellery's birthday thing's tomorrow night. Madison invited a lot of the old gang to come for the party. I was going to drive over and back tomorrow, but I thought a little getaway would be nice. I've been working hard lately and—"

Now that she knew her house was okay, a new panic gripped her. Clay and Ellery weren't close. Oh, sure, they still saw each other when Ellery and Josh went out for drinks or went to watch a football game at a friend's house, but she knew Ellery still had issues with the boy who'd once wronged her, which made what Daphne had done with him ten times worse. "You shouldn't have come, Clay."

"Why not?"

Daphne glanced around to make sure no one could hear. "You *know* why not."

"No, I don't."

"You're not even friends with Ellery. You're here because . . . I'm not sure why you would do this."

"I told you. I wanted some time away." He shrugged and averted his eyes.

She got a strange feeling. "Clay, what's this really about?"

"It's about you giving me a chance. It's about you seeing me in a different light."

"Seeing you in a different light? Clay, we've already had this conversation."

"No, you told me what you thought I want, but I've been doing a lot of thinking, and I think you're wrong about us. When Madison told me what y'all were doing, I felt like it was an opportunity. I wanted to show you that I can be what you want."

"Clay, there's no us."

"Because you've spent the past two weeks running from what we could have."

"No, I've accepted that what happened was . . . a one and done. You and I just can't do this. You said it was just sex. Remember?"

Clay contemplated her for a few seconds. "That's what I thought. But I keep thinking about you, and I think you've been thinking about me, too. Only you've convinced yourself it won't work because of what everyone else will say. Especially Ellery. But here's the deal—why does Ellery get to have whatever she wants, but you have to live like a monk? And the whole age thing is so passé. Who cares?"

Daphne didn't know how to make him understand that she wasn't merely hiding from what others thought. She and Clay made no sense. At all. "Clay, you need to think about your future. I'm not your future. You need to date women your own age, girls who want to get married, have babies, and—"

"You're assuming I want that. Who said I want a picket fence and a playpen of babies? All I want at present is to be with you. I'm asking for a chance, Daph."

Daphne wanted to press her hand against his mouth, not just because she didn't want anyone in the restaurant to know her business, but because she didn't want to hear the words emerging from his mouth. "I don't know what to say. I can't even imagine us being . . . in a relationship."

"Because I'm too young? Or you're too scared?"

Both. Absolutely both. But she wasn't going to admit to her fears.

"Go back to Shreveport, Clay," she said, pushing by him, wondering how her one night of throwing caution to the wind had come back to smack her in the face. Who would have thought a twenty-five-year-old Lothario would want second helpings from a nearly forty-year-old woman?

The thought he'd come to Texas to win her was so ridiculous she wondered if someone was playing a joke on her.

If she could, she'd press rewind and refuse that third—or was it fourth?—glass of wine. Then again, if she were truthful, she would own up to that wine as only an excuse, a bit of liquid courage that allowed her to act on what she'd wanted for weeks. Something hot and needy had bloomed in her, twining itself around the need to feel something. She longed for the stroke of a hand on her hip, the delicious weight of a man pinning her to the bed. To say she needed to get off wasn't wholly accurate. She'd wanted human connection, too.

But that didn't mean she wanted a relationship with Clay.

The more important relationship with her daughter was already a tenuous spiderweb in a hurricane of blame, jealousy, and resentment. Oh, these emotions between them were ones she was aware of. What they engaged in was a push and pull of two women trying to find their footing in new lives. Daphne didn't know how to remove what sat between her and Ellery, but she knew picking up what Clay Caldwell was laying down—no matter how spectacular he was in bed—wasn't anything that could help.

"Hey, hey," Clay said, catching her arm. "Stop just a minute, Daphne."

She whirled. "What?"

"You can't be the only person who decides."

"Actually, I can. That's how it works, Clay. When one person wants something, and the other doesn't, it doesn't happen." Daphne uncurled his hand from her arm and held it tight. "You are a great guy—"

"But—"

"Whatever you envisioned happening this weekend isn't going to." Daphne walked away, hurrying through the arch that framed the opening to the restaurant. She didn't have time to deal with Clay or the mistake she'd made with him, so she hoped her words were enough to drive him to climb back into his big pickup truck and head east.

Daphne was so flustered that she didn't pay attention to where she was heading and ended up in the wrong wing of the bed and breakfast. Of course, she didn't realize this until she'd reached the last bedroom at the end of the hall and discovered it was room number three and not room number six. She did an about-face and ran straight into someone standing behind her.

"Whoa, hey," the man said, gripping her upper arms and steadying her.

Daphne brushed the hair out of her eyes and glanced up.

Whiskey. His eyes were the exact color of the nightcap Rex had poured himself each night. A mellow amber with marigold bursts, those eyes dared a person to get lost in their intoxicating depths. Or maybe she'd turned into too much of a writer and needed to rein in her need to embellish brown eyes.

"I'm sorry. Wrong way," she said with a self-deprecating shrug.

"Daphne?"

She paused. "Yes?"

"It's Evan," he said, tapping a hand against his chest.

Evan. The owner of the vineyard. She'd seen a picture of him in one of the brochures that Madison had forwarded to her over a week ago. In the brochure, he wore a cowboy hat that covered his high forehead. He was taller than Rex, maybe six foot two or so. His hair was a thick reddish brown almost exactly the color of her own. Of course, she now got her color from a box, but she'd matched it to the shade her hair had always been. "Evan McCallum. Of course."

She felt the full measure of the smile he delivered, and her first impression was utter warmth. "I'm so glad you're here at the vineyard. What do you think so far?"

"Oh, it's lovely. I haven't been out to the actual vineyard or tasting room, of course, but I love my room."

"Yes, the Jonquil Room's the best. Nothing like hot tubbin' in a vineyard, right?"

Daphne smiled. "I haven't tried that yet, either, but I love how I feel like I'm in California. Or even Italy. If you look out the window, you can't imagine you're in Texas. Outside of the place having a friendly Texas feel."

"I knew you'd like it," he said, turning as if he would walk with her.

The hall was narrow, which meant his shoulder brushed hers occasionally as they walked toward the open area that held the registration desk, small bar, and opening to the restaurant. His overly familiar manner felt odd, but maybe that was part of the charm. Flowers, a personalized note, and treating guests as if they were long-lost family.

They emerged into the foyer, and Evan stopped, nodding at the young woman who worked the desk.

"Well, it was lovely to actually meet you," Daphne said, extending a hand. "Oh, and the flowers this morning. My favorite. I have no idea how you found peonies, but what a lovely touch."

He chuckled. "Well, I'm trying my best to—"

"Daddy!" a little girl interrupted, slipping out from what looked to be the door of an office.

Daphne grinned at the redheaded little girl, who looked about six or seven. "This must be Poppy."

Evan caught the hand of the little girl as she grabbed his and executed a perfect twirl. She crashed against his leg and looked up at Daphne with brilliant-blue eyes. "Hi."

"Yep, this is my Poppy girl. Do you recognize this lady, Pop?"

The little girl narrowed her eyes, and then they widened. Finally, she squinched her eyes at Daphne. "Where's your hat?"

"I didn't wear it this weekend. No pearls or white gloves, either. Just me."

"Where's Dixie? And Mahalia?" the girl asked, her gaze roaming around the foyer. She looked concerned.

Daphne glanced up at the child's father. His eyes laughed at her.

"Well, Dixie is home with my friend Tippy Lou. She's working on a new case, you know. Someone stole Mr. Izuzu's suitcase, and she and Mahalia are on the trail of the culprit." Daphne touched one of the girl's braids. "I admire your hair. You know, mine was the exact same color when I was a girl, and I had adorable freckles across my nose just like yours."

Poppy grinned. "I don't like my freckles. Have you read the book called *Freckle Juice*?"

Ah, this small child was a young bibliophile. "I have. That's a big book for you."

"My aunt Marin read it to me. She comes in and reads my bedtime stories for me. And makes sure I brush my teeth. My uncle Jared's a dentist. I think he makes her check and stuff."

Daphne smiled at Poppy's father. The man looked at his little girl like a man truly in love. Daphne's heart may have skipped a beat or two at that look. Rex had been much the same over Ellery. Everything Ellery said was adorable, even when she was sassy. "Well, your teeth *are* important. I brush Dixie's, and she doesn't like it, but she also likes to eat and sort of needs her pearly whites."

"You brush a dog's teeth?" the little girl asked, her eyes popping.

"I try to. Dogs aren't always as agreeable as little girls." Daphne thought about the few times she'd chased Jonas down and tried to use the finger dog brush and meat-flavored toothpaste. Her trusty hound had been insulted and shook his head so hard that Daphne had to pick the disgusting-smelling toothpaste out of her hair. Jonas wasn't a fan no matter what the paste tasted like, and honestly, Daphne had feared he'd bite her finger. "I suppose I should be on my way. It's my little girl's birthday this weekend, and I have a party to oversee."

"You have a little girl, too?" Poppy asked.

"Well, she's not so little anymore," Daphne said.

Evan tucked Poppy against his side, curving an arm around her to pin her in place. The child's feet were already twisting. "If you need help with anything, let Caroline know." He nodded toward the young woman at the desk.

"It was so good to meet you and your daughter."

"Well, we've been waiting to meet you in person. I'll pull away from things later this evening and catch up with you," he said, bestowing a big smile on her.

Daphne wondered if the man was always so familiar with his guests but decided that his personality was one that spilled over onto the people around him. Ellery could be that way. Rex damn well made sure his personality assaulted those around him. Evan wasn't like that, per se, but he certainly treated her like an old friend rather than someone he'd only just met. "That would be lovely. Bye, Poppy. Have a good day."

"I'm out of school. It's fall break," she said, her eyes shining brightly with the joy only a day of no school could bring.

"Well, have fun. I'll probably see you around, and maybe we could read some books together."

"Yes!" the child said, hopping and punching the air with her fist.

"Now you've done it," Evan said as she pulled her keycard out of her pocket.

"See y'all later," Daphne said, giving the child a happy wave and then lifting her gaze and catching the eye of her father. The expression on his face reflected warmth and familiarity. An odd prickling of something—warning, maybe?—skittered up her spine. His demeanor seemed incongruous with how a host might treat a guest. It was as if he knew her, but she was nearly certain she'd never met him before. She'd done a lot of book signings in the area, but she would have remembered a tall, handsome Texan and a chatty redheaded child.

She wondered if he was married.

Just as she had this thought, she passed the bar, which looked to have just opened, and saw Clay sitting there, chatting with the bartender. He nursed a Bloody Mary and looked morose. Daphne had a sneaking suspicion Clay wouldn't do as she asked.

This weekend was going to be more difficult than she'd expected, because the only two men she'd slept with in her life had become unexpected guests.

Daphne couldn't catch a break.

CHAPTER TEN

Dear Evan,

Sorry I haven't been in touch. Things have been busy around here with the renovation, and I have been working from home. I loved your analogy about the wine. So true that the bad times in life can make the good times sweeter. Thanks for sharing that with me. Good news—I'm taking Ellery on a little birthday-surprise weekend. She's been so down, I think it will be good for both of us to get away from the dust, noise, and reality. Yeah, I know what you're thinking after our last discussion, but escaping reality is a must sometimes, right? I should have an answer for you regarding the date in a few weeks. Pencil me in. If I don't have any unseen obligations with my publisher or the studio, I will be there. I look forward to seeing you soon.

Best,
Dee Dee

Ellery stared at the email she'd sent Evan last night and tried not to panic at the thought of sitting on the couch of Vine House at One Tree Estates. She could still hear the echo of her best friend's voice as they exited the interstate outside Tyler, Texas.

Surprise, Elle! We're doing your birthday weekend at your favorite vineyard! Happy birthday!

Any other time, she'd have been ecstatic that her friends had come up with such a cool birthday weekend. But since the owner of the place was her secret obsession, she was less than thrilled. More like panicked that Evan and her mother would find out she'd been masquerading as a stalker.

No, remember, you're not a stalker.

Pretending to be the talented, pretty Miss Dee Dee O'Hara and maintaining a friendship, albeit a flirty and somewhat intimate one, wasn't stalking. It was . . . something that she'd obviously convinced herself she needed because her fiancé was . . . something.

God, why couldn't she figure out *why* she was doing what she was doing? Why couldn't she sort through her emotions as easily as she sorted through what would be on trend for the upcoming spring season? Her once-perfect life was so smudged around the edges that there were no lines left.

Every time she thought about Josh and the way she no longer seemed to matter to him, jagged pain split her heart into two halves. She didn't know what to do, but she'd decided this weekend she would do her best to reel him back to her. When her mother had mentioned that a weekend away was a go, she'd convinced Josh to leave the books, the study group, and the stress behind for just one night. She'd bought a leather bustier and stockings, ordered a few sex toys to try from a discreet online company, and gotten a Brazilian wax. This weekend he was going to notice her if she had to park her ass in his lap and . . . okay, not make him have sex with her, but make it really hard not to.

But that was before, when she thought they were getting rooms at a swanky hotel in Dallas. She had been almost certain her mother and friends would arrange a shopping weekend and spa treatments.

Nope.

Lord, what had she gotten herself into? Why had she ever started flirting with Evan . . . building a secret relationship with him? Her house of cards faced a tsunami.

"Elle, check this out. It's stocked with a bottle of every type of wine they grow here," Madison said, opening the wine fridge. "Birthday perks, birthday girl. So which one should we open?"

"Mads, technically my birthday is tomorrow." She now felt silly for wanting everyone to make a fuss over her birthday. She should have insisted on the simple dinner her mother first suggested. But she knew why she'd let them plan this celebration. Because deep down under all the "I'm totally an adult" facade, she wanted the cake, balloons, and epicness. Because a nice dinner out had sounded too much like what everyone else did. Like it wasn't special enough.

Ellery didn't want to admit that her life had become ordinary. Ellery had graduated from being on the homecoming court to being a basic bitch. She might as well drink pumpkin spice lattes, carry Michael Kors, and wear yoga pants to the grocery store. Totally basic.

And she didn't want to be that woman. If she were going to have the fabulous life she'd wanted for herself in NYC, she had to be interesting enough to be in the spotlight. And if she and Josh were going to make it, she had to be more interesting than his books and cadaver.

Her biggest fear was that she was neither. That she had already peaked, and everything was downhill from hereafter.

"Uh, you get to celebrate the whole month if you want to," Madison drawled before grinning, causing her two precious dimples to come out to play. Her friend's blonde hair spilled over her shoulders, and her mossy-green eyes surrounded by sooty, long lashes inspired jealousy in other girls. Madison Cunningham had been Ellery's BFF ever since they'd both worn the same Supergirl costume to kindergarten on Halloween. Rather than see the other as competition, like Mia Dinkins and Claire Toby, her other close friends who had both dressed as Tinkerbell, Mads and Elle had declared themselves soul mates . . . and still had the connection that going to two different colleges, pledging two different sororities, and crushing on the same hot celebrities couldn't break.

"That's right. We're making up for lost time," Claire said, selecting a plump strawberry from the fruit plate Ellery's mother had set out. Her mom had decorated the rented house on the edge of the vineyard with fresh flowers, pink balloons, and a cute birthday sign that hung from the two light fixtures. The island bar was covered with party poppers and confetti. No doubt her mother had a vacuum in her car ready to tackle the rental after Ellery and her friends departed. This was the kind of mother hers was—always prepared, committed to making everything perfect, and never leaving a mess.

Problem was, her mother couldn't fix the downhill slide Ellery felt she was on. So while she felt grateful to her mother for always picking her up, she also resented that while she was plummeting toward an uncertain future, her mother was on a meteoric trajectory toward fame. This small, petty part of herself she hated, but she couldn't seem to make it go away. The only thing she'd felt good about was being engaged to Josh, and now that part of her plan was in jeopardy.

There were times she wondered if Josh had proposed just to get her to shut up about their future . . . or as a consolation for her getting smacked down by J.J. Krause. The glow of wearing that diamond had faded, and often she felt like she was merely another piece of business he needed to complete so he could get the dream he wanted with a woman whose plan coincided with his own. Dr. Josh Prince, plastic surgeon, upstanding husband, doting father, and rich as shit.

But that wasn't true. They were more than just a plan. They were in love.

Or had been.

"Elle? Wine?" Madison asked again, jarring her out of her too-difficult thoughts.

"Huh? Oh, yeah, let's crack open a white." *'Cause I'm going to need it. Maybe two bottles before the cocktail hour.*

Madison smiled and looked so pretty it made Ellery wish she hadn't done the microdermabrasion on her cheeks and chin. Both were now red and splotchy, even though her face felt remarkably smooth. She just needed an hour or two more for her skin to calm down.

"Gotcha," Madison said, rooting in the drawers for a wine opener. Claire continued munching on the fruit, snagging a cookie that her delicate frame could well afford. Claire had short, dark hair, a lithe runner's body, and a weakness for watching *Gossip Girl*, *Mean Girls*, *Gilmore Girls*, or any kind of show with *girls*, *pretty*, or *gossip* in the title. Claire was studying to take the CPA exam while working for a firm in Baton Rouge. Gentle Madison was working in the pediatric intensive care unit at a hospital in Monroe. Both were already ten times more successful than Ellery, not that either would say anything about Ellery failing to net the internship she'd crowed about all last year. They'd heard about her failure months ago, offered encouragement, and then promptly gone about their own business. Ellery was the one who had to live with the choices she'd made. Or choice. She should have listened to her adviser and applied for more than one internship.

She'd just been so certain that the position would be hers.

"I wish Mia could have come today, but at least she'll make it tonight," Claire said, swiping crumbs off the granite. While Madison and Claire had elected to go to LSU for college, Mia had gone with

Ellery to the University of Georgia, where she'd stayed to do law school. Still, the four girls had stayed very close, going on spring break together every year, texting each other at least once a day, and spending the holidays shopping, vegging while watching *CSI*, and sipping apple-pie moonshine before going out to their favorite haunts in Shreveport.

Ellery accepted the wine Madison handed her. "Josh *is* coming, right? You made sure? Because he's become very slippery here lately."

"Yep, and he is part of Mia's job. She's grabbing him on the way over, and she's vowed to stand over him until he gets in the car. They'll be here in time for dinner. JB, Thomas, Matt, and Wade are coming, too. Oh, and we invited a few people from high school for the party tomorrow night, along with your work friends Rachel and Fiona. But it's no more than, like, fifteen or twenty people." Claire grabbed a glass and poured herself a hefty portion of the white wine.

Ellery didn't want a ton of people coming. Why would her friends invite a bunch of people? Of course, a bigger group would keep her plenty busy, which meant she might not even run into Evan. Or the sneering, sexy bartender who'd popped into her mind more than she wished. Gage. His name seemed prophetic, like he could see inside her and tell her where she was in her life. Yeah, she knew they were spelled differently, and she'd only met him that once, but still he'd unnerved her with the way he could *see* her, and not the good part of herself she always presented to everyone else. The part she was ashamed of. The part she tried to hide. "I hope they don't show. I like it low key."

"When have you ever wanted fewer than, like, fifty people to come to your parties?" Madison drawled.

"Um, like, tomorrow when I turn twenty-three." Ellery took a sip of wine that was cold and sharp on her tongue. The finish was mellow and golden. "Sorry. Things just feel so real. I mean, we have jobs and bills and—"

"Jell-O shots," Claire interrupted, pulling a box of cherry Jell-O from the depths of a grocery bag along with a bottle of vodka.

"You didn't," Ellery said. Claire loved to make Jell-O shots . . . or any shots, for that matter. Last Christmas they'd stayed half-drunk the entire holiday on something with RumChata and Fireball.

"Um, yeah, I did. It's a party, and it's been, like, forever since we hung out. It's a miracle the stars lined up and we all got off work. Especially since it was short notice, so we're going to make like college freshmen and forget about time clocks and performance reports . . . and do shots," Claire said, looking over at Madison. Mads raised her glass.

Ellery immediately felt like a shit for not being in the spirit. Claire was right. It had been a long time since they had all been together, and they had done this for her. "Okay, bring it."

"There's the Ellery we know and love," Claire said, opening the doors of the cabinets. "I'm going to whip these up, then shower. Your mother said cocktail hour is at five, and I still have one thing I have to do online before I totally surrender myself to booze and bitches."

"I'm going to take a nap. That shift switch to get off for the weekend is kicking my ass," Madison said, moving toward the bedroom she was sharing with Claire.

Ellery needed to get pretty before they headed to the distillery and the cocktail bar housed within, but she felt angsty. Like she needed some time to herself. "I think I'll take a walk and enjoy the foliage. Just breathe some of this nice cool air."

"Don't get lost," Madison said, pointing a finger toward her, her mouth curving with amusement.

Ellery had once gotten lost on a Girl Scout outing. The troop leaders were about to call the police when Ellery wandered back into camp, scratched by brambles and tear streaked from her four-hour-long ordeal. To her credit, she'd been ten, and she'd just watched *Friday the 13th* at a friend's house, so she was freaked out and a bit overly dramatic about getting lost. She never went camping again. "I won't. And if I see a guy in a hockey mask, you'll hear me. I've been practicing that scream since I saw that dumb movie."

Ellery hurried to the master bedroom she'd share with Josh that night. The big four-poster bed dominated the tastefully decorated room and held her suitcase. After donning running shorts, a jacket, and her trusty Brooks trainers, Ellery slipped out the french doors onto the private patio attached to her bedroom and moved around to the front.

The rental house at One Tree Estates was called Vine House and was built of stone and wood, evoking a European chalet. Perched on the edge of one of the vineyards, it butted up against a young copse of woods, decked out in autumn finery. Rocking chairs sat on the stone porch, where a barrel of mums and pansies spilled over. As if on cue, a gray cat strolled onto the porch, stretched in the patch of sunlight, and sat, regarding her as if she were the intruder.

"Hello, fella," Ellery said, walking over and extending her hand. The cat meowed but ignored her.

She shrugged and walked down the path marked with natural stone pavers that matched the house. A gravel drive led up to the main winery and bed and breakfast where her mother was staying. Her father had texted earlier and told her he'd try to make it for whatever her mother had planned. Once upon a time, he would have never considered *not* making her birthday party, but that was before her parents split. Sometimes she forgot that her parents weren't together anymore. Every time she forgot and then remembered, the loss stung more. She wanted to believe that some things in life lasted . . . that people could truly be committed to each other. Because that's what she would have with Josh.

She was determined.

Ellery started walking along an unmarked path that led into the vineyard. She glanced around for a sign that might warn her it was for staff only but didn't see anything. The path rose through the vineyard to the top of a gentle hill. Once she reached the top, she could see acres of dark, twisted vines that looked to be in the first stages of pruning. An abandoned truck sat near a fence line that backed up to a subdivision, but she saw no evidence of workers. To her left, the hill sloped down to a small pond, and beyond that a pasture of bovines lazily chewed cud. Brilliant autumn foliage from scrubby trees tumbled toward the rippled water, and the midafternoon sun had started its descent, encompassing the scenery in warm, soft light.

It was the perfect place to gather herself and do a few breathing exercises.

Her shoes slid on the gravel exposed by erosion, and the sun warmed her shoulders even as the breeze caused goose bumps to dot her legs. Someone walked to the pond regularly, because the path was beaten down. Once she reached the pond, she spied a shady spot to the left that looked level and still gave her a view of the serene water and swaying reeds. It was too cool for snakes, so she should be fine folding herself into Sukhasana and searching for her center.

Sinking onto a soft carpet of pine needles that were flattened to such a degree they didn't prick through her lululemon shorts, Ellery positioned herself into a relaxed pose and straightened her spine, dropping her head to her chest, closing her eyes. She allowed her hands to rest palms up on her knees. She drew in a deep breath, making herself aware of the birds chirping overhead, the earthy scent of wood and decaying leaves, filling her lungs with cool autumn air. She tilted back her head and allowed her breath to escape. She did this three times, each time feeling the tension leave her body.

"You're not supposed to be out here. It's private property," said a voice to her right.

Ellery yelped, her hands going to the ground, pushing herself back.

Her gaze found Gage standing several yards away, watching her like she was a bug he wanted to squash. Or maybe that was his usual expression—bored disdain.

"What . . . I'm sorry. I needed some time to myself," she managed to say, pressing a hand against her chest so she could stop her galloping heart. "You scared me."

"There are signs that should have told you this area is not for guests," he said, setting his hands on his hips. He wore running shorts and a long-sleeved athletic shirt that fit so closely she could tell he had a spectacular body. His dark hair was damp, his skin sheened with perspiration. He wore trail-running shoes, an armband with his phone strapped to his biceps, and earbuds draped around his neck. Her memory of Gage the barkeep had been spot-on.

Grumpily sexy.

Ellery lifted her chin. "I didn't see a sign, so I wasn't aware I was trespassing. You might want to take this up with whoever is supposed to put up signs."

Gage's eyes narrowed. "Wait. Do I know you?"

"No. You most *definitely* do not know me."

He studied her for a second or two, and she saw recognition dawn in his eyes. His mouth twitched. "Yeah, I do. Minnie Mouse."

"That's not my name."

"I know it's not your name." He made a thinking face. "Uh, Hillary, right?"

She could feel the momentary tranquility she'd held on to slip away to be replaced with irritation. "Wrong. Not Hillary."

Gage didn't look as if he were in a hurry to leave her alone, so she unwound her legs and pushed herself up to standing. Brushing stray pine needles from her shorts, she folded her arms and waited for him to say something.

His mouth quirked, and it was totally sexy. But she didn't care if it was sexy, because he was an ass.

Finally, he tilted his head. "So are you going to tell me your name?"

Ellery ran her tongue over her upper lip because her lips felt dry. His gaze caught that, and a flicker of something in his eyes gave her pause, sending a little thrill of awareness inside her. "Ellery. My name is Ellery."

"Ah, I was close," he said.

"But wrong."

"But close." He looked around. "What were you doing? Yoga?"

She shook her head. "Just centering, trying to feel myself in this space."

His eyebrows lifted. "Oh. Well, I'm heading back to the winery. Why don't you join me, since this isn't part of the property where guests are supposed to roam. I know it's pretty, but it's still trespassing."

Her inner rebel stamped its foot at being told what to do, but Ellery also didn't want to be a bad guest, even if it was only to this guy who had been so quick to judge her and now was quick to hustle her out of serenity and back into the reality she so wanted to escape. "Fine."

"I'm Gage, by the way." He turned so that she could scoot past him. He could have turned and started walking, expecting her to follow him. Instead, he'd been somewhat gentlemanly. She'd give him a point for that.

"I remember."

"You left your wineglasses. My cousin tried to catch you before you left. I think they're in the gift shop with your name on them."

She'd forgotten about them. Or maybe she had wanted to forget about them because she'd embarrassed herself driving to One Tree Estates that day. What she'd hoped to find was still a mystery . . . or not such a mystery. She'd been chasing after someone who made her feel like she mattered. If she'd paid better attention in her psychology class, she'd probably understand her inclinations. "So if you know my name is on them, why didn't you remember my name?"

He glanced at her. "I don't make a habit of memorizing the name of every person who leaves something behind."

"But you knew they were mine."

Gage shrugged. "I remembered you."

Ellery couldn't stop her smile.

He made a face. "It's not what you think. You have a fiancé, and I don't go traipsing around another man's pasture. Unlike you, I can read signs."

So he remembered she had a fiancé, too. Something warm and almost wonderful bloomed inside her fickle heart. Gage wasn't the kind of guy she'd go for in a million years. His very demeanor was bristly, contentious, and somehow a challenge. But knowing he had totally botched her name on purpose—she was almost certain he had—dragged her bruised ego up at least a notch or two. "But you also remembered I had a fiancé. Huh."

The look he gave her said more than any words, and that made her smile harder.

They ascended the hill, and he moved slightly in front of her. She noticed the way his legs flexed as he climbed, and that he had a tattoo of a dead tree with only a few green leaves on the back of his calf. Four green leaves and a vine with a single red rose. Above the tree, mountains created a space for a lone bird. It was artsy and somehow earthy.

"What's the tattoo about?" she asked, trying to not slip on the loose rocks.

"Which one?"

"On your leg."

He glanced back like he didn't know what she was talking about. "Oh, uh, just a tree."

So he wasn't going to talk about it. But why had she asked? She didn't care. It just looked like a puzzle . . . something that would give her a glimpse into who Gage was. Not that she cared. Of course. "It's . . . nice."

He turned back to her, and at that moment her foot slipped. His hand was like a manacle on her upper arm, and he caught her before she went down. Her hand instinctively clasped his forearm. The man was sinewy and strong. And warm from the sun. His torso dipped toward her, and she caught a whiff of clean soap and salty perspiration. For an awkward moment, she thought about kissing him.

Ellery straightened and released his arm, trying not to blush. That's when she remembered that she wore no makeup and was blotchy from the earlier microdermabrasion. Her hair was a tangle, and her eyes were puffy from lack of sleep. She might think Gage looked like the cat's meow, but she resembled more closely what the cat threw up. And, of course, that was how she would look when facing the guy who'd played dodgeball with her thoughts over the last couple of weeks.

Ellery pushed her hair from her eyes. "Thank you."

He shrugged. "Sure. If you want to take a walk or find a place to sit and do your breathing exercises, there's a curated path that runs through the adjoining neighborhood."

Ooh-kay. So she had been slammed with an awareness of Gage, but he'd reverted to employee of the year as if she were nothing more than a total nuisance.

They reached the top of hill, and Gage pointed toward the winery. "I think you can find your way back from here."

Ellery glanced over at him. "I could have found my way back from the pond. I'm not directionally challenged. By the way, where are those signs that warn visitors from this area?"

Gage stabbed a finger toward a small sign attached to a tree. Ellery couldn't make out the letters but assumed it said something about trespassing or not finding a place to center oneself when faced with a fiancé who no longer found her attractive, a mother who thought she could fix the world, and a future that felt like it teetered on a tightrope. She totally hadn't seen the sign earlier. "Oh, well, maybe you should put it lower or something."

His mouth was as disapproving as a catfish. "Enjoy your stay."

Then he turned and walked away. Ellery couldn't help herself. She watched for a few steps, enjoying the view of a tight butt, chiseled calves, and wide shoulders.

Hey, Ellery may be engaged and in love with . . . um, Josh . . . but she wasn't dead.

Some things deserved a second glance.

Finally, she tore her gaze away and headed back toward the house she was sharing with her best friends. She wasn't going to think about Gage or Evan or anything else that was unsettling in her life. Center not found, but she'd pretend it was. At least for the weekend.

Time for life to deliver her some goodness.

God, she really needed something to go her way for once.

CHAPTER ELEVEN

"Everyone, everyone," Rex called out, tapping his spoon on his water glass. "Let's have a toast."

Daphne stifled the sigh that tried to make its way to the surface. Her ex-husband had shown up sans Cindy, wearing a new Rolex and a pair of Italian loafers he'd bought last spring in Milan. Daphne only knew this because Rex had told her a few minutes before. He was sitting next to her on Ellery's suggestion, and Daphne suspected her daughter still clung to the desperate thought she could somehow get them back together. Daphne had read a book on dealing with the dynamics of divorce and knew that almost all children hoped that their parents could reconcile. It was natural, but Daphne also knew it was now impossible. That ship had sailed. Not right away, because for a month or so, she'd clung to possible reconciliation, but after the initial panic of facing a life without the man she'd pledged to love, she'd accepted and even made sure that ship was no longer even on the horizon.

Starting over had felt like a relief, especially when she realized her new life was exactly what she wanted.

Rex cleared his throat, his smile as big as the state they were currently in. "Tonight we are celebrating my darling girl. She's the apple of her daddy's eye, and I'm so proud of her. Next year she'll be in New York setting the world on fire with her designs. Get ready for Ellery Witt, people!"

"Hear, hear!" someone called.

Earlier they'd met at the cocktail bar in the distillery. Not only did One Tree Estates have vineyards and a winery, but they also distilled their own vodka. A gift shop was attached to the wine-tasting room, which sat to the side of the craft cocktail bar called Branches. Daphne had spent most of the cocktail hour chatting with Ellery's friends, keeping an eye on Ellery, who spent most of the time checking her phone. At one point, her daughter had excused herself to step outside, and Daphne had caught a glimpse of Ellery talking to who she assumed was Josh. Tears had sparkled in her daughter's eyes, and her disposition upon coming inside was not celebratory.

Ten of them had traipsed over to the restaurant for dinner—Ellery, Rex, Daphne, and several of Ellery's friends. Madison's high school boyfriend, Claire's fiancé, and their buds had arrived to make the occasion more festive, but Josh had yet to arrive. Ellery said he was en route and would arrive before the entrée made it to the table.

"So let's raise a glass of this delicious wine to our Ellery! Sláinte!"

"Sláinte!" everyone echoed, clinking glasses.

Ellery sat at the end of the table, looking as beautiful as she ever had. She wore a violet wrap dress that accentuated her peachy complexion and hinted at the curve of her high breasts. Her blonde hair was artfully arranged, and chandelier earrings framed her face. Her makeup rivaled any runway model's, subdued everywhere but the eyes, which were shadowed to look smoky, a perfect background for the intensity of blue irises. But if one looked closely, she could see the strain, the doubt. Ellery's mouth was strung tight, though she smiled often. Daphne knew it was because there was still an empty chair next to her daughter.

She wanted to kick Josh's ass from here to Mexico. When she'd first met her daughter's then-boyfriend, he'd charmed everyone within a mile. Josh was handsome, mannered, and utterly sincere. Daphne had not thought she could select a better fit for her daughter, but then the two had moved to Shreveport, and Josh had changed. Oh, he could still turn on his hundred-watt smile at will, but he'd been distracted and mostly absent since he'd started school.

Still, if there were a line for ass-kicking, Josh could get in line behind Rex.

Her ex was grandstanding, acting as if this weekend was his idea. That's what he'd always done. But this time, she felt personal about his taking credit, especially after the front desk had called an hour ago, asking if his room should be billed to her account. Seems when he'd checked in, he'd said he was part of the Witt party. Daphne hadn't wanted to make a scene, so she'd told the front desk it was fine and to add it to her card, but she would tell her ex-husband he had to change it over to his card before he left. She wasn't paying for Rex's room for the night. Hell to the no.

"Thank you, Daddy," Ellery said, smiling at him with the adoration she'd always held for the man who'd spoiled her rotten. "And everyone for coming. I know it was hard for y'all to get away! So cheers!"

Everyone clinked again and then sipped the wine, conversation returning to normal.

Daphne trampled her annoyance at not being thanked. Rex, who did nothing but show up, got thanked. She supposed she'd have to settle for being "everyone."

"Mrs. D, the decorations at our rental house are so cute," Claire said.

Rex anchored the end of the table, and Daphne was to his right. Claire sat directly across, next to her fiancé. The two had gotten engaged at the end of college, right before Ellery. Sometimes, Daphne wondered if that was why Ellery had become so enamored of diamonds, china patterns, and bridal Pinterest boards. Ellery liked to be first at everything . . . she also liked to do things bigger and better than everyone else. "Thanks. I thought it would be festive. You know I love a theme."

"You always think of everything. I wish my mom was more like you and thought about cute things like that. You're so good at details. That's probably where Ellery gets it from." Claire unfolded her napkin and sat it in her lap. "My mama's always on the road and losing track of things. She actually forgot my birthday this year."

Rex raised his eyebrows. "Your mama still work for that drug company?"

"Well, Mr. Witt, they like to be called a pharmaceutical company, but, yeah, she's still with them," Claire said with a smile. "How are things with the AC business?"

"Perfect," Rex said, his eyes lowering. He reached for the basket holding rolls as if signaling he didn't want to talk about his business. Something inside Daphne reared its head. Something felt wrong. Rex was way too jovial, and now he deflected an opportunity to talk about his business? He loved to talk about himself and the company he'd built into a "veritable empire." That was the word he loved to use. *Empire*.

"And you, Mrs. D? How is our favorite poodle?" Claire asked, passing the butter to her fiancé, who'd nudged her.

"Very well. Production has started on the show, and I have a new book coming out in January. It's a Mardi Gras caper—a stolen king cake."

Daphne felt Ellery's eyes on her.

"Mom is about to do a book tour in a few weeks," Ellery said, sipping her wine and trying not to look at the empty seat or her phone, which she'd set at her elbow.

Everyone around the table looked toward Daphne. She didn't want to attract any attention to herself. Not at Ellery's birthday party. She gave a nervous laugh. "Ellery's doing such a good job. See? She's promoting me even when she doesn't have to."

Her daughter shrugged. "Hey, I guess I'm qualified to answer emails and fetch coffee."

An uncomfortable silence descended on the table.

Claire set her glass down. "Yeah, but it's not too far off what you'd be doing in NYC, right? Nothing like getting good practice before being thrown to the wolves." Her tone was light, meant to diffuse the tension.

Instead Ellery's eyes flashed. "Oh yes. Thanks for reminding me that I had to come home to Shreveport to practice pouring coffee."

"Elle, you know I didn't mean that," Claire said, her cheeks heating but her eyes hard.

"Of course you didn't," Daphne said, shooting Claire an apologetic look. "And this weekend is about fun and celebrating being together, so let's not talk about work, all right?"

Thankfully, at that moment Evan McCallum walked into the dining room and headed over to their table. He looked handsome in a pair of jeans and a navy blazer. His auburn hair swooped across his forehead, making him look boyish, and his smile was wide. "Ah, our birthday celebration. How's everyone this evening?"

Everyone made satisfactory noises. Ellery's face pinked, and Daphne wasn't certain if it was because she was embarrassed that she'd made the dinner awkward, or if it was because she was on her second glass of wine. She seemed to be imbibing more than she normally did.

"Good, good. I'm Evan McCallum, one of the owners. If there's anything we can do to make your stay more pleasurable, I hope you'll let us know. Now where is the birthday girl?" He turned toward Ellery and smiled. "Ah, of course, it's this beautiful lady. Happy birthday, Ellery."

Ellery's color had deepened. She glanced up quickly and then back down at her empty plate. "Thank you. I love what you have done with the vineyard. It's lovely."

"We tend to like it," he said, giving her a nod. "I hope you're enjoying your weekend so far."

Ellery's smile this time was genuine. "I am now. I have my friends and family around me, and they couldn't have picked a better place for a celebration."

"Great," Evan said, smiling at Ellery, who pinked again before he moved around the table toward her mother. "And, Daphne, I wanted to thank you for reading with Poppy earlier. Made her day. Heck, made her week."

Evan's gaze was warm, and she couldn't help but notice how much more handsome he seemed in the glow of the dinner lighting. His ruddy skin and whiskey eyes projected health and good spirits, his square jaw a certain ruggedness, and his body was evidence that he worked out daily. Everything about him made her want to learn more . . . and it struck her that he was exactly the kind of man she should be interested in rather than the twenty-five-year-old, who she'd learned earlier had not checked out and gone back to Shreveport as she'd suggested. "I was glad to do it. Poppy's a delight. So smart, too."

"You read a book to his daughter?" Ellery asked, her tone . . . odd. Almost accusatory.

"Yeah, this afternoon after I finished up everything. Poppy's a fan of Dixie Doodle."

"Oh, well, we're fans of Dee Dee O'Hara, too," Evan said with a wink before turning back to Ellery. "Though I have to say I can't believe that Dee Dee has a daughter your age. You look more like her sister."

He turned his attention back to Daphne, and she could feel both her daughter and ex-husband bristle.

"I'm pretty sure she's my mom. I've seen pictures of her preggers," Ellery joked, but her eyes weren't exactly happy. But then again, when were they ever happy these days?

Daphne had to wonder about why her daughter would react as she did. After all, Ellery had started pushing her to get "out there" and start dating, and here stood a man who fit the bill, and her daughter acted . . . jealous? It was out of character and alarming because it felt like the tension that existed between them that summer was building. Daphne didn't know how to fix it. Ellery wouldn't let her. It was as if she liked the discord.

Rex stood and extended his hand to Evan. "Rex Witt. I'm Ellery's father."

Evan gave her ex-husband's hand a brief shake. "Evan. Nice to meet you. You have a lovely family."

Rex preened. "Yeah, but you should see my girlfriend."

Daphne's mouth dropped open. Everyone at the table looked goggle eyed. Even Ellery looked uncomfortable.

"Just messing around. Daphne here's my ex-wife. Just clarifying that because she's on the market if you're looking," Rex said with a braying laugh, like he hadn't just insulted the mother of his child, the woman who had picked up his questionable underwear, the woman he'd knocked up because he hadn't known condoms had an expiration date. "Yeah, nice place you have here, Evan. Very quaint. I like the wagon-wheel lights and all."

Daphne knew her cheeks were aflame. How could Rex say something so . . . obtuse? Bragging about Cindy and then referring to her like she was cattle on an auction block. The awkwardness was palpable at the table. No one made eye contact, and everyone seemed to be really into sipping their drinks.

Evan leveled an undecipherable look at Rex. "Thank you, I think."

Then Evan looked at Daphne. She was fairly certain she could read his expression. *What the hell?*

She gave a small shrug and tried to smile.

"Okay, I need to go to the back for a few minutes. Enjoy." Evan lifted a hand and shot her a sympathetic look.

Ellery frowned at her father but didn't say anything. Instead she picked up her glass and took a big gulp. Daphne started to send her a warning glance but decided that maybe Ellery had the right idea. Booze might be exactly how she could get through this night.

Thankfully, at that moment the waitress arrived with a huge platter of appetizers and a second round of drinks. Everyone at the table looked relieved to have a break from the awkward moment and turned to individual conversations.

"Nice, Rex," Daphne muttered.

"What? I was joking." He shoved a stuffed jalapeño into his mouth. "You need to lighten up."

"Oh, that was always my problem, right? I wasn't any fun. I think that's what you told the judge." Daphne could feel ire rising inside her. Animosity fueled by hurt always hovered beneath the surface when she was around Rex. She played nice for Ellery, but she wanted to eviscerate him with the words she always held back. He was a complete jerk, an accomplished ass clown, and head of the douchebag patrol. All the little things he'd done to aggravate her were magnified by ten when they'd married, and they'd been magnified by a thousand when they'd divorced.

Rex hissed. "Don't start with me. It's Ellery's night."

It was always Ellery's night, and that was probably why Ellery couldn't deal with life's disappointments. Daphne had only herself to blame. She'd always stepped back and let her daughter have the spotlight. The same way she'd done with Rex. When she was sixteen, she'd crawled into the back seat with Rex and given him her virginity. And she'd allowed herself to stay there until her books had yanked her out front. "After that speech, maybe that's something *you* need to remember."

Passive aggressive much? Way to sink to his level.

Deciding she needed to get out before she said something she'd regret, Daphne scooted back her chair. "Excuse me for a moment. I need to check on something."

She had already been assured by the restaurant manager that they had the chocolate sheet cake she'd made Ellery yesterday ready. They would serve it after dinner replete with candles and champagne. Tomorrow they would have a big store-bought cake, but Ellery had always loved her chocolate cake, and since there didn't seem much about

Daphne that Ellery liked these days, she'd sacrificed valuable writing time to bake the cake.

She walked briskly through the foyer and pushed through the carved mesquite double doors onto the wide porch. The night air cooled her heated face. She sucked in the air and looked up at the twinkling stars overhead. *I'm losing it, God. I mean, I really might throat punch Rex and slap my ungrateful daughter silly. Violence, Lord. I'm about to do violence. Please help me to keep my temper in check.*

"Amen," she whispered.

"Hey, you okay?"

Daphne turned to find Clay standing behind her, looking concerned.

"Oh God," she said, remembering that sometimes God reminded a woman of her transgressions rather than merely answering her prayers. "So you're still here?"

"Yeah, I told you I was invited to the party tomorrow night. I've been in the bar drinking that wine we had a couple of weeks ago." Clay looked unruffled and oblivious of the distress in her voice. "You know, you look like you could use some."

"I could use a baseball bat, Clay," she muttered.

"Who do I need to knock around?" he asked with a twitch of his lips. He moved so that he was in front of her and could look her full in the face. "Seriously. Are you okay?"

Daphne put her hands over her face. She'd worn a pretty dress of evergreen that hit her right above the knees. She had allowed her legs to be bare and had pulled on cute kitten heels. Her autumnal hair was worn loose around her face, and she'd taken care with her makeup. No crow's-feet yet, thank God. And her neck was still smooth. She should be happy and feel good about herself, but her good-for-nothing ex had made her feel fat and frumpy. Total heifer. For sale cheap, cheap.

And here in front of her was the cure for feeling old and sexless.

"I'll be okay," she said, dropping her hands and sighing. "I have to get back. I just needed some air."

Clay caught her by the elbow. "Hey, hey."

"Clay, you're such a nice guy and really good for my ego, but I can't do this right now."

"Let me come see you tonight. Please. We'll just talk. Sometimes you need someone to listen to you . . . someone to care about you and what you want." His eyes were so sincere and his face so handsome. Daphne remembered the way he'd made love to her, the way he'd moved beneath her, his honeyed words and firm touch healing something deep inside her.

The irony about her world at present was that no one cared about what she wanted except this good-looking man. He wanted to help her feel better. To listen to her. To hold her. To sex her up.

Giving in to what he offered was so tempting. One word, and he'd come to her room that night. Then she could lose herself in his arms and feel something besides . . . second rate. But that was no reason to further a relationship that made no sense. "You're kind, but no. I . . . I wish things could be different. We're just too different to work, Clay."

He dropped his hand. "Damn, but you're a stubborn woman."

She shrugged. He wasn't wrong.

Clay leaned in closer, and she could smell the wine on his breath and the cologne that made him somehow more sensual. "Thing is, Daph, I've had you, and I can read you. You want me. I want you. But you're too afraid to take what you want."

His words were true. She wanted him to sweep her away from the reality of her life, but wanting to have good sex and escape from the world wasn't a good enough reason to give in. She was more than her sexuality. She needed more than what Clay could give her, and Clay Caldwell deserved more than a divorced, premenopausal woman.

"I have to go," she said. She pushed on his chest so he stepped back and walked toward the bed and breakfast. Out of the corner of her eye, she saw Mia and Josh walking across the parking lot. They hadn't seen her with Clay. Thank God.

Now maybe her daughter would snap out of her mood and start having the fun Daphne was paying for. Time for people to start doing what they were supposed to be doing this weekend. Ellery would laugh. Clay would go home. And Rex would choke on a bone. The thought of her ex-husband's eyes going wide and face suffusing with color as he grasped at his throat made Daphne smile.

Okay, she'd give him the Heimlich and let him live, but she could at least enjoy the thought for a few seconds.

CHAPTER TWELVE

Dear Dee Dee O'Hara,

You're here at the vineyard. Ellery's birthday surprise is also my surprise. Though I have to say that I'm feeling weird about it. We've been corresponding for a while, and I know we're friends. Still, it's . . . am I the only one feeling awkward?

Do you want to meet for a drink later? I don't know how to handle this, and I'm not sure why you didn't tell me that the surprise weekend was here at the vineyard. I'm confused.

Best,
Evan

Ellery slid her phone from her cute crossbody bag and sighed. No messages from Josh. She'd thought he'd text her something. An *On the way* or *I can't wait to see you, beautiful,* but he hadn't made any contact since she'd hung up on him earlier. And ever since she'd seen Evan's email about his being confused, she'd avoided responding to him. Because, hell, she was confused, too. She didn't know what to do about him and the lunacy she'd perpetuated by emailing him almost every day.

She looked around the dinner table and at that moment hated everyone.

Even stupid Evan.

The man had looked so warmly at her mother, and Ellery could see he was attracted to her. It was supposed to be *Ellery* he was entranced by. *She* was the one who'd laid her heart bare and made the connection. When he'd glanced her way, his expression had been friendly but impersonal. Of course, it made sense that he'd feel that way. Ellery's deception had hog-tied her into a prison of her own making. She wasn't supposed to want Evan to be attracted to her. She wasn't supposed to have sexy dreams about the insufferable, judgy bartender. She wasn't supposed to have these doubts about her fiancé.

What she was supposed to be was happy, but that felt impossible.

Why were all these people even here? Because her mother was footing the bill for a stupid birthday party for a stupid girl who thought the world owed her streamers and cake? Was that it? Free booze and a room for the night? Hell, she couldn't even rely on her fiancé, a man who supposedly loved her, to show up for her birthday weekend. Okay, fine, he was coming, but only because she'd essentially threatened him with ending their engagement in order to get him there.

And even after threatening to give his ring back, when she'd called Josh earlier, the man had tried to get out of coming that night.

He'd greeted her with a simple "Having fun, babe?" and then launched into "Hey, listen, I'm not sure I can make it." At those words, she'd felt like he'd ripped her heart out. Hurt had poured into her like a flash flood overwhelming a sewer drain. For a moment she thought she might not be able to breathe past the pain.

Then she got angry. Really, really angry.

"You better get your ass down to Mia's car when she gets there, Josh. I mean it," she'd said in a calm but furious voice on the phone.

"Elle, I know you want me to come, and I know I promised, but you don't understand. Schwartz rescheduled the exam for no reason. We're going to have to put in extra—"

"I don't give a fuck when the test is, Josh. You have put off every-thing for the past month. No! *Two* months. I've been going solo to everything we've been invited to. This is my *birthday*, and though I really don't care about the party and balloons, I do care that my fiancé spends time with me. You promised me one night where you would not study, would not talk about school, and would not treat me like a leper. I'm claiming it, buddy. So tell your study group you have plans, and get your ass downstairs."

"Elle, baby—" he started in his plaintive, you're-being-so-irrational voice.

"Do you love me?" she'd demanded, pacing outside the bar where her mother and friends sat swilling craft cocktails and laughing. Like normal, happy people.

For a second . . . two seconds the line was silent.

"Of course I do," he said.

Something in his voice sounded weird. Like maybe he was lying. But that couldn't be true. She'd done nothing to extinguish any part of the love he'd sworn he felt for her. She'd done everything right. She'd supported him, given him pass after pass, made him cookies, taken him cupcakes, even drawn him a freaking Epsom salt bath when his back hurt from studying too long. No, Josh loved her. They were perfect for one another. Everyone knew it. They were going through a rough patch. That was all.

No sense in projecting her insecurity or letting doubt creep inside her head. "If that's true, if this ring you gave me means anything, if our future together is worthwhile to you, you will be a man of your word and come to Texas."

"It's not like I don't want to be with you, Elle," Josh said.

"It feels that way, Josh. If this is how it's going to be—you choosing your career over me every time, then we can end this thing now," she said.

At that exact moment, Gage the barkeep emerged on the stairway that led to the large patio covering the back of the property. He wore a plaid shirt over a blue T-shirt, tight jeans, and a pair of half motorcycle boots. He looked like J. Crew collided with the Hells Angels. Cool, sexy, and scruffy. His eyes met hers, and he crooked an eyebrow. Then his mouth twitched into a small smile at catching her watching him.

Heat flooded her. She turned away.

Damn it.

"Elle, I told you it would be hard. I'm not choosing anything over you, but if our plan is going to work, we both have to make sacrifices."

"I'll see you in a few hours. If I don't, I will know what you have chosen," she said, clicking off the phone, refusing to turn around and see the knowing smirk on Gage's face. She hadn't been checking him out. Not at all. She was in love with Josh, who *was* going to come to dinner.

Because if he didn't show, she had a hard decision to make.

But now, sitting at the table with her friends, she was relieved that she didn't have to figure out a new future because Josh *was* coming. Mia had texted and said they were on their way. Josh had chosen Ellery, and that night after they celebrated with their friends, she was determined to reconnect, to make him fall in love with her all over again.

"Miss, is the table ready to order?" the waitress asked her for the third time. Appetizers had been cleared away, and almost everyone was on their second or third drink. If they didn't order soon, they'd all be trashed. Her mother's chair remained empty. Couldn't blame her mother because her daddy had been out of line. Sometimes Rex didn't think before he spoke. Her mother had looked wounded, and Ellery felt immediate kinship. Dudes didn't know the power of their words or actions.

"When my mother returns, we'll order. Thanks," she said, lifting her glass and sipping more wine. Madison sat next to her and tossed her a concerned look.

"I'm fine," Ellery said, trying to summon a smile and not look at the empty chair next to her.

"He's coming. Mia called half an hour ago, and they had almost reached Tyler," Madison said, running a finger around the melted water on the table beneath her glass. Mads didn't drink a lot on account of her father. Seeing your dad in rehab three times was sobering. No pun intended. But it had kept Madison from some of the addictions that plagued many of their other friends.

For the first time that evening, Ellery noted the restaurant was full and festive. A huge fireplace covered one wall, flanked by bookshelves containing Texas authors and native artwork. An attractive bough of autumn leaves festooned the hearth where the crackling fire danced. Evan's place was nice, and that thought gave her a blip of happiness. Over the past few months, she'd gotten to know exactly how much the vineyard meant to Evan. He'd poured so much of himself into making One Tree Estates more than just a place to harvest and make a product, but a destination that brought families together. After the death of his wife, something he shied away from talking about, he seemed to find comfort in creating a legacy for his daughter. His wish seemed to have come true, if the smiles on the faces of those dining around Ellery were any indication.

At that moment Daphne walked back into the dining room, skating through the tables filled with chatty diners. Her mother looked more together, and when her gaze met Ellery's, she smiled.

"He's here," her mother mouthed.

Immediately, Ellery felt the oppressive pall that hung over her dissipate. Funny how suddenly feeling valued did that to a person. She'd been so afraid he wouldn't show . . . even though Mia had sworn that she had him in her car and was heading their way. Something about his voice when she'd asked if he loved her had caused doubt to worm its way into her conscious and lay waste to what little confidence she had left.

But her concerns were silly. She and Josh had chosen each other for a reason, and that knowledge would get them through every bump in the road. This was where she differed from her parents. Daphne and Rex had had to get married. That was the way they did things back in the day, but Ellery and Josh had weeded through a lot of wrong ones to find the person who would suit them best. They balanced each other and complemented each other. On paper and in life, they made sense.

Ellery sucked in a deep breath and smiled at everyone at the table. "Josh and Mia are here. I think it's time we order and get this weekend started."

"Finally—I'm starving," Claire said, shoving the empty bread basket to the center of the table and looking up at the waitress. "I'm ready to order."

Ellery looked over as Mia and Josh appeared in the doorway. Her fiancé looked gorgeous in a cashmere sweater and jeans that hugged his frame. His blond hair glinted in the flickering light cast from the fireplace. This was a beautiful man.

And he loved her. Or at least Ellery thought he did.

CHAPTER THIRTEEN

Evan,

I'm sorry if I made you feel awkward. It's awkward for me, too, and there are so many things I want to say to you, but I haven't had the courage. Sometimes I don't know myself . . . or why I do the things I do. Let's set aside time to talk, and then maybe you'll understand why I didn't tell you I was coming to the vineyard. Would you come to the party? I'll make sure we have time to talk. Again, sorry for the confusion.

Dee Dee

Ellery tossed her phone on the dresser, ran her fingers through her hair, and contemplated the turned-down bed in the room she was sharing with her fiancé. It was nearly eleven o'clock, and she'd expected Josh to be back at the rental house by now.

After dinner they'd all gone to the small bar off the restaurant to have an after-dinner drink. Ellery was surprised to find Clay Caldwell there. Seemed Madison had invited him when she'd run into him at Elmo's Bar last week. Ellery couldn't think why he would want to come for her birthday party outside of him being bored with his regular scene. But whatever. All the guys stayed behind to have one more bourbon before turning in, which suited Ellery fine because she wanted to shower, dab some perfume between her breasts, and be absolutely prepared for seduction when Josh locked their bedroom door.

She'd been sitting there for the last twenty minutes, trying to figure out how to get the party in their bedroom started. Sliding into bed and reading by the soft lamplight would look as if she weren't waiting to sex him up. He might not get the idea. But then again, hiding the sexy dominatrix-vibe lingerie beneath the demure robe could make for a naughty surprise. Or she could toss the satin robe aside and spread herself out on top of the coverlet. Obvious, true, but the leather bustier and fishnet stockings held up by the satin garters showed a lot of flesh. He'd be stupid not to understand her intentions. The downside was she'd never role-played anything remotely BDSM. Either Josh would jump her bones . . . or run.

Picking up the phone, she checked her texts for the third time in five minutes.

Clicking his name, she read the last text she'd sent him again. **Coming to bed soon? Key word is coming. <naughty devil emoji> <whip emoji>**

Josh had responded with a kitty cat emoji and a high five. Seemed promising.

Ellery went to the antique dresser and fluffed her hair, then wriggled her breasts up in the bustier, turning to make sure her ass looked firm and high. Check. Check. Check.

She could hear her friends laughing outside in the common area as they watched late-night television and drank wine. Usually she would stay up with them and talk the night away, but Ellery had confided to Madison that she needed some alone time with Josh. So when they'd arrived back at the rental after having a final glass of wine—that Ellery really hadn't needed—she'd said good night and slipped into the master suite. And now she was waiting, slightly drunk and bored.

She could always pull off the uncomfortable lingerie and join her friends, but she wasn't going to surrender an opportunity for intimacy with Josh. They needed to reconnect on all levels, and sex would be a good start. But what if he didn't like the racy thong and bustier she wore? Some guys weren't into black leather. Josh liked the fantasy of her being a nerdy, smart type. He loved when she wore his button-down shirt and little else. He'd gone nuts when she'd once worn a man's sleeveless undershirt and barely there panties. She may have gotten everything wrong tonight with the heels and leather.

But shouldn't she already know what turned her man on? Maybe or maybe not. They'd dated for a year and a half, and sex had always been good. Well, as far as she knew. She'd never had it with anyone other than Josh. Many people would find that surprising because she'd dated a lot of guys, but she'd never been willing to give her virginity away to someone she wasn't committed to. She hadn't wanted to end up like her mother and father—forced to marry. When she gave herself to a man, it would be forever.

Ellery looked around the room, catching sight of Josh's backpack.

Hmm . . . he, unlike her, probably had his laptop with him.

Porn. Most guys watched it, didn't they? And in her limited experience in viewing it, she knew they catered to all sorts of fantasies, like big boobs, older women, or even lactation. Of course, if any of those were Josh's thing, he'd be out of luck. A guy in her finite math class had admitted to having a thing for pantyhose. She'd had a fascinating and eye-opening discussion with him about how all guys (and some girls) had things they were into, whether it was feet, lesbians, or redheads.

Ellery had done a little research that night and had been shocked at what was out there.

So what was Josh's true fantasy?

If she could find out, there was a possibility she could make it happen.

But that would be wrong. It felt skeevy going through his web browser. Still, some women did it. One of her friends had told her she'd once spied on her boyfriend to see what he liked in bed, and their relationship had been better for it. Ellery wasn't sure she had time to figure out Josh's fantasy trigger, but she could try. It would either pay off in a sexy dividend or be a huge invasion of privacy.

Do or die, Elle.

Ellery slipped over to the bedroom door and locked it. If she was going to snoop, she didn't want him to stumble in on her. No need to kill the mood and start a fight. She might not find anything anyway. Josh didn't strike her as the type to have a porn habit. He was too busy studying and bonding with his fellow future doctors. Besides, if he caught her, she could say her computer had died and she needed to fire off an email or two.

Lying already?

Ellery waved away the imaginary angel with her hands folded in prayer perched on her shoulder. Instead she embraced the sexy little devil on the other shoulder, who said, "Find his perversion and use it." So she grabbed his backpack and pulled out his MacBook Air.

When she opened it, she faced a password page.

Damn it.

What would his password be?

His dog from childhood. What was his name? Grover? Homer? No, it was Howard. Ellery typed in *Howard* and pressed ENTER.

Nope.

HOWARD0206

Nope.

Not a dog. What else would he use? She tried a few more birthday-pet-family-member names before smiling to herself.

DoctorPrince0206

Bingo. His dream job plus his birth date worked like a charm. His homepage came up, and she clicked on his browser history. A bunch of searches for medical jargon and research stuff came up. She scrolled down. Nothing that looked like porn. Part of her was relieved that he wasn't looking at porn all the time. If she'd found a bunch of sites listed and paired that with the fact they hadn't had sex in a long time, she'd be worried. But nothing looked remotely alarming other than he'd gone to Nordstrom a lot.

Before she shut his computer, she clicked on his bookmarks. Lots of research, stores, Facebook, etc. A few popular sites like YouTube and a luxury-car forum. Nothing, really. On a whim she clicked on his iCloud. Lots of medical papers and notes. Then she saw a video clip titled "The Experiment." Ellery frowned at the title because it was an odd way to phrase it. Something tingled at the base of her spine.

She hovered the arrow over the file and clicked.

A window opened to a video that looked to be filmed with an iPhone, grainy because it was dark in the room. Someone stepped into the shot and sat on a bed. He was a big guy, who wore scrub pants and had a broad, hairy, muscular chest. She squinted at the footage, trying to recognize the man and process the location, but she recognized neither. She turned up the volume but could only hear the rustle of movement in the background. The man on the bed crooked his finger to someone out of the shot. Another man, this one slightly built, stepped into the shot. The footage was blurry enough that she couldn't tell much about the new guy, but his hair looked lighter beneath the baseball cap he wore. From what she could tell, he wore a dark sweatshirt. This guy immediately sank on his knees in front of the larger man. The man on the bed reached out and tenderly cupped the other man's head while at the same time tugging the drawstrings of his scrubs. The man kneeling reached out and pulled the man's pants down so that an enormous erection sprang loose.

Ellery gasped and covered her mouth with her hand.

"Take it all, baby," the guy said, grabbing the kneeling man's neck and pulling his head toward his jutting—

"Oh God," Ellery said, slamming the computer shut. She shoved the computer across the bed and stared wide eyed at her reflection in the mirror of the dresser. Ellery looked as if she'd seen a ghost . . . or a video of one man giving another man a blow job.

Wait, she couldn't leave the video open. She had to close it, or Josh would know she'd found the naughty file on his computer. God, just what *had* she found?

Was the guy kneeling Josh?

"No, it can't be," she whispered, pulling the laptop back so it sat in front of her.

Josh wasn't gay. They'd had sex, and she would know if he were. Besides, Josh never wore ball caps. He said they were for guys who had bad hair, and she was certain the only sweatshirt he had was one from Harvard that his best friend from high school had sent him. No. That guy couldn't be Josh. But was the bigger guy his friend Drew? He sort of looked like Josh's study partner, but she couldn't tell for certain.

She opened the computer, and the window popped back up. She clicked the video off and closed the browser. Part of her wanted to watch the entire video to see if she knew either of the guys. The other part of her wished she'd settled for getting into bed and reading. She'd listened to the devil on her shoulder, and this was what a gal got when she went snooping under the pretense of trying to please her boyfriend.

Gay porn?

Was it that big of a deal? She'd seen lesbian porn before, but that didn't mean she was gay. She'd been curious, was all. Maybe that was what the video was for Josh? A curiosity. Or it could have been something someone sent him as a joke? *Here's what doctors have to do to get ahead. Pun intended.* Or wait, what if the video was blackmail? Maybe someone had caught another student engaging in such behavior . . . but, no, was being gay and filming sex a blackmailable offense? Not in 2019.

Ellery jumped off the bed, shoved the computer back into Josh's backpack, and zipped it closed.

Again, she saw herself in the mirror. She stood there looking like most men's wet dream. Boobs spilling over the bustier, legs clad in the ridiculous and tacky fishnet hose. The mouth she'd painted red looked garish against the paleness of her shocked face. Panic rolled over her, threatening to smother her. Suddenly she couldn't breathe.

"Holy shit, Elle," she whispered, sucking in big gulps of air.

Ellery dashed toward her open suitcase, grabbed a fuzzy hoodie, and pulled it on. Then she riffled through her clothes and found a pair of baggy gym shorts and wriggled them over her fishnets. Shoving her feet into her UGGs, she grabbed a ponytail holder and her phone and slipped out onto the small private patio off their bedroom.

Outside the stars sparkled, unaware Ellery had just found gay porn on her fiancé's computer. Bastard twinkling stars. How dare they look so happy against the Texas sky.

At least out here she could breathe. She sucked in the cool air and squeezed her eyes shut, begging the horrible crushing anxiety to stay away. Before she could think better of it, she jabbed her phone into her hoodie pocket and started walking. Her feet led her onto grass that was dying but not crunchy—the pine needles made a soft carpet, so her footfalls were silent as she rounded the house. She didn't want to go toward the bed and breakfast. People were there laughing and drinking. No, she needed some time to think. To figure out what that video meant. Maybe it meant nothing. Maybe it meant everything.

She headed toward the path she'd taken earlier in the day. Yeah, she would be trespassing, but at that moment she didn't care. That small patch of heaven beside the small lake would isolate her from everything, give her a place to think . . . give her a place to hide.

Her breath came in small puffs as she climbed the hill. It was chilly out, and she should have been shivering in the damp coolness, but she wasn't. Her body felt on fire, flushed from the knowledge that something was off. Or not. God, she didn't know. Maybe what she'd seen was no big deal, something they'd laugh about and tell friends at dinner parties.

One time, my friend sent me a crazy video as a joke, and this woman here—Josh would jab his thumb toward her—*thought I was gay. Can you imagine?* Then everyone would laugh, and Ellery would shrug and roll her eyes.

God, she hoped that was what it was.

No big deal.

When she got to the top, she angled toward the area she'd gone to earlier, the place where Gage had found her and forced her to abandon. She ground her heels against the earth as she made her way down so she wouldn't take a tumble. No one needed to find her body the next morning. Especially since she still wore her bustier and fishnet stockings beneath her mismatching Tri Delt hoodie and shorts. Her corpse would look like a hooker collided with a sorority girl.

"Hey, hey, stop," a voice called from behind her.

Ellery turned to see Gage standing at the top of the hill.

"Damn it," she uttered under her breath. She didn't stop. Just kept trucking toward the lake.

"I told you that—"

Ellery lifted her arm and gave him the finger. And kept going. If Gage didn't want her to sit by the lake and figure out her goddamned life, then he could put her under citizen's arrest. Drag her kicking and screaming off the private property. But she wasn't going willingly. Nope. Not this time. She'd be a bad guest.

"Ellery," he called. She could hear him coming after her, and that pissed her off. What the hell did he care if she took a moment for herself in the quiet Texas wilderness? Okay, semiwilderness. She doubted there were any coyote packs running around ready to dine on blonde au gratin. Bobcats were lone creatures, and she could probably survive one of them ambushing her. Snakes were snug in their snake beds. She wasn't going to jump in the lake and drown. So why didn't he turn around and go pour some wine for tourists and leave her the hell alone?

"Hey, Ellery," he said, catching her elbow.

She spun around and growled between her teeth, "What?"

His eyes widened. "What's up with you?"

"Nothing. I need some time alone. So go do whatever it is you do, and leave me alone. I won't trample the flowers or steal a cutting or whatever people do to steal grapes. Just let me be." She turned back toward the lake, knowing her voice broke on the last sentence. She reached the place hidden by the knotty pines. The moon shone on the lake, reflecting a path on the still waters. The wind had died, and night surrounded her.

Tears had gathered in her eyes, but she wiped them away. She wasn't going to cry in front of stupid Gage. He didn't like her. Disapproved of her. Made her prickly and defensive. So, no, she was not going to give him the pleasure of knowing she was about to fall apart.

But, of course, he didn't listen. Because she could feel him standing to her right, silent and perplexed at this defiant princess flipping him off and then allowing her stupid emotions to get away from her.

"You must need a doctor to check your ears. I told you I wanted to be alone," she said, not turning toward him. She didn't want him there.

"And I told you that you're trespassing."

"So sue me. Arrest me. Call the police. I don't care."

He moved closer. "I could do that, but all those flashing lights and depositions are such a drag."

"Who says something's a drag? What are you? From a fifties time warp?" she said, glancing over at him, trying to get him to feel her displeasure at his presence. "And how is it you are the one who keeps finding me, huh? Stalk people much?"

"I was on my way back to my place when I saw you climbing the path again. You're wearing a light-blue sweatshirt."

Ellery turned her attention back to the lake and said nothing. So she had worn something not so covert. She hadn't been thinking about subterfuge. Just getting out of the room and breathing the cool air.

He moved to stand beside her, and they both stared out at the lake. He didn't seem to be in a hurry to leave or toss her over his shoulder and haul her out. Instead he stood, hands tucked into his jeans pockets. The coolness of the air brought a crispness to the contrast between the water and bushes embracing it, and the moon seemed benevolent, as if pleased to cast some of the darkness out. In the center of the lake, a fish broke the surface, making ripples in the stillness.

They stood like this, cloaked in the intimate night.

Finally, he looked at her. "Who hurt you?"

"No one. I'm just . . . there's just stuff."

He didn't say anything.

She looked at him then. "Have you ever seen gay porn?"

That took him aback. He literally shrank from her. "What? Why would you ask me that?"

"Just tell me. Have you ever watched gay porn?"

He stared at her. "Are you asking me if I'm gay?"

She hadn't thought about that. "No. Are you?"

"No."

"Good. I mean, for my purposes, it's good. I just need to know if guys look at gay porn."

"You mean like girl-girl action?"

"No. I mean guys. Like, two guys." She coughed and averted her eyes back to the water. She didn't know why she'd asked him such a question. Other than that she needed to know if it was normal or something to worry about. He was a normal guy—or at least she thought he was—so he should know.

"No. Can't say I've seen two guys having sex. I mean, we snuck and watched *Brokeback Mountain* when I was in grade school because my friends and I had heard about it, but that wasn't porn."

"Oh." Her phone vibrated in her pocket. She ignored it.

She could feel tears rising in her eyes, and she wanted to stop them. Her body seemed to have a mind of its own, though, because the damned things kept coming. She blinked and felt one drop onto her cheek.

"Ellery, is this about your fiancé?" Gage asked, his voice now absent of its normal edginess.

Something about the sympathy in his tone made everything ten times worse. She swiped at her eyes. "Of course not. I just needed to know, is all. Sorry to have asked something so personal. I barely know you and—"

"Shh," he said, stepping in front of her. "Just . . . it's okay. I'm not upset or shocked. I'm concerned because the woman standing in front of me is not the one I met weeks ago."

Ellery sniffed because her nose felt runny and then dashed more tears away. "News flash: women have a lot of different sides to them. I'm just having a bad day."

Or a bad month. Or a bad year. Take your pick.

"We all have them. I'm not sure what that has to do with what you asked, but know that everyone has bad days, and sometimes what you think you know, you don't," Gage said, his eyes somehow soft in the moonlight.

"I guess," she said, wishing she could redo so much about this night. So much.

"Do you want to talk about it?" he asked.

"Not really. I want to forget about it. That's how I deal. I just smile and move on because that's what you have to do sometimes. Some things are beyond your control, and you have to . . . just suck it up." Ellery looked up at the sky and gave a little shake of her head. "I'm not really good at sucking it up sometimes, but lately life's been giving me lots of lessons that have dropped me to my knees."

As she said the words, the image of those two guys popped into her head. She shivered and folded her arms across her chest, rubbing her arms. How would she ever get that home movie out of her head? How would she ever summon up the courage to ask Josh about why he had it on his computer? How would she know if it was harmless or . . . something more?

A prickling rose on the back of her neck.

"Here," Gage said, shrugging out of his jean jacket. Beneath he wore a long-sleeved black T-shirt. Or maybe it was navy or some other dark color. She couldn't tell.

He draped his jacket around her shoulders, and immediately she was enveloped in warmth and the smell of Gage, which was a cross between a men's cologne Josh would never wear and something almost homey. At that moment she'd never smelled anything better, and she fought the sudden inclination to pull it to her face and use it to block out the world.

She should say thank you or refuse it, handing it back, but instead she hugged his jacket closer to her and tried to think what a slightly drunk, very disillusioned woman did when standing on forbidden land with the sexy bastard whose mocking smile had haunted her for weeks. Everything was wrong about what she was feeling . . . what she was doing here in the dark with a stranger she'd had fantasies about. A reckless disregard for everything she'd planned for her life with Josh urged her toward something dangerous. With a flick of a finger, she could tip the domino and undo the careful pattern she'd meticulously set up.

All it would take would be to reach out to Gage and make it happen.

Gage didn't seem to know what to do with her silence. He stared at her for a moment, and then he did something rather unexpected. His arms came around her, and he pulled her into . . . a hug.

Ellery didn't struggle, because being pressed close against Gage felt better than anything she'd felt in a long time. She tucked her head under his chin, her forehead resting against his bare skin, her nose nestled against the soft T-shirt, and stood still in his embrace. His hands gently rubbed her back, and though minutes before she'd thought about something that wasn't as innocent as a hug, she found herself feeling the comfort she'd been needing so desperately. For a few seconds, she closed her eyes and allowed herself to relax against the warmth of his body.

Eventually, Gage loosened his arms and stepped back. "Good?"

She looked at the center of his chest and nodded.

"Ellery?" he asked softly.

When she looked up, she knew she'd see sympathy in his eyes, and she didn't want that. She lifted her gaze anyway, but in the grayish-green depths of his eyes, she didn't see compassion. No. She saw a man who wanted more but wouldn't allow himself to take it.

The thought that he wanted her but cared enough to do nothing more than hold her did something to her.

So she stepped closer.

"What are you—"

Ellery silenced him the best way a woman could silence a man.

The moment her lips touched his, something inside her broke apart. One hand went around his neck, the other his waist. Liquid heat poured over her as she opened her mouth and tasted him.

For a millisecond, Gage seemed stunned, but she knew he wanted her no matter how much he liked to pretend he didn't. His arms came around her, and this time there was nothing comforting in his embrace. Hot, hard, beautiful passion spilled from every pore of his body. He cupped her face with one hand and devoured her mouth.

And sweet baby James, the man could kiss. For the first time in her life, Ellery felt nearly dizzy with desire, out of her mind with the need to have this man. She reveled in the passion because she'd never, ever felt so turned on by a man. It felt delicious and not so very wrong at all.

His tongue moved against hers, and he made a growly sound in his throat. He pulled her tighter against him, and she shivered in delight at the hardness of his body.

"Mmm," she groaned, sliding her hand beneath his shirt. His skin was warm and smooth, and she wanted to feel his naked body against hers. She wanted nothing between them. "I want to . . . I need you to . . . please, Gage."

He seemed to understand she needed his hands on her body. Gage slid a hand beneath her fluffy hoodie and stilled when he encountered the leather bustier. He wrenched his mouth from hers. "What are you wearing?"

Ellery opened her eyes. "What?"

Gage stiffened as if he realized exactly what they were doing. His hand dropped from her back as he looked down at her. "You wore that for someone else. I can't . . . I just can't. This is wrong, Ellery."

Ellery stared at him, realization landing with a plop. It *was* wrong. So wrong. "I know. I'm sorry."

She stepped away.

Gage rubbed his face and shook his head. "I shouldn't have done that."

"You didn't. I did. It's on me." Ellery pulled his jacket from her shoulders and held it out to Gage. He searched her expression when he accepted it but said nothing more. Ellery gave him a small smile. "Thanks for . . . just thanks."

Then she turned back toward the slope she would climb to take her back to a world she no longer understood. She shouldn't have kissed Gage. All that had done was make her world even murkier than before, and it was already dark as Mississippi Delta mud.

When she reached the top, she turned around. Gage hadn't followed her and remained hidden in the pine-dense copse. It was better that way because she was now not only confused but embarrassed that she'd forgotten who she was and allowed her baser instincts to take over.

Or maybe it wasn't baser. Maybe she'd had a need to feel something good. Just one moment of something good in a day that had felt, well, not so good.

Ellery walked briskly back to the room she was supposed to share with her fiancé. At this point, her plan for the night lay like cold ashes in a forgotten grate. The room was dark when she slipped back through the doors. In the moonlight she could see Josh curled into a ball beneath the coverlet. At the click of the door, he didn't budge. Ellery slipped her phone from her hoodie pocket and saw he'd texted her three times.

Where are you?

You okay? I thought you were waiting up for me?

I'm going to bed, babe. So tired.

This time Ellery didn't try to stop the tears that slipped from her eyes.

CHAPTER FOURTEEN

Daphne's morning had started out nicely.

After a disastrous, tense dinner next to her ass of an ex-husband, she'd fled to her room before she could bump into Clay or have to spend another moment listening to Rex talk about scuba diving in Belize. Seemed it was "amazing," and she should "totally go."

Hey, she would have loved to leave Shreveport behind and sun on a beach somewhere. Rex knew this because she'd talked about getting certified and taking some trips once Ellery was in college and they no longer had the grind of soccer games, cheer camp, and National Honor Society inductions. They would take long weekends, leaving Pinnacle Heating and Air in the capable hands of Betsy Morgan, a cute, young divorcée who had taken over most of the office management when Daphne had to scale back in order to write and keep up with the demand of Dixie Doodle. But divorce had come before rest and relaxation. Then Cindy had not liked the attractive redhead spending time with Rex, so Rex had let Betsy go. Cindy had taken over, leaving her part-time RN position to do the receivables. Daphne knew Cindy didn't have a background in office management or bookkeeping, but it was no longer her business. She kept ownership of her intellectual property, and Rex kept ownership of Pinnacle. That was agreed upon in mediation during their divorce.

So, yeah, she would love to go to Belize, but at present her deadlines would keep her at her computer.

When she woke that morning, Daphne passed on a cup of tea and instead pulled on her old trainers, a pair of running leggings, and a pullover, then went for a jog.

The path through the gated neighborhood wound around a community lake and undeveloped woods bright with fall foliage. The slap, slap of her feet on the pavement paired with the zing of coolness on her face did much to improve her mood. Her favorite playlist—a mix of Van Halen and Aerosmith—was the perfect accompaniment even if she found the hilly terrain an extra challenge. Her normal route back in Shreveport was fairly flat, and in the last few months she'd decreased the amount she ran because her knees had started aching. Getting old sucked.

As she came around a corner, she nearly crashed into Evan McCallum, who leaped aside at the last minute.

"Hey," he said, jogging in place and flashing her an engaging smile. He didn't even seem out of breath.

Daphne tugged her earbuds out and leaned over to grasp her knees. Breathing hard, she managed, "Lord, I'm not used to these hills."

Evan stopped jogging. "Yeah, they can get you sometimes. I'm on the last leg of my run. Want to join me?"

She wasn't sure she could keep up. "I'm not a fast runner."

"That's okay. I'm cooling down. Come on," he said, jerking his head toward a side street she'd avoided on her first pass.

"What the hell," she muttered and followed him down the leaf-strewn street.

"This is the loop where my family lives," he said, his breath coming in short bursts. His body was taut and compact, legs long, and his shoes ones *Runner's World* had touted as the shoe of the year for avid runners.

Auburn hair glinted when the sunlight hit it, and the teeth that flashed in a charming grin were glacier white. Overall, he was a compelling, fit man. "Up there is my sister Marin's house. She and her husband have three children, ages fifteen to eight. Next to that is my sister Maureen's house. She doesn't stay here year-round because she's a travel photographer. Her son, Gage, lives there and helps at the winery. He's a programmer who writes games. Like video games. He's really talented, and some big firms have been after him. He's moving out west soon."

Daphne managed a nod and was glad she could do that. Evan's stride was much longer, and she was having trouble keeping up. Her breath tore from her lungs, but she had too much pride to fall behind.

Evan glanced over at her and slowed his pace. "Sorry. I didn't realize I was killing you."

"No problem," she gasped, trying to look like she wasn't about to fall over. "I love that house." She nodded at the large rustic home constructed of stacked stone, stucco, and large cedar beams. Orange cypress trees sat against the evergreens embracing the house that looked straight out of *Log Cabin Today* or whatever those magazines were called that had the huge rustic houses overlooking lakes and mountains.

It looked like the lake house she and Rex had always dreamed of building on their lot on Caddo Lake. They'd scoured blueprints and clipped magazine photos in preparation for building a house on the land where an ancient cabin now sat. Rex had been saving money for the down payment, but that had gone to pay for the court costs of their divorce. Oh, the irony.

"That one's mine," he said with a grin.

"Gorgeous," she managed now that he'd slowed down. "I always wanted one like that at the place we have on the lake. Currently my lake getaway is one stiff wind from collapse."

"It's not that bad. At least you have a pier."

"You know I have a pier?" Had she blogged about that? Maybe Ellery had. She vaguely recalled something over the summer about swimming and jumping off the pier. Ellery loved to embellish things and had probably made their lake house sound more chic than the simple old house that was a glorified shack.

"Yeah, of course," he said with a laugh.

Again she got a weird feeling. He was so familiar with her. Maybe she'd met him somewhere and forgotten about it. She'd done things like that. Being a writer meant being in perpetual la-la land, and when she was working an idea or brainstorming an illustration, she could get so wrapped up, she forgot where she was. Once she'd sat for thirty minutes on the toilet at T.J. Maxx when she'd gotten a breakthrough on a direction for the story line she was stuck on. No lie. So she may have met Evan before. Yet surely someone as attractive as Evan would have imprinted on her brain. He was yummy with a cherry on top.

She wanted to ask him about his wife. When she'd looked up information on the bed and breakfast and the vintner, she'd discovered an article on Evan spotlighting him as a single dad. The attached picture of him and Poppy riding on a donkey had made her smile, but the article had been vague about his wife's death. Of course it would be rude to ask.

"Well, it's beautiful."

"My wife's idea. She was from Colorado and missed the mountains. It was our compromise when I moved back here to help my father run the vineyard when he was ill. Building this house made her happy for a while."

Did that mean she was unhappy? She wanted to ask more but knew it would be too nosy. "Texas *is* a big change from Colorado."

He laughed. "You think?"

He slowed and started walking. "You okay to walk the rest of the way? I did five, and my legs are protesting."

Praise Jesus. She didn't know how much farther she could have gone. Daphne slowed to a walk, wiping sweat from her brow and trying not to sound like Jason beneath the hockey mask with her breathing. "This is good. Those hills . . . whew. Killer."

Evan smiled, and that grin did something to her stomach. The man was incredibly good looking. "Heather grew to appreciate Texas, but she never got over the heat. I lost her a few years ago, you know."

"I'm sorry."

"I am, too. Especially for Poppy. She misses her . . . or at least she misses having a mom. Heather suffered from depression. I mean, I know you probably already guessed as much." He gave her a cryptic look.

Daphne did not guess that. How was she supposed to infer that his wife's death was related to depression? Had she committed suicide? The thought was horrific, and she didn't know quite what to say. So she said nothing.

"Sorry I took the conversation in that direction. We were having a good time." He physically shook himself and pasted a smile on his face. "So how is your daughter enjoying her weekend? I hope everything is meeting her expectations?"

Daphne couldn't very well admit her daughter was so complicated she needed a road map to discern Ellery's emotions. There were times she knew Ellery enjoyed herself. Like last night when Josh had finally arrived and then doted on her the entire meal, even spooning the hazelnut crème brûlée into her mouth and insisting she have an extra dessert. Ellery had finally looked pleased and reverted to her former glittering self. Daphne had found great pleasure in Ellery laughing and enjoying herself.

When Daphne had slipped off to bed, she'd glimpsed Ellery's gang clinking glasses in the bar—Clay with them, thankfully unaware she'd peeked in. All looked to be laughing and happy. Daphne had hit the pillow comforted by the thought the weekend might turn out to be successful. Rex had even paid for the meal last night, which had been a nice surprise. "We surprised her with this destination, so she didn't really have expectations, but she's really enjoying it. We are doing the tour of the winery today and a tasting. I think everyone's looking forward to that."

"I'm so glad you came, Daphne. I've been waiting a long time to meet you."

"I'm really glad to be here."

Evan looked inordinately pleased at her remark. "Okay, so we have a couple of tour guides, but I'll make sure you get Gage 'cause he's the best. He truly has a feel for the whole process of wine making. I've been trying to talk him into staying here and making One Tree Estates his career, but he's been here longer than intended and has his own dreams. I don't know much about what he does because I'm not a gamer. I played *Tecmo Bowl* back in the day, and that was about it."

Daphne smiled. "I don't even know what that is."

Evan laughed. "You didn't miss much."

They'd stopped by his mailbox. "I better go. Poppy just woke up."

"How do you know?"

He twisted his wrist, and she saw his Apple Watch. "I have a camera in her room. This button blinks when there's movement. That allows me to go out for a jog each morning. Poppy knows how to use Alexa to call me. I got one for her room."

"That's smart. The things you can do with technology, huh?" Daphne said, impressed with his attention to detail. The waitress had said as much yesterday morning.

"See? That's her now." At that moment his watch lit up. Evan pressed a button. "Morning, pumpkin."

"Morning, Daddy. Where are you?" a sleepy voice asked.

"Right outside your window talking to Dee Dee O'Hara," he said, giving Daphne a wink.

The whole thing was so sweet that Daphne's heart warmed. Or perhaps that was because she was sweating beneath her three-quarter-zip pullover. Either way Evan McCallum intrigued her with his genuine demeanor and nice body. Oh, and that he was such a good daddy didn't hurt, either. Really, the man was like a beacon to single women everywhere.

They saw the blinds in the far-left window part. Two little eyes peeked out. Daphne laughed and gave Poppy a wave. The little girl grinned and waved back, her tiny fingers wiggling against the pane.

"I need to get back myself. A delicious breakfast awaits," Daphne said, jabbing her hands into the small pockets on either side of her pullover. The morning was cool, and she could feel a chill coming over her.

"It's maybe a fourth of a mile back. Enjoy that breakfast. I'm having a protein drink and banana." Evan turned and jogged up the driveway. "See you tonight, Daphne. We'll talk more then."

Daphne raised her hand and made her way back to the bed and breakfast, her mind turning over the pleasant surprise of a jog with Evan along with so many questions. How did he seem to know so much about her? And what had happened to his wife? Being a single parent wasn't easy. Far from it, in fact. In that, she was glad she'd had a partner.

After a cup of hot tea, a soak in the hot tub (heaven!), and a quick shower, Daphne made her way to breakfast, where sunlight streamed into a rather busy dining room. No little name cards greeted her this morning. Seemed Saturday was a free-for-all on table grabs, but the aroma of coffee and bacon, though she didn't even drink the former, sent her stomach into a growl. Maybe this morning, since she'd nearly killed herself on the early-morning run, she'd have some pancakes. The thought of her jog with the attractive owner of the vineyard made her smile.

"Well, you're all smiles this morning." Daphne turned to find Rex sipping a cup of coffee at a small table near the entrance to the dining room.

"It's a beautiful morning, and I get to spend today hanging with our daughter and drinking wine. What's not to love about that?" Daphne said, stuffing away the leftover irritation she'd felt last night and trying for lightness. New day. New Daphne.

Rex waved his coffee mug at the empty chair opposite him. "Join me. It will keep a table open for someone else."

She didn't want to eat breakfast with her ex-husband, especially after dining with him last night had given her a permanent case of ex-husband indigestion.

Her hesitation must have shown, because Rex made the "forgive me" face she'd seen a million times before. "Daph, I'm sorry about dinner last night. I drank a bit too much bourbon and acted like an ass. The guy that owns the place just rubbed me the wrong way, and I got all puffed up. You know how I am."

"I do," she said, eyeing an empty table on the other side of the room that sat beside a large picture window that overlooked the vineyard. She didn't love eating alone but—

At that moment Clay walked in. Of course, half a dozen female heads turned to watch him meander toward the very table Daphne had been eyeing. He looked across the room and spied her, quirking his mouth in the most adorable (and too sexy for so early) smile.

"Come on. I won't bite you," Rex said.

Those were the exact words Clay had used the night she'd lost her ever-loving mind and had sex with him twice. Guess those were the words that worked on her dumb ass, because she pulled out the chair opposite her ex and sat down. "Fine."

Rex seemed pleased, which was odd. Since they'd split, their relationship had been schizophrenic. Sometimes fine. Other times barely civil. That in itself had bothered her. If anything, she and Rex had always been friends. But divorce seemed to have a way of making one forget. Or maybe it was Cindy. She'd developed a healthy dislike for Daphne based solely on the fact she was Rex's ex.

"Want me to order you a pot of tea?" he asked politely.

"I can order for myself. But thank you," she said, feeling uncomfortable across from a man she'd spent over half her life with. So strange to know so much about him but be so far away from who she'd been with him. "Are you sure Cindy isn't going to be upset with you for . . . this?"

"We're just eating breakfast, Daph." Rex laughed, his eyes actually warming as he regarded her, and she recalled that he wanted to talk to her. Did he think to make another run at reconciliation? She'd been shocked when he'd shown up at the house last April and wanted to talk. He'd started with an apology and then proceeded to tell her why they had made such a mistake in splitting. She'd reminded him that he'd been the one to leave, but he'd inferred that he'd only done so to shock her into seeing she was making a big mistake by continuing the path she was on. Daphne had stared incredulously at this man who wanted her to take the blame because instead of begging him to come home the minute he left, she'd discovered a new life without him. Finally, after he'd talked about how he'd been thinking that they could make it work again, she'd risen, opened the back door, and told him that she was happier being exactly who she was and wasn't interested in reconciling. Rex hadn't taken her refusal well. He'd stormed out and made life much harder for her. But lately, he'd been better. Well, sort of.

She glanced over at where Clay was sitting. He sipped coffee and watched her, which was sort of creepy and flattering at the same time.

Rex leaned forward. "I see Clay is here. How's he been working for you?"

"He's better than I imagined," Daphne said, suppressing a smile even when she knew she shouldn't take any pleasure in the double entendre only she knew about. It was an odd thing to sit with one man she'd slept with while the other one gave her come-hither looks. *Twilight Zone* music played in her head.

"That's good," Rex said, his gaze narrowing. "What?"

"Nothing."

Thankfully, at that moment the waitress arrived and handed Daphne a menu. Daphne turned back to Rex. "The house is nearly done. When you're out that way, you should come by and see it. The bathroom looks amazing. You wouldn't believe the difference, and the kitchen is almost complete. It's going to look like a totally different place."

Conversation about the house they'd shared for years seemed like a safe topic.

Rex nodded. "I suppose the old place needed some updating. We never got around to doing what we said we would. Time seems to fly when you're having fun or raising a kid, right? I mean, she's turning twenty-three. How can that be?"

"I know. Out of college, looking to take the world by storm. Well, maybe for Elle, it's more like a gentle shower. That whole J.J. Krause thing set her back a little."

"Yeah, but I didn't like the idea of her living in New York City by herself anyway. A looker like her in that place is like a little mouse in a roomful of alley cats. This gap-year thing so many kids do now ain't a bad thing. Get their feet wet in a puddle they're familiar with."

Daphne thought about that. "Maybe. She doesn't seem very happy, though."

Rex studied her. "Why do you say that? Every time I'm around her she seems fine."

Because she never showed her displeasure to you. You're her daddy, the man who always gives her the moon and stars. I'm her mother, and my job is to keep her from burning her fingers on all the stars you rope for her.

"Maybe I'm wrong," Daphne said, giving the waitress, who had returned, her order. "I'll have the pancakes, side of bacon, and a cup of fruit."

Rex's face wasn't exactly judgmental, but she knew what he was thinking. *All those carbs will go straight to her ass and thighs.* That's how Rex rolled. Didn't worry about the paunch he carried, but damn sure said something to her if her pants were the least bit snug. Daphne didn't care. She was going to relish every damned bite.

"Listen, part of the reason I came here this weekend is because I need to talk to you," Rex said, getting a look on his face she knew all too well. He wanted something from her.

She was almost afraid to ask. "What?"

"So this is a little embarrassing, but I don't really know where to turn, and since it deals with the business we built, I thought you'd be more willing to—"

"Wait a second," she interrupted. "The business *we* built? I think I remember you telling the judge that it was *your* business."

"Daph, I admitted that you kept the books and helped me run Pinnacle, just like you readily admitted that I held down the fort when you were off peddling your books."

"It's not peddling," Daphne pointed out.

"I know. I misspoke. So here's the deal. Pinnacle is having some cash-flow problems. Cindy took over doing the books, and she didn't know about payroll taxes or even estimated taxes. We had an audit. That's why I had to get those files from the house, remember? Anyway, we owe a pretty penny. So between the new mortgage and paying all these credit cards, I'm almost overextended on the line of credit."

"You got a line of credit?" Daphne asked, feeling her appetite fleeing. It was true that she didn't have a stake in Pinnacle Heating and Air any longer, but she'd helped Rex build that business into a profitable, solid company with a stellar reputation. They had been fair and efficiently run. She knew Cindy would screw things up when she fired the office manager. "Rex, the company was in good shape two years ago. How have you run it into the ground?"

But she knew. All those trips and fancy gifts. Rex had always liked nice things, but she'd been there to temper his harebrained schemes and impulse buys. Cindy wasn't the kind of girl to say no to Italy. Or Belize.

"It's not run into the ground. We just have a little cash-flow problem. End of the year is coming up, and you know I have to give bonuses to the guys. Plus, that first tax payment is due. It's just . . . a lot I have to pay next month. I wondered if you would be willing to . . . uh . . . maybe lend me some help."

Alarm bells paired with flashing emergency lights went off in her head. "Define *help*."

"A short-term loan. I have to pay the IRS close to eighty thousand, but that's on an installment plan. I also have to start paying the bank back for the line of credit. Business is good, and so I'll have money coming in. Just not enough to cover everything right now. I don't want to get another loan, Daph. So I'm asking you to help me save the business. At the very least, if you'll pay Ellery's credit cards and rent for the next year, that would help, too."

The waitress sat a stack of delicious-looking pancakes in front of her, along with the crisp bacon and fresh fruit. "Will that be all?"

Could you bring me a sledgehammer?

Daphne didn't know how in the world to handle this request. Rex had constantly gaslighted her their entire marriage, making her feel as if she were a fuddy-duddy because she said no to extravagant vacations and a two-story mansion in Southern Trace. Seemed being financially responsible wasn't much fun. So while it was horrifying that Rex had gotten Pinnacle in so much trouble, it was also very gratifying to know he had been wrong. But even as that tiny thrill of "I told you so" nee-ner-neenered in her head, she felt disheartened that Rex had endangered so many other people. He had twenty employees and several hundred customers who depended on him not to toss what little common sense he had to chase ridiculous dreams pulling Louis Vuitton luggage behind him. "So this was why you came to me in April? That whole 'let's try again' thing was about fear . . . about wanting me to help you fix things?"

He didn't have to answer because she could see it in his eyes. He hadn't wanted *her* back; he'd wanted security. For some reason, that made her furious.

"Okay, so I knew there was a problem in April when George looked at our taxes, but . . . it wasn't about just the tax thing. I missed you. I missed what we'd once had. I know you don't . . . but I did."

Her anger sulked off at the sincerity in his voice. "I didn't want to split up, Rex, but once we did, I realized that I had lost part of myself. I have that back, and I like my life. So I didn't want to try to work things out, but that doesn't mean I never loved you. But I'm not going to fix this for you. It's your mistake. You got your business into this shape, and you're going to have to be the one to get yourself out."

Rex looked at her with a pitiful expression. "But I don't have anyone to turn to, Daph. Mom and Dad have already loaned me money, so that door is shut. I had to cancel our trip to Scotland. That's why Cindy's not here with me. She's not speaking to me. I don't know where else to turn. You're about to sell the house and land, and your business seems to be really taking off. I mean, you're working with Disney. They're a cash cow, right? Or rather a cash mouse." He tried to smile, but it fell short.

Daphne reached over and tapped Rex's Rolex. "What are you doing, Rex?"

He pulled his arm back quick as spit. "What do you mean?"

"Rex." Daphne used her soft voice on him.

He looked up, his eyes full of . . . regret? "I don't know, Daph. I thought I wanted a different life. It's not your fault I'm this way. It's me. I thought I missed out on so much, you know? That one mistake we made defined my entire life. I tried to make the best of it, right? For a while it was fine. I liked our life."

They'd had a good life, and they'd done a pretty good job of making a silk purse from a sow's ear. She and Rex had raised an accomplished daughter, built a business, had very little debt, and loved each other . . .

at least for a while. Maybe they hadn't chosen how they started, but they'd gotten along pretty well. But his words said everything about who he was. *That one mistake we made defined my entire life.* Rex only saw himself as the victim of her getting pregnant. It was *his* life that was important. Not the young girl who'd had stretch marks at seventeen and, instead of going to senior prom, nursed a colicky baby. Daphne's dreams hadn't mattered. Only Rex's.

That was why they would never reconcile.

Because Daphne dared to want more than being Rex's wife.

She poured syrup on her pancakes, her joy in a carb-loaded, decadent breakfast as dead as the vows she'd shared with the man in front of her. "You said *short term*. How short?"

"I don't know." Rex rubbed his hands over his face and blew out a breath. "Six months?"

"And you said *credit cards*."

"What?"

Daphne took a bite, noting that even though she felt upset, the vanilla-flavored pancakes were delicious. "You said Ellery had credit cards and rent. Like multiple credit cards that *you* are paying?"

Rex blinked. "I've always paid her credit cards."

"Well, yeah, when she was in college, we gave her an allowance. She had a debit card."

Rex looked away. "You know how credit card companies are with college kids. They seduce them with free T-shirts and prizes. She got a couple of them. I didn't mind. Kids need things."

Daphne set her fork down, irritation at her daughter gathering in her gut. Of course Ellery thought she needed things . . . usually designer things. How many times had she heard her daughter say things like "They expect me to show that I know what is in style" or "Dress for the job you want, not the job you have." Their daughter knew the words to say to get what she wanted. She always had, and her father was her favorite parent to manipulate. He was a cream puff awaiting a good squeeze. "Rex, Ellery has two jobs and should be standing on her own two feet. You gave her a car for graduation, one too nice for a twenty-two-year-old, I might add. Your job is done, and she should be footing her own bills, not running up credit card debt for her daddy to pay off."

"Well, I don't know about—"

Daphne held up a hand, and Rex snapped his mouth shut. "At her age, we were driving a used van and attending kindergarten open house. You worked twelve-hour days, and I went to work at Saint Peter's. We were twenty-three and twenty-four respectively, and we adulted very well. Ellery has to learn how to hear *no*."

"She heard *no*. That designer—"

Daphne held up her hand again. "That was Ellery's fault, Rex. She didn't apply for other internships."

Rex inhaled and then blew his breath out, looking utterly miserable. "Maybe so."

"Look, our daughter is a good person. She is. But our love for her has crippled her, and it's not just you paying her credit cards or giving her a Lexus. I enable her, too. I swooped in with a job for her, and I'm paying her way more than anyone would pay an inexperienced assistant. And this whole weekend was because I felt guilty."

"Why did you feel guilty?"

Because I screwed her ex-boyfriend and then watched her current fiancé do to her what you'd done to me our entire life—disappoint and then make her feel like it was her fault.

She shrugged. "I guess because she's not happy."

Daphne felt the movement behind her before Ellery spoke. "For your information, Mother, I don't need your fucking sympathy, and I don't need your stupid made-up job, either."

"Ellery." Daphne turned to find their outraged daughter behind her. Ellery looked beautiful in a pair of skinny jeans, a slouchy sweater, and UGGs. She also looked pissed, with tears glistening in her eyes. "Honey, Dad and I were having a *private* conversation."

"Oh, it's real private." Ellery glanced around, her eyes glittering with rage. "You want me to be an adult, but you still treat me like a child. Like this whole divorce thing. What broke you and Dad up isn't some big, dark secret. You wanted a different life. You wanted fame and fortune . . . and nothing from your old life. Oh, and don't think I don't know about your trip to Chicago, the one where you slept with someone else. See, Dad told me everything because he knows I'm a fucking adult and can handle it."

Ellery might as well have taken the sledgehammer Daphne almost jokingly requested from the waitress and slammed it into her. *Slept with someone else?* "What are you talking about? Rex, what's she talking about?"

Her ex-husband looked like a dog caught eating the Christmas goose. "Uh, now, Elle. I said I thought . . . uh . . . I never said that it was for sure—"

"You told our daughter that I slept with a guy in Chicago? Who did you think I slept with? My agent? Paul is nearly seventy years old. Why would you tell her something like that?" But even as Daphne said it, she knew. Rex had been angry that Daphne hadn't fallen in line when he'd come groveling back. He also didn't want to be the bad guy and have their daughter think the end of the marriage was because he'd walked away first.

"I never said specifically that you *physically* cheated. It was more like emotional cheating. You gave your heart to your career, which was as much a betrayal as if you had given your physical self to someone else." Rex seemed to be addressing his orange-juice glass.

"What kind of psychobabble bullshit have you been peddling to people? I can't believe you, Rex. First you accuse me of emotional abandonment because I dared to pursue something other than getting stains out of your T-shirts, then you tell our daughter that I *cheated* on you? Oh, and let's not mention that you asked me for a loan because you decided to go to Belize instead of paying your taxes. Have you lost your damned mind?" Daphne knew people were looking at them, but she didn't care.

Ellery no longer looked pissed. Instead she looked like someone had slapped her. "Mom, I didn't know . . . I thought . . ."

Daphne stood, shoving her barely touched plate back, her chair banging into the table behind her. "What did you think? That I cheated on your father? That's what you think of me? That I'm an adulterer who went to Chicago to get sexed up? Really, Ellery? Really?" Daphne could feel tears slipping down her cheeks. She always cried when she was mad, a bad side effect of her emotions running rampant.

"Mom, I'm sorry. I didn't know. I mean, all of a sudden you were so busy with your new career, and it was like you were a different person, someone I didn't even know. You wouldn't talk to me about the divorce. It affected me, too, you know. I lost my family."

She stared at her daughter, realizing she, too, was making this about her. The apple didn't fall far from Rex's tree. "You didn't lose your family. It just changed."

"But it's like you want to erase everything from before. I mean, you're selling our house. You're signing up for online dating. You're just a different person now," Ellery said, her hands open in a plea.

"I am not a different person. I'm the person I always was. You"— she pointed at Rex—"and you"—she pointed at Ellery—"never saw me as anything other than someone to fix things for you. But I'm more than that."

Daphne angrily swiped at her face and looked for her purse. Where was her damned purse? She finally saw it under Rex's foot. She must have kicked it toward him at some point, so she crouched down to grab it, slapping his leg so he moved. When she rose, she slammed her head against the bottom of the table, making something on the table above spill and blinding pain rip through her. "Shit."

"You okay?" Rex asked, scooting his chair back.

"What do you think?" Daphne hissed, rising and pushing past Ellery. "And so you know, I'm selling the house because I don't want to live by myself in a house that holds all my memories, memories that are gone now. I just wanted a blank slate." She thumped her chest, knowing her eyes were blazing even as tears continued to course. "I deserve a blank slate."

Then with everyone in the restaurant watching, Daphne spun on her heel and tried to make a dignified exit. Except Clay stood in her way.

"Hey, you need some help here, Daph?" Clay asked, looking concerned.

Something about the tenderness in his eyes almost undid her. She nearly collapsed into his arms. Because at least someone was on her side. Hell, she was tired of being so alone, shouldering everything by herself. "Thank you, Clay, but not now. I can't deal right now."

Daphne shoved past him, digging for her keycard. She needed sanctuary, somewhere to process what had happened in the last ten minutes. Rex's news about the business, Ellery's revelation about what she thought about her mother, her biggest mistake appearing in Texas like a bad penny. It was all too much.

Thankfully, she didn't meet anyone on her dash to her room.

The morning that had started so well had just become a dumpster fire.

CHAPTER FIFTEEN

Daphne,

Hope it's okay that I call you that now. I feel silly calling you Dee Dee or Miss O'Hara. I really enjoyed jogging with you this morning. Felt nice to have someone at my side. When I learned you liked to run, I kept thinking about how it would be to have you beside me. Looking forward to our chat tonight. I hope you're not feeling awkward anymore and know that I have been enjoying getting to know you as a real person and not merely on the computer. I believed it when I said we have a bond that transcends distance or connection speed. I hope you feel that way, too.

Until tonight,
Evan

When Ellery had checked her email on the way to the bed and breakfast that morning to get Josh some coffee, she'd been panicked at the thought that her mother had figured out she'd been indulging in a relationship with Evan. That panic had wrestled with irritation. Evan had gone for a run with her mother and hadn't clued in to the fact that the woman running beside him was nothing like the one he'd shared such intimate thoughts with? How obtuse could a man be? And how come her mother hadn't figured it out yet? The woman could smell the one puff of a cigarette she'd smoked when she was fifteen but not this?

Then again, Ellery had bigger fish to fry than Evan McCallum, namely at this moment dealing with her father and the apparent lies he'd told her last summer. She looked down at where Rex still sat at the breakfast table, looking like a fox with feathers in his mouth.

"Daddy," she said, her voice full of disappointment.

His shoulders seemed to sink even lower before he took a deep breath. "Come on, pumpkin. Everything's okay. Your mom is just overreacting as usual."

"She's justified, Daddy."

Rex turned to everyone who had been staring at the spectacle that had unfolded and pressed his hands against the air. "It's okay, folks. Just a simple misunderstanding. Sorry to interrupt your breakfast."

Ellery stared at him. He had lied to her. He'd purposefully allowed her to think her mother was a philanderer who had traded her husband and her boring life for the high life. Or as high as life could be as a children's author who dressed like a southern matron. Her mother may have chased fame and fortune, but she hadn't cheated on her father. Mom hadn't walked away. Dad had. So why had her father led her to believe everything was her mother's fault?

Around her she could feel people returning their attention to their eggs.

Thank God.

"Just sit down," her father said, indicating the chair her mother had shoved into a small table that held menus and extra silverware.

"I don't want to sit down."

"Please, sugar. We've already made quite a scene, so maybe we should try a calm conversation without the drama," Rex said.

Her father didn't look like his normal self. Usually he exuded energetic confidence and vitality, but this morning he looked older and more tired than she'd ever seen him. His summer tan had faded, and the crow's-feet were more pronounced. She hadn't noticed before that moment. "Fine."

"Look, I know you're pissed, but I didn't mean to mislead you about your mother. Not exactly."

Ellery narrowed her eyes at him.

"Okay, fine. I was mad at her." Rex turned his hands over onto the table in a plea. "You have to understand that when she first started this whole book thing, I was happy for her. I always thought she needed something more than tending to us. But then she was *always* gone, *always* on deadline, *always* distracted. Then there were the huge paychecks and all the people lining up for her autograph. She felt different, not like the Daphne I had always known. I didn't tell you, but this past spring, I went to see her and asked if we could try again. She told me no."

She'd throbbed with anger, then outrage, and now felt something akin to pity for the man who hadn't been able to accept and support the woman in his life being more than a doormat. She was nearly certain the pity had edged in because she herself had felt those same things toward her mother—jealousy, hurt, incredulity. "I get it, Dad. Mama fell into something she never imagined—a career she loves. Did you think she would give all that up to be the person you wanted her to be again? I understand the way you feel, but you should have been proud of her and not threatened."

Even as Ellery said those words, she knew she was guilty of the same thing. She'd spent years resenting her mother. How many times had she been snide when Daphne couldn't make a luncheon or given her mother the silent treatment when Daphne forgot to mail chocolate chip cookies before exams? How many times over the past months had she been angry that her mother had happened into a successful career without even *trying*, while Ellery's own carefully constructed plan had netted her nothing but folding socks at Selber's? How often had she stifled irritation at people asking about her mother rather than asking about her?

Yeah, Ellery had been a shit to her mother . . . as much as her father had. Which meant Ellery had character flaws. Serious ones. She was ashamed of herself for being so envious of her own mother, especially now that she knew the truth.

Her behavior brought a fresh sheen of tears to her eyes.

Her father rolled his eyes. "I'm *not* threatened by your mother's success."

But the way her father said it made it obvious he was. Ellery had never thought about her father being jealous of her mother's unexpected fortune. When he'd talked to her over the summer about why their marriage had failed, his slant had made her mother seem in the wrong. He'd been the victim. Ellery had fallen for it hook, line, and sinker. For some reason it was easy to believe her mother wanted more than what she had. Daphne had spent her life at the ironing board, in the kitchen, wiping preschooler faces, and reorganizing the pantry. When that editor had called, it had been like her mother had woken up and seen what life could be. She'd been Dorothy over the rainbow, and her world was suddenly vibrant and unfamiliar.

Of course, when Ellery's father had first suggested Daphne had slept with some exec from a publishing house, Ellery hadn't believed his insinuation. Her mother was . . . her mom. Daphne may have wanted more than the lemons life had handed her, but she wasn't making martinis and swilling them while crooking her finger at random dudes. Ellery knew this for certain.

She'd even said as much to Josh an hour after her father had implied her mother had been unfaithful, and it was her fiancé who had allowed doubt to shadow her opinion.

"Well, you don't always know people, right? We see what we want to see. We have expectations for the people in our lives, and if they step outside that, we're unwilling to distort that version of them. So we ignore what is in front of us. Did your father confront her?" he'd asked as they stood outside the rental house in Seaside, Florida.

"I don't know. Dad just said it like he was ticking off all the reasons things went bad for them, and that little bomb was one of them. It was weird," Ellery had said, clutching the balcony of their beach house, the sea breeze tangling her hair as the waves crashed onto the beach. "Should I ask her?"

"Will she tell you the truth?"

"I don't know. Probably not." Ellery had turned to Josh, so glad that he was there for her. His solid shoulders and warm embrace ready to shelter her. She moved into those arms and closed her eyes at the pleasure of his closeness. "She *has* changed. Highlights, better wardrobe, and she holds herself differently. Maybe everything went to her head a bit. Her life has been small until recently, and you're right, sometimes people do what you don't expect. Maybe she wanted more than what she had."

Josh kissed her head. "Maybe she did."

But now sitting at that table across from her father—a man who had lied and made Ellery doubt so much of her mother—she wondered if she'd believed the untruth because she was discontent with her own life.

Ever since her stumble out of the gate, she'd been pasting on a smile, pretending everything in her life was gravy when in fact she hated the life she lived. She'd convinced herself there was nothing wrong with taking a year off, being a supportive girlfriend, and making lemonade and all that bullshit. So maybe it wasn't her mother who wanted more.

It was Ellery.

"Elle?" her father said, jarring her from her disturbing thoughts.

"Oh, sorry. All I'm saying is maybe you didn't want to be threatened by Mom's success, but you were," Ellery said, watching the syrup drip from her mother's abandoned pancakes. They looked really good. Ellery picked up a clean fork and stabbed a bite. "Thing is, Dad, I understand because the crazy success surprised me, too. And you're right—everything changed. Still, the more I think about it, the more I realize we were unfair to Mom. Something wonderful happened to her, and instead of celebrating it with her—I mean truly celebrating it, not just the clink of the champagne glass—we resented how it inconvenienced us."

"That's not true. Once you're in a marriage, you'll understand what I mean. You have to balance things. Before her career, your mom and I were fine. And then we weren't."

Easy for her father to say. He'd owned the balance of power in that relationship. Her mother had owned the power of Spray 'n Wash. And really, Ellery had no business analyzing anyone's relationship. Last night she'd kissed another man after finding gay porn on her fiancé's computer. If anyone was "unbalanced," it was the gal picking apart her mother's now-cold pancakes. "Daddy, I'm not saying how you felt wasn't valid. I'm just saying I may have been a jerk over the past year or so. You and Mom getting a divorce wasn't something I ever expected, and I didn't handle it well. I pretended to, but I didn't."

She set the fork down.

Rex looked at her. "So how long were you standing there? I mean, you overheard your mother talking about some things."

Ellery nodded. "I heard her essentially talk about what a spoiled little bitch I am."

"You aren't." Her father always defended her, something that comforted. But it was also a bit like wearing shoes that pinched her feet. She had to own her flaws, not have them smoothed over by her father. Or anyone else.

"Eh, I can be." Ellery shrugged, holding on to the truth with one hand while she pinched her nose with the other. Being honest with herself wasn't pleasant. "I also heard you say something about her paying my rent."

He swallowed. "Look, baby, I'm having some cash-flow problems. The divorce and some other stuff have made it harder to pay the bills lately, but I don't want you to worry."

Ellery felt something panicky gnaw at her. She'd relied on her father too much. It wasn't like she didn't know this, but it had been easier letting him pay for her life than taking ownership of her own poor decisions. Of course, she wasn't sure if she could afford her share of the bills and pay off the credit cards. She had three now, one her father didn't know about and that she had been paying on her own. "It's fine. I need to start paying my own bills. I mean, it will be challenging, but I have two jobs and have to do better at managing my money."

Her father lifted his eyebrows. "Really?"

Ellery shrugged, pushing aside the fear that clogged her throat. God, everything was so screwed up, and now she had to truly grow up. Bills, relationships, and a future that felt uncertain. "I have to start living on my own."

Rex nodded. "I guess it's official—you're a big girl."

"Ha." Ellery pushed her chair back. She needed to find her mother and apologize for thinking the worst of her. Why hadn't she asked her mother about Chicago? She wasn't sure. Maybe because she liked the anger she felt toward her mother . . . even enjoyed that her mother didn't know why Ellery was so distant. Daphne was the kind of person who was good at everything—she never left something undone, never half-assed, never screwed up. Ellery had found perverse comfort in the thought her mother wasn't so damned good after all. Somehow it made Ellery more of an equal, as if the blemish on Daphne's morality counteracted Ellery's own failure. That thought was fucked up, but Ellery knew it was true. "This big girl has to go apologize to her mother for believing the absolute worst of her."

"That would be nice."

"And perhaps you need to do the same, Dad. Take some of that therapy you've been immersed in and apply it to your life. Own your mistakes."

She didn't wait for her father to argue. Instead she turned and left the restaurant. Her phone buzzed in her pocket.

Where are you? Thought you were getting coffee?

Ha. *She* was the one who needed caffeine. The events of the night before had tag teamed her dreams, making her toss, turn, and doubt everything she'd so carefully planned. Her fiancé hadn't moved when she'd crawled into bed after leaving her stupid leather bustier on the bathroom floor with the pooled fishnet stockings. She'd scrubbed the red from her lips, wishing she could scrub away the taste of Gage as easily. It felt as if he'd imprinted himself on her. The way she'd felt in his arms, the taste of him, the smell—all of it conspired to undermine her intentions for her life.

When she woke that morning, Josh had been sitting next to her, tapping away at his computer. Alarm slammed into her, making her eyes fly open. Oh God. Did he know she'd been on his computer? Had she done enough to cover her tracks?

But when he felt her wake, Josh turned to her and smiled. "Morning, sleepyhead."

"Morning."

"You weren't here when I got back last night," he said.

"I went out for a walk. I felt . . . cagey for some reason." *Or maybe it was the gay porn on your computer.*

"I tried to wait up, but that bourbon snuck up on me." He stopped tapping on the laptop and reached over to run a hand through her hair. "Gosh, you're pretty when you wake up."

Guilt threatened to strangle her. She was such a bad person. Horrible. "I'm sorry I wasn't here."

Josh's blue eyes softened even more. "I get it—it's all these people. Tonight will be even busier. Don't know why your mom and friends thought this would be fun. I mean, it's nice, but kind of . . . I don't know, pretentious."

Ellery pushed her hair out of her eyes. "You're the king of pretention. Aren't you wearing designer pajama pants?"

He looked down at the material between his computer and lap. "You bought them for me."

"Touché," she said, wiping her no-doubt puffy eyes. "I'll make some coffee."

"Good luck. The coffee maker's not working."

"What? No coffee for you? Great." She slid from the bed. Since she'd abandoned her sexy lingerie, she'd had to sleep in a T-shirt and the thong. The thong had been as comfortable as dental floss up her ass. Granny panties were so undervalued by people her age. "I guess I can run up to the bed and breakfast and grab you some. I'll also let them know the coffee machine is broken."

"I could do it," Josh said, his attention already back on his computer.

"You finish whatever you're doing so we can have breakfast together."

"I have a lot to do, babe."

Ellery sighed.

Josh looked up at her. "But we will have breakfast. I have to get back to Shreveport for a big review for the test next week, but I will stay for the tour. How about that?"

"Goodie." Ellery may have sounded sarcastic. Okay, she totally sounded sarcastic, but she didn't wait around to listen to Josh's stupid apologies or excuses. She'd heard them all by now. *Their future. Every test mattered. He had to pull his weight for the group.* Yada, yada, yada.

She pulled on jeans, boots, and her abandoned hoodie, inhaling like some lunatic to see if there was a trace of Gage left. Then she climbed the hill toward the bed and breakfast and followed her nose to the place where she smelled coffee. Then she'd seen her parents sitting close to the entrance. Then she'd heard her parents.

This was what people got for eavesdropping—the same thing a gal got for snooping on her lover's computer—something she didn't want to know.

And she still didn't have the damned coffee.

Coming.

Ha. She wished.

Ellery spun back toward the dining room and hailed the waitress. She'd take Josh the coffee just as soon as she apologized to her mother. She couldn't continue the weekend with things this wrong between her and her mom. And while she was at it, she would admit to emailing Evan. Clear the air once and for all.

It was a solid plan, and by the tour, everything would be okay.

"Ma'am?"

Ellery smiled. "Can you get me three coffees to go? I'll be back in five minutes to grab them."

All a girl needed was a plan.

Daphne made it back to her room without running into anyone else who might see the utter desolation in her eyes.

All the tension between her and Ellery now made sense. Ellery had been nursing a secret falsehood, petting it in the recesses of her heart. And why? Why hadn't she asked Daphne about what her father had suggested?

But Daphne knew why—Daphne had discouraged any talk of the breakup. Any time Ellery brought up the divorce, Daphne sidestepped the conversation or out-and-out told her daughter that the details of what happened weren't any of her business. She wanted to protect Ellery and refused to bad-mouth Rex in front of her. She'd taken the high road . . . and Rex had taken the low, dragging their daughter's opinion of her down with him. That's what Daphne got for trying to be the better person.

She pushed into her room and then collapsed on the unmade bed, where she gave free rein to her tears. It had been a long time since she'd cried, and it felt like a plug had been pulled and everything inside had to come out before it could get better.

So Daphne let it.

Eventually her sobs subsided into sniffles, and she heard a quiet knocking at her door.

Ellery.

Daphne struggled into a sitting position and grabbed a tissue from the box covered with a needlepoint image of a rose. Mopping her face, she went to the door and opened it, expecting Ellery to be standing there looking contrite.

But Clay stood there instead.

"Hey, I thought I would check on you," he said, looking worried.

"I'm fine," she said, sounding more like a frog than an actual person.

"You don't look or sound fine. What was all that about?" He glanced down the hall, seemed to note someone there, and looked back at her. "Can I just come inside so we don't have to hold this conversation in the hallway?"

Daphne stepped back. "Sure."

He slid inside, and she shut the door. This morning Clay wore his regular tight, worn, romance-cover-worthy jeans, a denim button-down, and worn cowboy boots. His eyes matched the shirt and looked startling against his sun-kissed skin. He looked good. More than good.

Stop noticing, Daph.

"Great room. It's bigger than mine," he said, glancing around at the elegant fussiness of the room. "You have a porch and hot tub? Nice."

"Clay," Daphne said, trying to draw him back to their conversation so she could get him back out the door.

"Sorry," he said, turning toward her, taking in her tear-streaked face and swollen eyes. "You sure you're okay?"

"I told you I'm fine. Just some family drama that's been simmer-ing for a while." Daphne ran a hand through her hair, aware she was a mess. She didn't want to worry about what she looked like to Clay, but in this small space with that big bed so nearby, her libido overrode her common sense. She licked her lips and tried not to look so pathetic.

The thing was, Clay was standing here in lieu of either Ellery or Rex, the two people who should have cared enough to follow her and apologize. Neither of them had—this man she'd had mind-blowing sex with weeks ago had been the one to come check on her. No one in the world seemed to care for her but the one person she didn't want to have a relationship with.

"They gang up on you?" he asked, moving toward her. "I got the sense they were."

"A little, but it's nothing I can't handle. It was upsetting, but I'm fine now."

He stopped in front of her, so sincere and . . . warm. "You keep saying that, but your eyes say something different. I hate to see you sad, Daph. You sure the hell don't deserve to be sad."

Then he wrapped his arms around her and held her.

At first Daphne resisted, pulling back, but he held her firm, tuck-ing her head beneath his chin. His hands rubbed her back. Clay was solid . . . and warm . . . and so much what she shouldn't want. But she did. God help her. His arms felt so good.

Which meant she stayed exactly where she was even as the mood shifted from comforting to the point where arms were not just arms and the hardness she pressed against not intrusive but very welcome. Her body took over before her mind could catch up.

His lips brushed her temple, and she felt that once forgotten but newly awakened liquid heat ignite in her pelvis. It would be so easy to give herself to him. Temptation scratched at her resolve.

What would it hurt?

Clay moved his hands lower, cupping her ass and pressing his erection against her belly. Damn, the man got hard fast.

Daphne lifted her head. His blue eyes were limpid pools of *Come on in, baby.*

"Daph," he whispered, his gaze dropping to her lips. He lowered his head and brushed his lips sweetly against hers. Somehow the bare glancing of his mouth over hers was ten times more erotic than if he'd kissed her fully. He made his way down her throat, and though she had every intention of stopping him, she allowed it for a second, two seconds, because it felt so good to be wanted. His fingers slipped the top two buttons open, and the rasp of his whiskers against the tender slope of her breast made her catch her breath.

She wanted him so badly . . . but she couldn't go there.

Couldn't make that mistake again.

They had to stop.

Just as Daphne was about to press her hands against his rock-hard chest, a knock sounded.

"Clay, stop," she said, shaking her head and stepping backward.

Clay did indeed stop the sweet torture he was performing on his way to her breasts. In that he was an obedient man. But then he took the three steps to the door and opened it before Daphne could protest.

Ellery stood in the hall with her hand raised in a fist.

Clay stood, looking at her daughter, his eyes still dilated, his tight jeans framing his arousal in an in-your-face display of manhood.

Daphne clutched her shirt, which gaped to reveal the edge of her lacy bra and probably the outline of her hardened nipples. She knew she looked flushed, turned on, and out of breath.

And totally busted.

Ellery's hand dropped as her eyes widened. Then she snapped her gaping mouth closed as she took in the scene before her. Daphne could almost see the wheels turning in her daughter's head. Mom with her shirt half-unbuttoned. Spin. Click. Clay standing with an unapologetic erection pressing against his fly. Spin. Click. Intimacy almost as thick as the overly plush rug in the hall. Spin. Click.

"Can we help you, Elle?" Clay asked. His tone told Ellery in no uncertain terms that she was interrupting something. Daphne could see exactly when her daughter understood what was going on. The realization crackled in those pretty blue eyes she'd stared into as she nursed her . . . as she taught her to ride her bike . . . as she betrayed her with her ex-boyfriend.

"I came to . . ." Ellery shook her head, her mouth pressing into a tight line as her angry blue eyes narrowed. "You know what? Never mind."

"Ellery, honey . . . ," Daphne said, starting toward the door. "Don't go."

"Nope. I can see I interrupted. Carry on." Ellery reached out for the doorknob. Clay still held the door ajar, but as Ellery tugged at the knob, he released it.

The last thing Daphne saw before the door shut was the absolutely devastated and furious glare of her only child. Daphne's heart hit her toes, and her stomach immediately cramped.

"Oh my God," Daphne said, doubling over and clutching her middle. She backed up, hitting the tapestry chair in the corner of the room. "She knows. Ellery knows about us."

"Who cares? We're adults," Clay said, moving toward her. He'd started unbuttoning his shirt, and the amount of gorgeous skin on display that had once been tempting now made her want to retch. Her daughter now knew she was intimate with a man way too young for her. After the earlier conversation with Rex, Daphne now looked like a horny slut who would do anyone who came along.

Great. Just great.

She looked up at Clay. "You can keep your shirt on."

"What? Don't be ridiculous. You want me, and I want you," he said, grabbing her hand and pressing it against his large and still very hard erection.

Daphne snatched her hand away. "Are you insane? My daughter just caught us. You think I still want to screw you?"

Clay's laugh grated on her last nerve. "Ellery isn't a child anymore. She knows the score and what adults do in the bedroom. She doesn't care who you sleep with, Daph, so let's make each other feel good. Life's short, baby."

Daphne stood and pushed him back. "You treat sex like it's commonplace. It's not, okay? At least not for me. What I did with you a few weeks ago isn't going to be repeated, Clay. I thought you understood that. I'm looking for more than you can give me."

"I gave you plenty if I remember correctly," he said, hurt flashing across his face before being replaced with a belligerent hardening. He followed her to the other side of the bed. "I've also given you plenty of time to see that you and I can work. That's why I came here this weekend. I can be more than your contractor. Come on, I know what you need, Daph."

"Yeah, okay, you turn me on. That's apparent. But I want more in life than getting off, and I damn sure don't need a man who thinks he knows what I need better than I do. Been there, done that, buddy."

"That's not what I'm saying, and you know it. And I want more than sex. That's what I'm trying to say."

"Well, you're doing a shit job of it, Clay. I can't deal with this at present. You need to leave my room. In fact, you need to leave the bed and breakfast."

"You're being ridiculous."

"So you've said, but I prefer to think of it as knowing my own damned mind. So please go. Now."

Clay hurriedly buttoned up his shirt. "Jesus, I can't believe you. I really thought you were cool and someone I wanted to pursue a relationship with, but it's obvious you're caught up in some Victorian code of conduct."

"That's because I'm *old*," Daphne shouted at him. "That's what I've been telling you this entire time. I don't hook up. I don't see sex as an action equal to . . . eating a Reese's Peanut Butter Cup."

"Don't make me sound like a guy who was in it for pussy, because I can get that anywhere."

"I'm well aware, Clay," she said, her voice slightly sarcastic.

Clay's gaze hardened, but she could still see the hurt reflected in his eyes. She wanted to tell him she didn't think that about him, but if her hard words would get him to leave . . .

"I thought you would never treat me like I'm nothing more than a big dick in tight jeans, but I was wrong. You're too afraid to take what you want. You're too busy kissing Ellery's ass and being scared someone might think something about you dating a younger guy," he said.

Was that what she was? Scared to fall for Clay? No. She wasn't interested in Clay as a long-term, or even short-term, relationship. It was horrible to feel that she had used him to feel better about herself, but it was the truth. "I know what *I* think, Clay. That's the most important thing."

Clay shook his head. "Whatever. I tried to be what you wanted. I cared about you, but I can see you don't want me."

His pained words took the starch out of her. Oh, she was still irritated at his misogyny masked as good intentions, but she also knew

Clay was a good person. He was hurt, and she'd done that to him, knowing it had to be done. She couldn't have the temptation of Clay around her. Her vulnerability dictated she push him far away. "This is for the best. I wasn't trying to hurt you, Clay."

He walked to the door, shook his head, and walked out.

Daphne sank onto the bed, covered her face with her hands, and whispered, "Fuck."

She wasn't one for cursing much, but sometimes there was no better word for a situation such as this.

CHAPTER SIXTEEN

Ellery zombie-walked down the hallway. She may have passed someone. Or not. That's how messed up she was after shutting the door on her mother half-dressed with Clay Caldwell.

So not only was her fiancé watching a video of a guy blowing another guy, but her mother, who Ellery thought had cheated to end her marriage but was now innocent of cheating, was, in fact, screwing the only guy who'd broken her heart.

Which was worse?

Adultery or pedophilia?

Okay, it wasn't pedophilia, but it felt creepy and dirty and plain wrong that her mother would sleep with Clay. Yuck. Gross. Ugh. Wrong.

All Ellery knew at that moment was her life was completely upside down, and she had no idea how to spin it right side up again. Maybe she wouldn't. Maybe fucked up was her new normal.

She emerged into the common area where the reception desk and small bar were located and immediately saw Evan McCallum. His gaze met hers before she could rip it away and find a place to hide.

"Ah, Ellery," Evan said, setting down the papers he held in his hand onto the reception counter and walking toward her. "Good morning. Hope you had a nice time last night."

"Oh, it was dandy," Ellery said before immediately wishing she'd banked the sarcasm and proceeded with politeness. Maybe she was done with being polite. The fake veneer of cheerfulness she'd pulled on when she first arrived at One Tree Estates had worn off. Bitter deceit and bad behavior tended to abrade cheerful fronts.

Evan frowned, and she noted for the third or fourth time how handsome he was. He wore jeans and a deep-green Henley shirt that stretched across his broad shoulders. He looked Colin Firth–esque, and it dawned on her that she'd probably romanticized Evan to that exact degree. "What's wrong? Was it the food? Or something at Vine House?"

Ellery shook her head and waved a hand, wishing she could talk to him as easily as she did behind the keyboard. When they corresponded, he always had good suggestions and an insightfulness that dug beneath her shallow worldviews. Maybe he would know how to handle finding one's mother diddling the much-younger help. Okay, Clay was the contractor, but still, wasn't that sexual misconduct? "It's not that. The house is fine. I'm just dealing with family stuff."

"Oh, well, I understand that," he said.

She looked at him and saw he did indeed understand. Or thought he did. Her father's comments last night had been inappropriate, and Evan probably thought what she dealt with was the fallout. Ha. She wished this was about Rex acting like an ass. Nope. Way bigger. "Yeah, dealing with family can be . . . impossible."

Evan smiled. "But what would we do without them, right?"

"Yeah," Ellery said. "I do wonder sometimes. In fact, maybe I need to find out."

"Hey, while we're on that subject, I wanted to ask you something. Your mother and I have been corresponding for a few months, just a general friendship struck up when I sent her an email about speaking at Poppy's school. Your mom's a special lady."

Ellery swallowed hard and tried not to look guilty. Here's where she should say: *Funny thing, Evan. I answer email for my mother, and, surprise, you've been chatting with me all this time.* But she didn't say that. Maybe because she was embarrassed about the deception. Or maybe because she wanted to continue the secret relationship because in that she could be herself . . . or not herself. Whatever. Evan always made her feel like she was perfectly okay being the hot mess she was, but of course he really didn't *know* her. You never really knew anyone. "Yeah, she's certainly *special.*"

"I'm thinking about asking her out. Maybe drive over to Shreveport for dinner? You think she'd be open to that? I know she hasn't dated much since her divorce."

Evan wanted to ask her mother out?

Ellery's vision flashed brighter, and something ugly tore loose inside her. No. Her mother didn't get to have Evan, too. She'd tossed aside her father, screwed Clay, and now she got a shot with Evan? Nu-uh. No frickin' way.

She didn't want Evan to see the truth in her gaze, so she glanced away.

Of course this would happen. Hadn't she suspected as much? Evan had said he thought they had . . . what had he called it? Oh yeah. A connection that transcended distance? But that connection was as false as Ellery's eyelashes. Somehow the fact he had no clue what was going on made her even angrier. If they had a connection, why hadn't he noticed Ellery beyond simple niceties? How come he couldn't feel that it was with her he shared the zip, zing of something more? And not with the woman doing Clay five doors down?

"You know, she's in her room. I just left there. Maybe you should go ask her," Ellery said, turning on her heel and heading toward the front door. Maybe Evan would catch her mother in flagrante and understand exactly what he was dealing with—a woman who was more messed up than the one he had actually been feeling a "connection" with.

And maybe Ellery was as screwed up as her mother. After all, she'd cheated on her fiancé. Okay, it wasn't cheating really. A kiss meant nothing in the grand scheme of things.

Except it did to you.

"Stop it," Ellery whispered under her breath to her stupid inner voice.

"Wait, Ellery," Evan called from behind her.

But she wasn't stopping, because the handsome man who'd been Ellery's little secret all along asking her whore mother out on a date was the last straw. The absolute, final insulting slap of hard reality that Ellery had been running from. Hell, she never even knew she was running from anything. She'd thought she was making lemonade from lemons, but the truth was she hadn't been handed lemons. She'd been handed a steaming pile of crap to deal with, and a gal couldn't make anything with steaming crap. All she could do was throw it at someone else.

She stormed down the hill toward the house where Josh probably sat with earbuds in, eyes on his computer. Or maybe he was jacking off in the bathroom to his little video. Or maybe he'd already left without so much as a *See you later* to the woman he was supposed to love. But didn't.

Ellery now knew this.

Josh didn't love her. Not like he was supposed to love her.

Angry tears threatened to spill from her eyes, but she willed herself to stop being pathetic. *Suck it up, buttercup. You know how to do this. Slap a smile on your face and pretend everything is A-okay. Stick to the plan.*

As she approached the house, she glanced over to the trail she'd taken twice already. Her feet wanted to take her there, to that place where no one could find her. Except Gage.

But Gage was a crutch. She'd used him to feel better about herself. Or maybe that wasn't true.

If anything, she'd been her real self with him. She hadn't tried to make Gage like her. Instead she'd let all her ugly out. And he'd kissed the hell out of her in spite of her warts.

She didn't want to go back in that house to face Josh . . . or make merry with her friends. Her life felt too much for her at present. Decisions had to be made—should she confront Josh? She had to at some point, even if it meant admitting she'd snooped on his computer. Should she confront her mother? Eventually, but she couldn't deal with the thought of what her mother and Clay had been doing. And how in all that was holy was she going to pay her rent and credit card bills? And finally, she still had to do something about Evan. God, her life was so effed up!

Just run away.

The voice inside her screamed the solution. Ellery could climb in her car and leave. Drive fast and go where no one could find her. Someone would pack up her abandoned leather bustier and warming lubricant. Someone would eat her stupid cake and do the Jell-O shots. Someone would pick up the pieces of her life and put them somewhere for safekeeping.

"Hey, you," Madison said from the rocking chair.

Ellery squeaked and clutched her chest. "Damn it, you scared me."

"I know. You look like you've seen a ghost." Madison held up a coffee mug. "I got the coffeepot working. Josh had pressed all the wrong buttons."

"Figures. I sort of forgot to bring him coffee anyway," Ellery said, walking to the rocking chair next to her friend.

"I put on the kettle for you and found a tea bag in my overnight bag from last time. Your mom left us everything but tea."

"She's been distracted, I guess." *Doing Clay and flirting with Evan.*

"What's wrong, Elle? I thought after last night, you'd be . . . well, happier. I saw the bustier and stockings. Did Josh like-y?"

"Josh fell asleep before he could even see me in it." Ellery couldn't believe she'd actually admitted Josh's disinterest to her friend. Even with Madison, her absolute best friend, she never wanted to present herself as anything but totally together.

"Oh shit, E," Madison said, her toe stopping her rocking motion. She turned to Ellery. "I'm so sorry. Maybe it's all the stress he's under. Med school's so tough and such a commitment."

Ellery stared at the mums blooming brightly from the barrel between them. "That's what they say."

Madison reached over and took her hand, squeezing her fingers. "It won't last."

"I don't know, Mads. Everything is so screwed up right now. My dad is in financial trouble, and my mom . . . well, she's . . . sleeping with someone."

"What?" Madison's eyes got big. "That's crazy, but in a way good. I mean, your mom deserves to be happy, right?"

Ellery inhaled deeply. "Sure. But you don't get it. It's a younger guy, Mads."

"Reeeally?" Madison drawled, her mouth dropping open for a few seconds. "I never would have pegged your mother as a cradle robber, but good for her."

"No, it's disgusting. She's turning forty in December, and he's . . . he's too young for her. And I don't want to talk about my mom having sex. It's so disturbing."

"You know she has had sex, right? I mean, at least once," Madison said with a grin.

"Just stop," Ellery said, wondering why she had even sat down. She wanted to leave. Just get in the car. Not look back.

Madison sobered. "I'm sorry, Elle. I hoped you would forget all the bad stuff this weekend. I know things have been tough, but you have a fiancé who loves you, and when you get an internship next year, everything will look different."

If she got an internship. She had filled out the applications online but had yet to submit her portfolio or send any follow-ups. Something inside her had died when J.J. had delivered her email of doom. That one rejection had started her on the slide down the hill she now tumbled. She felt lost and didn't know how to get the old Ellery back. "Yeah, maybe so."

"Oh yeah," Madison said, sitting up and craning her neck like a meerkat. "There he is."

"There who is?" Ellery asked, leaning over so she could see around the large cypress beam. Walking from the parking lot below the vineyard tasting rooms was Gage. He wore tight jeans, hiking boots, and a flannel shirt, and he carried a motorcycle helmet. His jaw looked carved of granite, and she could have sworn his gray-green eyes darted toward where they sat on the patio before he started his climb toward the place where he worked. Ellery looked back at the parking lot and spied a shiny Harley-Davidson motorcycle sitting beside a truck marked with the One Tree Estates logo. Of course he rode a hog. Because of course.

"That delicious treat who works the bar, that's who."

"Gage?"

"You *know* him?" Madison turned to her.

"Sort of. We've met a few times."

"Any chance I can meet him? He's adorable and hot and tasty and—"

Ellery actually managed to laugh, even as something ugly rose within her, which seemed to be becoming a habit. But this ugly screamed "Mine," and she had no such reason to feel that way. Other than the fact that she'd kissed him last night beneath the October moon, and it had been incredibly moving. Like an awakening. Like something she suddenly longed to do again. And again. And again.

Gage disappeared into the building like a message.

Not for you.

Madison snapped her attention back to Ellery. "You want breakfast? Your mom brought some Danish and muffins. Oh, and fruit."

"Go ahead," Ellery said, nodding at her friend. "I'll be in later. I'm enjoying the morning."

Madison rose and opened the door. "You sure you're okay?"

"I'm perfect."

But Ellery was a liar. Nothing was perfect at the moment. Nothing at all. So she sat in the rocker, contemplating how she could change her trajectory, but she could find no answers. No answers at all.

Sliding her phone from her hoodie pocket, she stared at the many messages on her screen. Several from her mother. Please. Let's talk. Please answer. I need you to talk to me.

Ellery ignored those messages and pressed the center button with her thumb. The home screen appeared. It was a picture of her and Josh on the day he'd proposed. She looked stupidly happy. Josh looked pleased. Suddenly she hated the picture, so she pressed the email icon, making it disappear.

She scrolled.

No response from Evan on the email she'd sent him that morning. After Evan told her he was asking Daphne out, she had to figure out what to do. She felt like doing nothing. Radio silent. Ignore him. Maybe he'd get the message.

She scrolled up to one of her favorite past emails he'd sent her and clicked on the subject—My Philosophy of Life According to Wine.

Dee Dee,

We saw geese flying over our small lake this morning. They honked and made a ruckus, making Poppy giggle. She said they sounded like the lunch ladies at her school, who obviously spend too much time fussing. Funny how children can hear or see something and make it amusing. Ah, daughters. I know you're worried about yours and her relationship with her fiancé. I hate to hear there are concerns. Making a marriage work is much like making wine. You can plant the best vines, rejoice in the sunlight, and take comfort in the rains, but in the end, what you end up with inside the bottle is unexpected. Every little element the grape encounters changes it, whether it be temperature or soil or something unexplained. Often what you think you'll pour out isn't what you get. Sometimes you have to embrace the unexpected.

Evan

Embrace the unexpected.

Ellery cast her gaze once again on the winery and tasting rooms where Gage no doubt prepared for a busy day. The passion Gage had sparked in her had been unexpected. His lips against hers had been like one of those unmeasurable elements and had birthed too many questions inside her. His kiss had been different. Right. Good. Sweet as the wine they made here.

She rose without thinking and walked toward the unexpected.

Five minutes later she pushed into the winery, which housed the tasting room and gift shop. Here was where she'd first seen Gage, looking remarkably grumpy, sexy, and intriguing. She'd disliked him as much as he'd turned her on. Yet she could not deny he'd awakened something inside her, something she couldn't even put a name to. For some reason, she had to know if what he'd started inside her was real.

The tasting room wasn't open yet, but the door was unlocked, so she entered to find Gage alone behind the horseshoe-shaped bar, drying glasses and counting them.

He glanced up, looking automatically annoyed at the interruption, but his eyes softened when he noted it was her. "Oh, it's you. Hey."

"Hey." She stood just inside, allowing the door to close against her back. The click of the lock against the strike seemed to reflect her decision to come here.

Too late now.

He glanced back down at the glasses. "You know we're not open yet."

"I know. I didn't come for the wine."

Lifting his gaze to her, he hooked an eyebrow. It was gorgeously sexy. "So . . . ?"

"So I think you should know that my fiancé doesn't love me, my mom is screwing my ex-boyfriend from high school, and my dad is broke and can't pay my credit card bills."

Gage's eyes widened. She bet he hadn't expected her to lead with something like that.

"Also you should know I lost an internship in New York City to a guy from Minnesota who pretends to be Italian. He also wears orange wing tips. Then I took a job working for my mom because I couldn't cut it anywhere else."

Gage set the glass down on the counter and tossed the towel next to it. He moved around the edge and started walking toward her. "Never been a fan of orange wing tips."

"No one is." Ellery held up her hand. "But that's not all."

He raised his eyebrows. "There's more?"

"My daddy bought my car for me, I cheated on an ethics test, and I got a Brazilian wax that is not very comfortable at all, especially when wearing a thong." She knew her face was red, but for some reason she needed to tell him exactly what a wreck she was. He had to see her, the real her, not the one who pretended to be this together chick with a designer bag and glossy lips. She needed to say all this to someone, and for some crazy-assed reason, she wanted it to be Gage.

"Is that all?" he asked, stopping in front of her, his expression unflappable.

Ellery shook her head.

He was so close that she could reach up and trace his lips. She had the sudden inclination to do that. Just trail her finger slowly across his bottom lip. His gaze dropped to her lips, lower to the hoodie she'd worn last night. She wondered if he remembered what she'd worn beneath. Did he want her as much as she wanted him? Because she wanted him. Ellery wanted him naked beneath her. She wanted to trace his tattoos with her tongue, explore every inch of his body, watch him when she knelt before him and did what that guy did to the other guy on that horrible home movie on Josh's hard drive.

Gage's gaze rose back to capture hers. "What else?"

"Last night when you kissed me . . . that was the best thing that has happened to me since I won Miss Louisiana Redbud Queen and got this giant crown that absolutely no one could ever wear. I do believe that kiss was better than that, and it's all I can think about. I mean that other stuff is pretty . . . uh, there . . . but the way I felt with you last night was . . ." Ellery swallowed.

"What?" Gage asked, his voice so soft her heart squeezed.

"Real." She looked up at him, knowing that she was being completely honest. "I want—"

He caught her words with his lips. Her head and body collided with the closed door as he kissed her. She opened her mouth and let him in, let him take every bit of doubt, worry, ickiness she'd been carrying with her for the last few hours and replace it with hot, wet wonderful. He caught her hands, lifted, and pushed them over her head, pinning her against the rough cedar of the door.

Then he proceeded to kiss the hell out of her.

Ellery arched her back, and the delicious friction of her breasts against his chest sent her to a new level of desire. At that moment she'd do whatever Gage wanted her to do. Drop on all fours and howl like a dog or rip her clothes off and do him right here in the middle of the winery.

His mouth punished her, but she could feel how much he wanted her. He devoured her like she was something sweet to eat, and Ellery loved the way he made her feel.

She was out of control, and hunger for him gnawed at her convictions, drove her to abandon any sort of propriety, and made her forget everything she thought she was.

"Ellery," he whispered against her lips. "Baby?"

"What?"

He bit her bottom lip and lifted his head. "I want this. You know I do."

"I do, too." Her breathing was ragged and her body on fire.

"But you gotta fix some things before we can do this. You understand? I want you, but I'm not jumping into something so fucked up I can't get myself back."

Their breaths mingled, rasping, short, turned on. She wanted him to shut up and kiss her. Not tell her she had to fix anything.

"I don't know how," she whispered against his lips.

He released her hands. "You know what you need to do. You just said it. Be real."

"But I can't fix everything that's messed up. I can be real with you. I can let you see me."

Gage stepped away and wiped his mouth. "You can't use me to make things better for yourself. I can't exist in some pretend world in your head. I want you, but *you* have to fix you."

Ellery didn't say anything. The empty space between them felt profound.

Gage watched her. "Do you understand? What we just did is a temporary fix to make you feel better."

"But a good one," Ellery said, feeling aggravated. Why did he have to think? She didn't want to examine anything other than the way their bodies fit each other. She needed something good, even if it was wrong. Just one little bit of something that made her forget her life.

His laugh was almost bitter. "Babe, I've known women like you. I know what you want. I can give you that, but the thing is, I'm sorta done with putting myself out there so someone like you can get off and feel good about herself. I want more in life, Ellery."

"What are you even saying?" she asked, her gaze narrowing.

"I'm saying don't use me. I'm saying fix your shit. And I'm saying when you figure out what you really want, then come see me. Until then"—he took her forearm, pulled her from the door, and opened it—"don't let the door hit you on the ass."

"Gage, I wasn't . . ." Ellery's words died because she didn't have the words. She didn't think she needed words . . . she wanted action. She wanted to capture what she'd felt beside that moon-soaked lake last night. Standing with him beside that water had been the best she'd felt in forever. She wasn't using him. Not really. He made her sound like a horrible person, and she wasn't.

"I'm not a Band-Aid, Ellery. You can't patch over the bad with someone like me. It's not fair. It's not healthy. If you want to talk, I can do that. But I'm not going to screw you and then watch you sashay away with the guy who gave you a big diamond because you're too afraid of living honestly. That's what I'm saying."

Ellery swallowed and tried to stop the angry tears gathering in her eyes. Back to square one on the crying thing. Back to the starting line on the race through a shit-strewn uphill path. Back to feeling out of control in the worst of ways. "I don't know how to do what you want me to do."

"That's the thing, babe. This isn't about what I want. This is about *you* stripping all this shit away until you're down to bare bones. This is about you examining who you are and then deciding who you truly want to be. You may not understand what I'm saying, but I hope you do. I hope you want more than what you've allowed yourself. Because, Ellery, I want you, but if I'm going to have you, I want *all* of you."

His words did something to her. *I want all of you.*

Pursing her lips together, she rounded the open door, passing by him as he held it open. "Thanks for the insight, Dr. Phil. And so you know, I wasn't trying to use you."

"Maybe not, but you would have."

At that moment she hated him because she knew he was right. Her life was in shambles, and she reached for someone to save her. The sexy bartender who seemed to see right through her could have made her feel better, but she hadn't given one thought to what it might have done to him to give her the sweet escape she needed. Her hand curled into a fist, and she thought about hitting him, which was the most idiotic response she'd ever had, but the truth he'd handed her was almost too much to take. Anger laced with humiliation trampled her common sense.

How dare he kiss her like that and then lecture her as if she were a child?

He noticed her closed fist and caught her hand before she disappeared through the doorway. Uncurling it, he reached into his back pocket and pulled out a Sharpie. Capturing the cap between his too-white teeth, he put the pen to her palm. Then he curled it back closed. "Call me when you're ready."

Then he walked back to the bar.

"In your fucking dreams," she called back, slamming the door, wanting to rub off the phone number he'd written on her skin . . . but also praying she didn't smudge the number because obviously she was completely nuts.

She stood in the foyer of the winery looking at the glass door of the gift shop. She had the irrational urge to kick the door. But then Marin, Evan's sister, appeared outside the winery's main door. She juggled two grocery bags and a ring of keys. She paused when she saw Ellery standing in the foyer, looking, no doubt, angry as a spitting cat.

The older woman opened the unlocked door, looking confused, but managed a passable smile. "Uh, hi. Can I help you?"

"Only if you have Xanax and a time machine," Ellery said, hurrying past her.

"You and me both, sweetheart," Marin called as Ellery headed for the exit.

Ellery didn't stick around to apologize. Instead she hustled toward the winding staircase that would take her back to Vine House. Where her keys sat on the dresser next to the "do me" red lipstick she'd carefully painted on last night.

Only one thought pounded in her head.

Run.

She couldn't deal with touring the vineyard with her mother like what had happened that morning was no big deal, and the thought of bumping into Clay made vomit rise in her throat. Josh would be off to Shreveport to meet his precious study group, and though her friends had made such a sweet effort on her behalf, she was almost certain they were as happy about a free weekend out of town as they were about celebrating Ellery's birthday. But the absolute biggest reason that she had to run was because she'd just thrown herself at a guy who obviously had the moral conscience of a priest.

He'd told her to get her shit together and then come see him. Ha. Screw him. Like she needed him to tell her that her life was shitty. She *knew* that.

So Ellery Witt did something wholly immature, totally selfish, and freaking spineless. She climbed into the Lexus her father had bought her and pecked out an email to Evan.

Dear Evan,

I'm not the person you think I am. I should have been more up front with you from the beginning. You're a nice guy and don't deserve to be jerked around. I am having some issues and can't pull myself away tonight. Please understand that my life is crazy right now. Has nothing to do with you. You've been great.

Dee Dee O'Hara

Ellery stared at the way she'd signed the email and wondered if she should have put something different. Not having an answer, she hit the send button, put her car into drive, and drove away from everything that knotted so hard in her life that she would never get it untangled.

CHAPTER SEVENTEEN

"Hey, boy. Did you miss me?" Daphne asked, setting the braided leash on Tippy Lou's bar and stooping to rub Jonas behind the ears. Her dog gave her a very calm lick and then sank onto his haunches and sighed. No doubt he longed to stay with the woman who fed him broth, rice, and pumpkin over the canned diet food he'd been prescribed by the vet. "Ready to go home?"

Tippy looked up from where she seemed to be balancing her checkbook. "Of course he's not ready. He's in love with me."

"Everyone is in love with someone who spoils them the way you do that dog. Thanks for letting him stay here with you."

Tippy made a chuffing noise and gave a nod. "Tea's on. Have a cup, and tell me about what's going on."

"Well, I think the best description of what is going on is a shit show."

Tippy smirked and readjusted her readers. "I surmised as much from the expression on your face. Your aura is putrid, honey."

"Yeah, I would say that's accurate." Daphne managed a wry smile as she made her way to the kitchen, Jonas dogging her steps.

"Did you find Ellery?" Tippy asked.

"Sort of." Daphne blew out a breath and sank onto the stool opposite Tippy. Jonas moved to a patch of sunlight streaming through Tippy's sliding glass door. Outside the world was bright and shiny, a foil to the storms brewing inside Daphne. She needed to stop the coming rains, but she had no clue how to abate the changing winds or redirect the dark clouds on the horizon. Ellery wasn't answering her texts, emails, or calls. "She went to Dallas. Rex called the credit card company and got them to check for activity. I think she treated herself to room service and nothing more. The last twenty-four hours have been about as awkward as I can ever remember. Eh, maybe telling my parents I was pregnant at sixteen was worse, but this was a close second. Throwing a party for someone who bails is a little uncomfortable. No one to blow out the candles."

Tippy Lou gave a flash grin, took off her readers, and set them on the bar. "Ellery's being an asshole."

Daphne shrugged. "Maybe she's got cause to be."

"That's what you think?" Tippy asked, rising and walking toward the stove, where a red teakettle happily chortled. Snagging two cups and a few tea bags, Tippy came back and poured the water. Dropping in a tea bag, she shoved it toward Daphne. A fragrant curl of steam unfurled, automatically making Daphne feel better. Somehow a cup of tea always made things look a little brighter. "How do you figure?"

"Well, for one thing, she caught me with Clay."

"Whoop-de-do. I mean, you're a person, Daphne. Not her virgin mother," Tippy said, sinking back onto her stool and pushing her checkbook aside. "Big deal. Everyone has sex . . . or at least wish they could again."

"Don't act like you're too old to have sex, Tippy. You're in your sixties. Not dead."

Tippy laughed. "I'm not too old. I'm too set in my ways. And weird. Don't forget weird."

Daphne smiled. "You're wonderfully weird."

"I've always thought so," Tippy said, flipping her gray braid across her shoulder in dramatic fashion. "But we digress. We're talking about your daughter's unwillingness to accept that you are a person. And that she herself, in fact, is a grown-up. Grown-ups don't pitch fits and run away merely because they disagree with what a person—mind you, an adult person who has every right to have some happiness—does. She has no right to approve or disapprove of your life. Thus she's being an asshole."

"Tippy, she's my daughter. And this isn't a cut-and-dried situation. There are a lot of nuances—her failure to get the internship, her fiancé ignoring her, and her father cutting her off. Add to that me messing around with Clay, and that's a lot to take in. For heaven's sake, she came into my room, and I was half-undressed with the man."

"Well, bully for you, my dear." Tippy cupped her teacup and leveled a hard stare at Daphne. That look in her eyes was one she'd used on Daphne for too many years to name. When Daphne had lost her mother when Ellery was three years old, Tippy had made a concerted effort to fill the shoes of the woman she'd been best friends with for years. Tippy and Daphne's mother, Norma, had grown up together, more sisters than neighbors. As Norma lay dying of breast cancer, she'd made Tippy Lou promise that she would look after both Daphne and Ellery. Tippy didn't make promises lightly.

Ellery loved Tippy Lou and her outrageous and horrible sense of style. One would think Ellery would find overalls and tie-dye offensive to her stylish sensibilities, but her daughter loved to visit Tippy, curling up on her green tweed couch to read feminist tomes or flip through old photo albums, smiling at the faded photos of days past. Ellery agreed with almost everything Tippy Lou suggested, whether it was voting women into political office or planting verbena in the hanging baskets on the front porch, and Tippy Lou had adored Ellery from the time she crawled across the linoleum with her hair in blonde pigtails to the time she opened her college graduation gift and cooed over the vintage

Yves Saint Laurent scarf. Still, that didn't mean that Tippy Lou didn't know Ellery's (or Daphne's) flaws and point them out whether she was asked or not.

"I didn't want her to find out about Clay, and I damn sure didn't plan to repeat the mistake I made with him," Daphne said, renewed misery pressing in on her. Everything was so . . . awful, and she didn't know what to do about it.

"So why was your shirt unbuttoned?"

"Because he was consoling me." Daphne looked at her teacup.

Tippy Lou laughed so hard she nearly fell off her stool. "Oh, well, then. Clay should get hired on at Coburn's Funeral Home. People would no doubt pay double to be consoled by him when their loved ones bite the dust."

"Stop laughing."

Tippy wiped her eyes. "Okay, okay. I'm sorry, but that was funny."

"I didn't mean he was actually consoling me. It's just that Rex showed up and acted like an ass on Friday night, embarrassing me in front of a very cute and very single vineyard owner. Then Rex invited me to sit with him at breakfast and proceeded to tell me all about his financial problems. Then—"

"Wait," Tippy interrupted, holding up a hand. "Rex, the best businessman on the face of the planet, is having financial problems? Of course, I know exactly why. It's called pussy."

"Tippy." Daphne frowned. "Stop using that language."

"Why? That's his problem. I know Cindy and her tastes. She had her hand out before she spread those legs. I heard they've been traveling all over the world wearing matching Rolexes. Ain't that cute? And let me guess . . . he wants *you* to fix it for him."

Daphne wanted to argue with Tippy but couldn't because the older woman had hit the bull's-eye. "You're good. You should have been a detective."

Tippy Lou's eyes danced. "Can you imagine me being a detective? I would end up in jail 'cause I would have to slap someone . . . or kill them. People are too stupid for me to be carrying around a gun. I'd do us all a big favor and clear out the shallow gene pools."

Daphne stared at her fingers curved around the mug. "Yeah, let's not give you a badge or gun just yet. Besides, Rex is a good business-man as long as someone is there to remind him that what is in his checkbook isn't what he is actually worth. I was the one who had to monitor his desire for a bass boat or a new hunting rifle. But anyway, Ellery overheard me fussing at Rex for paying all of her bills instead of making her do it. She was angry that we were talking about her, and then she said something that flabbergasted me. Ellery accused me of cheating on Rex."

"What?" At that Tippy finally stopped looking gleeful. Color flooded her cheeks, and anger crackled in her normally serene eyes. "How in the world did she get that idea? Oh, wait, I know."

Daphne caught Tippy Lou's eye, and in unity they both said, "Rex."

"He implied that when I was traveling for a writing conference I betrayed him. Have you seen the guys who go to children's writing conferences? I mean, there are a few decent ones in the bunch, but a Clay Caldwell they ain't."

"And Rex told Ellery that you cheated on him? I can't believe that shit."

Daphne blew out a breath and took another sip of tea. "Oh, he tried to back out of it by saying he never said for certain, but it was as plain as the nose on my face that he'd led Ellery to believe that garbage. I don't know. It just upset me that she would think that I would do something like that. How could she think I would end my marriage because I wanted to get laid?"

Tippy picked up her cup and sipped. For a few seconds, the older woman stared out the window where the autumn sunlight danced through the dying trees. "You know, Ellery has had a lot of trouble accepting your career. It's always been odd to me that a girl who claims to be progressive and forward thinking would get so caught up in a net of familiarity that she would forget it's a net."

"I don't follow."

"Ellery claims to be a feminist, but she's not putting that claim into practice. She creates the perception of a career woman determined to succeed while at the same time holding on to traditional norms. You were a mother who sacrificed all for a daughter. You worked so she could have ballet lessons, tutoring for AP calculus, and clothes for formals. Ellery liked you as you were because she understood your role. You were her mother, and that meant in itself an ultimate sacrifice for her pleasure. When you signed your first book contract, Dixie Doodle began to compete with her for your time. Traveling as Dee Dee O'Hara meant you were sharing yourself with other little girls. You weren't always at mother-daughter sorority teas, soccer playoff games, and you sometimes couldn't bake the cheer squad cookies. Maybe you stopped sending her little 'thinking of you' gifts and stopped surprising her with visits to the spa. She may have said it was no big deal when you apologized, but deep down she noticed and didn't like that you weren't the same mother you'd always been. She started building up resentment against your career. Pair that with the fact her career never left the gate, and you can see why it was easy for her to believe Rex. Easy for her to be angry at you."

Daphne sat stunned at her friend's insight. Ellery was angry because Daphne hadn't given her the attention she thought she deserved? Or angry because she thought she deserved the success Daphne had? "I always thought she was pleased about my success. I spent so much time feeling embarrassed that I wasn't a career gal like her friends' moms. Yeah, I had to sacrifice some things, but I didn't think she cared. Ellery always seemed annoyed when I volunteered or made a fuss."

Then she remembered Ellery's words from a few months ago . . . something about it being unfair that Daphne had bumbled into something she hadn't even planned for, but that someone like Ellery, who had prepped and planned for her life, had failed. Daphne had wondered about the envy laced in that comment.

"Never had kids, but I taught a few. They say one thing and mean another. They push, they pull. They'll tell you the truth you don't want to hear, and they'll lie as easy as a hot knife through butter." Tippy sat back and folded her hands over her broad stomach. Her brown eyes watched Daphne.

"Yeah, but overall my career has brought a lot of good things."

"To you. But not her. Your career changed you, and she doesn't want you to change. She wants you to be who you always were—making her cookies, married to her dad, and bending over backward to make life easy for her. It's quite natural in one way, but it's impractical for a girl who is growing into a woman. She can't have her cake and eat it, too. Right?" Tippy's eyes stayed on her, searching her emotions.

"Yeah, I get it, but she has a right to be angry about Clay."

"Ellery doesn't want Clay. So why can't you have him? I think we know this is not about age but about competition."

"If Ellery wanted Clay, she could have him." Daphne ran her finger around the lip of the cup.

"No, I don't think so. I think that's part of it. He's the only guy who ever dumped her."

Daphne thought back to that time in her life. Rex had just bought a new building and made Pinnacle a multibranch company, and she'd started taking watercolor classes since Ellery no longer needed a ride to school. It had been the first step in her new career. Ellery had a habit of falling in and out of love with various boys at the time—the child had been in love with the concept of having a boyfriend. Clay Caldwell had been the one she'd chased . . . and then wept over.

"Maybe that's true. I don't know." Daphne spread her hands wide and tried to wrap her brain around all Tippy had suggested. "But I don't want Clay. He's not the guy for me. I just had a lapse in judgment. I was upset, but the knock on the door snapped me back to reality and reminded me I don't want a relationship based solely on sexual attraction. Of course, when Clay opened the door and Ellery stood there stunned, I just wanted to die. Good Lord, her face when she realized."

"Again, that didn't give her the right to run off like a spoiled child."

Daphne pressed a hand against her chest. "Maybe not . . . or maybe so."

"Honey, you spent a lot of money on this weekend celebration, not to mention time. And I believe her friends did, too. Running away because she couldn't deal was a shitty move on Elle's part. Doesn't matter how upset she was with you."

Daphne had to acknowledge that Tippy made some good points. She definitely wore blinders when it came to her daughter. What mother didn't? But she also knew Ellery's behavior was a result of not being able to cope with what life had thrown at her. Instead of bouncing when adversity hit, Ellery had shattered and still tried to pick up the pieces. Daphne hadn't really known how to handle her daughter's disappointment, either. She'd tried to help by giving her a job, buying things for her apartment, and bolstering Ellery's ego every chance she got. She didn't want her daughter to feel like a failure or to be unhappy. That's what mothers did for their children. That was their job.

"I know you're right, but I have to figure out a way to reach her. She's so angry, and I suspect things aren't good with Josh. And now with Rex not paying her bills . . ."

"I've loved Ellery for a long time, Daph. I know how wonderful she is, and I also know how difficult she can be. She's always been worth the while, but some things she's got to figure out by herself."

"I know, but I also know that everyone needs support. That's my job—to support her."

"Actually, that's not your job, honey," Tippy said.

Daphne made a face.

"You know I'm right. If you make the way smooth, she'll never learn how to navigate the rocks and potholes. You can't fix the world for Ellery any more than your mother could have fixed it for you. We all learn to live with what life hands us, and if we're brave enough, we learn how to fight what the world gives us and forge our own paths."

"But she needs me," Daphne said, sounding almost desperate. Didn't Tippy Lou understand? Or maybe she couldn't because she'd never had a child, didn't know what ends of the earth a mother went to for her children. Daphne would sacrifice every bit of her own success to see her daughter happy.

Tippy tilted her head. "You remember when Ellery was in that LEGO phase?"

Where was Tippy Lou going this time? "Sure, I stepped on a million of those suckers that summer."

"Elle always wanted those elaborate sets, remember? The big ones that cost an arm and a leg? A few times she lost the pieces, and I can still see her wailing and flailing because the pirate ship couldn't be completed or the spaceship wasn't perfect. She'd fuss a little while, and then she'd tear it apart all the way down to that little green sheet thing. Then she would build her own project. Remember?"

"She was always so creative."

Tippy reached for Daphne's hand and gave it a squeeze. "Ellery's got some pieces missing right now, and that means she's going to have to figure out how to make something different of her life. You can't do that for her because it's her little green sheet thingy to build upon. You've got your own project, my love. So let her figure it out. You can't fix what's wrong with her this time, Mama."

Daphne felt her heart sink because she knew Tippy Lou was right. The older woman may not have had her own children, but her wide taste in reading paired with her astute observations after teaching for thirty years had given Tippy incredible insight into relationships. Her advice was usually spot-on. Daphne's mother, Norma, was likely high-fiving her old friend for the wisdom she'd imparted . . . if Daphne's mother were prone to high-fiving someone, which she was not because she was way too proper to slap hands in such an undignified manner. Well, at least she wouldn't have done it anywhere except behind closed doors. "That's good advice."

"So take it."

"I guess I will." Daphne finished the last of her tea, rose, and set the cup in the sink.

Tippy Lou cleared her throat.

Daphne turned. "I'll try really hard. I promise."

"Good."

"Let's change the subject. Did I tell you I have a date? Like a legit date?" Daphne glanced over at Tippy Lou, trying not to smile because she knew the older woman would be pleased.

"What? With who?"

Daphne grinned. "The vineyard owner."

"The one Rex embarrassed you in front of?"

"Yep. I'll be going on the first real date of my life next Friday night."

Tippy laughed. "Look at my girl growing up. Her first date."

"It's about freaking time," Daphne said, then whistled for Jonas. The mutt begrudgingly rose from his warm patch of sunshine.

Daphne totally understood wanting to bask in the rays. Something about being at Tippy Lou's made a person want to stay put and enjoy the simplicity for as long as possible. The avocado-green, harvest-gold, shagged comfort of the old farmhouse was a time warp away from the harsh reality of life outside the doorstep.

But eventually, a gal had to step outside and face the real world.

CHAPTER EIGHTEEN

Daphne,

Since you haven't answered my last few emails, I'm assuming we're moving beyond emails to texting? I'm actually good with that, but I have to say, I have enjoyed opening my in-box more in the past few months than I ever have before. There's something romantic (dare I say that?) about corresponding via the written word. Great love letters of the past have always intrigued me—there's something so intentional about writing a letter or, in our case, an email. I've felt a bit like Tom Hanks in *You've Got Mail*, wondering about you behind that screen. Still, I'm very pleased that we have moved beyond mere words to starting something more. I'm looking forward to dinner next weekend.

Best,
Evan

"You want some more pasta?" Ellery asked Josh before snapping the lid onto the bowl and setting it back in the fridge. She slid her cell phone in her pocket, berating herself for looking at email and messages when she finally had Josh's full attention. And she didn't know what to do about Evan. Obviously her mother and Evan were going out, so it wouldn't be long before the man figured out that he really didn't know Daphne. And that the person he'd been emailing was a phony.

"No, thanks. Dinner was good, honey," he said, sipping the last of the wine they'd opened. For once, they had eaten dinner together at their pretty glass-topped bistro in the nook of their town house. Ellery couldn't remember if they had ever used it after moving in. Usually the table held junk mail and Josh's study materials. She should have cleared it off, bought flowers, and set out real dishes before now, and maybe they would have had more dinners together.

Or not.

Josh didn't seem to be swayed about where he ate. Only by how much studying he needed to do. Still, she was happy that her renewed commitment to the plan was already working. She had assumed he wouldn't eat dinner with her and had set a place for one at the table. When she'd popped the cork on her discount wine, he'd wandered into the dining area and sat down at the table as if it were an everyday routine. In fact, she'd had to scramble to set a place for herself next to him at the table.

"I'm glad you liked it. Thanks for eating with me." She squirted the counter with cleaner and studied the man, who had come home earlier than expected. He'd seem preoccupied but had made a few jokes and eaten all the grilled chicken and veggies she'd picked up at a local Mediterranean restaurant.

"Sure. I'm sorry I haven't been home much. I'll try harder to study here more."

Ellery paused, surprised at his words. "That would be good. I've missed you."

He turned his head and smiled at her. Then and there she remembered why she'd fallen for him. His blue eyes were so full of . . . concern? Apology? She wasn't sure.

"I know it's been rough these past few months, Elle. I wish I could go back and do some things differently. This med school thing has been harder than I expected. I haven't adjusted well, and that's made it hard on you."

His words made her lower her eyes.

Josh *had* hurt her . . . but she'd created something destructive with that hurt.

Maybe now was the time to reveal that she'd been so lonely she'd started emailing a stranger and then proceeded to carry on a secret relationship with him. She'd just read Evan's email and knew that ticking time bomb was approaching zero. And if she admitted to a clandestine relationship with Evan, should she also admit she'd kissed Evan's nephew? Twice? And liked it so much she wished there had been a third time? How far was she willing to go to demonstrate exactly how lonely, unhappy, and . . . full of doubt she'd been?

Because she could no longer ignore whatever Gage had started in her when they had kissed. She didn't want to want Gage or to think about the way he felt against her, but she couldn't seem to control her thoughts. He was like the flu—she could tell herself she wasn't getting it, but she was. Those feelings scared her because nothing about Gage was in her plan for her life. Neither was snooping on computers or emailing handsome vineyard owners. Nothing she'd been doing for the past three months was good for her or her relationship with Josh.

"It *has* been hard, Josh. I can't lie. I feel disconnected, and I don't know how to get back what we had. It worries me. I wonder if I'm what you really want."

Josh gave her a sad smile. "It's not that bad, is it? I know I've been preoccupied, but I didn't realize how unhappy you've been until you bailed on your party. I need to pay better attention to you."

Like she was a dog or something. *Let me carve out fifteen minutes a day to walk you and play fetch.* So her crazed run from reality was what had done it for him, huh? Nothing like some bad behavior and drama to make people sit up and pay attention. Ol' Ellery, the squeaky wheel.

Of course, her flight from the weekend had done it for her, too, but she hadn't been able to turn the car around. She kept driving into the sun, heading west, imagining she was like one of those women who'd run from trying circumstances a few hundred years ago, escaping to a new future in a new frontier, embracing the hope a new life could bring. Of course, many of those pioneers had ended up dying from dysentery, so there was that. But Ellery couldn't go back and face her mother, her father, her fiancé, and the man who'd made her feel like a cat turd on a fancy deli sandwich. She just could not do it.

So she'd checked into a hotel near the airport, just in case Dallas didn't prove far enough. Then she'd shut off her phone, climbed in the big, soft bed, and turned on the Hallmark Channel. Because she needed to believe that life could be exactly like those movies. Perfect hair, beautiful autumn leaves, and a cowboy with a farm that needed a decorator who was spunky and made him forget his loss. Why couldn't life be like a Hallmark movie, huh?

Five hours later, she'd shut off the television, ordered a double cheeseburger with fries and a piece of cheesecake, and taken an hour soak in the Jacuzzi tub. Then she climbed back into the rumpled bed and slept for nine straight hours. When she awoke, everything was clear.

Last year when Josh had gotten accepted into medical school in Shreveport and told her he wanted to build a future with her, she'd formulated her plan. She would graduate, make the move to NYC, and spend a weekend or two a month with Josh. After a year, she'd net a fabulous job in NYC or parlay her experience into a job closer to Josh. Her dream was to have her own line, of course. She'd do something like Reese Witherspoon had done with Draper James—create a line that was fun, southern, and wearable—but might have to wait a few years before that could happen. By that time, she and Josh would be married, he'd be in residency, and they would be living a fabulous life somewhere that was not Shreveport.

What an idiot she'd been.

The most important elements in the equation were she and Josh. She should have been focusing on their future together, but she'd let herself get sidetracked by a healthy dose of self-pity and an inappropriate relationship with a) an older man who thought she was her mom and b) a hot bartender who thought she was a spoiled brat. Oh, and her world had been shaken by that video on Josh's computer, of course, but she was nearly certain that it was some kind of hoax. Or curiosity. So she decided to regather her intentions and make a new plan. She got dressed, sat down, grabbed a Hilton notepad, and started writing.

Eventually she settled on four goals:

One: She needed to recognize that anything worth having required sacrifice. Ellery needed to be more patient with Josh and herself.

Two: She needed to come clean to Evan about her deception. No more sneaking around and taking pleasure in something she had no business pursuing.

Three: She would take a break from her parents. That meant paying her own bills (somehow) and working from home in order to figure out how she wanted to handle her mother and this whole Clay thing. She was not going to rush into confrontation.

Four: She needed to be more practical when it came to her career. That meant opening herself to something outside of fashion.

Gage wasn't on the list because he could not be there. His role had been to wake her from the destructive path she was on. If she had been in her right frame of mind, she wouldn't have even looked twice at him, much less kissed him. She would erase him from her life because that was how it had to be. She was in control of her mind, and she refused to remember how he felt, smelled, tasted, or any other stupid sense that wanted to remember him. She'd already washed his number from her hand . . . and she *would* tear up the paper she'd written it on.

And that was that.

After writing down her intentions, she'd checked out of the hotel, texted a generic group text, I'm sorry—wasn't feeling well, to her family and friends, and then driven back to Shreveport determined to get her life back. When she arrived, she went to the market and bought sensible groceries and a sad half-price bouquet she'd spruced up with red maple leaves and goldenrod clipped from a field near their town house. Then she made dinner and served a subpar wine that was good enough but easy on the pocketbook.

Ellery Witt wasn't a quitter.

Josh smiled at her and patted his lap. "Come here, beautiful."

Ellery sank onto his lap and looped her arms around his neck. "I think we both have to be intentional with one another. Just think about each other's feelings a bit more."

He looked up at her, his expression warm. "That's a good plan."

"I'm good at plans." She kissed him, her heart knitting itself back together with her intentions and the way he squeezed her against him. They would be okay.

Except his kiss didn't feel like Gage's. It felt . . . forced.

No. She wasn't supposed to compare Gage to Josh. She loved Josh. He was her future, and Gage was nothing but a moment of insanity. *Erase Gage already.*

Ellery broke the kiss and looked into Josh's soft blue eyes. "Before we close this conversation and you go back to studying, I have to ask you something that's sort of uncomfortable for me."

"What?"

She sucked in a deep breath and exhaled. "Why do you have a video of a guy giving another guy a blow job on your computer?"

She felt Josh's body tighten before he shoved her off his lap. "What the fuck, Elle? You were on my computer?"

Ellery turned toward him. She'd expected him to be angry, of course, but not this upset. He was supposed to laugh and make a joke of it. "I used your computer to check my email Friday night."

His eyes were no longer soft. "And what? You thought you would snoop around? Look at my stuff?"

"Not really. I just happened upon the video. I didn't know what it was."

He swallowed hard. "Well, I don't even know what video you're talking about. I don't have anything like that on my computer." He shoved the chair back, looking livid, but she also noticed he didn't look at her.

"I mean, if you like, um, stuff that's . . . different, well, I think fantasies are good. Healthy."

"Are you shitting me? I'm not into . . . that." Josh shoved a hand into his hair, and his face narrowed even more. "Okay, first, I don't know what video you're talking about. Second, if that was on my laptop, someone else put it on there. Maybe as a joke or something."

Ellery didn't say anything, mostly because he reminded her of the kids she used to babysit when they lied about drinking cola before bed or hitting their brother. She was almost certain he knew exactly what she was talking about, but she wasn't sure. "I'm not mad. I just needed to ask you because we haven't been connecting, uh, sexually, that is."

"So you know, I haven't had sex with you because I've been stressed. My hair is falling out, and I can't concentrate on anything other than stupid school. I can't believe you're accusing me of . . . whatever it is you're accusing me of."

"I'm sorry. It's just you don't seem to be interested in me anymore. And then I found that video and my mind started jumping to conclusions, wondering if you're—"

"Gay? Is that what you're implying?" He stood rigid, flushed and as angry as she'd ever seen him. "What makes you think I want to be with a guy, huh? Is there anything about me that makes you think I am gay?"

Ellery shrank from his anger. "You're making me seem crazy. I'm not. Any woman would ask about finding such a thing on her fiancé's computer. Pair that with the fact we haven't had sex in almost three months, and you can see that I might be worried."

"You want sex? Let's go right now," he said, grabbing her arm and pulling her toward the stairs.

"Stop, Josh. That's not what I'm saying," she said, jerking her arm away. She wished she hadn't brought it up. They were finally having a nice evening, and he was spending quality time with her. Why had she asked him about the video now? It could have waited.

"No. Come on. Let's do it," he insisted, tugging his shirt overhead before unbuttoning his jeans.

"Stop. I don't want to have sex right now. I just want to be assured that you still love me and that everything we have planned is still on track. After everything you just said, how can you be mad because I asked a question any normal person would ask? Because I doubt how you feel about me?"

Josh paused and stared off into space, taking deep breaths. Finally, he looked at her. "I want what we've always planned. I'm sorry that I have been so obsessed with school. I want to do the best I can for us."

"That's all I needed to hear, Josh. This weekend was a disaster and made me wonder if this is what you really want." Doubt kept coming at her even as she wanted to cling to relief at Josh's denial.

"I know, and I'm sorry. I saw the bustier and fishnets and wished I had clued in better to what you needed. You shouldn't have to tell me." He rubbed his hand over his face. "I want to be the man you need, Elle, but I'm struggling with so much right now."

Her spidey senses tingled at those words. Was he saying . . . that he couldn't be what she needed? Were his doubts about school or her? He looked so miserable standing there with his shirt balled in his hand, his eyes so sad. "Josh, you're what I have always wanted."

She went to him and wrapped her arms around him.

"I'm sorry, Elle," he said, folding her into his embrace. "I'll try harder. Things are going to be okay. We got this."

Then he gave her a sweet kiss that promised her he meant what he said, and for those seconds, Ellery believed everything would work out exactly as they had planned.

Josh broke the kiss. "I don't want to fight anymore. Why don't we watch a movie?"

"You don't have to study tonight?" Ellery asked, almost afraid that he was joking. He'd complained about the time he'd had to spend away at the vineyard. A big quiz and something else that needed his absolute focus. So how did he suddenly have time for a movie?

"I do. Since I slept so much last night, I figured I could study after you went to sleep." Josh slapped her bottom and dropped his arms.

"What about Drew and your group?"

A twist of Josh's lips told her all she needed to know. He was peeved about something. "They can fend for themselves."

"Uh-oh," Ellery said, rising and running a hand through Josh's pretty hair. "What happened?"

"Nothing you have to worry about. I'm just tired of caring about things more than Drew does. And the others, too. They don't seem to be as serious as I am."

Ellery smiled. "They don't know how determined you are to reach your goal."

He caught her hand and brushed her knuckles with his lips. "I don't want to talk about it. I want to sit on the couch with my girl and watch something totally stupid and inane."

She set aside the knowledge that Josh only wanted to hang with her because he was upset with Drew and the study group and embraced the happiness that he was going to spend several uninterrupted hours with her . . . on the couch . . . snuggling and eating gummy bears. Because that's how they rolled. "I can make that happen."

Josh reached over and grabbed the bag of gummy bears from the snack basket beside the pantry door. "Let's get to it, and then maybe you can find that bustier and stockings. I'm feeling less stressed tonight."

So far her plan was working better than she could have ever expected . . . and all she'd done was put flowers on the table rather than her expectations.

Yeah, this patience thing totally worked.

CHAPTER NINETEEN

Daphne smoothed the shirt she'd finally settled on over her jeans one last time and then fluffed her hair. Her stomach knocked against her spine in a vicious nervousness that she'd only felt a few other times. She was going on a date tonight.

Her first real date.

She and Rex had never really dated. They had sat next to each other in geometry, a happenstance that Rex had taken full advantage of by looking at her papers, but they had never gone on a first date. Mostly because kids in school didn't really date. They hung out and hooked up, but a real ring-the-doorbell date never happened for Daphne.

Until now.

"You don't look like you're forty," she said to herself in the mirror. Of course, she wasn't forty yet. She had a few more weeks in her thirties. Still, she needed to bolster her ego because she felt more like fifty after the last week of sleeplessness and angst.

Daphne had changed her clothes a dozen times. At first she'd pulled on her favorite black dress and added a cardigan, but that had looked stodgy. She'd shucked that for a fire-engine-red shirt with a plunging neckline and paired it with a short black suede skirt. Knee boots in a matching suede had looked perfect, but then she wondered if it looked like she was trying too hard. Not to mention she didn't want to exude a vibe that she "put out" on the first date . . . though she had, in fact, weeks ago put out on the first date. If cooking "family" dinner, drinking too much wine, and having sex 2.5 times could be called a date. So she took that off and tossed it atop the growing pile of discarded choices.

Finally, she'd settled on a pair of tight, distressed-denim jeans rolled to show off cute camel leather booties. She'd added a faded-rose tunic and a fun crushed-velvet scarf that was soft gold. Ellery had helped her pick it out on their last shopping trip. Back when they were speaking to each other.

Daphne's heart sank when she thought about her daughter, but she quickly dashed the sadness away. Tonight she wasn't going to think about the choices she'd made that had led to her being estranged from Ellery. She was going to focus on dinner with a handsome, successful businessman she hadn't had to swipe right for.

The doorbell rang, and Jonas did his insane-barking thing.

Daphne sucked in a breath and left her bedroom, shooing Jonas away from the door. "Get back, Jonas. Back."

Then she opened the door to Evan McCallum, who stood looking gorgeous and clutching a bouquet of wildflowers.

"Darn it, sorry about the dog. He's a bit protective until he knows you," Daphne said, frowning as Jonas sniffed Evan's pants and made little growling noises. "Jonas, here."

Her hound slunk to her side.

Evan smiled. "It's good he's protective. I don't mind the man of the house giving me the business. The dog *is* a guy, right?" He held out his hand to Jonas and let the dog smell him. One second later, Jonas's tail wagged, and a second after that he was wriggling against Evan's legs.

"He approves, and you now have a friend for life," Daphne said with a chuckle.

Evan straightened from petting Jonas and extended the flowers. "I tried to think of something less traditional, but I know my wife always liked getting flowers."

He stopped after saying *my wife*, and his cheeks reddened.

Daphne took the flowers. "Evan, it's okay. We both have a past, and you didn't mess up by mentioning your wife. Come on in. I'll put these in water and grab my jacket."

Evan exhaled. "Whew, I almost blew it. This is the first date I've gone on in a while."

"You did not blow it, and the nervousness is mutual," Daphne said, walking toward the kitchen, which was almost finished. Evan's faux pas had actually helped the butterflies in her stomach to subside. They were both anxious and in uncharted waters. There was comfort in that.

He followed her to the kitchen, which still had a few unfinished cabinets and a half-completed floor. "Wow, I saw the sign advertising your house for sale. This looks terrific."

Daphne went to the storage area off the laundry room and found a crystal vase that had belonged to her mother. "Thank you. Since it's just Jonas and me, I am moving in town to a smaller house in a gated neighborhood. Time for another family to enjoy this place."

"Well, it's a terrific house."

"Thank you," Daphne said, filling the vase and glancing around the space that looked far too trendy. She preferred the simple kitchen she'd started her married life in, but she would never tell her Realtor that. "It belonged to my grandparents once upon a time. I've lived here a long time, and it's hard to say goodbye, but it doesn't make sense to stay here by myself."

She placed the bouquet in the vase and pulled the flowers apart to form an artful arrangement. Setting them in the middle of the island, she turned to Evan. "Ready?"

"I've been waiting to take you to dinner for a long time," he said.

Again, his words were odd. She'd known him for all of a week, but he acted as if they were old friends. Perhaps she could broach it at dinner and find out if they'd met somewhere that she'd forgotten. Daphne fetched the gray cashmere jacket her friend Karyn had sent her for her birthday last year and the small Tory Burch clutch that Ellery had no longer wanted because everyone else had one.

Fifteen minutes and lots of small talk later, they arrived at Sutton's Steakhouse. Daphne had eaten there several times and loved the old-school ambience with the honeycomb floors of black and white and the gleaming, dark hardwood and brass. The restaurant had an elegance that wasn't fussy, and the food matched the vibe by being elegant, substantial, and well portioned. The maître d' showed them to a cozy leather half-circle booth and delivered the wine list with a flourish.

Daphne immediately handed the list to Evan. "You're the expert. Feel free to show off."

He flashed her a smile and shook his napkin onto his lap. Cracking his knuckles in exaggerated fashion, he perused the extensive list. "Let's see what we have here."

While Evan debated between a 2015 red blend and a 2016 cabernet, she scanned the room. Full house tonight, but she didn't see anyone she knew. Which was a relief. Oddly enough, she didn't feel ready to chat with an acquaintance and have to introduce Evan. It all felt too new.

Evan ordered the wine and appetizer and then turned to her. "So tell me about your new book."

Frankly, no one ever wanted to talk about her writing and illustrating. Oh, they feigned interest, but usually the only people who ever debated plots or illustrations with her were other writers. "Well, I have the Mardi Gras book coming out in January. I'm doing a book tour in a week for my Christmas book. That came out last year, but my publisher set me up on a small regional tour because we're about to announce the network deal. Book tours are lots of fun because I really get to connect with the kids, but they are tough on my creativity because while I can do some work on the road, most of it is done at home in my studio. I'm more comfortable there."

"So do you paint or draw the actual illustration? I mean, like on an easel."

"No, I use mostly digital illustration, so it's like a big, blank page on a giant iPad, if you can imagine that. I still do the drawing, but I can easily manipulate the illustration, changing colors and moving images. It's really cool."

"How did you get into it?" he asked, nodding at the sommelier who arrived and presented the bottle. The man uncorked the bottle, offered the cork, and then poured a small amount in the glass. Evan studied the cork and then accepted the glass. He swirled it, narrowed his eyes, and then lifted it to his nose, breathing deeply. A quick taste, a weird chewing-looking motion, and then a sharp jerk of his head. "That will do fine."

Daphne knew she stared, but she found his routine fascinating. "So that's how it's done."

Evan smiled sheepishly. "Sorry. It's automatic with me now."

She accepted a glass and sipped the full-bodied cabernet. "Nice."

"Thanks. Now back to how you got started."

"Well, when Ellery was in middle school, I went to a local college for graphic design. Just a community college. I loved to draw as a child, and my art teacher in high school believed in my talent. I took some design classes, some painting classes, and enrolled in an online illustrator program to learn the various mediums. My hope was to parlay my degree into doing some graphic art designs, but I loved writing stories and drawing the illustrations that helped to tell the story. I dreamed up this dog and made little stories for the preschool kids I worked with as a teacher's aide. I never imagined my hobby of writing silly stories for my kids at work would take me to where I am now. I was truly an overnight success. It was sheer luck, really."

"And talent, too?" Evan arched an eyebrow.

"A bit of that, but mostly luck. I made Dixie Doodle books for my kids for Christmas one year. One of the parents had a family member who works at Little Red Barn books, and she sent it to her. She loved it. Suddenly I went from hobbyist to professional author. It was crazy."

Their appetizer arrived, and Evan set an empty plate in front of her. "I hope you like crab. I forgot to ask. See? I'm rusty."

"Ditto for me," she said with a smile. "And I love crab. So tell me more about you. I read about the vineyard and how your father bought the land thinking he'd raise cattle, but tell me about how you got involved with growing grapes."

"You already know. I think that was one of the first things we talked about when you told me you liked my wines."

Daphne tried not to look confused, but she knew he noticed.

His whiskey eyes met hers, and she knew that he knew that she had no clue what he was talking about. Evan cut a piece of the crab cake and set it on his plate. "We've been emailing each other for several months. I wrote you back at the end of July about speaking at Poppy's school in March, and we struck up a friendship. Email exchanges five or six times a week. I'm now sensing that you know nothing about this."

Daphne grappled with the information he'd imparted. So much now made sense—the flowers, the note, the warmth that first day at the vineyard. "I'm sorry to say that I've never seen an email from you, Evan. Ellery has been working as my assistant."

He set his fork down, and she could see he was upset. "I wondered why you acted so . . . distant when I was around you. I thought it was because sometimes when you meet someone who you've only known online, it's awkward, but we shared so much about our lives over the past few months. I told you about . . . so much."

Daphne took a bigger gulp of her wine and tried to wrap her mind around the fact Ellery had been emailing Evan. Her daughter hadn't said a thing about a relationship between her and one of Daphne's readers. Ellery had never been one for idle chitchat or to hold secrets. If anything, her daughter could be too forthcoming. That she had carried on what sounded like a fairly intimate friendship with another man while pretending to be Daphne was so incredibly odd and very out of character. But then again, Ellery had been doing a lot of things out of character lately.

And perhaps Daphne was the pot calling the kettle black.

"I don't know what to say, Evan. I mean, I thought it was strange how familiar you acted with me last weekend. Like the flowers and the personal note at breakfast. And every time we ran into each other, you were so familiar."

Evan shook his head. "I thought maybe you'd changed your mind about liking me, but then when we went for a run, I felt like you were somewhat interested. Then there was the weird email about you not being the person I thought you were. I mean, now I get it, but I'm feeling really embarrassed right now."

Daphne covered his hand with hers. His hands were large, warm, and if hands could be sexy and masculine, Evan McCallum could corner the market. "Please don't. I was interested. I mean, I am interested." When she realized how her words sounded, she felt a blush climb into her cheeks.

Evan looked at her. "So I don't really know you."

Daphne drew back her hands. "No, I guess not. I think Ellery's the person you've been emailing."

For a few seconds, neither of them spoke. *Awkward* wasn't the word for what Daphne felt, and she wished she and Ellery were talking so she could find out why in the hell her daughter had done such a thing without telling her, especially since they went to the man's vineyard and met him several times. Evan had asked her out, thinking they already had something between them. She'd been flattered that such a good-looking, successful man was interested in her, but now she knew he was interested in Ellery . . . who had been duping him.

God, what a tangle.

"Isn't Ellery engaged?" Evan asked.

"That she is."

"Hmm" was all Evan managed.

The waiter arrived. "Is everything satisfactory?"

Evan issued a dry laugh. "The wine and appetizer are fine. The rest of it, we're still deciding."

Daphne looked down at her half of the uneaten crab cake and wondered how to handle such a situation. She had no idea if Evan was angry or if he even liked her enough to continue the evening. If he thought he was embarrassed and at a loss, he didn't have to look far to find someone who felt the exact same way. Still, she liked him and had hoped that he might be a possibility. Lord knew she needed something good on the horizon of her personal life.

"Shall I come back?" the waiter asked.

Daphne looked at Evan, hoping he wasn't going to ask for the check. "I am ready. If you are, Evan."

Evan hesitated for a few seconds before looking up from his menu. His gaze caught and held hers, and she could see all his emotions whirling within the depths. She was fairly certain hers carried the same combination of doubt and hope. Finally, he nodded. "I think I am, too."

Inwardly, Daphne sighed with relief. At least her first date wouldn't end up like something in a *Cosmopolitan* dating article titled "He Thought He Was Going to Dinner With My Daughter! OMG!"

After they both ordered a steak, the waiter left. Evan drew in a deep breath and blew it out. "You know, this is a strange situation, but it would have been even worse if I had asked via email and your daughter had shown up. At least it's with you."

"I'm not sure if that's a compliment or not."

"It is. The moment I saw you, I was into you. Of course, I thought we already had a relationship, so I was prepared to like you." He gave her a smile that smoothed the wrinkles inside her. "That's probably a bit too much to think about."

Daphne gave him a soft smile. "It's not. I am happy that when you met me, the real me, you liked me enough to ask me out. I don't know why Ellery did what she did. She's going through some things right now, and we're not really on the best terms. But the truth is I'm very happy to be here with you."

His gaze reflected pleasure at her words. "Okay, so since we truly don't know that much about each other after all, I guess we get to do this whole first-date thing the way it was intended. So, baby . . . what's your sign?"

Daphne managed a laugh. "My birthday is next month. I'm turning forty, by the way. I'm approaching over the hill, so if you want to ask for those steaks to go, I'll understand."

"I don't eat cold steak, so you're stuck with me on this date. Besides, you look maybe thirty-one or thirty-two years old. If that."

"But I didn't get carded," she said.

"Well, it's a classy restaurant. They would never do something so lowbrow," he said with another grin.

"And if they *had* carded me?"

"Then they can see, quite obviously, that you look too young to drink."

"Good answer." She laughed.

The early discomfort began to melt, and for the next hour and a half, they chatted about everything from the upcoming holidays to places they'd traveled to favorite actors. By the time the check came, Daphne had almost forgotten about the odd circumstance that had brought them here. She'd had such a good time, enjoyed his charm and humor, and felt nice, warm fuzzies when she thought about the possibility of a good night kiss. It was a good first date.

Until Ellery walked by.

And saw them.

They were just about to slide from the booth and leave when Ellery walked by with two of her friends from work. They'd obviously just gotten off because they were dressed to sell.

Daphne opened her mouth to say hello but snapped it closed when she saw the coldness in her daughter's eyes. Total disdain layered with surprise, likely at seeing her mother with Evan, shone within the depths. Then her daughter turned her head and kept walking, giving her own mother a direct cut.

The hurt was like an ice pick plunged into the depths of Daphne's heart.

She must have made a noise, because Evan, who was smart enough to figure out the dynamics on display, stood and assisted her from the booth, taking her elbow and then tucking her close in a semihug that normally would have been the beginning of something flirty and intimate, but instead felt more like someone tossing her a life jacket in a sudden storm.

"Let's just go," he said, his voice tender.

He felt sorry for her.

It was in that moment that anger planted itself in her soul. Or perhaps the seeds were already there, sown by too many years of making the most of every situation, smoothing everyone else's ruffled feathers, and pretending her feelings weren't the most important. She'd spent last weekend lying for her daughter after she abandoned her own damned party. Then she'd spent the week getting terse emails and texts from her "assistant," who no longer saw the value in working from her mother's home and refused to discuss anything more personal than hotel accommodations for the tour. The week had been strained, and Daphne's nerves felt like taut piano wire awaiting the first strike.

She wanted to march over to her daughter, who sat with her friends, smiling at the waiter in that charming manner that rendered her the best service, and ask her how she was paying for dinner at an expensive restaurant when she had crushing credit card debt. Or ask her why she had lied to Evan and strung him along on a relationship that couldn't exist. Or . . . or . . .

She shouldn't. It was striking low and being petty.

But then she looked again at the sympathy in Evan's eyes.

"Let me just say hello to my daughter," she said before she could think better of it.

Straightening her shoulders, she plastered a smile on her face and walked toward their table.

"Hi, Mrs. Witt," Rachel said. The rather plain girl had come to the party last weekend, but Daphne hadn't spoken to her beyond a polite hello and "Pass the chardonnay." The other woman had been there, too, but Daphne couldn't recall her name.

"Hello, girls. I saw you pass by and thought I would say hello," Daphne said.

Ellery studied the menu and didn't look up.

"This is Fiona. I don't think you met her last weekend. She works at Selber's at the makeup counter. This is Ellery's mom." Rachel looked at Ellery, her face reflecting confusion at Ellery ignoring her.

"Rachel, are you having the wedding-cake martini?" Ellery said, not bothering to acknowledge Daphne. Her slight was as plain as the font on the menu.

A worm of ire coiled round Daphne's wounded heart. "Yes, you should all have that one. It was delicious. Well, I should get back to my date. Just wanted to say hello. Nice to meet you, Fiona. Have fun!"

Daphne hadn't had a martini, but they didn't have to know that.

"I'm sure he'll be the one having fun later. Or is he too old for you?" Ellery looked up at her with cold blue eyes.

Any other time, Daphne would have shattered at the one person she adored treating her with such disdain, but anger at her daughter overshadowed the pain. Daphne looked over her shoulder at the handsome man waiting apprehensively near the exit. "Oh no. I like them all ages, and that one will do nicely. I guess I should thank you, darling, for doing all the legwork for me."

Then she spun on the heel of her boot and walked away as calmly as she could manage. Beneath her frozen facade was a tumultuous tsunami of emotion, but she wasn't letting anyone in that restaurant know, especially not Ellery.

"You're welcome, whore," Ellery called.

A clattering of forks, a clink of glasses, the hum of low conversation all faded to silence. This time it was as if an arrow had thumped into her back, skewering her, making her steps almost falter. But she didn't acknowledge the insult hurled at her. No. Daphne refused to give her daughter the satisfaction. She kept walking because if she could just reach the man standing near the foyer with a befuddled and irritated look on his face, she would be okay. Just ten steps. Eight. Five. Two.

"Is everything okay, madam?" the maître d' asked, stepping in front of her, glancing over her shoulder to where Ellery sat with her friends.

"Everything's fine, but I think my daughter has had too much to drink. You probably shouldn't serve her any more alcohol." She looked at Evan, begging herself not to crack. "Shall we?"

His expression was dark, his gaze unfathomable, but he took her elbow once again, tucked her in close, and grabbed a mint. "Let's roll."

When they stepped outside, Daphne started to tremble. "I'm so sorry I caused a scene. I shouldn't have gone over there." At those words, her teeth began to chatter.

Evan pulled her to him and wrapped his arms around her, holding her close. The pimply valet drivers darted around them like planes circling a landing field. She pressed her cheek to his jacket and tried not to cry. A single tear escaped, a rebellious droplet determined to betray her mask of control.

"It's okay, Daphne. She had no right to say that."

Evan couldn't know that Daphne had slept with Ellery's ex-boyfriend or that her daughter had caught her with Clay, shirt half-unbuttoned and lips swollen from his kisses. Daphne giving in to her insecurities (and renewed sex drive) had created a huge fracture across the bridge of ice she and Ellery had skated on for the past few months. Or maybe that bridge was missing pieces. Perhaps it was completely gone.

Her daughter had just called her a whore in the middle of a restaurant.

That bridge was definitely gone.

"Thank you," she whispered against a cashmere scarf that smelled like English Leather. She knew it wasn't English Leather because what man under the age of fifty wore English Leather, but it was similar to what her grandfather had worn—familiar, warm, but not exactly grandfatherly.

Evan released her and handed the claim ticket to one of the valets buzzing around them. "Let's get out of here."

Daphne had never agreed with a suggestion more.

CHAPTER TWENTY

Dear Evan,

By this time I'm sure you know that I am not the creator of Dixie Doodle and am instead the assistant who answers fan mail. I have no good reason for doing what I did other than I liked you, and your emails gave me something to look forward to at the end of each day. My life hasn't been going according to plan, and it was sheer selfishness and weakness that made me do what I did. You made me feel normal at a time that is anything but in my life. I sincerely apologize. You're a very nice man and deserve the truth.

With that being said, if you're going to date my mother, you should ask her about what led me to call her that terrible word. I am sorry about doing

it in a public setting, but I stick to my belief that
she is indeed a whore.

Most sincerely,
Ellery Witt

Ellery pressed the send button and glanced at her friends, who had
gone back to talking about the upcoming holiday work schedule that
had been released. The waiter had politely but firmly refused to serve
her anything other than iced tea, which was rather odd, but she figured
Daphne had something to do with that. Or perhaps she'd been cut off
before she'd begun because of her outburst.

She supposed she deserved as much.

She, Rachel, and Fiona had decided to grab appetizers and martinis
after a long day, and Fiona had suggested Sutton's Steakhouse because
she was on the prowl and wanted a few wingmen to fly with her in the
adjoining bar later. Ellery had wanted to go home and pull on jammies,
but she knew Josh was studying and would be home late. So she reluc-
tantly agreed to the peer pressure exerted by her coworkers.

When she'd seen her mother sitting with Evan, it was like gasoline
being poured onto smoldering ashes. Swoosh! Her thoughts tripped
over each other. What the hell? Evan had a connection with *her*. Not
Daphne. Yeah, he didn't know that, but that didn't matter. Ellery was
the person he'd shared his troubles and dreams with. Not Daphne. Her
mother didn't get to have him. Not after what she'd done.

Ellery had pressed her fingernails into her palms and forced herself
to remain calm. After her initial reaction of sheer rage, she'd felt a bit of
relief. Evan and her mother would have figured everything out by now.
Now at least everything was out in the open. But then her mother had
approached their table. Ellery had tried not to be provoked, but when
she'd looked up at her mother, the glint in Daphne's eyes paired with
Evan standing in the background looking concerned had made Ellery

so angry that those horrible words flew out of her mouth before she could stop herself.

But she meant them. Or at least she meant the whore part.

"I can't believe Susan got both Black Friday and every Saturday in December off. What kind of bullshit is that?" Fiona drawled, sipping her martini and spearing another olive from their cheese board. "Ellery, snap out of it. Your mom's gone, and the maître d' has stopped shooting us dirty looks."

Ellery looked at Fiona. "I'm sorry. I shouldn't have come."

Rachel shot a sympathetic smile at her. "That was a little dramatic, but don't worry, we'll still hang with you. Come on, stop moping. You're a tough cookie, Elle."

Was she? She didn't feel that way. She felt more like a cookie that crumbled at the slightest pressure, leaving pieces of herself behind. Beneath her bluster was a blister, rubbed raw and never healing. How did one heal a blister? Oh yeah, they stuck to the stupid plan and stopped wearing things that made the blister. "Yeah, well, sometimes tough cookies crumble. It's been a suck-ass year so far."

"Says she with this on her finger," Fiona teased, picking up Ellery's hand so her diamond engagement ring caught the light above and looked extra bling-y. The classic, princess-cut diamond seemed to be mocking her because her one night with Josh had yielded no sex or intimacy. After the movie, he'd followed her upstairs, tucked her into bed, and avoided any attempt to talk him into staying in bed with her. He'd gone to study. She'd spent the rest of the week as she'd spent the others—alone and stir crazy—trying to stick to her plan of not complaining and giving Josh the room he needed.

And trying not to think about stupid Gage and the number she'd copied from her hand onto hotel stationery and slid into her wallet. The paper she was supposed to tear up and toss.

But didn't.

"Ha," Ellery said, pulling her hand away. "That's the only good thing about this year."

"You graduated," Rachel pointed out with a sigh. "I can't wait until I have a diploma."

"Stop changing your major and you will," Fiona said good-naturedly. Then she glanced over at Ellery. "I know you're pissed at your mom for whatever reason, but who was that hottie hotster with her?"

Ellery shrugged. "Just some guy. She's dating again. Obviously."

"Is that why you're mad?" Rachel asked.

"No," Ellery said, looking off, wishing like hell she could talk her waiter into a drink. She needed one. Or five. She waved at their waiter. He ignored her. "I'm not mad she's dating."

"Then why call her a whore?" Rachel asked.

Ellery leveled a glare at her friend. "I told y'all I didn't want to talk about it."

"But talking about things that bother you with your friends is how you get past it," Rachel said, sipping her vodka tonic and giving Ellery an earnest look.

But they weren't her friends. Not really. But then again, maybe they were. The girls who'd always been there for her seemed to have moved on with their lives. In fact, Madison had sent her a text saying she wasn't ready to talk to Ellery yet for bailing on the weekend like a "spoiled child." Maybe it was true that she was still a spoiled child, but Ellery preferred to think of her fleeing to Dallas as self-preservation. It wasn't like the party didn't go on without her. She knew it had because her mother had texted her pictures designed, no doubt, to make her feel guilty. Ellery *did* feel guilty, but she also knew that if she had stayed, something bad would have happened. She might have said something she couldn't take back.

Then again, she wasn't certain she could fix what her earlier words had done.

Whore. God, such an ugly word.

"Fine. My mother slept with a younger guy, someone almost my age, and then there's just a lot of other stuff. Stuff with my dad. With Josh. With my future. Is that what you wanted to know? That my life is falling apart, and the one person I should be able to turn to is my mom, but she's, like, way over there on the other side, and I can't even begin to figure out how to reach her or if I even care to. Because I'm pissed at her. And at my dad. And at myself for the decisions I've been making lately."

Rachel and Fiona probably hadn't expected her to unload that much crap, but, hey, Rachel asked.

Her work friends glanced at each other and looked uneasy. Fiona leaned forward and placed her hand on Ellery's. "You know, that really sucks."

"Yeah," Rachel said. "I mean, I knew you were sort of down about Josh studying so much, and then your mom said you got sick on Saturday. I didn't know you were feeling this way."

Ellery hadn't expected her admission to feel . . . so freeing. "Yeah, I have been trying to have a good attitude about things, but sometimes it's hard."

"We all have stuff we hide from everyone," Fiona said, signaling to the waiter, who veered their direction. "I'm so damned tired of every person I date being such a loser. And I still live with my parents. How's that for sad?"

The waiter arrived. "Anything else, ladies?"

"Yeah, I'll have another one of these, and my friend Ellery, who is not inebriated, needs a drink."

The waiter made a frowny face. "But—"

Fiona gave him a hard look. "Nope. Her mother is being a bitch, and she needs a drink. So bring her one of these."

The waiter glanced over at Ellery.

"Please," Ellery said.

"Fine," he said, gliding away.

"I slept with a guy last week, and I don't even know his name. Like not even his first name. We were over at my friend Sally's, and we drank a lot, and somehow I ended up in the bathroom with him. No clue what his name was. Thing is, I only did it because he told me my eyes were pretty." Rachel drained the last of her drink and thumped it on the table. "And I think I'm getting a C in Bio Chem. So, yeah, we all got stuff that we would rather not show others."

Ellery managed a smile. "So you're saying we all got problems?"

Rachel grinned. "Yeah. We all got them."

"Look, chicken, you're having a bad couple of months. It won't last," Fiona said, taking a drink from the waiter and passing it to Ellery. Taking her own, she lifted it. "A toast to bitches who persevere in the face of adversity. One foot in front of the other . . . wearing cute shoes, I might add, is our best defense."

"Hear, hear," Rachel said, clinking her glass to Fiona's.

"I'm down," Ellery said, touching her sugar-rimmed glass to the others. "Misery loves company."

"And we're good company," Rachel said with a laugh.

For the next half hour, they chatted about work, and Ellery tried to forget her troubles. Once she pulled her phone from her crossbody purse and checked messages. Nothing from Josh or her mother. There was one from her father, but she wasn't ready to talk to him, either. Both her parents had behaved badly, and she couldn't deal with them. She wasn't sure she could deal with much of anything lately.

"I know a great bar downtown where you can hear decent bands. Who wants to continue the night? After all, it's Friday, and we are young and mostly single." Fiona leveled slightly glassy dark eyes at them.

Normally, Ellery would beg off, but what did she have to do at nine thirty on a Friday night? Go home and mope? Yeah, that was pretty much it.

"Fine. I'm in," Ellery said.

Rachel clapped her hands. "Yay, this will be fun. Let's get the check, and I'll get an Uber."

Ellery smiled, and this time her smile felt genuine. A year ago if someone had told her she would be going downtown to hear a band with a bisexual black woman and a girl who wore socks with sandals, she would have thought they were smoking crack. Yet, at that very moment, even after calling her mother a whore in front of half of Shreveport, Ellery felt better than she had in a long time. Fiona and Rachel made her feel comfortable with herself. They made her feel like a better person. And she really needed to feel that way.

Because she was certain that she wasn't such a good person. Not if she'd called her mother a whore, lied to her fiancé, and still fantasized about a certain bartender even though she knew she shouldn't.

CHAPTER TWENTY-ONE

Nearly a week after her memorable date, Daphne caught Josh kissing another man in a CVS parking lot.

She'd just pulled in the parking lot of the CVS to fetch the Benadryl her father had requested in a panic at nine fifty-five on a Thursday night when she saw her daughter's fiancé. There were only a few clusters of cars sitting in front of the twenty-four-hour drugstore. It wasn't her regular place to grab a prescription or snack, but she'd stayed late at a book club meeting at a member's house in Keithville and was on her way home when her father called.

"I ate shellfish, Pickles," her father had rasped, skipping the greeting when she'd answered his call.

"Daddy, why in the world did you do that?" She sighed, glanced at her clock, and then looked for an exit. If she could find a CVS or Walgreens, she could grab an antihistamine and be at her father's assisted-living apartment in less than twenty minutes.

"Because those little suckers are seductive," her father managed to impart. Though it sounded more like Sylvester the Cat saying it. Thufferin' thuccotash. "Gonna need some of that medicine. My lips already look like those women who get all the plastic surgery."

"Can you breathe okay?"

"Yeah. Same as last time. Just swelling up."

"I'm on my way now. Hang tight."

"Thank you, honey," her father said, the apology in his voice scrubbing away her annoyance. The man loved shrimp even though he wasn't supposed to eat it. Thankfully, it wasn't usually a life-threatening allergy, but she knew that allergies were fickle and could turn into something more dangerous. Her father needed to be more responsible.

When she arrived at the drugstore, her lights flashed by an occupied car. She didn't pay much attention since she was reviewing a mental list. She needed to pick up some creamer for her tea and a roll of paper towels to tide her over. She shut the car off and reached for her purse, her gaze snagging upon the two men arguing in the car. The driver was emphatically gesticulating, and a coil of alarm went up Daphne's back. There had been a shooting a few nights ago in a different store parking lot. Someone had pulled a gun, and a bystander had been struck and gravely injured.

Just as she was about to crank her car to move it to the other side, the man in the passenger's seat turned his head.

Josh.

He hadn't seen her because he was too busy making his point to the driver, who himself was jabbing his finger on the steering wheel and shaking his head.

Daphne grabbed her purse, wondering if she should say hello or just get the goods and get out since the two men seemed to be arguing. Her hand touched the door latch right as the driver grabbed Josh's head and kissed him.

And it wasn't a friendship kiss. Not that guys really engaged in such . . . maybe a few guys from South Louisiana. They liked to smack a kiss on a cheek regardless of gender. But this wasn't one of those.

Nope, this was passionate, and Josh was very obviously into it.

A lump formed in her throat as disbelief slammed into her over what she was witnessing. The man was cheating on her daughter right before her eyes. Add to that it was with a guy. Did this mean her daughter's fiancé was gay? And if he were gay, why in all that was holy was he engaged to Ellery?

Daphne couldn't look away from the two men, who seemed to grow more and more . . . uh, turned on.

What should she do? Film them? Blow her horn? Storm up to the window and demand answers? Or pretend she'd not seen the encounter?

Her phone buzzed, and she ripped her gaze from the two men tangled in each other and glanced down.

Can you get me some Preparation H, too? Got a flare-up.

Why had she taught her father to text? He loved to send her lists. Of course, she always got him what he wanted, so she couldn't blame him for asking for what he wanted. Her father wasn't a dumbass. But the irony of needing hemorrhoidal cream while watching the asshole her daughter was engaged to blatantly cheating was not lost. Flare-up indeed.

Sucking in a deep breath, she glanced again at Josh making out with a rather good-looking guy in the middle of a parking lot and climbed out of the car. The area wasn't the safest, but the parking lot was well lit, and a security guard stood near the whooshing doors of the store. She could likely get in and out without Josh seeing her, but for some reason, she wanted him to see her . . . if he came up for air.

So she walked toward their vehicle, where luckily a stray shopping cart sat a few spots down. They didn't seem to notice her. They were busy. Obviously.

Daphne snagged the cart and swung it in a wide circle that took her even closer. They did not pull apart. She stopped and glanced at the storefront, where the security officer stood watching her.

Should she? Or should she not?

If she interrupted, Josh would know he was busted. What were the ramifications for Ellery? Well, for one, it was probably a given that there wouldn't be a wedding. If she moved along and ignored Josh's bad behavior and conflicting sexual identity, what were those ramifications? She could think of none that were the least bit satisfactory. Maybe for the lying bastard kissing another man, but none for her daughter.

Without any further thought, she approached the car and tapped on the passenger window.

The two men jerked apart, a shocked scramble to return to their seats, and Daphne caught the wide-eyed expression of the driver. But after the fear and shock subsided, Josh's expression was . . . honestly something that made her so incredibly sad that she forgot to be mortified and outraged at his behavior.

At first he was frightened, as anyone would be when someone knocks on his car window when the occupant's, uh, preoccupied.

Then Josh's alarmed expression changed as he focused on who it was knocking on the window. All the pieces clicked together. Kissing. Fiancée's mother outside. Cold-ass busted.

At that point, absolute misery covered his face.

He turned to the driver and shook his head before unlocking the door and climbing out.

Daphne had stepped back and clutched the shopping cart because it gave her trembling hands something to do. Josh shoved his hands into his hoodie pocket. He still had on the scrubs he wore to school, and he looked like he'd been kicked in the head.

For a few seconds neither of them said a thing. Daphne waited and Josh studied his feet.

"Josh?" Daphne said, after it was clear he wasn't going to initiate the conversation.

His shoulders sank, but he said nothing.

"Josh? You have to say something."

"I can't think of what to say. I really can't. I'm sorry? Don't tell Ellery? Pretend you didn't see that?" Josh glanced up at her, his eyes pools of despair and guilt. "I tried so hard . . . I really tried to stop this from happening, Daphne."

Daphne, as angry, shocked, and upset as she was, felt her heart break for the man standing before her.

"I don't understand," she said, because she could think of nothing else to say to such a devastating revelation. But she knew exactly what he meant. He had tried to fight against himself, but ultimately what had gone on in that car was something a person couldn't run from.

He rubbed his face, squeezing it as he winced. "I don't, either, because I love Ellery. I do. She's the best, but . . ." He trailed off and looked up at the moths dive-bombing the fluorescent lights high above them before returning his gaze to hers. "I didn't know . . . what love really felt like until I fell in love with someone else. I didn't want to. You have to understand that I really, really didn't want this to happen."

"You're not in love with Ellery." A statement. Not a question.

"No." He shook his head and returned his gaze to hers. "I want to be. I never imagined this would happen. It's not what I want for my life. My father's a pastor, and while he can overlook some things, having a gay son isn't one of them. But what I feel when I'm with Drew, well, it's real, and it's not going away no matter how much I try to make it."

Daphne released her death grip on the shopping cart. "You can't keep hiding this from her, Josh."

Tears sheened in Josh's eyes, and one made its way down his cheek. Facing hard truths about one's life wasn't a cakewalk, and she pitied Josh for the upheaval he would face in the coming weeks and months. Her daughter's happiness was like a beautiful ice sculpture, destined to melt under the heat of the truth. Yet the truth would have to come. Josh wasn't allowed to use Ellery so he could hide who he was.

Eventually, Josh inhaled and exhaled. "But I *want* to be the other Josh. The one who is engaged to Ellery. Maybe if I—"

"You can't pretend this away. You know that, right?"

He shrugged and swiped the tear from his cheek.

"Some people may have trouble accepting who you truly are, but the world has changed a lot, Josh, and for the better when it comes to being gay."

He flinched at the word. "What if I'm not? I . . . I've been with girls, and it was fine."

"And it's the same as when you're with him?" She pointed to the car where the other man waited.

Josh swallowed and slowly shook his head.

"You might find leading a life free from pretense a lot easier than you think, but that's not my decision to make. That belongs to you. But you have to tell Ellery the truth. You're not being fair to her . . . or faithful."

"I know. But how do I do that? I can't do this to her, Daphne." Agony in every syllable of every word.

"So your solution is to carry on a secret affair while she decides what flowers to put in her bouquet? Or maybe you'll wait until after the engagement party in March? Just how long will you put off telling her you're not in love with her and are sleeping with another man?"

"Oh God. That sounds so . . . I mean, I know I can't marry her. I just don't know how to undo all this." Josh ran his hand through his normally perfect hair and looked up as if he could get deliverance. "Her year has been so shitty, and I don't want her to feel rejected again. I thought if she could just get a job in another city, it would be easier to break the engagement and tell her the truth. Then she would be away from me, away from here, living a new life. Our breakup wouldn't matter as much."

"God, Josh, why did you propose to her in the first place?"

"Because I *do* love her. I mean, obviously not the way she deserves to be loved, but I didn't realize . . . I mean, I didn't meet Drew until August and—" He pressed his lips together, glancing back at the man sitting silently in the car. "I didn't know what it felt like. I wasn't trying to deceive Ellery. God knows she means so much to me, and that's why I have been staying away from her. I can't bear what I'm doing, but I can't seem to stop."

Daphne shook her head. "You're intentionally sabotaging your relationship. Is that so she'll dump you? What kind of manipulation is that, Josh? You can't make her think it's her fault. That she's done something wrong. If you don't want to own up to your sexuality, that's your business, but taking my daughter along on your train of guilt is *my* business."

"I wasn't doing that. I don't know, maybe subconsciously I was hoping she'd walk away from me, and that would be easier than breaking her heart. Mostly I stayed away because I've been carrying on this affair, lying to myself and Ellery and wishing I were brave enough to own up to what I'm doing."

Daphne was almost certain there were no books on how to confront your daughter's future husband about having an affair with whoever this guy in the car was, so she wasn't sure how she could help Josh. "The chickens have come home to roost. I don't care who you tell, or if you want to spend your whole life hiding who you are, but you're going to out yourself to my daughter. She will *not* think she's the reason you two didn't work out."

He looked down at his feet again. Scuffing his toe against the asphalt, he cleared his throat. "Don't you think I should wait? At least until she hears about the internships? Or maybe after the holidays?"

"No. I think she deserves to know right this very minute that the man she loves is sleeping with someone else . . . and that he's gay and has known that for some time."

Josh jerked his head up. "That's not true. I wasn't totally sure."

Daphne arched one eyebrow and gave him the "mom stare."

"Okay, I thought maybe I was bisexual or something." He lifted one shoulder, his mouth quirking into another guilty expression. "I tried not to think about it. I wanted to be normal."

"Normal? This might be your normal, Josh."

He nodded. "Maybe so. I just want to do the right thing."

"If you care about Ellery as much as you say you do, coming clean and letting her move on is the right thing." Her phone buzzed, and she remembered why she stood in the CVS parking lot. Benadryl for her father. Oh, and hemorrhoidal cream. "I am going out of town next week. When I return, Ellery *will* know about this. If she doesn't, I will tell her."

Josh made a pathetic noise. "How will I tell her? I don't know how to make her understand that—"

Daphne set a hand on his shoulder. "In this case, Josh, I think the old 'it's me, not you' line should work perfectly."

With that, she walked toward the sliding doors of the drugstore, her heart thumping from the adrenaline that had poured through her. Her fingers still trembled with emotion, and though she felt sorry for the man agonizing over his life in the parking lot, a deep anger had burgeoned within her. Josh had not only duped himself by thinking he could live a straight life when he was not straight, but he'd dragged her baby into his delusion. No wonder Ellery had seemed so unhappy these past few months. Josh was staying away for a huge reason—he was running from the truth in his life. Her Ellery was a casualty of his lie to himself.

Lies . . . they had such a way of catching up to a person.

But then again, hiding transgressions did the same. Or maybe it wasn't hiding transgressions—it was giving in to a bad decision in the first place. She'd allowed a few kind words (and a stupid book) to trip her into the tangled web of sleeping with practically an infant. At present she was still pulling cobwebs from her hair. But she wasn't the only one who'd made bad choices. Her daughter had allowed a simple request by a handsome widower to turn into a secret relationship . . . or at least from what she could tell. She assumed it started because Ellery was lonely and needed to feel like someone was interested.

Evan had been surprised and disappointed to learn Daphne was not the person he'd been having a relationship with for months. Daphne couldn't lie and say it hadn't put a damper on the excitement she'd had for going out with Evan. She was attracted to him and wanted to explore that fluttery feeling she got when she thought about him, but her life was so sideways that it wouldn't be fair to pursue something with him until she got it right side up again. She'd told him as much when they'd pulled into her driveway last Friday night.

"I would invite you in for a drink, but I know you have to drive back to Texas tonight. I don't want a Smokey to pull you over," she said as the headlight beams swept across the brilliant-colored Bradford pear tree and the detached garage painted to match the barn. After the showdown with Ellery, all she wanted to do was pull on her favorite pj's and climb into bed with Jonas. Her loyal hound would help her lick her wounds with his solid presence at her feet.

"That's okay. I would love to have one, but, yeah, I don't relish a DUI on my record. Though coffee isn't alcoholic."

"I can make that, but I wanted to say something to you before . . . I mean, I don't really know how to do this after that debacle of a dinner. Or rather the ending was a cluster, um, you know. But I enjoyed the actual dinner and conversation."

Evan looked over at her. "Daphne, it's okay."

"No, it's not. I want to be totally transparent here because I like you. I would love to get to know you better and continue what I think would be . . . good. I think it could be good between us."

He shifted into park and turned toward her. "I like you, too, but you threw me a bit of a curve tonight. I thought we already had something, but maybe that's not a bad thing. I mean, I'd like to ask Ellery why she pretended to be you for so long. Still, I can't say I'm not attracted to you. Dinner was pretty nice, well, up until the end." His smile was sheepish.

In the faint light from her porch, she could see how attractive he was. The clean-shaven jaw, firm lips, whiskey eyes. Her tummy did its flippy thing, so she turned away. "Yeah, and that's the thing. Ellery's angry at me. Ellery's angry at a lot of things in her life."

"Growing up is hard. She's still in that zone, truly moving from child to adult. That doesn't happen at eighteen. A switch isn't flipped and suddenly you're a taxpaying, über-responsible adult with all the answers."

"No, it's not. I never went through what she went through. By the time I was twenty-three years old, I had a six-year-old and had been married for almost seven years. No traditional college, no dating, no first job. Not to mention, the world is so very different now. You're right, she's at that place . . . which means I'm at that place, too."

He made a confused face.

"I'm newly single after being married for a long time, and I haven't dated until now. I'm still learning how to walk in my big-girl shoes. They feel high and wobbly at present."

"And you've never been with anyone other than your husband?"

Daphne's face must have shown surprise at his query, because his eyes grew wide. "Oh crap, I'm sorry. I wasn't exactly talking about sex. I mean . . . uh, I shouldn't have asked that. Rusty, remember?" Evan's face actually turned red.

Daphne managed a smile. "It's okay. And ironically that's what's sitting between me and Ellery. I . . . well." She sucked in a deep breath and exhaled. "I slept with someone she didn't approve of. She only recently found out and is very angry with me. So to answer your question, yes, I have been with someone else, but it was an embarrassing one-night stand that never should have happened."

She snuck a look at his face. He tilted his head and she couldn't read his expression. "I don't understand. Why would she be so upset? You said you've been divorced for a few years?"

Daphne hadn't wanted to come quite so clean. If she told him about Clay, she'd be so squeaky clean she might never see him again. But the upside would be starting a relationship with a blank slate—no secrets, no shame. For some reason, she was tired of hiding and pretending. "This is hard to admit because I'm such a rule follower and very conscious of my choices, but I went a bit crazy almost a month ago. I drank too much wine and slept with"—she sucked in another deep breath before closing her eyes and exhaling—"one of Ellery's ex-boyfriends."

A second passed, then another. Finally, she cracked one eye open and looked over at him.

Evan looked flabbergasted.

Cripes. She shouldn't have told him about sleeping with Clay. She barely knew him, and now he would think she truly was a whore.

But then Evan smiled. "You . . . you . . . did what? You slept with . . ." He started chuckling. "So that's why she called you . . . oh my God, that's . . . kinda . . . awesome."

Daphne opened both eyes. "Awesome?"

"I mean, not for her. And maybe not for me, because it's not like I want to imagine you with someone else, especially someone who's twenty."

"He wasn't *twenty*. Jeez."

"Look, I understand how those things happen. I mean, this whole rebounding thing ain't for the faint of heart. I made some missteps myself. I took out a woman my sister set me up with, and I pretty much did the same thing you did. We had a one-night thing, and suddenly she was planning our wedding. That got rough fast. Then I tried Tinder because one of my friends talked me into it. The woman I met at the bar was twenty-one and brought a flogger thing in her purse. She asked me if I was willing to role-play."

Daphne lifted her eyebrows. "A flogger?"

"Yeah, and we hadn't even finished our first drink."

"She wanted to whip you?"

Evan shrugged. "I dunno. She seemed excited about the possibility. I faked a text that my daughter was sick and told her I had to go. I may have actually jogged to my truck. The dating scene is crazy."

"I planned to do a dating site but kept putting it off. Maybe if I had, I wouldn't have done something so . . . impulsive. At least you tried to do it the right way. I just got hammered and lost my damned mind."

Evan seemed to grow serious. "This truly is all very new to you."

"It is," Daphne said. She looked down at her hands twisted together in her lap. "But I'm ready to move on with my life. I've grieved my marriage and spent several years trying to claim a life for myself. That being said, I need to fix some things, like my relationship with Ellery, before I jump into a new relationship. I don't want to start something feeling this bad."

"What if you can't fix things?" he asked.

Daphne squeezed her hands together hard, almost wincing at the pressure. "I can. As soon as I figure out how."

"Sometimes all it takes is time."

Daphne felt so warmed by his understanding. "You're such a gentleman. I'm fairly certain anyone else would have tossed me out of his moving vehicle and watched me roll in the light of his taillights."

"I reserve that right for the second date," he said with a grin. "So how about I walk you to the door and we do this first-date thing the right way?"

"And what does that entail?" she asked, unbuckling her seat belt.

"Me getting nervous wondering if you'll let me kiss you. Then wonder if a hug says I have no skills as a player but also know a handshake would portray no interest. And if I manage to get a kiss, how far should I take it? A light peck or. . ." He shrugged.

She crooked a finger at him. "Let me set aside your worries."

"I like the way you first date, lady," he said with an impish light in his eyes.

"Kiss me already."

So he did, his lips a soft whisper before growing bolder. He framed her face in his hands, so tender, as if he would drink from her, take from her, and it was hot and gorgeous and sexy all at once. The rasp of his jaw before she slid a hand to his thick hair, angling her head so he could deepen the kiss, sent desire lapping against her pelvis, uncurling sweet heat and desire. Evan tasted complex—wine and sex, moonlight and earth, old and new.

Finally, he pulled his lips from hers. "Not bad for a first kiss."

"You're implying there will be a second," she whispered as he stroked his big thumb against her lower lip. Want pounded within her along with the realization that this was right. This was what she wanted with a man. This. Right. Here.

"I'm planning on it," he said, telling her exactly what she wanted to hear.

Daphne was jolted from the memory of Evan and her date back to the present when the doors swooshed open—she was in CVS. She needed to buy hemorrhoidal cream, and oh, by the way, her daughter's fiancé was gay.

She'd told Evan she could fix her daughter, but Tippy Lou's words came back to her. Ellery had to fix her own world. Finding out her fiancé was gay and in love with another man would be the biggest blow of all.

"Can I help you, ma'am?" a store clerk asked from the end of an aisle.

"I need to find Benadryl?" Daphne asked.

"Aisle four by the pharmacy."

"Oh, and where's your wine?"

"Right up front where you can grab it quick, sugar," the woman said, returning to the empty checkout station.

If anyone needed a glass of wine after taking her father his requested sundries, it was Daphne Witt. And if there was anyone else who would soon need a glass of wine more, it was Ellery Witt.

Daphne could only pray and wait to see how things would play out. Would Ellery come to her . . . or would the silence between them continue?

CHAPTER TWENTY-TWO

Dear Ellery,

I accept your apology, but I disagree with you about your mother. That being said, I have no skin in this game between you. I hope that you will both soon see that life is too short to hold a grudge for long.

Best,
Evan McCallum

Ellery shoved her phone away from her and lined the shot glasses up across the bar. Five. At this point, she might as well go for six and break the record she'd established spring break of 2015. But if she did that, the floor would rise up to meet her because she'd been shooting tequila, and everyone knew that tequila made your clothes fall off . . . or made you barf. Probably both for some people.

All she knew was that no clothes would be dropping that night.

After all, she was drinking alone at Elmo's, wearing an old Victoria's Secret sweatshirt and jeans that she usually did yard work in. And house slippers. She may have brushed her hair before she called an Uber, but she wasn't sure. She *had* brushed her teeth after the crying jag she'd indulged in. She remembered that much.

"You don't want another, do you?" the bartender asked, looking like he hoped the answer was no. He was new to Elmo's, and she didn't know him. The regular bar manager had back surgery and couldn't work for another month. She really needed to remember to send ol' Charlie a get-well card or make him some cookies. Two regular waitresses, Tina and Kelsi, were working the tables, and Jeremy was assisting this new guy, who was pretty hot and getting plenty of looks from the women clumping in groups around the bar.

"Maybe in a minute," Ellery said, trying hard not to slur her words. She had to really focus on speaking clearly. "Hey, what's your name again?"

"Chris." He looked worried, but he didn't have to be. She was going to be fine. F-I-N-E.

"Yeah, that's right. You're new."

"I am," he said, glancing over at Jeremy, who shot him a bemused look.

"I know another bartender who looks like you. He's an asshole, though," she said, knowing that she'd totally slurred the word *asshole*.

"Don't sell me short," Chris said, popping off the lids of three Bud Lights and setting them on Tina's tray.

"Guess what? I got dumped today. Tina, did you hear? I got dumped. No longer engaged," Ellery said, frowning when someone jostled her elbow. "Hey, watch it."

"You told me already. I'm sorry about that, Ellery," Tina said, ignoring the tray of beers. Instead she walked around the bar, grabbed a bottle of water, and poured it into a clean glass. She set it in front of Ellery. "Try some water, honey."

Ellery stared at the glass. Chris reached over and stuck a lime on the rim. "I don't want water. I want more tequila. Let's all do a shot and celebrate how I'm single again."

Tina shook her head and shot Chris a look. "You need to call someone."

"No one to call," Ellery said, because even though the room looked fuzzy and could be tilting a little, she knew this to be absolutely true. Her fiancé was probably blowing Drew, the guy he was truly in love with. Whatever. And her mother wasn't speaking to her. Okay, it was the other way around, but the last person she wanted to come get her was her whore of a mother. But wait. Didn't matter, because Dee Dee O'Hara was on her book tour anyway. Ellery's friends were out of town. Rachel was on a date. She couldn't interrupt that because Rachel would kill her. Her daddy was on a trip with Cindy. New Orleans or somewhere fun. Whatever. Who cared? She didn't need any of them anyway.

She looked at her hand, the third finger on her left hand, and wiped a tear away. Josh had come clean about everything that morning. The video was his, or rather him and Drew filming themselves doing each other. He'd fallen in love with Drew, and that was that. Oh, Josh had cried and carried on, but in the end, it didn't matter. He'd left carrying her big engagement ring, and she'd started drinking. Eventually, she'd decided to come to Elmo's, though she didn't know why she'd made that decision. Drunk people didn't make good decisions.

Neither did people named Ellery who were dumb blondes who thought they could make things work when they couldn't make things do anything. Or something like that. Even her thoughts were broken.

Someone sat down on her left. She squinted at the person and frowned. "Well, of course, it's you. Why wouldn't it be *you* sitting next to me on the single worst night of my life?"

Clay Caldwell shook his head. "Elle, dude, you're wasted."

"Ding! You are correct, sir. That was my goal." She slapped her chest and noticed a stain on her sweatshirt. She hoped it wasn't drool. She may have dozed in the Uber on the way to Elmo's. "I rock."

Clay looked over at Chris, who was not nearly as cute as Gage, by the way. Not even close. "Shit, how many has she had?"

Ellery counted the upside-down shot glasses, tapping each one. "One. Two. Three. Four. Five."

"Jeez, Elle, drink some water," Clay said, sliding the sweating glass toward her.

"You may have fucked my mom, but you aren't my daddy, Clay Caldwell," Ellery said, poking his arm with her finger.

Clay's expression was mad. She could tell because his mouth made a line.

"I'm calling Josh to come get you." He pulled out his phone. "He gave me his number a few weeks ago."

"I bet he did," Ellery drawled. Or tried to drawl. She wasn't sure if it came out as intended. "But he isn't going to come get me. We broke up. See?" She held up her naked left hand.

"Then I'm calling your mother," Clay said.

"Fine, but she's in San 'tonio."

Clay set his cell phone down on the bar. "Then I'll take you home."

"Over my dead body," Ellery quipped, tapping the bar. "I'll have another. Now."

Clay shook his head. "You're cut off. Drink your water."

Ellery tried to slide off the barstool but stumbled and fell against Clay. She pushed off him and straightened. "Whatever. I'll go somewhere else. Where's my purse?"

"I don't think you have one," Chris said. The new bartender shook up a drink, the ice clattering obnoxiously as he made a martini or something fruity. It was probably for the ladies celebrating at the end of the bar. They'd been laughing, taking selfies, and being all-around happy for the last hour. Ellery hated them.

"Here," Clay said, sliding his credit card across the bar. "It's on me. I'll get her home."

"No, he's not," Ellery said, swaying a bit. She grabbed hold of the bar. "You know why? He slept with my mother. My *mother*. Can you believe that?"

"Elle, stop," Clay said, shooting her the look her father usually used when he was tired of her behavior. "You're making a fool of yourself."

"Really? You're the one who made a fool out of my mother."

Clay's mouth remained tight. His eyes flashed anger, too. "Stop. You're making a scene."

"Oh, so now you're worried about what people think? Well, I don't care. Look at me, Clay," she said, stepping back and looking down at her sloppy outfit. Her house shoes had kitty-cat whiskers. "Does it look like I care?"

Clay peered down at her feet. "Are you wearing slippers?"

"Yep. I got 'em on. 'Cause they're comfortable, and I don't care anymore. You want to know why I'm quitting my life?"

He sighed. "I'm afraid to ask."

"Because I'm so bad in bed, I drive guys gay."

She really didn't think that was true, but it sounded good. Her self-pity was at least a foot deep, and she found she liked wading around in it. Felt better than trying to make a stupid plan for her life that wouldn't work anyway or cutting up all Josh's clothes, which she had actually contemplated. She felt like going all Carrie Underwood with a baseball bat on his stupid car. Except as mad as she was, it wasn't so much at him. Could he help that he was gay? Nope. She was angry that her life had gone completely off the rails and her stupid plan to keep it all together had been smashed by a sledgehammer of reality. The fact was, she sucked. And her life sucked. So she was done with trying to hold it together. So done.

Clay looked at her like she was a curious bug that had hopped onto his pants leg. Swat it, or watch and see what it does? "I'm sorry to hear that, Elle, but I'm not totally surprised about Josh."

"Yeah? Well, I was. So don't save the date. Not that we had one, mind you. Because Josh kept saying we didn't have to be in a hurry." Her laughter was bitter as aspirin ground between one's molars. "I guess now we know why. He didn't want to marry me. He was lying to himself, to me, to everyone."

She may have sobbed on that last statement. Or was that a hiccup? "I want Gage. Can you call him?"

Ellery wasn't sure why she said that. Gage was too far away. In Deacon Point. Besides, why would he answer the phone when she had failed on every level of getting her shit together? Fix herself? Ha! She was spectacularly broken, lying in throbby little pieces all over the beer-drenched floor of a dive bar. But she couldn't stop thinking about him. About the way he felt against her. About how wrong he was for her. About why she needed him there with her.

He could help her. She knew he could.

"I don't know who that is, but I think you should sit down before you fall," Clay said, patting the stool and giving the people around them staring a look that said *Nothing to see here* even though there was. Watching a pretty blonde who'd once had everything at her fingertips crash and burn was thrilling for a lot of people. She understood. People took pleasure in some people's downfalls. Made them feel better about their own lives.

"I don't want to," she said.

"Why are you such a brat? Sit down. Or go. Either way, stop reeling around, knocking into people." Clay's expression grew less interested in what she would do and more prone to lecturing her the way her father would. Imagine that, the man whore of Shreveport lecturing her about her maturity.

"Why did you sleep with my mom?" she asked, ignoring his question and the fact he was insulting her. "Did you do it to make me jealous?"

Clay's hard laugh made her insides hurt even more than she thought possible. "You don't get it, do you? I'm not into *you*, Ellery. I *was* into your mother. She's beautiful, accomplished, and generous. She made me feel like a person, like I wasn't some schmuck who didn't have a brain. Your mother was exactly what I was looking for."

"But too old for you. She's my *mother*. *My* mother, Clay."

Clay signed the receipt Chris slid over to him along with his credit card. Then he looked hard at Ellery. "If there is anyone in this world who needs to get over herself, it's you, Ellery. Get an Uber, go home, and dry out. Then when you wake up and can think straight, you should really, really get the fuck over yourself and stop acting like a selfish princess."

With that, Clay stood up and walked away.

Her mouth was open. She should close it. But she couldn't seem to remember how to.

She wasn't a selfish princess. He didn't get to call her that. How dare he? How . . . tears started leaking from her eyes. People were staring.

So Ellery left, staggering toward the door of Elmo's, passing people she'd probably known her entire life, while wearing kitty-cat slippers and listing to the right. She stumbled only once before pushing out the heavy metal door into the cool night air. A carload of people climbed out of a car. She thought there was an Uber symbol on the window, so she knocked before the woman pulled away.

"Are you Uber?" Ellery asked.

The woman pointed to the window. "That's what that sticker means."

"Will you take me home?"

The woman made a face. "Use the app. You have the app, right?"

Ellery managed to complete the request and then climbed into the front seat.

"Don't puke in my car," the woman said before pulling away from Elmo's.

Ellery fell asleep as soon as the woman hit the interstate. She woke groggy, nauseous, and annoyed at something poking her. She opened her eyes to see a stranger, whose index finger was super pointy. "What?"

"We're here, princess," the driver said.

Ellery peered out the window at the town house she and Josh had signed a yearlong lease on. He'd taken a few things with him when he left that morning. He said he'd come back when she was at work to pack the rest of his stuff. Like she might get crazy if he came while she was there. Crap, how was she going to pay for the lease now? The fairly expensive town house was in her name, cosigned by a father who was no longer paying her bills. "I'm not a princess. I'm a pauper."

"Great. Looking forward to my tip." The driver unlocked the door and took off as soon as Ellery managed to shut the door behind her.

Ellery stood for a moment, watching the taillights fade into the darkness. A tear plinked onto her sweatshirt. Huh. She didn't realize she'd been crying until that moment. She wiped her cheeks, and a wave of nausea rose within her. She barely made it to the bushes out front before the tequila made an encore performance in the worst possible way. After her body finished its last heave, she used her sleeve to wipe her mouth, which was totally gross but all she had. It occurred to her drunken brain at that moment that she had, in fact, hit rock bottom.

Uncurling from a standing fetal position, she staggered toward the front door. It was upon staring at her cute red door that she realized she had no idea where her keys were. She tried her pockets, but they held only a gum wrapper and a hair tie.

"Great," she said to the door.

A strange sound emerged from the azalea bushes to her right. A yowling that could best be described as a dirge to the hopeless and forgotten.

Ellery peered at the bushes, hoping there wasn't a rabid raccoon ready to attack. Because that would be the cherry on top of her rock bottom. A rustling of still-green leaves yielded the ugliest cat she'd ever seen. Mottled fur of gray and black, one ear definitely missing a nice chunk. The feline hotfooted it toward her, making a racket that made her oddly sympathetic considering she'd never liked cats much. The lean cat twined about her feet. "You like my kitty-cat slippers, huh?"

Sinking down onto the stoop, Ellery extended her hand. The cat bumped up against it, twisting around so that she could tell it was an unaltered male. His purr was loud in the silence of the night around her. She shivered and wondered where Josh had hidden the spare key. They had one, but Josh had been insistent that it be hidden in a place no one would think to look.

Mission accomplished, because she had no clue where it was.

A single headlight swept over her, and she peered at the brightness hitting her square in the face. The loud rumble died at the same time the light turned off.

A motorcycle sat in the parking spot in front of her town house, and a figure clad in black, helmet covering his face, climbed off.

For a brief moment, Ellery wondered if this was how it was going to end for her—her mangled body found in the most hideous of clothing, hair matted, vomit on her sleeve. But then she realized it was Gage, and he was carrying a box.

She didn't get up because she didn't trust herself not to fall. The horizon still tilted back and forth, like she was in a fun house with crazy mirrors and optical-illusion floors that made her walk with her hands out. He pulled off his helmet and shook his hair, which was really too short to worry about, but it was probably a habit or something.

"Hey," she said.

He stood, helmet tucked under his arm, box in hand. "Hey."

"What's in the box?" Stupid question. There were so many better ones, like: Why are you here? Or: How did you know where to find me? Or: Do you have some wet wipes, because I really would like to wipe my face . . . and shirtsleeve? But she didn't lead with any of those.

"Your wineglasses."

"Wow, that's service. You came all this way to bring my glasses?" She knew it was another stupid question, but she'd made asking dumb questions the theme of the night. Might as well continue the streak.

"No. I came because you texted me and told me you were in trouble and needed help." He slid his phone out of his back pocket and waggled it. "About an hour and a half ago."

"I did?"

"You did. Luckily we had your address on file."

"Well, I'm drunk."

His lips may have twitched. "So I see."

"And I'm locked out of my house." The cat yowled pitifully, as if he were the choir joining in on the chorus of her pity song.

"That's definitely a problem."

"And Josh is gay. He broke up with me."

Gage moved closer, his boots almost touching her kitty-cat slippers. "I figured as much. Not about the breakup, but the other."

"Yeah." She looked down at her hands and the cat bumping against them, demanding attention even though she had never seen the fellow before. He was awfully demanding for a cat who didn't know her. "I guess I should have known, but I didn't. I'm stupid."

"Okay, enough with the pity party. Do you have a key hidden around here somewhere?" Gage asked, his gaze scouring the small porch with the bright, happy mums she'd planted a few days ago. A fat pumpkin sat beside the clay pot looking ridiculously festive, an insult to her current nonfestive mood. She wanted to kick the pumpkin for being so fallish, so perfectly round and pretty, but she'd probably fall on her ass.

"Somewhere around here, I guess."

Gage stepped past her and tried the doorknob. It opened. "Your door is open, babe."

She wasn't his babe, but it sounded so nice to be called that by him. She wanted him to call her that again . . . and for the world to stop spinning. "Told you. I'm stupid. I left my door unlocked. Irresponsible as hell."

"Ellery," he said, turning around. He set the box on the umbrella stand opposite the cheerful fall decorations and stretched out a hand. "Come on."

She tried to take his hand and missed. "Oops."

"Here," he said, lifting her beneath her arms and tugging her up. He was stronger than he looked because he practically lifted her. "Whoa, babe, you smell ripe."

"Yeah, I threw up." Somewhere in the recesses of her mind she was horrified at what was happening. Ladies didn't throw up. They also didn't wear house slippers to a bar. And they brushed their hair and wore lipstick. "I'm sorry. I don't remember texting you. I mean, I saved your number even though I told myself I wasn't going to. I didn't want to want you . . . I mean, I didn't mean to call you. I don't—"

"Sh," he said, turning on a lamp near the door. "Let me check the house since the door was unlocked. Stand right here."

Gage propped her against the wall and shut the front door. Then he prowled around her town house. She heard the opening and closing of doors. Lights flicked on. Then he came back for her, looking so gorgeous in the low light of her living room. The very moment she realized that he might be the sexiest man she'd ever met, her stomach flipped over and nausea rolled up from inside.

"I'm gonna throw up again," she said, stumbling toward the guest bathroom right off the living room. She barely made it before she retched again, her body violently jerking, heaving against itself.

A cool cloth touched the back of her neck. "Here we go. This will help."

His words were soft, and the dishcloth was cold and smelled like Gain fabric softener. Ellery wasn't sure she'd ever felt so comforted. "I'm sorry. I'm so sorry."

"Sh, it's okay. Let's get you upstairs. Uh, you probably need to shower. Do you think you can manage washing off?" Gage asked, taking her arm and helping her toward the sink, where she rinsed her mouth.

"I think so," Ellery said, noticing that her hair hadn't made it out of the way when she'd vomited. Where were her damned girlfriends to hold her hair back while she puked? Well, she couldn't exactly blame them since she'd taken an Uber to drink by herself—on an empty stomach at that. Total amateur move, but she hadn't been thinking straight. No, she'd been hurting and wanted something to kill the pain. Tequila had sounded like a good idea.

It wasn't.

Tequila was never an answer to heartbreak.

Gage helped her up the stairs and deposited her in the bathroom. "Look, I'm not going to come in, but just in case, don't lock the door. You're safe with me."

Ellery looked at him before closing the door. "I know I'm safe with you. You're a good guy, Gage."

His eyes flashed something indecipherable. "No, I'm not."

"I texted you for a reason . . . even if I don't know what it was."

She shut the door and turned on the shower, stripping out of her smelly clothes and kicking them toward the hamper. Steam curled up from the curtain, an invitation to scrub away the stink of the night. She'd wash her hair and bathe using her new honey-almond body wash, her last luxury for a while. Then she'd emerge and figure out why she'd texted the man she swore she wasn't attracted to, didn't care about, and never would.

And maybe she could also figure out why she was such a liar.

CHAPTER TWENTY-THREE

Rex was waiting for Daphne when she pulled into her driveway, road weary and not in the mood to deal with her ex-husband. She'd spent the last week driving around Texas and Oklahoma, smiling until her face hurt. She'd also worn tight floral dresses, a pearl choker, and high heels as her persona Dee Dee O'Hara demanded. Honey sweet and slightly ditzy as ol' Dixie Doodle herself, Dee Dee was more than ready to transform back into Daphne Witt, the pajama-wearing, makeup-free author who didn't have to laugh at every joke or smile even when someone asked her about why she continued to perpetuate patriarchal tyranny forced upon females by wearing said outfit.

She didn't have an answer for the angry mother of a little boy . . . who seriously had sat through her talk picking his nose and eating his finds. Maybe she *was* perpetuating a stereotype, but even as she longed for her yoga pants, she liked wearing heels (for maybe 1.5 hours at a time), a dress with lace or sequins (but never together), and the way she felt when she applied a shiny overcoat over Chanel red lip stain (somewhat glamorous).

Couldn't she enjoy being a lady and being a woman without being judged?

Rex gave her a half wave as she drove by and pulled beneath the new carport that had been spiffed up. Clay had covered the old wrought iron with cedar planks and added an arched farmhouse roof. It had gone from 1960s carport to fancy porte cochere.

Daphne climbed from the car, unleashing the flouncy skirt that was wrinkled from being bunched almost to her waist. Pantyhose made her sweat, so she'd shimmied out of those at the last rest stop. They lay like roadkill on the passenger floorboard.

"Hey," Rex said, walking around the side of the house and hitting the latch of her car. He pulled out her suitcase the way he'd always done when they'd been married. The action was so familiar . . . yet so foreign. She'd gotten used to taking care of herself.

"Hey," she said, closing the door after hooking her shoes in her hand. The pavement of the carport was cold on her feet, so she walked toward the back door.

She'd left an extra key with Clay so he could complete the work while she was away. Ellery had agreed long ago to come by and check on things and make sure the house was locked at the end of each day, but when Daphne had sent her a reminder, she'd gotten a message that Ellery was out of the office. Or rather Dee Dee O'Hara was out of the office, because Ellery was supposed to be Dee Dee and monitoring the business while Daphne was on the road.

"Have a nice trip?" Rex asked, pulling her rolling suitcase behind him.

"I did. Signed a lot of books, talked about the new series, drummed up support, tap-danced, all that fun stuff." She unlocked the door and pushed into her new mudroom. Clean white shelving, a bench, and a small mail station to house packages, outgoing and incoming. She'd designed this area herself, keeping a busy working mom in mind as she made a place for book bags and junk mail to stay out of sight.

She flipped on the kitchen light and gasped at how pretty the renovation was.

While she'd been gone, Clay and his guys had finished the remodel, and it was gorgeous. Swirling gray-and-bone Carrara marbled counters, white cabinets with transparent glass, vintage lighting, and a Viking range made a striking impression.

"Wow," Rex breathed behind her. "This doesn't look like our kitchen."

"It's not," she said. His words made her sad because as much of an ass as Rex had been over the past few years, they'd had a lot of good times together in this house. Rex had chased her around the old kitchen island wearing werewolf gloves and Dracula teeth while Ellery squealed in delight, Daphne had paced the floor in front of the old pantry holding a sick baby, and they'd dyed Easter eggs right beside the sink, praying they didn't spill and stain the grout . . . again. So many memories of families doing what families do in kitchens—sustaining their lives with food for their bodies and souls.

"Yeah, I guess that's true. I can't believe you're selling this place," Rex said, depositing her suitcase next to the open door.

"Sometimes I can't, either, but I need to start over. I don't think I can do that here." She set her purse on the counter and dropped her shoes onto the floor. "So what can I do for you?"

Her tone went from nostalgic to firm. She hadn't forgiven Rex for what he'd done.

Rex made a pained face. "Well, you know I suck at apologizing."

"If it were an Olympic event, you'd be the Michael Phelps at sucking at apologizing."

His mouth quirked. "Yeah, you got me there."

Rex looked tired, way more tired than she did, and she'd just done a six-city tour in seven days, answering questions, signing books, and sleeping in four different hotel beds. Her back was a disaster, and the bags under her eyes were so big they'd definitely have to be checked and not carried on. Her ex-husband's fatigue lay in the tightness of his mouth, the deep crevice on his brow, the sagging of the skin at his throat. He wore a ridiculous pair of jeans that were intentionally torn at the knee. For a moment she felt sorry for him.

But only a moment.

"Listen, Daph, I'm a dick. I shouldn't have led Ellery to believe anything bad about you. You didn't do anything wrong—you made a new life for yourself. After I left, you flourished. The truth is that I was jealous and looking for a way to make you look . . . look like you didn't want me. That the divorce was your fault . . . but it wasn't. It was mine."

Daphne stilled, thinking before she spoke. Because she wasn't certain she'd heard him right. Was Rex Witt apologizing? She thought he was, but she couldn't be totally incredulous at his attempt. She needed a source for this admission, a reason why he'd shown up on her doorstep. Rex always had a reason. "Did you get a new therapist?"

"No."

She turned toward him. "No?"

"I went by Tippy Lou's the other day."

Daphne raised her eyebrows. "*You* went by Tippy's? Were you trying to commit suicide by cop? How bad is the money situation?"

"It's not great, but I'm not checking out just yet. Oh, and she did bring a shotgun to the door. That might have been because she didn't recognize my truck, and you know Tippy Lou. She's . . . protective."

Daphne's mouth twitched into a smile. "As a junkyard dog. No, three junkyard dogs combined into a super guard dog. Why did you drop by Tippy's house?"

Rex ran a finger along the shining marble. "I hadn't planned to, but I remembered that I told her I would fix that gate. I never did it, and I wondered if someone had. And besides, I hadn't seen her since she stopped talking to me. I knew I had messed up so much about my life, and my therapist had mentioned that the only way to fix what's broken is to find out why it got broken in the first place. I really think she wanted me to just blame my parents like everyone else, but you know I couldn't. Pat and Judy are pretty perfect, as parents go."

Daphne nodded. Her once-upon-a-time in-laws were kind, considerate, and good spirited. They'd raised successful children and had always been available for babysitting, a cup of coffee, or good advice on buying a used car. "I miss them."

"You don't have to." Rex gave her a little smile. "I'm the one who screwed up, and even though we're no longer husband and wife, you're still family."

Daphne shook her head. "Not really. But thank you for saying that."

"Anyway, I somehow ended up on Tippy Lou's porch, her toting that gun and me not knowing why in the hell I had stopped. I guess I needed someone who would tell me the truth. Tippy Lou is good at that."

"Yeah, she is."

"Funny how she can see things so clearly. I didn't know people could see me the way she does. It's like she goes under your skin or something and tells you things you didn't even know about yourself."

Daphne made a face that said she totally understood because Tippy did that to her all the time. Of course, Tippy not only held up a mirror to a person, she planted seeds. Sometimes those seeds were needed to root a person or lead a person to harvest something she needed in her life. Tippy Lou was the person who had suggested Daphne go back to school, that she stop paying for Ellery's highlights, and that she treat her writing and art like it was a serious career and not a hobby.

And, let's not forget, she'd also suggested that Daphne sleep with Clay.

Wrong seed that time . . . but even as she thought about how Tippy had encouraged her to leave behind societal expectations and expired moral codes, Daphne knew Tippy's intent was right—she wanted Daphne to claim a life for herself, to not be afraid of being a whole woman and owning her needs and feelings. So even though that seed yielded an unintended consequence, it had a purpose because it had led to this moment.

"Sometimes we need someone to see who we are. We put on a lot of different masks in our lives," Daphne said, swishing her skirt to prove her point. "We all lie to ourselves, Rex. We all manipulate, avoid, and hide the ugly because who wants to be that honest in life?"

Rex swallowed hard and glanced away. "Who I am is not who I want to be. How is that for a midlife-crisis revelation?"

Daphne looked at the man, who avoided her gaze. She'd never seen him be so honest with himself, and briefly she envisioned Tippy Lou strapping Rex to a Chinese water torture board and forcing him to admit all his flaws.

Too many years too late.

If he'd had the revelation before now, if Rex had been a supporting husband, toting her books as she went to book signings and conferences, would she be happy at this very moment? She wasn't sure. Thing was, until Rex left her and broke her heart, she hadn't known that she was truly unhappy. Her life had been an endless cycle of making others' lives easier while she ignored her own self-fulfillment. She'd been a shadow, living in the dark, content with what little someone she loved tossed her way.

Like a dog who lived inside a small courtyard, she hadn't known there was a grassy open meadow next door. One did not miss what one did not know existed.

Now she knew, and though that meadow was sometimes scary with its unexplored boundaries, big anthills, and occasional thorns, she loved the freedom she had . . . a freedom she'd never had before.

"You know, Rex, it's never too late to start over, to find out who you really want to be."

"I guess you found that out."

"I'm trying to. I never thought my life would go like this, but that's the thing about living life. It throws you curveballs and surprises. Sometimes they are good. Sometimes they are not. But you never end up exactly where you thought you would be. Or maybe some people do. I don't know."

Rex glanced around the room. "So do you accept my apology? 'Cause Ellery isn't talking to me right now, and I think if you forgave me, it might go a long way in helping me repair the damage I did with her."

"I do, and I'm not so sure Ellery is going to care. She's not talking to me, either."

Rex jerked his expression to her. "Really? Why? I'm the one who lied."

Daphne had already admitted to Evan that she'd slept with a younger man, but telling Rex would be ten times more uncomfortable. Still, if Ellery told him, it could be worse. Better he found out from her. Clean slate. Honesty. Living strong and unapologetically. Those were words she'd been tossing around in her mind, professing to want, yet dancing around them to keep the peace. "I slept with Clay."

Her ex-husband blinked once. Twice. "What?"

Daphne sucked in a deep breath and let it go slowly. "I drank too much wine one night, he came on to me, and we ended up in bed."

"Our bed?" His words held shock . . . and hurt.

"No, *my* bed. You left, remember?"

Rex shook his head. "But he used to play badminton in the yard. Clay? Clay Caldwell?"

Daphne spread her hands out on the counter. "Yes, that Clay. I know it seems odd. I do. And Ellery's upset even though it was a one-time mistake."

"What in the hell were you thinking, Daphne? He's a kid. Ellery dated him."

"You're not telling me things I don't know, Rex, but I'm not apologizing to you for trying to get back the part of myself you trampled on when you walked out. You had a therapist telling you to take care of yourself. Did you stop to think what you did to me? You had been my everything, and you walked away from our vows, our future . . . me."

Rex's lips drew up. "We've been through all this, and I apologized. I can't go back and fix it. Still, Clay's so young. I can't even picture you . . . and him."

"I don't want you to. What I am asking you to do is realize that I'm a person who is . . . a person. Not someone who fixes things, takes people's shit, and feels guilty every time she does something that doesn't sit right with others. I deserve some happiness, Rex." As she said those words, something inside her moved and settled into where it belonged. Because for the first time ever, she truly believed those words. They weren't mere vowels and consonants strung together by someone else, a mere repeated platitude. They were real and true. She deserved to be as happy as anyone else, and if that meant hurting people's feelings or upsetting them with her choices—good or bad—then she would have to live in that space.

"I do realize you're a person," Rex said, but he sounded unconvincing. "I'm just surprised, is all. He's young, and . . . I guess when I thought about you moving on, I had a different picture in mind of the guy."

"I'm not moving on with Clay, Rex. But I *am* moving on. Finally."

When Rex glanced back at her, she saw the tenderness in his eyes. "Good. I'm glad. I mean, part of me isn't, because, well, you know. But the other part of me, the one who still knows you are my friend and will always care about me, is very pleased you're getting a new life for yourself. I do love you, Daphne. I always will. I screwed up our marriage, and maybe it was for the best in the long run. Who knows? But I own the fault in what happened between us."

"You weren't the only one who made mistakes, Rex. I chased that dream hard, and sometimes I thought only about what would benefit me. I didn't acknowledge or try to understand your feelings about my career."

Rex gave her a wry smile. "Yeah, but you didn't pack up and leave. I did. I messed up and didn't try to fix it."

"Water under the bridge now," she said.

Rex walked toward her and wrapped her in a hug. He set his big head atop hers, and for a moment, the old familiarity of his embrace washed over her. She knew his smell, the feel of his rib cage expanding, the small indention in his back—a result of a bike wreck when he was thirteen.

When Daphne released him, something inside her finally knitted together, and she felt at peace. "So come see the house. You're going to love the bathroom and wish we had done this when we were still married. It's got that rain-shower thing you always wanted."

"Sure, and when we're done, I have a few things for you to look over and give me some advice on," Rex said, dropping his hands and starting for the living room.

"Rex," Daphne said, trying to stamp down the irritation unfurling inside her. "If this is about Pinnacle or your finances, I'm not open to discussion. That's no longer my role, and if that's why you truly came by, you can turn right around and walk out that door."

He studied her for a few minutes, his shoulders sinking. "You know, it's not the reason I stopped by, but I can't deny that I respect your opinion and want your advice. But I get it. I shouldn't have asked."

Daphne paused and looked back at him. "Good. You're learning."

Rex's lips twitched. "Guess it took me long enough."

"Or maybe it took me long enough," Daphne said.

CHAPTER TWENTY-FOUR

Ellery woke to speckled sunlight dancing across her face. "Ugh."

She didn't want to open her eyes, because a thousand tiny hammers were tapping against the inside of her skull. Instead she attempted to roll over, away from the darts of light that were trying to kill her, but that made her stomach lurch. She stilled, eyes closed, and prayed that she was in fact in her own bed.

"Ellery?"

She cracked open one eye. "Yeah?"

"You okay?"

"Far from it. Who is that . . . Gage?"

He appeared in front of her, looking concerned and not at all hungover. "Yes, Gage."

Even though she was certain she was in fact in her own bed and could possibly be suffering from alcohol poisoning, her heart leaped against her chest. Gage was standing, looking right as rain, in her bedroom. "What are you doing here? How did . . . who brought me home?"

"I think you said an Uber."

She squinted as if she could see back in time. She vaguely recalled the tequila shots, Clay Caldwell, and no purse. Something landed on her bed and brushed against her. Ellery screamed and shot upright, swatting at whatever it was. "Oh my God!"

"Relax," Gage said, catching her arm and preventing her from falling out of the bed . . . which would have been totally embarrassing considering she was wearing—she looked down at herself—an old high school T-shirt and a pair of ragged gym shorts that she did not remember putting on.

"What was that thing?" she cried as the blur of fur bolted underneath her bed.

"It's your cat, Elmo," Gage said.

"Cat?" Ellery was now sitting up in her bed, her sheet tangled around her legs. "I don't have a cat."

Gage ran a hand through his hair. "Well, you had one last night. I could have sworn you said his name was Elmo."

"That was the name of the bar I went to. I don't know where that cat came from."

Gage bit down on his gorgeous lip as if trying not to laugh. "I mean, I thought he looked a bit thin and ragged, but he was friendly and seemed to know his way around. He slept at the end of your bed all night."

Ellery pulled the sheet up to her chin. "How did I get into these clothes and . . . did I take a shower? I think I remember washing my hair." She picked up a sticky chunk of hair stuck to her shoulder. It was obvious her hair had been shampooed but not rinsed.

"You passed out in the shower." Gage bent and looked under her bed. "Here, kitty."

The cat yowled.

"I passed out in the shower," Ellery repeated, her voice rising with each syllable. "Naked?"

"That's usually how one takes a shower," he said, lifting his head and looking at her.

Ellery was certain her entire body was the color of ripe raspberries. Gage had seen her naked. Naked, drunk, and . . . oh God, she'd vomited in the downstairs bathroom. "Oh my God."

Gage sat back and looked at her. "Hey, it's cool."

"It. Is. Not. Cool." She covered her face with her hands. The sheet fell, revealing the tight T-shirt that accentuated the fact she wasn't wearing a bra, but did that really matter? The man had pulled her passed out from the shower and dressed her for bed.

"Elle, it's okay. I couldn't leave you in there, and you insisted that you never slept in the nude, so I tried to help you put those clothes on. I mostly kept my eyes closed."

She dropped her hands and made a face. "You did not."

He grinned, and it was so adorable coming from such a grumpy, stick-in-the-mud guy that she couldn't be as angry as she wanted. Hell, she couldn't be angry at all. She'd drunk enough tequila to be a spokesperson for Jose Cuervo, vomited in the azaleas, and passed out in the shower. If anyone should be angry, it was the man she'd obviously drunk texted.

"Okay, I may have peeked, but in my defense, I've been wondering how you'd look naked for weeks now. I'm no saint."

He'd wondered how she'd look without clothes for weeks? So she wasn't the only one fantasizing about someone she shouldn't. Or maybe he hadn't set stupid rules for himself. Maybe he'd given himself permission to imagine every square inch of her body. That thought made her stomach warm . . . or perhaps that was the nausea making a reappearance. "I'm so sorry about this. I don't even know what to say."

"It's okay."

"Why did you come?" she asked, suddenly desperate for water. Her voice sounded thick and cottony.

Gage reached over to the bedside table and handed her a chilled glass of water. He'd even placed it on one of the stone coasters from downstairs. "Here. You need to rehydrate."

Ellery greedily gulped the water. It was cool heaven sliding down her throat. "Thank you."

"I came because you said that you wanted me. Only me. And that it was an emergency."

Ellery's eyes widened. "I said what?"

Gage pulled his phone from his back pocket. He wore faded pale jeans that molded to his body, black motorcycle boots, and a tight Kinks concert T-shirt. "Please come get me, Gage. It's an emergency. I need you. Only you. This is Ellery, BTW." He waggled the phone.

"I was drunk."

"No shit, Sherlock. I kinda figured that out."

"But you came anyway." She swallowed hard and shook her head. "I don't know why I did that. Why I asked you to come and scared you that way. I felt so alone . . . and . . . I think . . . ugh."

Gage watched her as she grappled with the situation. The strange cat crept out and leaped onto the bed. Ellery turned to look at the ugly beast. He was rangy, mottled, and ugly as sin, but he purred sweet, and his green eyes fastened on hers with something eager in their depths.

Love me.

The cat bumped her knee, then ducked his head under her elbow. She was almost certain he was covered in fleas, but she still gave him a pat anyway.

Gage sank onto her bed. "You know, I think the best thing to do in moments like these is have something to eat."

Ellery gave him a small smile. "That sounds better than me waffling around in embarrassment, trying to figure out . . . my entire life."

"Mmm . . . waffles. Those sound good. Let's have that." He petted the purring cat. "This cat has fleas."

"I know."

"I'll put the cat out, and you get dressed."

"No," Ellery said, sliding from the bed. She crossed her arms in front of her breasts, even though she knew Gage had already seen her in her glory. Or rather not in her glory at all. Ugh, she'd probably looked sweaty and close to death. "I mean, I'd like to give him some tuna or something. He looks hungry."

Gage lifted an eyebrow. "I knew underneath all that glitter and bluster beat the heart of a softie. I'll find him something." With that, he scooped up the agreeable tomcat and shut her door. Ellery eased back onto the mattress and grabbed the cell phone Gage had placed on her bedside table, trying to ignore the thump, thump of her head. A quick glance showed she had a few Snapchats and a text from her mom with a cut-and-dried directive about procuring the date at Evan's daughter's school. Evan. Gage's uncle. Gage.

He'd driven an hour and a half to come to her.

What did that mean? Something? Nothing? She wasn't sure. What she was sure about was she needed to get the heck up and wash the sticky shampoo from her hair . . . then she could try to salvage her image with sexy bartender guy.

Fifteen minutes later, with the stray cat fed and put on the patio, Ellery sipped ice-cold water at a Waffle House. Gage sat across, nursing black coffee and studying her.

"You're not going to puke, are you?" he asked.

"I don't think so." Though she wasn't sure. Her stomach had rolled during the motorcycle ride to the restaurant. Of course that could have been because she was wrapped around Gage, the wind ripping at her still-wet ponytail, as she prayed not to die or vomit on Gage's back.

"Food will help."

At that moment the waitress slapped down a plate with eggs, bacon, and grits followed by another plate containing a waffle. Gage had the same, except he'd gone for hash browns instead of grits. "Here you are. Get you anything else?"

Ellery shook her head before picking up her fork and diving in. She ate half her plate before she looked back up at Gage. "I feel better."

"Nothing like Waffle House after a night of drinking."

Ellery had never been to a Waffle House before. Josh wouldn't be caught dead here. He preferred an overpriced, trendy brunch spot over on Line Avenue that featured remoulade and hollandaise sauces, but the basic food here was pretty good, and the cheerful banter between guys in work boots driving big, white trucks and the sassy waitresses made her smile. Clattering dishes, cooks yelling "Order up," and the friendly sunshine streaming through the glass window front were comforting.

"I'll try to remember that. Or perhaps I should try to not do what I did last night ever again."

Gage didn't say anything. Mostly he watched her with gray-green eyes that seemed as impenetrable as Fort Knox. What was he thinking? He'd said he wanted all of her, but she had to get her shit together. She was fairly certain her shit was not together. Not even close. Instead she was worse than before.

"Why did you come?" she asked, setting down her buttered toast.

His shoulders may have twitched into a shrug. "I wish I knew."

For a few seconds neither one of them said anything.

"Josh and I broke up. Turns out I don't have the right equipment for him."

"And how does that make you feel?" Gage asked.

What kind of question was that? How did he think she felt? "Hurt."

"Because he couldn't want you? Because he deceived you? Or because you're no longer living your plan?"

"My plan?"

"You said you had a plan, and he—I'm assuming Josh—messed up your plan. Last night when you were crying, it didn't seem to be over him, but over the fact nothing has worked out the way you planned it."

Ellery looked down at her plate. "Well, yeah. I guess that's some of it. I thought I loved Josh. He's a great guy, and he always treated me like I was . . . I mean, now I can look back and see that he was doing what he thought a man does when he loves a woman. Maybe I was doing the same thing. I thought we made so much sense. Everyone said so.

The things we wanted in life lined up, you know? But to answer your question, I wanted the life he and I had planned."

Gage's expression seemed to say, *How's that working for you?*

"Nothing's been going my way since last spring, Gage." *Other than meeting you.*

That thought popped up out of nowhere, and before she could talk herself out of it, she knew it to be true. Ever since she'd fizzled in her career, she'd been making bad decisions, one right after the other. Or maybe some of it wasn't because she'd made bad decisions. Maybe this was how life was—that in spite of one's best efforts, things didn't always work. Some of what had happened to her over the last few months was what life had given her. Another thing she knew for certain was that Gage . . . oh crap, she didn't know his last name . . . was meant to be here in this time and place.

"I get it," he said, tucking into his breakfast while still giving her cryptic looks.

"What's your last name?" she blurted.

He chuckled. "Nacari."

"Gage Nacari . . . you sound like a European race car driver or a soap opera star."

"Nope. Just a guy who slings wine. Well, for another week anyway. I'm leaving for Seattle right before Thanksgiving."

"What?" Ellery jerked her gaze from the pooling syrup on her half-eaten waffle to Gage. "You're leaving?"

"There's this job in Seattle. One I've had my eye on for a long time."

"You're *leaving*?" She knew she shouldn't be upset. Gage was a guy she'd met exactly five times, if last night counted as a meeting. They'd shared a few kisses. That was it. But for some reason, his casual mention of leaving next week was like someone kicking her in the stomach. He couldn't leave now. They had chemistry, the beginning of something that she wasn't ready to put her finger on but that existed all the same.

"I started the interview process last month. The Seattle office called last week, and I have an interview. It's *the* opportunity I've been lusting after for a while now."

He was excited. She could see that in his eyes. "But you don't have the job yet?"

"Not yet."

"What if you don't get it?" She knew how it felt to not get the job you thought you would. Sometimes it didn't work out, so why move to Seattle when he didn't have a sure thing?

"Then I'll find something else. It's time for me to go after what I want in life. I have a degree from UT in computer engineering, and I've been waiting for the right opportunity. This is it."

"Well, that's brave. Seattle's a cool place. I went once when I was in college. Nordstrom is headquartered there."

Gage's gaze searched her face. "You should come with me."

Ellery dropped her fork. The clatter was loud, and a few people in the next booth turned toward them. "Sorry." She picked up the fork and set it next to her plate. "Are you crazy? I can't go to Seattle with you."

"Why not? You just said it's a cool city."

"It is, but you don't have a job. I don't have a job."

Gage's mouth quirked, and damned if it wasn't sexy. "So? We'll get some."

"That's . . . it doesn't make any sense."

"Because it's not in your plan?"

Ellery stared at him like he was crazy. "That and I . . . I have a lease and a job . . ."

"Sublease your place and quit your job." He gave her a shrug. "You're young, probably too young for me even, but that's the best reason to roll the dice. Why let life happen to you? Come with me to Seattle. You can sleep on my couch, put out some résumés, and start over."

Let life happen to you.

Those words might as well have slapped her in the face.

She'd been letting life happen to her. What had she done to change her situation? Not much. She still hadn't sent in the internship applications and had been avoiding everything that was difficult in life. Her life here in Shreveport was pathetic and safe. But moving to Seattle on a whim? That seemed extreme.

And somehow . . . exciting.

Gage was right—she was young, and if she were going to make mistakes, now was the time to make them. There was nothing left for her here . . . outside of parents she wasn't talking to. Maybe a crazy, out-of-the-blue Seattle move was exactly what she needed. Maybe this was the break she'd been waiting on. No, it wasn't a break. It was an opportunity. If things didn't work out in Seattle, she could come back home. Or find a new opportunity. She didn't have to have a plan. Ellery could create her life as she went.

"How old are you?" she asked.

"Twenty-nine," he said.

"That's not too old for me," she said.

His answer was a small smile.

"Are you flying to Seattle or going on your motorcycle?"

He wiped his mouth with a napkin. "Well, I sold my bike to Evan, so I thought I would rent a car. I've already shipped my computer and most of my clothes to the one-bedroom loft that's costing an arm and a leg."

"If I come, I can bring my car, so we have transportation. Once I get a job, I can help with rent and stuff."

"We can figure it out," he said.

"Are you sure you want me to come with you?" she asked, wondering if she had lost her mind. Because she was seriously considering going to Seattle. With a man she barely knew. With no job. She was crazy, but this kind of crazy felt good.

It felt right.

Everything about Gage had felt right. The first time she'd met him, she knew he could see through her outside veneer. He challenged her on every level, and he was a hell of a good kisser.

When Gage smiled at her, she felt something inside her snap into place. "Weirdly enough, I do want you to come with me. We met for a reason—fate, kismet, whatever the world puts out there that makes things happen. That's why I came here last night. Because I can't seem to get you out of my head. When I said I wanted all of you, I meant it. Thing is, Ellery, you have to decide if you want to take a chance on Seattle. And on me."

His words were like magic. He wanted all of her—the good, the bad, the Ellery who threw up in the bushes. This man who she knew next to nothing about, had too many tattoos, wore concert T-shirts, and kissed her like the devil could never be planned for. Didn't matter. She wanted him. She wanted a new life with him in it.

"Okay," she said.

"Okay, what?"

"I'm going with you to Seattle."

CHAPTER TWENTY-FIVE

Daphne stared at the email on her computer and tried not to scream and dissolve into a puddle beneath her desk.

Her daughter had lost her effin' mind.

Skipping Thanksgiving? No Christmas? And Ellery was resigning as her assistant?

"What in the hell is wrong with this girl?" Daphne said, releasing the mouse and spinning her chair toward the large window that framed November leaves whirling against the gray sky. Thanksgiving was two days away, and she'd given her daughter plenty of space to absorb her mother's transgression and come to her senses. Of course, Daphne wasn't sure Ellery would, in fact, come to her senses. Or ever be accepting of what her mother had done, but as Clay had been so fond of saying, *they were adults* and *it was just sex*. Ellery would get over her mother's poor decision, even if it remained a pebble in her shoe on the road of life. After all, Daphne was Ellery's mother, and her daughter loved her. This she knew. Still, skipping the holidays and resigning at the first of the year felt spiteful and not the decisions of a woman who had had enough "space" to figure things out.

No one figured life out anyway.

Daphne clicked off her email, making the resignation letter disappear.

But maybe this wasn't solely about Daphne and what she'd done with Clay. Josh had texted her last weekend and told her that he'd told Ellery about the affair he'd been having with his study partner, and that they'd both agreed to end the engagement. Daphne had wanted to respond with something flippant about how of course they'd ended it. Who wanted to be married to a guy who was unfaithful and not in love with her?

Ellery hadn't called her, crying, wanting her mother to give her comfort like Daphne had hoped. No, Daphne's texts had gone unanswered unless Ellery was responding to something to do with Dixie Doodle. Her daughter had continued to answer email, monitor social media, and conduct contests. But that was all.

No doubt Ellery's decision to remove herself from the holidays was more about grieving the loss of her fiancé and less about her mother. In that, Daphne understood. Nothing fun about eating turkey while avoiding prying questions and pretending away whispers about what had gone wrong. Broken engagements were no fun.

Still, after three weeks of silence, it was time for Daphne to face her daughter and end the stretch of discord. Time healed wounds, but Ellery ignoring the elephant in the room and avoiding the one person who loved her beyond all others wasn't going to help anyone move ahead in life. Besides, a girl needed her mother.

Daphne grabbed her purse, pulled on a jacket, and headed out to the carport. The Realtor was showing the house later that afternoon, so Daphne would have to be out anyway. Might as well go to her daughter and get the tears, anger, and reconciliation out of the way. She missed Ellery and couldn't stand this breach between them. Daphne had to fix what was wrong so she could move forward. Evan McCallum waited in the wings, and Daphne wanted to stop treading water with him. She enjoyed their friendship, long talks, and getting to know one another, but she also wanted that second kiss.

Twenty minutes later she pulled into the cul-de-sac where her daughter's town house sat. Two unfamiliar cars sat in the drive, and a guy Daphne didn't recognize came out the front door carrying a box. Ellery's work friend Rachel emerged from a U-Haul truck, carrying a laundry basket full of pots and pans.

Daphne parked and climbed out, walking toward the front of the house so she could intercept the woman. "Hey, Rachel, you remember me, right? Ellery's mom?"

The young woman smiled. "Of course. How are you?"

"Fine. You moving in?"

She nodded, her face flushed from the exertion. "Yep, finally getting out of my parents' house. They're thrilled."

"That's great. I'm glad Ellery found someone so quickly." Daphne took a few pots off the top, hoping to lessen the weight for the girl. "Here, let me help you."

Rachel grinned. "Thanks, these are heavier than I thought."

Daphne eyed the basket. "You must cook a lot. Ellery will probably appreciate that."

Rachel looked confused. "Yeah, but she's leaving, so I doubt she'll get much of a chance to sample my bad cooking. I have to tell you that I'm going to miss her. If you had told me I would have gotten to be close to someone like her, I would have thought you were crazy. I'm bad about judging people sometimes. I hope I can go see her in Seattle. Never been there before."

Daphne stopped in the middle of the yard. "Seattle? What are you talking about?"

Rachel's steps faltered and she turned toward Daphne, her eyes panicked. "Oh shit. She didn't tell you."

It was a statement, not a question.

"Tell me what? I assumed Josh moved out and you were moving in to room with her. Why would Ellery leave? Seattle? Did she get a job?" Daphne felt weak in the knees at the thought. Ellery was leaving Shreveport without telling her own mother?

Rachel bit her lower lip and rested the basket on her knee, shifting the load to her other arm. "Um, I think you better talk to Ellery."

"I think I should talk to her, too." Daphne set the pots back on top of the pile in the laundry basket and stalked inside her daughter's town house. Sure enough, the couch and chair she'd tried to talk Ellery out of financing had been replaced by a faux-leather monstrosity that Fiona was wiping down.

The woman paused and watched Daphne as she ascended the stairs.

Anger, shock, and hurt increased with each step she took. Her daughter was moving to Seattle? And she forgot to mention that little detail in her letter of resignation? And how about not bothering to mention it when she told Daphne not to expect her for Thanksgiving or Christmas this year? How dare Ellery think she could up and move away and not even let her own mother know. Who did something like that? After all she'd done for Ellery, this was how her daughter treated her?

With each step she grew more and more aggravated at her immature, spoiled daughter.

Daphne rounded the corner and entered Ellery's bedroom, but it was empty. A bed frame sat propped against a wall, little bits of paper were scattered across the floor, and a few boxes marked with the name Fiona sat stacked in a corner. The bathroom was bare, hooks hanging from the shower-curtain pole. Her daughter had indeed moved out and left nothing of herself behind.

When had this happened? Why had she done such a thing? To punish Daphne? Or was the broken engagement actually that humiliating? She had no clue why her daughter was doing this.

"Mrs. Witt?" Fiona called from the doorway. "I'm Fiona. We met before."

Tears threatened to choke Daphne. "I remember."

Fiona walked inside the room. "I'm sensing you didn't know that Ellery moved out?"

Daphne shook her head. "I don't understand why she didn't tell me. Rachel said she was going to Seattle. I have no idea why she would do such a thing."

Fiona paused for a few seconds. "She's young, and Gage is easy on the eyes. After getting her heart broken, maybe it's not such a bad idea to start over in a new place with a new guy."

"But she and Josh broke things off just a little over a week ago," Daphne said, turning a full circle in the empty room. "And who the hell is Gage?"

Fiona's eyes widened. "Uh, she met him in Texas. At the vineyard?"

"Evan's nephew Gage?" Daphne asked, her voice rising with each syllable. She felt as if she were in an alternate universe. Her daughter was running off with Evan's nephew to Seattle? It didn't make sense. "This is ridiculous. Do you know where she is right now?"

"I'm not sure. I think she went to Texas yesterday. Rachel said she was staying at the vineyard for a day or two before making the drive."

Daphne brushed by the woman. "Sorry. I have to go."

She ran down the stairs, nearly knocking over Rachel in the process. "Sorry. I have to find Ellery and stop her before she does something idiotic."

She hurried to her car, pulled out her cell phone, and sent Ellery a text.

Call me. *Now!*

Then she called Rex as she turned the car toward the interstate. He answered on the third ring. "Hey, Daph."

"Did you know that Ellery is running off to Seattle with some man she barely knows?"

"What? Running . . . Seattle?" Rex's voice rose in alarm.

"Yes, Seattle. I just went by her house because I'm sick of this silly silence between us, and two of her coworkers were moving in. They said she had gone to Texas, and that from there she was going with Gage, a bartender from the vineyard, to Seattle."

"You're joking. A bartender?"

"I wish I were," Daphne said, driving west, hoping she could get to One Tree Estates before Ellery left. She had to talk sense into her daughter. Obviously the events of the last few weeks had driven her to lunacy. Quitting her job, running away with a virtual stranger, going to a place where she had no job and no support? She'd lost her damned mind.

"What are we going to do?" Rex asked.

"I'm going to Texas to stop her."

"Do you want me to go with you?"

"I don't have time. I'll call you when I get there. I don't know what is going on with our daughter, Rex. I think I'm responsible for this."

"No, Josh is responsible for this. Don't blame yourself."

Daphne shook her head. This was partly her fault. Her actions had kept her daughter from her at a time when she had needed her mother the most. This was what she'd reaped from her mistake with Clay—a dangerous gulf between her and Ellery that had driven her into the arms of a stranger and onto a desperate path.

When she didn't answer, Rex said, "Let me know what I can do to help, Daphne."

Daphne hung up and called Evan. No answer. She glanced at her phone and saw no response to her plea for Ellery to call her.

Damn it.

An hour and fifteen minutes later, she roared up the road that led to One Tree Estates, feeling more panicked than ever. She'd been unable to reach Evan, Ellery wasn't responding to any of her calls, and when she'd called the winery, the person who'd answered could only take a message for Evan to call her. The receptionist had said Gage no longer worked there and she didn't know who Ellery was.

Feeling unhinged, Daphne pulled into a reserved spot and shifted into park with a jolt. She palmed her keys and leaped out, scrambling toward the entrance, not caring that she looked a bit mad. She had no makeup on, wore yoga pants, a tunic shirt with a bleach stain on the hem, and running shoes that had seen better days. Her curly auburn hair was likely snarled, and her cheeks held the high pink of a panicked mother.

"Hello," she said, bursting into the lobby and turning toward the reception desk.

The girl behind the desk cheeped in alarm. "Oh, hello."

"I'm looking for Evan McCallum, please. Is he here?"

The teenager behind the desk blinked and stepped back, looking unsettled. "He's out in the fields at present. I can try to call him."

"Do it," she said, glancing around, hoping to catch a glimpse of her daughter or that surly bartender with his pretty smile and obvious silver tongue. But she saw no one familiar. Then she remembered that Evan had said his nephew lived in the house next to his. His sister's house.

"Never mind," she called to the receptionist as she bolted out the door of the winery and back to her car. Several guests looked at her in alarm as she hurried through the parking lot. She may have been muttering bad words under her breath, or maybe her panicked disposition was enough to make them pause. At that point she didn't care. Her only thought was to get to Ellery and end the madness her daughter seemed to be determined to conduct.

She tried to follow the speed limit as she wound down the drive but found herself anxiously pressing the accelerator. Evening approached, and the shadows were long and golden. If she hadn't been in such a state, she might have appreciated the dying day more, but she was focused on one thing—the most precious person in her life, a child she refused to lose because she'd made one mistake.

She came to the house Evan had pointed to as being his older sister's while on their run and turned into the drive. No car sat in the driveway, and the house was dark. It looked as if she were too late.

"No," she breathed, killing the engine. "No, no, no."

She climbed out and heard someone call her name.

"Daphne," Evan called again, striding across his yard, crossing into the yard of the house she'd pulled into.

"Evan," she said, closing the car door and moving toward him. "Is Ellery here?"

"She and Gage left several hours ago," he said, his expression narrow and concerned.

Daphne felt as if he'd dealt her a blow. "No. Oh my God, this is unbelievable."

"You didn't know?" he asked, looking taken aback at the thought. "She didn't tell you?"

She shook her head as she blinked back the tears gathering in her eyes. Her daughter had essentially run away from all that she had known, willy-nilly, without care, caution, or enough sense to fill a boot. "She's still not speaking to me. She resigned from being my assistant and told me she would not come to Thanksgiving dinner via email, but she never said anything about your nephew or Seattle."

Evan's eyes widened. He reached for her hand. "Come with me. Let's sit down and talk."

Daphne shook him off. "I don't want to talk. I want to go after her. This is the stupidest thing she has ever done. Evan, she can't just up and leave like this. Like she's punishing me."

"I don't think that's what it's about," he said, his voice quiet.

"How do you know? You don't know her," Daphne cried.

"Actually, I kind of do. We've been exchanging emails with each other for months now. I know a bit more than a stranger would. Come on." He took her arm again and gave a slight tug. "You're not going to catch them."

Daphne went because he was right. She was hours behind her daughter, and it wasn't as if she could put an APB out on her grown daughter who wasn't actually missing . . . except for maybe missing her common sense.

Evan's hand was warm on her elbow. She wished it felt comforting, but she wasn't sure if she could be comforted at this point. Her heart felt completely broken, and her stomach churned with adrenaline.

"I'm sorry you didn't know about Ellery going with Gage," Evan said, sinking onto a cedar bench that blended perfectly with the landscaping. "That wasn't very well done of her."

"How does she even know him? I guess they met that weekend, but . . . I just don't understand what has gotten into her lately."

"They've been a bit more than acquaintances from what I understand and from what I've seen over the last twenty-four hours. But you don't have to worry about Gage. He's a good guy, more responsible than any other twenty-nine-year-old I know."

Daphne crunched through the fallen leaves, trying to grapple with all Evan had revealed. "They were here overnight? Why didn't you call me? We talked yesterday, and you said nothing about Ellery being here."

He held up a hand. "We didn't talk. We texted, and it was about brining a turkey. I assumed you knew Ellery was going with Gage. Besides, I didn't know she was here until last night when Gage and Ellery came up to the restaurant. And I called you this morning, but you didn't answer . . . and I texted you to give me a call when you had a chance."

In that he was right. She'd planned on calling him that afternoon once she finished with the last storyboard. Asking for an extension was something that went against every fiber of her being. She didn't like to sign a contract and then break it, but the last few weeks had been more than stressful, and since her publisher had requested the book tour after she'd signed the contract, she didn't feel as bad asking for a few more weeks. Still, she'd rededicated herself to setting aside time to work, putting aside her worry so she could do her job. "You did. I'm sorry. I didn't mean to sound accusatory. I'm just really upset that she would do something so ridiculous, and not tell me that she was doing it."

Fresh heartbreak welled inside her. Her daughter had pulled herself so far away that she didn't want or need Daphne in her life. How had that happened so quickly? Sure, they hadn't been the same for the last half year, but to leave home and say nothing to either of her parents? It was immature, inconsiderate, and thoroughly selfish. Irritation burgeoned inside her, fighting for a place beside the hurt.

"It seems extreme, but she's searching to find herself," Evan said, his voice soft.

"Find herself? What a stupid millennial concept . . . and I don't even know if she's a millennial, but either way, it's an excuse for bad behavior. Her father and I have given her a pretty spectacular life, and this is how she treats us? This is how she treats her mother?" Daphne stood up abruptly, the anger taking hold now.

"Daphne, I don't think she's doing this to hurt you. I think she's trying to be an adult."

"An inconsiderate jackass of one," Daphne said, turning and staring down at Evan. "You're not defending her, are you? Because it sounds like you are."

"I'm not necessarily defending her. I'm trying to get you to see this from her point of view."

"Well, I could have done that if she would have bothered to tell me that she was taking off to the West Coast with a stranger. Maybe I could have shown her just how stupid it is to make such a snap decision and leave all her plans and family behind for a whim. She doesn't have a job, she doesn't have a plan, she doesn't—"

"—need one. She's twenty-three and will have to figure out how to get a job, pay her bills, make mistakes, and live her own life on her own terms."

Daphne rolled her eyes. "Really? And you know this because . . . ?"

Evan's brow furrowed. "That's what I had to do. I mean, isn't that what you did?"

"No," Daphne said, whirling back toward the horizon, where the sun had begun to sink, streaking the sky like an impressionist painter's palette. The beauty was incongruous with the ugliness battling inside her. "I didn't have the opportunity to do any of that because I had a kid and a husband. Making mistakes meant my kid didn't eat or we didn't have running water. Living my life on my own terms ceased to exist on that last push when my daughter emerged, screaming her lungs out, from my teenage body. I didn't get to figure my life out. I was handed a life, and it was handcuffed to me. I didn't get to 'find myself.'"

Evan stared at her for a few seconds. "So this is about you?"

"No, this is about my daughter being a complete ass and running from her problems."

"Or maybe she's doing what you're doing—starting over with a blank slate. That's what you told me on our date. You said that you were done playing by everyone else's rules. You were claiming your own life. So perhaps Ellery is doing what you're doing. She's trying to find a new life for herself. When you do that, you can make missteps. You admitted to making one with a younger guy, right? But that's what happens when you decide to live your life on your terms."

Boom. Mic drop.

Daphne didn't want Evan's words to make sense. He was supposed to side with her. He was supposed to be outraged for her. "Okay, so if Poppy did what Ellery did, you wouldn't be upset?"

"Sure. I want Poppy to make good choices, but I know she won't sometimes. My job is to prepare her for the road ahead. Not pave it for her. You have said over and over that you've given Ellery so much and she owes you. Does that mean she owes you the gift of managing her life? Of fixing it for her?"

Daphne watched as the sun set, lighting a path for her daughter. "No, not necessarily."

"Hey," he said, reaching for her hand and threading his fingers through hers. "I'm not saying you shouldn't be upset. It's justifiable to feel the way you do, and if I were in the same situation, I'd be upset my child didn't tell me about her plans. I'm not saying you can't own that you're hurt and frightened for your daughter."

Daphne sank back onto the bench. This time the tears fell, and she didn't bother to try and stop them. "If I hadn't done something so stupid, she would have come to me. I could have helped her figure things out. Her fiancé turned out to be gay, her engagement a sham, and her ego probably pancaked, and because I screwed up with Clay, she doesn't trust me or—"

"Daphne, you can't persecute yourself because you were less than perfect. Everyone messes up. Everyone makes bad decisions. You're holding yourself to a crazy standard."

"Of what? Being a decent person . . . a mother doesn't allow her baser needs and insecurities to put her in a situation that brings about this."

"Daph, this didn't happen because you slept with someone, no matter how old he is. This is about the decision Ellery made, one you're going to have to live with because she's an adult now."

Daphne sniffled. A partial sob may have escaped. "But this is horrible. She won't acknowledge me other than sending me a stupid resignation letter. It's almost intolerable, and I don't know what to do to make it better."

"Ellery loves you. I know that much through corresponding with her. She'll come around, but you have to let her go. You have to not push . . . or fix . . . or force something. I learned this with my wife. Sometimes you can do nothing but love that person, and even that won't be enough."

His arm came around her and pulled her to him. She allowed herself to fall against his solidness. Evan was warm and smelled like fresh laundry. "I'm not good at doing nothing, Evan."

"I understand. It's harder to do nothing than to do something, sometimes. We're parents, so our first inclination is to protect and repair. But Ellery is safe. Gage will see to that. I trust him implicitly. As to repairing Ellery, that's up to her. Let go of the wheel and see what happens."

She tucked herself deeper into his side, wiping the tears still spilling down her cheeks. Deep down inside she knew Evan was right. It wasn't her job to fix Ellery, but the thought of sitting back and watching her wreck her life was almost too much to think about.

But what if her daughter didn't wreck her life?

What if Ellery was doing something that Daphne had waited almost too late to do in life?

Taking a chance. Rolling the dice. Jumping in with both feet.

Evan kissed the side of her head, and this time comfort stole over her. For the past few weeks, she and Evan had texted and talked a few times on the phone. He'd told her he would give her space, but their communications held promise for something more. Sitting here, lower than she'd been since Rex had filed for divorce, having someone to lean on, to give her necessary truth and to hold her with a sweetness she'd forgotten she needed, told her all she needed to know about her future with Evan.

Sure, that was putting the cart before the horse, but she was willing to put herself out there. Maybe that was the thing she had to do. Stop thinking, stop trying to control every aspect of her world, and let life come to her.

"How did you get so smart?" she asked.

"I make wine. There is nothing certain, nothing I can control except the label," he said, a little bit of disgust tingeing the acceptance that his career had taught him.

"I like your label," she said, allowing herself to completely relax against him and enjoying the feel of his arms around her.

"Gage designed it. You know, if you think about it, Ellery's like a good wine. She just needs room to breathe. Pop the cork, Mama, and give it time." She could hear the smile in his voice, and that made her feel like perhaps things weren't so bad.

"You should write wine-ology," Daphne said.

"I'll leave the writing to you," he said, dropping another kiss atop her head.

For a few minutes they sat there, snuggled on the bench as the day turned into evening, surrendering the rays of the sun to the soft gray of dusk. As the light faded, a chill permeated her tunic and made her shiver. Her heart still hurt, but his words had found their mark. Ellery needed room . . . to make mistakes . . . to try new things . . . to breathe.

"Come inside. I'll build a fire and pour some wine. Poppy's over at Marin's, playing with her youngest, so we will have a bit of peace," he said.

"I should get back," she said, pushing herself upright.

"Why?"

"Well, I burst in here like a madwoman. I'm sure you have things to do," she said, now feeling a bit embarrassed about her panicked storming of the winery. It wasn't like Evan had been sitting around with nothing to do but talk a crazy mother out of an all-out manhunt for her grown daughter. She'd interrupted his evening.

"I do. With you."

She turned to him. "That might be the nicest thing anyone has said to me in a long time."

"You're not hanging around the right people," Evan said, rising and holding out a hand. "I know things in your life are feeling uncomfortable right now, but I'm really glad to see you, Daphne."

She took his hand. "It's odd, but after feeling like my world was falling apart, I'm glad to see you, too."

Her toes did a small curling thing when he gave her a crooked smile. Then he brushed his lips softly against hers. "And that's the nicest thing *I've* heard in a long time."

Evan pulled her toward his house, and she went with him, her heart not completely healed, but her fear quieted. "Thank you, Evan."

He squeezed her hand and turned to look at her. "We've had a little breathing room ourselves. I think I'm ready for that first sip. You?"

"I've been holding on to my glass for a while now."

"I'd say let me fill it, but that sounds a little weird," he said with a sparkle in his eye.

"I'm down with wine-uendos," she joked.

His laughter surrounded her with the warmth she'd been looking for. "Dating a wordsmith is going to be fun, I see."

"Hey, I just make up stuff for a living."

CHAPTER TWENTY-SIX

Four months later . . .

Ellery pulled the rental car into the driveway of the house where she had spent her childhood. The house looked different with its fresh paint, new landscaping, and updated shutters, but even so, it still looked like home.

A sharp pang struck her as she shut the engine off and looked at the tree she used to climb. She'd carved her initials on the branch right above the small platform she'd built, her base for a tree house that never materialized. Not too far away was the old well that she was never supposed to get close to, but, of course, the warning made it all the more seductive. She'd thought she would throw pennies down the well, making her wishes for a pink bike, a kiss from Hayden Harvey, and a training bra come true. But the old well had ended up being dank and weird smelling. She'd slid a penny under the concrete lid and never heard it plink below.

Here her childhood sat, ripe with memory but not with regret.

No, her regrets were more recent.

Ellery picked up the cake pan, climbed out, and walked around to the kitchen door, which no longer had a bang-and-slam screen door, but instead a pretty french door with a striped awning above. Her mother's car sat in the carport, which had also been given its own makeover. Ellery climbed the steps, expecting Jonas's bark. The dog didn't come skidding to the door. Instead she caught her mother's figure walking past.

Daphne moved toward the door, her eyes widening only slightly. For a moment the two of them stood, each on a side of an unfamiliar door, both perhaps wondering at the metaphor.

Finally, her mother opened the door. "Ellery."

"Hi, Mom."

She could tell her mother wanted to ask her a barrage of questions, but for a moment, she merely took her in. Ellery knew what she found was likely a surprise. Ellery's hair was no longer flat ironed within an inch of its life. Instead, she'd opted to let it curl naturally, a softer look. Her makeup was minimal—her Seattle look, as she liked to call it. She wore a slouchy sweater because March was still cold in Louisiana, perhaps the coldest month because spring tended to hold on to the chill as if it knew the torrid heat of June would soon render it a distant memory.

"You look good, honey," Daphne said, something warm in her eyes. "Gained some needed weight."

"It's cold in Seattle . . . and rainy. I've been eating more. And I've gone curly," she said, twining her hair about her finger. "I can no longer afford a blowout every week. Or maybe I never could."

Her mother's mouth twitched. "Come on in. I would offer you tea, but the kettle is packed."

Ellery stepped inside the warmth. The mudroom was empty and smelled of new paint, and the new kitchen was gorgeous but also bare. It didn't look like home. Tears prickled in her throat, but she swallowed them down. She set the pan on the counter right as her mother wrapped her in a hard embrace. Ellery didn't fight it, because she needed her mother's arms, needed to smell the Chanel N°5 she wore on special occasions, needed to breathe in home. She wrapped her arms around her mother's back and laid her head against her shoulder. Her mother's hands rubbed her back, and Ellery closed her eyes and pretended there was nothing hard between them.

Daphne eventually dropped her hands and pushed away, wiping tears from her eyes. "You came home."

Ellery nodded. "But only for a visit. I needed to see the house before you handed the keys over, and I wanted to be here for the luncheon. Tippy Lou called me and told me about the award."

Daphne set her hands on the marbled island. "She's a meddling old woman."

"Yeah, and always has been," Ellery said, joining her mother at the island. Daphne glanced over at her. It was obvious her mother had been looking for her composure but hadn't found it. Tears streamed down her face.

"Sorry," she said, wiping her cheeks. "What's this?"

Ellery pulled the aluminum foil off the top of the cake pan, revealing a chocolate sheet cake with sprinkles. "I missed your birthday."

Daphne's gaze met hers. "You baked me a cake? A chocolate Texas sheet cake?"

Ellery looked down at the cake covered with sprinkles. "It's the first time I've ever baked something. I had to do it at Tippy Lou's house. I'm not sure the almond milk worked so well."

Her mother stared back at the cake. "No one has baked me a cake since my mama died."

Ellery felt the unshed tears perched in the back of her throat move to choke her. "Well, I did. I should have done it long ago."

Her mother grabbed a napkin from the lazy Susan and noisily blew into it. After a few seconds, she looked up. "I missed you, honey."

"I've missed you, too," Ellery said, her sigh slowly leaking. "I'm sorry about the way I left. It wasn't cool of me. At the time I was angry at you, and maybe I wanted you to be as angry at me, too."

"I was," her mother said.

"Are you still?" Ellery asked.

Her mother shook her head. "Not really, but I'm confused by a lot of what you did. I have had time to think about what happened between us. We both hold fault. Our actions caused our own problems, I think. Or at least some of them did. My mama always said that you reap what you sow. Or maybe that's the Bible, but either way, I came to terms with the fact that my decisions pushed you from me."

"You haven't tried to contact me," Ellery said, twining her fingers together. "I didn't expect that. I thought you'd fly out and drag me back."

Daphne issued a snort. "Well, when I found out you moved, I drove like a bat out of hell to Texas to try and stop you."

"I know. Gage talks to Evan, and Evan told him that you scared some guests. There was a complaint about people driving too fast in the parking lot and a recommendation of speed bumps." Ellery smiled through her tears at the thought of her mother nearly mowing down people on her mission to stop her from leaving.

"He never told me that," Daphne said, looking concerned.

"So you're dating Evan?" Ellery asked.

"You're dating Gage?"

Ellery laughed. "If you call living with someone dating, yeah. I mean, we're figuring stuff out. He's an ass sometimes, don't get me wrong, but he calls me out on my bullshit. At the same time, he gives me validation in a way I never had. He's teaching me a lot about life and how sweet and hard it can be. Looking back on my relationship with Josh, I can see so much wrong."

Daphne tilted her head. "You didn't love Josh?"

"I loved the idea of Josh, and bless his heart, he really did everything he could to play the part. It's like all those prom-posals and crazy romantic gestures every girl thinks she wants—well, that was what Josh was. He was good at doing what he thought was love. He was bad at actually loving me. Of course, maybe he wasn't capable. But no, I wasn't in love with Josh. I was in love with the idea of love."

"Easy to do."

"Yeah, I wanted to believe I was doing the right thing. Like there was a perfect guy, a perfect career, and a perfect life. When that wasn't enough, I made some bad decisions. Like Evan."

"Did you think you were in love with him?" That question from her mother was loaded with so much—worry, fear, understanding.

"Nah. He seemed to understand so much about me. He was funny, flirty, and wise. After the first time he wrote—a really amusing email, I have to say—I searched for him on the internet. I don't have to tell you he's easy on the eyes, but the pictures on the website showed him with Poppy, and he looked so . . . capable and loving. That sounds weird, but he looked like a guy who would love a person for who they were. It's really stupid, but the more I corresponded with him, the more I couldn't stop. The first time I saw him, I knew I had built a sandcastle in the air, but I didn't stop until he knew what I was doing. Then I was mad at him, too." She gave a hard laugh. "I was messed up, Mom."

Daphne slid a hand over to hers, untangling her fingers. "I made it worse for you, though."

"I made it bad for myself. I own that."

"But why did you run away? You didn't have to leave."

Ellery turned her hand over and threaded her fingers through her mother's. "I'm choosing to think of it as not running away but running toward something I needed. I had a lot of self-truths I needed to face. Parts of me were unlikable, vain, manipulative, and too afraid to actually do the things I said I would. I allowed you and Daddy to fix things for me. Relied on Josh to fill the empty space when my ego got crushed.

Made excuses for myself and blamed everyone else when things didn't go my way."

"You weren't that bad. You were trying to deal with disappointment."

Ellery knew what her mother was doing. It's what all mothers did. They loved too hard to really see their sons or daughters as anything beyond wonderful. "I thought I was making lemonade from the lemons life handed me."

Her mother nodded. "Exactly."

"Like you did when you got pregnant at sixteen. Like you continued to do for years. You were married to the man you *had* to marry, committed to a job you *had* to take, saddled with a child you were too young to have. You made lemonade."

"It wasn't bad lemonade. My life was good, Ellery. Don't doubt that."

"But you didn't want it back, and I think that knowledge sat inside me and soured. Dad told me he tried to reconcile with you, but you told him no. I'm not going to lie, that made me furious. A selfish part of me wanted you to sacrifice yourself so I could have my old life back."

"Ellery, I couldn't go back. Your father wanted someone to make his life easy again. By that time, I didn't feel for him what I once did. I loved your father. I did. He's not a bad guy, but you're right, I never dated anyone else, and I did have to make the best of the situation Rex and I got ourselves into. I don't regret my marriage, but that didn't mean I wanted to give up the part of me I had discovered just to make it easy for your dad . . . or for you."

Ellery smiled. "You took those lemons he tried to give you again, and you threw them back."

"Well . . . maybe."

"I think that's what part of my anger was about. My mother had said to hell with lemonade and made her own damned drink. And I had tucked my tail and come back home, accepting my failure. I didn't throw lemons back, Mom. I took them and proceeded to turn them into muddly mush."

"Don't paint me into something I'm not. I'm no trailblazer. I stumbled into the whole Dixie Doodle author career, just like you said."

Ellery smiled. "No, you prepared. You did the work. I remember you staying up late drawing and creating. I knew the book was good. I didn't tell you that, but I knew. And when opportunity knocked, you didn't hide. You jumped in and owned it, Mom. Yeah, maybe you got lucky, but it wasn't luck that made you Dee Dee O'Hara. That was you. So I think I wasn't so much jealous of you and your career as I was upset with myself that I didn't have the grit I needed to do what you had done."

Daphne squeezed her hand. "It's damned gritty to start over again. You did that."

"I had a good role model." Ellery looked at her mother. "You showed me I could start over. That I had to put in the work, and if luck came my way, I had to be prepared. I couldn't rely on my wit and charm, but I had to have the chops. Let me show you something."

Ellery pulled out her phone and clicked on a button.

She handed her phone to her mother. Daphne's brow gathered, her eyes narrowing as she studied what was on the screen.

"Ellery and Elmo Designs." She paused. "Elmo?"

"He's my cat."

"You have a *cat*?"

Ellery laughed. "He's the ugliest thing you've ever laid eyes on, but I love him. I liked his name, and it was sort of a joke between me and Gage. I like the assonance of the name, and I used whiskers in my branding. It's sort of hokey, but I like it. It's kind of Kate Spade–ish whimsical, but my clothes aren't nearly as structured. Of course, I'm making custom pieces through an online vendor, but it's keeping me occupied when I'm not working."

"You have a job?"

"In a vintage-clothing store. I really like it. It's inspiring me. Oh, and I work in a coffee shop on the weekend. Sold the Lexus Dad bought me and paid my credit cards off. Gage and I have a one bedroom that's about the size of a postage stamp. He got the job he wanted, and it pays well, but he refuses to move until he's saved enough for a sizable down payment. He's way too reasonable for me," Ellery said, but she said it with a smile. Because Gage made her feel that way—irritated, turned on, treasured, independent. In other words, he gave her exactly what she'd needed. Not to mention she'd learned very quickly what good sex was. Whether they would last, she wasn't sure, but that was okay. She was done with planning her life to a T.

Her mother flipped through the designs. "You made all these in a few months' time? They're really good, sweetheart. Creative, bold, but wearable."

"I had time on my hands while I searched for a job. Gage encouraged me to do something productive, and he's so good at computer stuff. He built the site, and I bought a used sewing machine with the money I had from selling my furniture."

Daphne's eyes shone with pride. "I'm so proud of you."

"What's really cool is that I'm proud of me. I took a chance, and I don't know what is around the corner, but I'm doing it on my terms. The way you showed me."

Daphne set the phone on the countertop. "You amaze me."

"I'm happy, Mama. I'm really, truly happy . . . well, most days. I sling coffee and work hard, but I love it." Ellery pocketed her phone. "I think you probably need to go, right? The luncheon starts at eleven thirty. It's nearly eleven now."

"Are you coming? I mean, you said—"

"Can I be your plus-one?"

Her mother squeezed her so tight. "You're always my plus-one, and I don't care if I'm getting an award from the president of the United States, you're ten times more important."

"The award is from the president?" Ellery asked, hugging her mom back.

"No, the Shreveport Ladies Auxiliary Guild for Woman of the Year," her mother said, stepping back.

"Whew," Ellery said, pretending to wipe her brow. "I have a dress in the car, but it's not presidential. I'll be quick."

Daphne grabbed her hand before she escaped out the back door. "So we're good?"

"I brought you a cake, didn't I? I had to bake two of them. I burned the first one."

"I love you, Elle. You're the best thing that I ever did."

Ellery felt all the twisted pieces left inside her turn and click into place. "I love you, too, Mom, and thank you for doing so much for me. I see you now. You're not just my mom. You're you."

With that, she turned and slipped out the door, tipping her head up to the sky, breathing deeply of the early spring morning air. For the first time in a long time, she felt totally at peace. Her life in Seattle had been hard to adjust to at first. She'd cried when she sold her car, but when she'd paid off her secret credit card, cut up the card, and mailed her father a payment on the ones he had been paying, she'd felt a wave of pride in herself. Gage had taught her how to budget and how life could be good without carrying a Birkin bag and getting her nails done every two weeks. He even made a sexy game out of pedicures. And she'd worked hard, so hard that if she'd had those fingernails done, it would have been a waste. Busing tables ain't so glamorous.

But she'd done it, and she loved the inspiration she got at the vintage-clothing store. Design school was one thing, but repurposing vintage haute couture and being inspired by 1970s Halston, 1980s Bob Mackie, and the Coco Chanel sailor dress she found a few weeks back had given her real-world experience with iconic clothing. The owner of the store, after seeing her window display, had given her free rein in organizing and showcasing classic finds. Ellery often wore the dresses she discovered and sold them right off her body.

She'd busted her world wide open, but the thought of things left unsaid between her and her mother had left a hole. For a while, she'd held on to her anger. She figured her mother owed her the apology. After all, she'd slept with Clay. Yet, as the days wore on, the harder Ellery had worked, the more sacrifices she made to pay her bills and help Gage with rent and groceries, the more she realized how she'd behaved and what she'd expected from her mother.

Then she'd seen a funny dish towel about lemons and making lemon-drop martinis and started thinking about her whole philosophy when she'd gone home to Shreveport after college. Which led her to thinking about her mother. Perhaps it was a sort of epiphany when she realized that she was modeling her mother. She'd taken a chance, not settled, and rolled up her sleeves.

For the first time in her life, she'd realized her mother wasn't just her mother.

She was Daphne. She was Dee Dee O'Hara. She was a person.

When Tippy Lou had called her to tell her the house had sold, and then mentioned that her mother was getting an award, Ellery had sold her Lanvin bag and bought a plane ticket.

It was time to mend what was between them . . . and she had.

When she reached her rental sitting in the drive, she slid into the driver's seat and pulled out her phone. Scrolling back several months, she found the email she'd been looking for—the last email Evan had sent her thanking her for confirming her mother's appearance at Poppy's school. She hit REPLY and changed the subject to A Final Message.

Dear Evan,

I'm sure you're surprised to hear from me after so much time, but I need to apologize to you a second time. I once told you that I stood by the words that my mother was a whore. I was wrong. Very wrong.

My mother is a person. Both she and I have made some mistakes, but there is one thing that was no mistake—you. If I had not corresponded with you, I never would have met Gage, and my mother never would have met you. My mistake turned into something good for both of us. You once told me your philosophy—that when you grow your grapes, there are things you can't control, like the weather or temperatures, but in the end, you still have something worthwhile. But you forgot the most important element. Someone has to plant the vines, someone has to pick the fruit, and someone has to make the grapes into wine. There are things we can't control, but if we do nothing, we get nothing. Thank you for that lesson.

Ellery

PS Be good to my mom. Be deserving. She's worth the effort.

ACKNOWLEDGMENTS

I would like to thank my editor, Alison Dasho, who has such faith in me and my ability to write books that matter. To Michelle Grajkowski, my fabulous agent, whose conversations about raising young adults led to this book and whose guidance is invaluable. Thank you both for believing in me and this book.

I would also like to thank Selina McLemore for her editorial insight; Phylis Caskey, Jennifer Moorhead, and Ashley Elston for the long walks, the support, and helping me reach my goals; and the Fiction From the Heart Ladies, who inspire me every day to be a better person and writer. I would also like to mention my Tuesday "Lunch Bunch," who helped me come to terms with Ellery and the authentic twenty-three-year-old she needed to be. And, finally, the wonderful Robyn Carr, who always sets me straight and gives me the advice I need, not the advice I want. I am blessed by these women in my life.

ACKNOWLEDGMENTS

ABOUT THE AUTHOR

Photo © 2017 Courtney Hartness

A finalist for both the Romance Writers of America's prestigious Golden Heart and RITA Awards, Liz Talley has found a home writing heartwarming contemporary romance. Her stories are set in the South, where the tea is sweet, the summers are hot, and the porches are welcoming. She lives in North Louisiana with her childhood sweetheart, two handsome children, three dogs, and a naughty kitty. Readers can visit Liz at www.liztalleybooks.com.